LAST TIME WE KISSED

A SECOND CHANCE ROMANCE

NICOLE SNOW

ICE LIPS PRESS

Content copyright © Nicole Snow. All rights reserved.
Published in the United States of America.
First published in April, 2018.

Disclaimer: The following book is a work of fiction. Any resemblance characters in this story may have to real people is only coincidental.

Please respect this author's hard work! No section of this book may be reproduced or copied without permission. Exception for brief quotations used in reviews or promotions. This book is licensed for your personal enjoyment only. Thanks!

Cover Design – CoverLuv. Photo by Wander Aguiar Photography.

Website: Nicolesnowbooks.com

DESCRIPTION

I just ran into the girl who got away.
   Holding a hate letter addressed to me.
   And now we're stranded.

Last time we kissed, I broke her.
   My best friend's little sister worshiped me.
   She teased. She provoked. She goaded.
   Rubbed forbidden in my face till I went off the chain.
   Making her beg was inevitable.
   So was my sacrifice.

Last time we kissed, she demolished me.
   Her rich family thought I was perfect.
   I took Amy Kay under their noses.
   And then I kept taking.
   I promised too much. Loved her too hard. Left too soon.

Last time we kissed, he betrayed me.
> Her backstabbing brother. My ex-best friend.
> I never saw it coming.
> He'll pay for his sins ten times over.

Last time we kissed, it was final.
> I wasn't supposed to see her again.
> Not in this city. On this elevator.
> The moment it craps out, stranding us overnight with animal cravings and fencing lies.

Last time we kissed, how could we know our next might truly, madly, beautifully restore us?

I: TIMES LEFT BEHIND (AMY KAY)

Words from a letter I never sent, and still want to every damn day:

I HOPE you go to hell, Trent Usher.

Buy yourself a nice long ticket and enjoy your stay.

I won't be waiting when you get back.

The worst thing you did wasn't leaving my father on his knees, screaming in tears. Or the fact that you left me flattened against the wall with my heart pounding, watching the color drain from Jace's face.

It wasn't even the things you whispered to me the morning after our night. Our first and last and only.

The last night I'll ever be this young, this stupid and this trusting. I believed in you too much.

It wasn't the promises you made, or how you strung me along with the magic and mystery I'd always wanted to hold, if just for an instant, in your bottomless blue eyes.

The worst thing you did was leaving without a word. Without an explanation. Without an apology.

I waited, Trent.

I waited so fucking long.

I thought you'd drop me a goodbye. Even if you had to in secret, just to say I want you, or I'm sorry, or there's some deep screwed up part of me that never meant for any of this to happen.

Now, I wonder if you meant it all along. Maybe a sick, deranged part of you enjoyed what you did to us, what you're STILL doing to me.

We opened our home and gave you the world. My parents treated you like another son. Jace loved you like a brother. But nothing like I did, drunk on your toxic promises and sadistically enchanting smirks.

I loved you, asshole.

You loved making me a fool.

I found your address in Portland. You wouldn't be reading this if I didn't. Don't worry – I'm not turning you in.

Even after everything that happened, you're safe. Even with every shred of common sense I have left screaming 'do it,' I can't.

Just can't.

So, I'm going to make sure you read this, and then I'm doing the next best thing to driving down there and kicking your crazy ass: forget you ever existed.

Move on. I suggest you do the same. Whatever dirty, evil stuff you've gotten into will play itself out. That's not my problem. Not anymore. I've wasted too many tears.

But if I'm able to make you think twice before doing this to another girl, leaving her heart a battered wreck, I'll have done my job.

If I find a conscience somewhere behind those beautiful blue eyes and hard body, I hope I stab its heart.

This isn't some guilt trip. It's the bleeding truth. Plus a nice big dose of 'fuck you,' written on my hundredth night in tears since you left, after I've spent too many hours alone in dad's wine cellar.

Stay in hell, Trent.
This lifetime and the next.
Don't come calling.
Fuck you very much,

"Precious"

* * *

It's three hours since I stepped off the plane, checked into my rental, and I'm right back in la-la land. Downtown Seattle is as dreary and bustling as I remember. It's separated from my aching eyes by a sheet of thick glass. The orange lit lobby of this huge tower is like a second home, as it should be for any daughter who grew up in the shadow of a powerful law firm.

I rub my eyes, still trying to forget that stupid letter. I found it just yesterday, digging through my things, taking a break from packing to pick through old trinkets I haven't seen since college.

Six years ago, I penned a Fuck You letter to the man who once meant the world. I never sent it.

For some ungodly reason, I tucked it in my purse. I read it three more times at the airport and once since I landed, like some strange homecoming ritual to this city where life showed me love and promises are fairy tales. Nothing more.

Tucking the long green straw from my iced coffee into the corner of my lip, I suck angrily, draining the last third of watered down coffee.

This isn't a freaking mud run, Ames. Let's pull ourselves together and get this done.

If only it were that easy. I'm feeling my jet lag as the building goes quiet for the day, employees scurrying out the door by the dozen. The guy at the front desk is the last to go, throwing his computer in his case, giving me a weak, unsure grin.

I turn to the man in the leather chair across from me and –

And my heart damn near stops.

My eyes go wide. The anxious electric hum prickling my blood has nothing to do with the caffeine hit.

Deep breath.

Deep freaking breath.

This isn't happening.

It's totally not him. Totally not sitting there in a magnificent suit, navy blue to match his eyes, his strong jaw covered in a delicious bristle of five o'clock shadow. Totally not staring me down, pinning me to my seat, locking my body, mind, and soul to the leather with the same uncanny ease he did when we were kids.

No. Dang. Way.

I blink, look away, and hold my breath. This is silly.

But God help me, I can't bring my eyes back his way. Can't look the man who ruined me and everyone I love dead in his baby blues.

I can't even face his spitting image. A person who

looks exactly like him because all the logic in the universe dictates he's not the real Trent Usher.

There's a shuffle of movement to my side. I exhale slowly. When I look back, predictably, he's gone.

If he ever existed and this wasn't some feverish hallucination.

More air hisses out of my lungs. So fast I almost choke.

It has to be the letter, I tell myself. Bad luck. Stress.

I should've burned it the second I pulled it out of that box with the old travel magazines. Should've burned it *twice* and thrown the ashes to the breeze. Before it ever made it on this trip.

I'm such an idiot. This is my fault, no one else's.

My own dead angry words put Trent Usher's dark stamp on my brain. So does being back here, a universe away from the comfy bed and breakfast chain I've built with my bare hands on the other side of the Cascades.

I miss Spokane. It's smaller, simpler, cleaner than the Emerald City. This place is forever tainted with things I've tried so hard to forget.

Stress does crazy things to a person, too. That's another reason I'm seeing ghosts.

The man who was in front of me a few seconds ago couldn't possibly be him.

Trent Usher is in Oregon. Portland. That's all I know.

All I really care to, really, after the way he baited my heart and then blew it to smithereens.

This is present day Seattle. I have family business.

Whatever this place was to me before, whatever happened here, it won't be the same again. History doesn't repeat itself. Not as tragedy or farce.

It's my burned out brain playing tricks. Nothing more.

Just like Edgar Allan Poe's raven said. Or was it *never?*

I have to remember I'm safe. There's a better chance of being struck by a meteorite while I've got the winning lotto numbers in my pocket than encountering the man who destroyed me here.

I'm still telling myself how impossible it is, casting glances around the room for the mysterious stranger there's suddenly no trace of, when my phone vibrates in my purse.

"Yeah, Jace?" It's hot the instant I press it to my ear.

"You up there yet? Listen, I wanted to talk about that old green crap in dad's office, the jade theme? I want it gone. Replaced with something modern. Hell, maybe blow out the other wooden panel on the wall and throw in another window. That's an awesome fucking view up there, Amy Kay, and I'd be an idiot not to make the most of it. I –"

"Whoa. Calm down, bro. I haven't even gotten on the elevator yet," I snap. "Jesus. I'm barely off my plane, and you're already bombarding me with details about a section of the place that won't do a lick of good for client retention?" I want to reach through the phone and slap my older brother.

"Well, taking clients into the board room for the big talk over coffee was dad's thing. Mine's treating them more like old friends. More whiskey shots at the sushi bar down the street, less sipping scotch. I've got a better shot at sealing the deal when they're at my desk, drinking in the best goddamn view of Rainier they've ever seen."

"Only thing you're *sealing* right now is my patience. Putting it in the same ugly box holding all those questions, like why the hell I bothered coming back here. I'm *not* an interior designer, Jace."

"Yeah, but sis, you do homey so well. You've got an eye for it. Friendly decor, ambiance, that's what really matters these days – especially with all this online bullshit. Making things look pretty, that's your strong suit. I've seen pictures of your rentals in Spokane. Don't be so modest. Business is booming, isn't it?"

It's up and down, like always, but of course I'm not telling him the truth. I also don't want to have to swallow my pride with a lie.

My inns are also business I desperately need to return to once this ridiculous stint decorating the family firm ends. I've got competent people running the show while I'm away, but nothing lasts on auto-pilot forever. "Jace, I'm here to do you a favor. Don't make me regret it. I can't work miracles."

"Shit, sis. Not like I'm asking you to walk on water and turn dirt into gold. This is for our parents. Mom's health. Dad's sanity. They've worked their asses off our whole lives. Least we can do is make sure they've got a comfortable retirement."

Yeah. Retirement.

Like this isn't actually about my older brother finally getting his shot at dad's empire. My older, slower, lazier brother who's very prone to screwing up. And letting his greed own him.

"I'm still waiting for the office to clear out so I've got the space to myself. I'll see what I can do." I sigh.

"You'd better. Because if I keep hemorrhaging clients dad held down left and right, we're definitely in deep –"

"Correction: you are. This is *your* rodeo, Jace. Not mine. I never wanted it. I left this town for a reason."

"You ran, sis. I'm the one who stayed behind and took this crap by the horns. I couldn't stand to let our family name die once dad decided he'd had enough. We're part of Seattle. Chenocott turf forever." Jace takes an arrogant breath. "I get it, I guess. Your situation. You had to start over. It was harder on you than anybody, what happened, after that traitor fucking asshole –"

"No. Not now. I've got work to do and we don't have time to dwell on things we shouldn't. We're making this as brief as possible and then I'm *done*." I stand, eyeballing the elevator.

It's a sober, tall, 1980s-looking thing. Glass and stainless steel. Part of Chenocott and Wick's illustrious heritage. "We'll talk in the morning. After I've been up there, I really need to check into my room and crash for a few."

Jace says something, but I don't bother listening. I've had it up to here with my brother's petulant, demanding, and always ungrateful attitude. I just want to get this done and rest. Maybe soak in a few drinks at the high-end sushi place down the road to take the edge off bad memories.

I grab my purse and head over to the elevator. It's getting dark outside. I hear a security guard's footsteps patter down the hall from the deserted lobby.

I tap the button, expecting a long wait for the elevator's silver doors to slide open. But it's late. Empty. Every normal person in this building who isn't stuck working overtime is gone. The elevator pings a second later and the doors grate open.

I step inside, punch the button for the floor I need, and slump against the wall. It never moves.

The door slides open again for another passenger.

My heart leaps in my throat for the second time this evening.

Mr. Totally Not Trent steps past me, adjusting his tie.

If the man in the suave navy suit isn't just a figment of my imagination, then he's a drop dead gorgeous mirror for the man I hoped I'd never see again.

A doppelgänger. A double. It has to be.

Has to!

But the longer I look and the harder I stare, the more my desperation sinks in. Slowly winding around my throat like a vicious snake, running its venom into my heart.

Of course, I barely realize how long it's been since I blinked. I'm wide-eyed, bewildered, and lost in my own head.

A perfect opening for the stranger to smirk and speak in a voice stolen from the gods. "What floor?"

More like what universe.

I practically crawl up the opposite corner from him. His crystal blue eyes are unrelenting. They're on me, waiting for an answer. Probably wondering if I'm a crazy person or just mute.

"Thirtieth floor please," I say. I can't remember the last time I ever sounded so weak, so mousy.

So scared, if I'm being honest.

Clenching my fist on the gold railing behind me, I softly exhale my relief as the stranger's eyes wander to the small digital screen above the door.

"Same place," he whispers, stabbing at the button. The doors pinch shut.

We're going up fast. There's that heavy weight in my legs and a mechanical *whoosh*. It might as well be a dentist's waiting room, the only place in the world I'd thought with the miraculous ability to stretch time. Until now.

And there's plenty reason to start staring again. Gawking, really, my eyes fixed on a face that's older, handsomer, and eerily familiar. *It can't be. It's not. It's impossible.*

Not him.

Not here.

Not now.

Oh, but his voice...that's different. I haven't heard Trent speak for almost seven years.

This man's cadence sounds richer, smoother, older and wiser than the cocky boy I remember. Too much like how he'd sound if the playful confidence he always carried had aged, matured, and developed a soul.

It'd be a lot like this stranger's voice – all four words he's spoken.

Four. Holy crap.

This really *is* getting insane, isn't it? This isn't me. Amy Kay doesn't go all stalker freak and stare at strangers.

It's this place. This trip. It's set me off, tangled nervous, left me jumping at ghosts. I have to make it stop.

Just when I'm about to force myself to look through the window at the slowly illuminating evening city below, the stranger clears his throat.

His eyes shift to mine. More than a sideways glance. Like he's scoping me out, too, trying to place me in some tragic past we've both tried our damnedest to forget.

Or so I imagine. If this isn't real, then why the curl in his lip?

If he's not Trent, if there's any justice in this universe, then there's no way – *no freaking way* – his lips should be carbon copies of the ones I traced with my tongue countless times over one fatal summer.

This doesn't make sense.

Nothing about him ever did, it's true.

But this is a whole new level of coincidence, of hell, that shouldn't be possible.

Such a tall, handsome, improbable death blow to every set of odds, every sense of logic, can't be standing in front of me...right?

But he is. Right there. And now he's staring back.

That's where we're stuck for the next three seconds, the longest of my life, before my eardrums explode and everything spins in a furious metal shriek.

* * *

IT'S DARK, but it doesn't mean a thing to the merry-go-round in my vision. I struggle to place myself, put my hand against the glass. Everything feels...off, somehow.

It's crooked. Slightly angled. One more thing that shouldn't be happening on an elevator ride to assess the furnishings upstairs. I see Seattle's lights through the cold glass and instantly start to sweat.

They're all wrong.

Too crooked. Too strange. Too sideways.

We're wrecked. Dangling God only knows how many feet in the sky.

Gasping, I twist my head to face my companion, who

up until a few seconds ago was my biggest problem. "Jesus! We're –"

"Stuck, Presh. What are the chances?" Apparently, the horrific mortal peril we might be in doesn't faze his cool, or that smirk I'd really like to wipe off his face with a nasty flick of my palm.

The pet name doesn't register. Not at first.

When it does, my heart stops beating. My blood runs cold. A chill swarms up my spine.

Presh is something I haven't heard for years. Not outside my nightmares. That name is a ghost rising up, whispering in my ear, draining my life away.

Presh was what *he* called me.

Presh breathed sunny warmth into the coldest afternoon swept by the Pacific wind when it hung on his lips.

Presh is engraved forever in my mind.

How he groaned it mid-thrust, owning me, painting every inch of me with fire.

Presh, sometimes Precious, but always Presh. Always.

I was his precious girl. That means this stranger, this madness, is no one but...

"Trent?" I whisper his name. Half-curse, half-denial. Entirely get-me-the-hell-out-of-here.

The disinterested spark of recognition flaring in his eyes worries me a whole lot more than the world going crooked outside. He's too distracted to torment me as much as he'd like.

Proof positive there's something terribly wrong with this elevator, and one wrong move might send us plummeting to our deaths.

His smirk becomes a smile. The man, the bastard – Trent – nods.

"Like poetry, isn't it? Perched above the world with the Reaper at our necks. Hell of a delay I didn't really expect. Guess this is a bad time to say you're looking well, darling?" It's not just the elevator that's slanted.

It's him, his hand stretches behind him, holding on so gravity doesn't send him crashing into me. The floor is bent at such an angle it isn't easy to stand on his side without assistance.

"Delay? What?!" My brain hits its limit. It shuts down. I can't process what the hell's happening between the fear, the shock, the loathing that sweeps through me, curdling my blood. "What...what do you mean?"

"You didn't stop to wonder why I'm on an elevator heading up to your family's office? Shit. You've been through a lot in the last sixty seconds, Presh. Couldn't have been much fun twisting around, nearly bashing your head on the glass, this rusty old thing crapping out...so I'll go easy. " He pauses, taps behind him on the glass, a sound that ricochets through the small compartment like a bullet. "Let me fill in the blanks for you, darling, because you were never much good at puzzles. I'm back in town to pay your fuckhole brother a visit. Back for justice. Fancy meeting you the evening I swore I'd get even."

The air I've had trapped in my lungs for what seems like forever hisses out. For a brief second, I imagine the cold glass behind me giving way, cracking, putting me out of my misery. Tumbling through the chilly spring air and impacting solid concrete seems easier than this.

Far too easy.

Luck, Fate, and Heaven itself just trampled me in the mud and laughed. The years I've spent running marathons, trying to forget, ruining endless pairs of sneakers in sticky muck haven't prepared me for anything.

Not for today. I'm at least twenty stories up, hanging in mortal danger, trapped with the boy who trashed my family and left my heart a burning ruin.

"Presh –"

We lock eyes the instant I cut him off. "Don't, Trent. Just don't."

There's more clinging to the tip of my tongue, a proper lashing, heavy and bitter, but I just can't get it out. It's still caught in my throat when the elevator shakes a second time, groans, and drops.

I'm thrown into a deep inky blackness before I can breathe the last words I want to say on this Earth.

Don't you dare, Trent Usher. I still hate your fucking guts.

II: MEMORY LANE (TRENT)

She's out cold. Can't say I blame her.

I'm wondering if it's a mercy. This damn elevator is acting like it *really* wants to kill us.

When I hear the loud grinding noise, feel the mechanism overhead giving way, I think our little reunion is about to end with a life ending splat.

But the spinning, the growling, the brutal plunge stops.

Drops five, maybe ten feet and then catches, jerking us up again.

I'm still gripping the gold banister. My fucking arm nearly rips off my shoulder, burning as the thing bounces once and then catches again.

Miraculously, it holds. Stops. Leaves us suspended, closer to eye-level with the Seattle nightscape. I see the Seattle Great Wheel by the waterfront lit bright and slowly spinning, turning over like a clock counting down the impending end of our lives.

It's stupid, really. I should care more about the

prospect of becoming a pancake in a designer suit if we hit the bottom. More about the fact that I'm not sure if the way my arms just jerked back into their sockets will leave permanent damage.

But all I can do is hang off the railing like a monkey, gazing at the woman under me. And for once, she's pinned under my body in a way I never wanted.

She's as beautiful as I remember.

Hell, maybe *more.*

Hips for ages, chestnut hair, emerald green eyes. The color of those tawny locks I used to love curling my fingers through, she got from her ma. The ripple in her hair came from her old man.

The elder Chenocotts couldn't have created a more perfect wonder. Or a bigger bastard in her brother, Jace. Have to hand it to them: they forged an angel and a demon from the same blood.

Presh groans gently. I forget musing over the good and evil in her family DNA.

Fuck.

Six goddamn years, and *this* is how we reconnect?

Somewhere, somebody's laughing. It's a colossal cosmic joke, our predicament. A knee-slapping, tongue-biting, sucker-for-punishment sorority prank, and it just might be the last one we ever get to throw an acid laugh at.

A new pain burrows through my shoulder. My wrist tightens, but I can't hold on.

The angle is too steep. My bones can only take so much. I wish I'd kept up rock climbing, but there hasn't been much time for that since leaving Washington in the rear view mirror, piecing my life back together, plotting my revenge.

I grit my teeth. If only it were Jace, not Amy Kay, stuck here with me. I'd go out in a blaze of bloodletting, throwing the fucker who torpedoed my life through the glass.

It's not him, though. It's her.

Unthinkable, abandoned, still hot-as-the-devil's-fireplace Presh.

She, who I wasn't supposed to ever hear from again.

Much less lay eyes on.

Much less wind up trapped in a ruined elevator with.

A woman – and what a woman! – who's blossomed since I turned my back, left her behind, and told myself a million times I had to.

For her good. For mine. For everyone's.

"Trent?" Her lips open, whispering my name, but her eyes stay closed.

First time since our run-in I can't detect raw hatred in her tone. My eyes crawl her limp, half-conscious body. She's slumped against the glass with one heel knocked off, lying in the corner. It's crunched underneath my briefcase, which I lost the first time the elevator went haywire.

"I'm here," I bite off.

Her eyelids flutter shut. I get nothing back.

Shit.

I'm trying to decide whether to move, wake her the hell up, figure some way out of this together. But she'd just as soon give me the same treatment I've planned for her asshole brother, I'm sure.

Worst part is, I can't even blame her. Not in this lifetime.

Still, she could be hurt. I can't just stand here like an idiot, waiting for her to come back to life and breathe fire. I let my legs give, dangling, rocking my weight, testing the elevator's stability, hoping my weight won't be the last straw. *So far, so good.*

It won't drop us again. *I think.*

Only one way to be sure...I let go of the gold railing and let myself fall. I hit the edge of the metal divider between the glass, rolling next to her.

It takes another minute to struggle into a crouching position. The elevator sways gently.

Good. One less worry about the cord or whatever the hell's holding this thing snapping like a twig.

"Presh?" I take her hand, squeezing.

Nothing. Adrenaline hits my veins.

"Presh!" I do it again, adding pressure, watching her eyelids flutter. Hoping she didn't bash her head in harder than I thought. "Come the hell back here. You hear?"

Nothing again. She just twists her neck, moans a little, something soft and small and indistinct.

Goddamn, this better not be a concussion.

For all my brains – and they've worked miracles – I'm not a doctor. I reach up, testing the emergency button for the intercom, yanking the phone off its cradle.

No tone. Dead silence. The more I press it to my ear, the heavier the void.

Fuck.

Whatever caused this one-in-three-million mishap, it's knocked out communications. And I'm betting our cell phones don't work either. The enclosed shafts of these old buildings are notoriously crappy for reception.

Worst part is, I'm too busy to even try. I'm stuck, focused on my breathing, trying to still the fierce ache in my joints. Worried as hell Amy Kay will never wake up again.

Tightening my hold on her hand, my eyes flick to the briefcase.

"Shit!" Growling, I bash my fist into the solid steel part of the wall that's become our floor with everything spun nearly ninety degrees.

This isn't how it was supposed to go down. Not at fucking all.

I was supposed to come up here alone, find a comfy seat to perch for the night, and be there bright and early before the morning crew arrived. I was supposed to make my special delivery to Jace Chenocott in person, documents I've spent the better part of the last year piecing together. Tactical nukes made of paper.

Unbelievable. This entire thing, starting with the fact that he used to be my best friend.

Amy stirs, whimpering a little. With no better options, I scoop her up, hold her to my chest, and send a silent prayer through the glass.

If there's anybody left to hear, I want this over, A-S-A-fucking-P.

But I'd really like her to walk away alive a whole hell of a lot more.

I close my eyes, waiting for her to come back to me, my patience for miracles running thin.

Can't tell what's spinning faster: my head or every breath shaking my lungs.

Before I know it, I'm back in Madison Park, almost a decade ago. You know that load they feed you about facing impending death and having your life flash before your eyes?

I'm living it. Except my life didn't start until age seventeen, world hanging from my balls, face-to-face with the most beautiful woman in the world who'd ever learn to hate me.

* * *

Nine Years Ago

"ANOTHER ENGLISH PAPER? Jace, what the fuck?" I look up. He doesn't even ask, just drops it on my desk, a shameless grin digging at his dimples.

"Hot date tonight. I'll pay you double to get mine done. Look, I realize old man Matheson is up everybody's ass, wanting us to have some original spin on this James Joyce crap." He pauses, rolling his eyes. "Guess the old fart's never heard of Google. I could find a ghostwriter overseas to spin college papers all damn day."

"Dude, don't. It's not just professors lining up to check plagiarism now. You fuck up that bad, you're out of Maynard. Besides, you know you'd get junk-ass quality. I'll write your crap again, okay? Just give me double, like you said. And wrap *it* the hell up if your date tonight's Georgia. She's been screwing those La Crosse players numb for the past semester."

Grin growing wider, Jace extends a muscular hand. We're about the same size and strength and it's always a small pissing contest when we shake.

Then I turn back to my screen, cracking my knuckles. Another long night of writing lays ahead instead of trying to get my dick wet.

That's for rich kids who can afford to be irresponsible. Guys like my boy, Jace, who lives in a damn Madison Park mansion. He's got a rotating harem of girls from millionaire families.

My blessing is brains. Better work ethic, too. I'm living about as much as I really want to, taking money to crib Jace's papers, and hell yes I charge him *big.* If anybody ever found out, I'd be out on my ass like lightning.

It's in my interest to make sure my best friend doesn't do something stupid that gets us both cooked.

Exclusive academies like Maynard don't fuck around. I'm one of the few students there on merit, rather than money or blue blood. There's more pressure than ever on the principal to crackdown lately, too. Ever since the Randolph kid did the unthinkable on school property.

An accident, they said. A bad fight that got out of hand. A complete clusterfuck.

It was the big, ugly finale to a whole lot of corruption tarnishing the academy well before I ever enrolled three years ago.

"You can stay here and work. Ask mom for dinner," Jace says, tapping his fist next to my laptop. "Shit, sometimes I think my parents like having you around more than me."

His confidence dims. I give him a crooked smile, unsure what the hell to say to that.

The Chenocotts are good people.

Like any high class Seattle family, they're also demanding. Sometimes, I think they've already given up on Jace.

He was grounded for weeks last year after pulling a C in chemistry. It's more likely they're putting their chips on their daughter.

Amy Kay.

Fuck.

Don't even think about her, I tell myself. There's a very good reason.

Amy Kay Chenocott is on my mind way more than she should be. She's everything Jace isn't: soft spoken, sweet, intelligent, and way too fucking young.

She's only in her freshman year. We're Seniors. I've always told myself I won't be one of those assholes who hooks up with the fresh meat and leaves them high and dry. I *definitely* can't be the prick who does it to his best friend's little sister. For more reasons than I've got time to list.

"I'll get it done and then I'll eat the shit out of your ma's chocolate muffins." I grin, slapping my friend on the back. I have to deflect the wicked thoughts his little sister always manages to give me somehow.

"Gross, Usher. If you weren't so damn good at what you do, don't know why we'd be friends."

"Because you need to shore up your GPA if we're heading to Bellingham next year. Blood pact, remember?" I turn back to my screen, well aware he's still staring through me.

"You're a madman for turning down the Ivies. I've seen what's on your desk at home – Yale, Princeton, Stanford. Fucking scholarships out the wazoo. Beats me why the fuck you want to stay local, getting rained on up and down this dreary coast." Jace walks across the room, yanking an expensive craft root beer off the counter, bringing one for me. "If I had the grades...shit. I'd be down in SoCal so fast and I'd never look back. The world's a whole lot bigger than Seattle and months of no sun."

I shrug. "Why do a stupid thing like that when there's money to be made? Big coin."

That gets him smiling. Or maybe he's got me half-tuned out already, picturing his latest conquest. Georgia Evans goes down easy for most guys, and for Jace? He'll probably be home early with her panties in his pocket.

"Seriously, man, I like those ideas you floated a couple weeks ago. Started brainstorming in my little black book. It's a nice distraction during Euro history." He reaches into his backpack, grabs his small leather notebook out of it, and flips it open. "This solar shit...it's gonna change everything. Won't even be hard to line up the venture capital with my old man's connections. You've got the brains, and I've got –"

"People," I finish for him.

I don't need him saying the other word, money, rubbing in his status.

I have an idea what it takes to grease the wheels if you want to get anywhere in life. I also know how high a mountain I'd have to climb alone, without him, raising funds for an untested technology startup.

I nod, trying to be encouraging. Truth is, Jace barely understands what a solar panel is.

He hasn't spent the hours like I have, ass deep in government white papers, exploring markets and pinpointing needs that'll make this thing a success, right out of the gates.

"Yeah, that's it. People." His phone starts buzzing. Throwing his notebook back in his bag, I watch him toss it over his shoulder, and race toward the elevator leading to the garage.

Yes, their house has its own elevator, as insane as that is.

"Gotta run! Email whatever you've got over by midnight and I'll pay up tomorrow. Thanks again, dude, I owe you."

"Bye, Jace." He's already out the door.

I should consider myself lucky he's taking this business talk so seriously. His support, his family, can open more doors than any degree. I'm lucky we're friends, even if it's frustrating as hell sometimes.

Whatever his faults, we make a good team.

* * *

"Alone again, Mr. Usher? Where's Jace?" Maxwell Chenocott appears behind me a few hours later, dropping his usual formal greeting. He's a strapping older man who looks like one of the playboy executives from *Mad Men*. He's a lot more reserved than the guys on TV, though, and more buff than any guy in his fifties should be. Probably the hikes in the Cascades he does religiously.

"Oil change and a library run, I think. Said his car really needed it. I decided to stay here and get cracking on our paper. How's business anyway, Mr. Chenocott?"

"Another day, another dollar." He smiles, throwing his raincoat on the bamboo hanger by their door, then returning a minute later with a drink in his hand and a coffee for me. "Will you look at that view? Goddamn magnificent this evening."

I turn to where he's staring out the massive windows.

It's late evening and the city's lights are a half-smeared twinkle, distorted by the rain and darkness like a Grimshaw painting.

"Always is, Mr. Chenocott. You've got an awesome place." I'm honest.

Deep down, maybe I'm a little jealous. They've always been good to me, but my folks will never have anything like this. Sometimes the chasm their money opens between us swallows me.

"Don't be covering for my boy if he's left you high and dry, okay?" His voice sharpens and he casts a sideways glance. "Jace has to learn to sink or swim on his own. No carrying his load if he's off screwing around, you hear?"

I do.

Doesn't change the fact there's only one sane thing to do every time he probes me over Jace: lie through my teeth.

"He's getting better at the details. Honest, he is. Just last week, we knocked around business ideas all evening. Even seemed excited to take another crack at the SATs."

"He'd better. I didn't raise a loser. Hoping something rubs off before he finds himself in a world of hurt, Trent. You're a good kid and a better friend. He'd be worse off without you."

Before I can say, "thanks," the door swings open. There's a clatter of shoes.

Mrs. Chenocott sways across the room, falling into her husband's arms, greeting him with an enthusiastic kiss. She's a slender, regal woman. An admiral's daughter, supposedly. I burn my eyes into the screen, ignoring the fifteen year old shadow materializing over me, stabbing my fingers at my keyboard. Harder and harder so I don't have to live her torment.

"You again? Guess that means he isn't here," Amy Kay whines, lowering her eyes. Her parents stop making out in front of us long enough to give a concerned look. "Jace promised he'd run me over for my uniform tonight."

"Oh, Orcaettes?" Mrs. Chenocott smiles. I've heard she was on the academy's dance team back in the day, too, which is probably why she still has a trim figure. "I'll take you, hun. Where *is* Jace, anyway?"

Shit, shit. His cover story's growing thinner by the second. And picturing Amy Kay in the black and white tights that make up our school colors for the dance team does me no favors.

I've never been able to figure out if the Orcaettes get their name from the islands north of here, or the whale. Either way, the girls all look more like mermaids than any lumbering ocean beasts.

"Oil change and library books, Mrs. Chenocott. Should be back soon." Yeah, I'm a royal heel for BSing like this. But there's a chance it could still be true, *if* my blood brother finishes getting his dick wet sometime this century and calls it an early night.

"Mom, forget it," Amy says, shooting me a lingering look. "Too bad you don't have a car yet, Trent."

"Yeah, too bad." My family's relative poverty slaps me in the face. I try not to bite my tongue.

"Peanut! Not nice. Mr. Usher does perfectly well with his bicycle, just like most kids. Vehicles are very expensive to operate and often unnecessary. Hideous carbon footprint." Mr. Chenocott's hand slaps my shoulder, trying to be reassuring.

Fuck, my guts just want to turn inside out. I don't need him coming to my defense, getting on his moral high horse about the environment or the logic of urban living. "Listen to your mom. She'll run you over for the uniform. Why don't you two go now while I figure out dinner?"

"Oh, Maxwell, not more takeout from that sushi place again?" His wife gives him a knowing look.

"Never, dear. It's so much better fresh. We're all going out tonight. Assuming Jace gets the hell back here in the next hour to join us." He looks at his ten thousand dollar gold watch and taps the glass. "On second thought...screw it. We're not waiting up for him. Trent, I hope you'll join us. Proxy for Jace. It's the least we can do for not having a home cooked meal ready after helping him out."

"That's very kind, but I'd better check with my folks," I say, reaching for my phone.

It's just a formality. Ma never says no. Hell, she loves when I hang around the Chenocotts. Their money, prestige, and class impresses her.

I also think it's balm for the guilt she feels, in a twisted way, adopting me and being unable to provide anything like the culture these millionaires can.

Amy Kay's eyes are on me while I'm deep in thought, dialing mom's number.

Despite hanging around Jace and his family, their high culture hasn't exactly rubbed off. Not in my soul. I'm a thousand times more at home in the salt of the earth fish markets by Pike's Place than eating fancy sashimi. Too bad I'd be rude and foolish saying no.

A quick call to mom goes off like I expect. She doesn't even hesitate, tells me to have fun, and enjoy. It makes me just as determined to buy her and Pops a four hundred dollar dinner someday.

While I'm busy talking, the door crashes open again. Jace drags himself inside. Amy Kay and Mrs. Chenocott instantly shoot him dirty looks.

"What? What'd I miss?" Jace locks eyes with me.

He's grinning ear to ear. It's insanely difficult not to shake my head.

"You're just in time," Maxwell says. "Go wash up and see if Trent needs help wrapping up your project. Soon as you boys say you're good, we're calling a ride and going to Satoshi's."

* * *

Dinner is surreal.

I sit next to my best friend, doing my damnedest to pick over raw fish and rice. I'm sure I'm breaching etiquette a hundred times overloading every bite on my chopsticks full of wasabi, but I can't bring myself to care.

Ophelia Chenocott prattles on excitedly, telling us how nice her visit to the local university was with Amy Kay in tow. She dragged her daughter to some cancer research benefit, one of many charities she has a hand in.

I barely hear a word. My eyes are drunk on the site across from me, shyly hoisting bites of sushi to her ruby red lips.

Merciful Christ, is Amy Kay wearing lipstick tonight?

If she is, it looks damn good. Also sends jealousy storming through my blood, imagining who she's wearing it for.

Is this practice for some guy?

Another rich fuckhead I see every day in the halls, rubbing his paws together, hoping he'll be her first? Hell, is she *already* seeing somebody?

I hope to hell not. And not just because everything involving her and me is a bad idea.

She's too young, too innocent. Practically bait for the rich pricks who make up the majority of Maynard's male population. They're more like Jace than I care to admit. A willing cock carousel who burn through girls like their parents' money.

"Hey, dad, you still going to that thing in Olympic Park this weekend?" The excitement in Jace's tone gets my attention.

"It's October, dear. Your father wouldn't miss his last good chance at the trails before they turn freezing for anything." Mrs. Chenocott smiles, waiting until her husband nods. "Speaking of getaways, if you boys promise to behave, we were thinking –"

"Ma, you can trust us anytime. Hell, me and Trent were just planning to box ourselves in all weekend so I can study my SATs," Jace tells her cheerfully.

I don't even have to look at my friend to know he's already got something diabolical planned.

"You're trying awfully hard to sell us, son. Makes me want to think twice about breaking in my new hiking boots before the season's over." Maxwell stops mid-bite, eyeing Jace through his thick spectacles.

A plump shrimp roll slips out of Amy's chopsticks, slapping the plate underneath. She sighs. "Does this mean I'll be cooped up all weekend with these clowns? Mom?"

I hold her eyes, longer than I need to. Damn, those

jade green irises are dangerous – the kind that'll drown a man in stupid if he lets them.

They're also mysterious. Unpredictable. Consuming.

I can't tell if she actually hates my ass or maybe there's another reason she wants under my skin.

"Hon, you can bring a friend over too, if you'd like. I'm sure it'll be okay...we've got Trent to keep everyone in line. Consider yourselves lucky." Mrs. Chenocott runs her hand along Maxwell's. He gives her a knowing look.

Gross. They *really* need that weekend getaway, probably to finish what they started after she came home today.

Mr. Chenocott nods. "Jace, I'm trusting you. You know the rules: no strangers, no drinking, and don't you *dare* set foot in the boathouse."

Jace's eyes are on me, prickly as ever. I wonder if he resents having me appointed big brother, but it seems like he doesn't really care. Having the whole house to ourselves overshadows whatever weird anxieties his parents keep pounding through his head.

I know one thing: this weekend is going to be balls to the walls insane.

"Dad, I don't know. Seems like a bad idea." Amy Kay won't let go. I can't tell who's giving who the dirtier look – her, or Jace.

"Peanut, there's a lesson here for you, too, I'm sure. If it makes you feel better, keep an eye on them, and call us anytime. We'll keep our phones on." Maxwell never says what that lesson is.

Amy Kay's eyes meet mine again for a burning second, before she resumes stuffing her little mouth with sushi. Her hands stay busy the entire time. Clearly, it'll be a while before she makes peace with Jace running the house.

I just hope I'm able to diffuse the wicked heat this girl pumps in my blood, without blowing everything to kingdom come.

* * *

I'M at the Chenocott's place bright and early on Saturday morning. The beer I bought off an older kid's big brother last night swings under my coat, hiding from any servants who might still be lurking around. Same tactic I used with Ma and Pops. The Chenocotts rarely have their cleaning people by on the weekends, but I'm not taking chances.

Jace will be royally pissed if I screw up the booze. Sure, there's greater likelihood any missteps will be on his end, but a small part of me also wants to make the most of having this massive place to ourselves for the weekend.

I only ring the doorbell once. Jace's big hand comes out, grabs me by the wrist, and yanks me inside with all his might. "Get the fuck in here, my dude. We've got clear weather!"

"Weather?" The bottles rattle in my hand, secure in their cardboard container.

Behind us, I hear a shrill giggle. Fucking Georgia.

"Oh, Jaycee, you *sure* we need this beer with everything else? Hi, T!" Georgia waves. I try really hard to see a brain behind her manikin smile.

I give a weak hello and wave back. Don't know who I feel worse for: Georgia, for hanging off him like a damn puppy, or Jace for leading her on. He's bought himself a hell of a time getting rid of this one after he's had his fun.

"Forget it, babe. The more, the merrier. Usher, we're fucking loaded. Already raided the liquor cabinet dad hasn't touched in ages. Time to hit the waves."

The boat? Shit.

Jace is wasting no time landing us both in hot water.

"The boathouse?" I'm shaking my head, more obviously than I should. "Dude...you heard what your old man said. If anything happens to the Wilkie –"

"Usher?" He pauses, an irritable flicker in his eyes. Jace yanks one of the bottles from the box and rips the cap off, shoving it to my lips. "Drink. It'll help you chill the fuck out and, you know, not blow our only chance in months at finally having some goddamn fun."

Checkmate.

A rich dark Porter bubbles on my tongue. Higher alcohol content, of course, just like he wanted.

I shut my yap and suck it down, following Jace and Georgia through the garage, out the side door, and down the little stone walkway through Ophelia's manicured gardens. It's a decent walk across the huge property to their boathouse.

I've lost the war before it started.

There's no convincing him. He's made up his mind, and when there's pussy involved, Jace always aims to impress. No better way to do that than a four ton stand-in for his dick size that could sail all the way to Alaska. Overkill for Georgia, who's already wide-eyed and starstruck at the crown jewel of the Chenocott's enormous wealth.

Inside the boathouse, even the beer hitting my empty stomach can't completely silence the voice in my head screaming, *this is a bad idea.* The ship beckons in the dim light, big and proud, a seriously complicated machine.

The SS Wilkie is more than a rich man's yacht. It's a twenty person luxury liner. A freaking whale crafted from the finest wood. Right now, perched safely in its nest for at least a few more minutes.

A small part of me hopes Jace doesn't have a clue how to get this thing off the dock. He's already scrambling up the staircase leading to the main deck, grinning as he helps Georgia along. Predictably, she giggles her little ass off, pecks him on the cheek, and whispers something about "captain."

Awesome. We're not even out to sea, and I'm already fighting the urge to yak up breakfast.

"Usher, you coming?" Jace's tone is a warning. Not a question.

Lucky more booze hits my blood, giving me the liquid courage I need to get on with the insanity. I run up the stairs and bang my fist on his. "There's my man. Let's roll. I'll show you guys how hard I rock at steering this thing."

He'd better be right.

* * *

It takes over an hour to get the boat into the Puget Sound. Jace doesn't really know what the hell he's doing.

Rather, he knows just enough to spool the engine up and get us cruising along the coast at a lazy clip. Good thing these yachts are meant to be idiot proof.

Traffic on the water is light today, thank God. The other owners of fancy docks on this exclusive stretch of coast must be out of town for the weekend like the Chenocotts.

It doesn't take much time with Georgia on his lap before Jace gets distracted either. "Yo, why don't you take over, Usher? It's easy. I want to show my girl the rooms downstairs. Give her a little tour. Think you can handle this big bitch without running us aground?"

Georgia's eyes light up the second he says "my girl."

Fucking *woof.* I've never seen any of his conquests happen so fast.

"I'll try," I say, running my eyes along the control panel.

It looks more like the fucking space shuttle than any boat I've ever known. But hell, it's not like I've ever been in the nerve center of anything more complicated than a car. Good thing I like a challenge. "Run along. If I run into trouble, I'll holler."

"See? Told ya we could count on him." Jace silences Georgia's laughter with a long kiss, and then they're gone.

Shit. I'm buzzed, but not so far gone I've lost my common sense. I plop down in the captain's seat and dig through the cabinet on the right.

Surely, there's a manual. A guide. *Something.*

I'm practically a genius and a decent driver, despite not having a car yet. I got my license easy and drive Pops' truck somewhere every week. Figuring out how to navigate this thing shouldn't be impossible.

The boat drifts along, stable and safe, buying me precious time to look for the instructions. It's a mess inside the compartment. There are old maps, an atlas, maybe half a dozen thick travel magazines, each of them stuffed with pamphlets for ritzy resorts from old family outings.

The screaming that starts up below deck doesn't help.

What now? At first, I think it's just Jace screwing with her, but she doesn't stop. Georgia is howling bloody murder.

I bolt up, race to the stairs, wondering if somebody fell and broke bones, or if this is just how loud they get when they're drunk and going at it.

Then I hear Jace's voice. "God dammit, Amy Kay! I ought to throw you overboard and make you swim the fuck home."

"Hey, hey...She's just a kid." Georgia's voice. "You said this ship is good for how many? Like twenty people? It's not like she'll interrupt anything if we just let her hang."

"No, Georgia, you don't get it. This little stowaway *will* rat us the hell out the second she's got her phone to her ear. Speaking of which – where's your phone, sis? Hand it over." More rage floods his tone by the second.

"Jesus, calm down! It's not like I was going to say anything. Honest. Just wanted to know what you guys were up to. We already both know messing around with the Wilkie is a butt kicking in dad's book. We've been out here for more than an hour, Jace." She pauses, sighing. "Don't you think I'd have called dad by now if I really – hey, hands off!" It's the last thing Amy Kay says before the discussion, if you can even call it that, breaks down into three way teenage screaming.

This is getting out of hand and very fucking dangerous. We can't have a slap fight and nobody at the controls for long. I have to break this shit up.

I pound into the main living area like a tornado. Amy Kay is in tears, locked in a tug of war with her idiot brother, while Georgia looks on and clucks her tongue, making the world's weakest attempt to make peace.

"Guys, for fuck's sake. Guys!" I rush between them, shove Jace off her, ripping at the phone in his hand.

He's caught off guard and goes spinning back against the wall, stabbing a dirty look through me. "Screw you, Usher! What the hell do you think you're doing? Didn't you see –"

"I've got it right here in my hand," I growl. "You're paranoid, man. I'll keep this safe if you're worried about her squealing."

Amy stands up, wipes the stray tears off her cheeks, and takes a good long look at me.

I catch her green eyes, try to telegraph a warning into her brain. *Quiet. Let me handle this.*

"That's not the fucking point!" Jace roars, storming over. He's in my face, shouting, something I've never seen him do in the three years we've known each other. "She always ruins my shit – *always*. She's a little rat. Her life's so damn boring she's always got to rub her nose in mine, where it doesn't belong."

"Like I care, asshole! Don't flatter yourself." She stumbles forward a couple steps.

For once, I'm grateful for Georgia, who grabs her, whispering a few choice words.

Jace ignores the scene, too busy barking more rancor, spitting in my face. "Fuck you, man. You know how wrecked I am if dad finds out we've got his boat? Any fucking clue?"

Yeah. Maxwell will nail him to the wall, put him under house arrest.

Jace'll be lucky if I'm even allowed to drop by to write

his papers and help with SAT drills. He'll be useless, set back, an even bigger liability for getting our business off the ground.

I gather my words, ignoring how good it'd feel to punch him in the face.

"Remember what you told me earlier? Relax? That's what we're here to do today, right?" I'm speaking slow, measured, like I'm cornering an escaped beast at the zoo. "She won't be making any calls. Trust me. Let's just forget this crap and have our fun."

He narrows his eyes. I see it in his face, he doesn't want to let go. "Fine. But damn, any more antics, and I'm dead serious about making her *swim*."

"Screw you!" Amy Kay lurches forward, catches Georgia's arms, beaming raw hate at her brother. "You're all lucky I'm here. Somebody needs to be sober on this ship. I swear, Jace, if you bring this boat home beat up, dad'll –"

A high pitched scraping sound drowns her out, giving heart-stopping emphasis to her words. *Fuck.*

It only lasts a second, maybe two. At least it shuts everyone up. We're glued to the floor, staring at each other, fear replacing anger in Jace's eyes. "Oh, Christ," he whispers.

"Let me take a look. Amy Kay, you've been out on this thing a few times, haven't you?" I look her way, see the same terror filling up her face. Slowly, she nods. "Come with me. Georgia, Jace, you two stay here. Cool your heels. If we're in deep shit, you'll hear it from me."

I hear them bantering back and forth while Amy follows me upstairs. She's still blotting at her eyes with her sleeve. It's a maroon sweater and a skirt today, concealing her curves, but barely.

I'll take it. I don't need distractions while I search out what we hit, praying it isn't another boat.

"No manual for this thing?" I ask her, rummaging through the cabinet again after a quick check through the windows. I don't see any obvious collision objects or damage. Maybe – I hope – it was just a huge rock or the edge of a navigation buoy drifting by.

"I...can't remember. Dad always steered. Like second nature to him. He had a few years in the navy, spent a few summers with our grandpa's fishing company, I think." She sniffs, still clearing her tears, shaking her head. "Okay. I've seen him do this a million times...once or twice he even let me have the wheel. Supervised, of course."

Quietly, she comes close, peering over my shoulder. "Sensors look good. Whatever it was, I don't think it did any major damage, but we should try to dock to look things over."

I shrug. "If we're not taking on water, I think we're okay. Good for however long Jace wants to stay out here, I mean."

She twists her lips sourly. "He's a dick. Don't know how you stand him."

Can't argue today. I'm trying to focus and let go of the shit storm with my best friend.

It's raining, big fall Pacific droplets pelting the hull. So much for the clear weather Jace promised, wiped out by the abrupt rains that always manage to attack a beautiful Seattle day.

I'm hoping this doesn't pick up, or visibility will become a struggle.

I look through the glass, ignoring how she leans on my shoulder. Her heat is another vicious distraction I don't need. "Your brother's not an asshole constantly. Sometimes, hell yeah. No denial. He thinks with his reptile brain and doesn't know how to shut it off."

"His...huh?"

"Reptile brain. You know, the part where all the animal instincts are. Fight, flight, and –" I stop myself right before I say *fucking*. "Feeding. Point is, that's what he lets lead him around. Causes a lot of trouble sometimes."

"Is that why you enable him?" She casts a bitter look. "He'd have flunked out of Maynard or gotten a real tutor by now if you weren't writing his papers. Too bad you can't take his tests, too. Best he ever does on those are Cs."

I ignore her, eyes ahead of me.

Think I see an island in the distance, one with those small channel harbors where they used to have fisheries and whaling houses a hundred years ago. Probably a heritage marker now. Chances are there's a run down dock or two, the perfect place to wait out this storm, if I can get us there in one piece.

"Sorry, Trent. That was rude of me, I guess." She sighs, looking down. "His crap isn't your fault. I'm just...really frustrated. We all are." Her voice softens. So do her fingers, running along my neck, causing something evil and electric to dart through me. "I'm scared he won't come home one day. Mom, too. Or he'll wind up in big trouble, something so bad it hits the whole family. Call it a gut feeling. An ugly one."

"He's going through some shit. Letting his dick and his inexperience lead him into trouble. Finding himself or whatever. Pretty typical seventeen year old acting out."

She laughs, a high tinsel sound. A smile digs at my cheeks while I'm looking for the rudder controls, trying to turn this thing, point us toward the docks in the distance. "On your left, old fart. You don't have to correct very much. The computer does it automatically."

"Old fart?" I raise an eyebrow.

"I mean, you talk like you're not the same age as Jace. Like you've been there, seen that, done it all. Come on. You're a kid, Trent. Just like the rest of us. Or does that tortured high IQ orphan thing make you a wise man, too?"

"Shut up," I grumble, half-playfully and half-serious. She's touched something I've tried to bury. "Never gone looking for sympathy. Not even once. My parents are great people. They've given me the world, and I'm grateful. Couldn't care less about the nobodies sharing my DNA."

I bring the ship closer to the island, keeping a safe distance. There's an outline of something on the shore. An old fishery, I think, or maybe just a touristy place with docks.

If I'm right, it'll do.

"Ouch. Sorry for trying to figure you out." She pats my shoulder playfully. Then she leans over, bringing her lips dangerously close to my ear, a whisper falling out. "Didn't know you were so easily offended, Usher."

Great. More fuel for those wet dreams I'm trying like hell to forget right now. "Trent, Amy Kay. That's my name. Everybody says my last so much it's been run into the ground and then some."

"What, I thought you were a Poe fan? House of Usher? You've got that broody, tall, dark mysterious thing going on. Kinda fitting."

Her voice flows in my ear, thick as honey.

Definitely softer.

Dangerously sweet.

Almost addicting.

Also, so damn close to making me crack and tell her she can call me whatever she pleases.

No. Focus. I'm *not* running this ship into a cliff because I can't stop imagining what her sassy lips would feel like on mine. She's wearing a new shade of lipstick today, I see, a light maroon that makes her face look more grown up.

I say nothing, easing the ship forward as best I can, until Amy Kay squeezes my shoulder. "You're coming in too fast. Don't crash."

Turning, I slowly look her over, studying the curved smile on her lips. "You've watched your dad a million times, you said?"

She nods. Slowly.

"Then stop being a tease and show me." I take my hands off the controls. She laughs, maneuvering her hands down my arms, taking her sweet time on the muscles I've sculpted the last four years in the weight room after school.

"This," she says, guiding my hand to a lever on the side. "It's just like a brake. It'll help you slow, make sure we don't rip the dock clean off."

I test it slowly, pushing where she showed. There's a faint creaking sound. We're losing speed. A brutal weight lifts off my shoulders.

It takes ten minutes to guide the boat into a large space tucked in the beat up marina. I see one of the museums perched above it, already closed for the rainy season and the end of the tourist rush.

"You think it's safe? I mean this is private property..." Amy's burst of confidence is gone. I see the sweet, shy daddy's girl again, so afraid Jace's stupidity will land her in the thick of trouble.

"It'll have to do. Rain's picking up. We'll take our chances nobody else notices or cares. Do I need to anchor, or what?" She takes my hand, guiding it to another panel on the side. I push the button and there's another groaning sound, smoother than before.

The swaying from the wind and water eases. We're docked, probably through the evening. Amy's soft hands leave my skin slowly, no longer having an excuse to linger. I watch her smile and trot to the edge of the glass. Her eyes search the rain, the trees, the thickening gray clouds choking off the sky.

"Sucks we can't go on land. I can't believe I forgot my umbrella."

"It's frigid as hell, Amy Kay. Consider yourself lucky. Hear how hard it's coming down? That's rain like ice." Finally relaxed, I reach for the beer I brought aboard, cracking open another porter. The rich dark brew helps take the edge off.

She turns, wrinkling her nose when she sees me flopped back in the captain's seat. "Can't believe you're drinking that stuff. We're definitely *screwed* if the cops pull up for an inspection. No boat license, underage, and intoxicated. I thought you were like crazy smart?"

I lean forward, smiling. "Here's a tip, Amy Kay: your brain gets bigger when you learn to pull that stick out of your ass. Quit worrying and live a little."

Her jaw falls open. Somehow, I like her a whole lot more when she's looking at me bewildered.

Makes the fierce urges running through my blood a whole lot easier to control. "Whatever. Not sure I'd call screwing off and almost flunking classes living, Trent. Or stealing dad's prized baby just so I can have a fancy room for a quick lay. That girl, Georgia...she'll be in tears next week. Jace is just sad." She whips her head around, then looks back, adding, "So are you."

Standing, I walk forward, taking another swig off my bottle. "Sad? You say that like it's a bad thing. No yin in this life without the yang. Sad has its place, darling. Sometimes sad means being young and stupid, making mistakes. Living just to learn."

I'm closer than I intend. She turns, her eyes widening.

They're huge, green, and so fucking bright.

Just for once, I wonder what they'd look like truly lit. Like if I take her little face in my hand, pull her in, and leave her with something electric.

Something worth thinking about far more than fretting over her dumbass brother.

"I don't need a lecture, Mr. Usher." She imitates her dad's voice when she says my name. "Look, I know you've got my parents and everybody else fooled. They think you're the good son they never had. Brains, morals, nose to the grindstone, wizard-like responsibility. They all trust you."

My hand grazes her cheek. She gasps, her sweet body wriggling under the maroon sweater. Deep purple dipped in rust red, a color calling to every dirty, dark thing I've had on my mind since the first time Jace invited me over a year ago, and I saw his little sister for the very first time.

"And you don't?" Can't figure out if it's the booze warping my mind or just her sass.

Fuck. I'm playing with fire, throwing it around in fistfuls, begging to have my ass kicked if Jace or Georgia wander up here while I've got my hand on Amy's face.

"No." She says firmly, but I sense hesitation. "If you were really so different from Jace, you wouldn't be hanging around him all the time. Definitely wouldn't be planning to take off to college together, hatching your silly solar business. I'm not stupid, Trent. You're using my brother, my family. It's money you're after, isn't it? Ours."

That...that isn't fucking true. Arrow, meet chest. My playful smirk fades. It's hard not to pinch her cheek until she squeals.

I mean, in a round about way, part of the Chenocott allure *is* what they can do for me. No denying it. But hell, I didn't creep up to Jace in gym the day we met just for money, offering to spot for him while he hit the bench press. I didn't have a clue how rich he was then, or why his take-no-shit attitude pissed off most of the other guys in our class.

I damn sure didn't start hanging around to bleed him dry. I'm not a manipulator. I actually appreciate my little chats with Maxwell Chenocott, and if I've got an ulterior motive with Ophelia, it's scarfing down her latest batch of cookies.

"What? Too real for you?" Amy Kay whispers, her green eyes twitching as they pour into mine. They're nervous.

A wry laugh rattles in my throat. She stares harder while I shake my head. "You're precious, Amy Kay. Never change. I mean it, too. Nobody else but you could insult me to my face and get away with it, calling me some kind of fucked up gold digger who's just out to leech because I'm the orphan kid, or whatever."

"Hey, now. I didn't say you wanted to marry him or anything. Don't think Jace swings that way." She thinks she's being funny.

Fuck this. I've had it with her insults, her insufferable looks, her words. Everything she's patented to make my blood run so hot it scorches my blue veins black.

Tightening my hold on her face, I bring my lips home. I kiss the brat with half my soul. Plus a wild need to shut her up.

She melts in a fury of shock and awe and disbelief, her little tongue bending against mine. More eager than I expected, soon as she's gotten over the initial shock.

Sweet. Fucking. Mercy.

Her taste is equal parts temptation and wrong. So off limits, so good, so real I don't want to stop.

But I haven't lost it. However much I'd love to drink her over and over, let my hands roam freely across her, I realize our predicament.

Jace and his latest fuck are too near. We're marooned here until this rain stops. And if I keep drinking with Amy Kay Chenocott in close quarters, we might do things that'll land me in far deeper shit than any reckless driving with this yacht.

I can't let that happen. Not with my best friend's little sister. Not with a girl who's a freshman.

I tear myself away, leaving her lungs working overtime. She flattens herself against the huge window for support. "What...why...why did you stop?"

"Stay precious, Presh. You can't do that if the dirty

orphan boy you don't trust is the first to break you in." I turn, grabbing my beer, heading for the stairs.

It's the only sensible thing. I don't have a death wish.

"Trent? You...you're disgusting!" She belts out the last two words when I'm well on my way below deck, whistling to myself to drown her out.

Fuck.

I'm smiling when I find the empty room at the end of the hall and flop down on the bed. Behind the wall, I hear heavy breathing, grunting, the sound of something heavy and solid creaking like it'll break.

Jace and Georgia are going at it. Thank God for the beer, or I think I'd have the world's worst case of blue balls.

I work through my beers slowly, playing with my phone, staring out into the twisted, rain-beat beauty of the Washington coast.

It's hell getting my mind off that kiss. Meaning it's even worse for her, somewhere on this ship, wherever she slunk off to after we got up close and personal.

I meant to leave her breathless, shaken, humbled.

Instead, I'm the asshole feeling rustled, wondering if it was too much, too soon.

Is she somewhere on this ship crying her little eyes out? Fuck, was that her first kiss?

Don't know why I care about the answers.

She's a spoiled, annoying, beautiful brat. Sooner or later someone was bound to teach her some respect. Not like this, though.

Goddammit. Having a conscience sucks.

After a couple hours, flat on the bed, listening to Jace

snoring in the other room while him and Georgia take a breather, I've reached my limit.

I get up, push through the narrow door, and walk into the main living space. Amy Kay lays curled up on the big leather sectional built into the ship, a gas fire going nearby for extra warmth. She looks so fragile asleep.

Guilt stabs at my chest. Again when I see the faint salt lines left on her cheeks, the slight redness lingering around her eyes, obviously from crying.

Ass. Hole.

You pushed her too far.

Still, I won't apologize outright. Drifting behind her, I put my hands on her shoulders, point my lips at her ear, and whisper as slow and careful as I can without waking her. "Didn't mean to come down so hard, Amy Kay. Leaving you in knots was the last thing I ever wanted. Yeah, you piss me off with your entitled, know-it-all crap, but you're a sweet girl at heart. Never change. Never. Not from Jace's antics, not for any guy, not for me. Stay forever precious."

Precious. The word echoes in my head over and over like a bad guitar riff.

Only because it's true.

She might be a thousand things in the years to come: actress, singer, scientist, wife, mother.

To me, she'll always be the same playful Tinkerbell with the lush green eyes and the lips that never know when to quit. Precious.

Presh to her very soul, too deep, and far too deep in mine.

She murmurs, turning over, clutching at my hand. I freeze, wondering if she's heard everything, but her lips move in the sleepy sing-song way that only happens in dreams. "Trent..."

I close my eyes. Hearing my name on her soft, tired lips – the same I want to taste again – is fucking torture.

What's one more sneaky taste? Giving her little fingers another squeeze, I bring her hand up, and plant my lips gently on her skin.

She stirs again, harder, my cue to get the hell back to my room for the night.

The next twenty-four hours are a blur. I'm tossing and turning long after midnight, trying to fight the Chenocotts out of my head. Both Jace's BS and Presh's weird crush, now hanging out in the open, haunting me.

I can't make a bad situation worse. I have to let her down easy. Best way to do that is pretending nothing happened here, in a boat we shouldn't have, on this island that might as well be at the end of the earth.

I vaguely remember hearing Jace and Georgia going at it again, fixing a pizza in the kitchenette, then my best friend screaming in the rain, wild and high as a kite.

Clearly, booze wasn't the only thing he snuck on board. I crack my window, smelling smoke from at least one joint.

I'm the only one sober or awake the next day. Remembering what Amy showed me, I manage to get the ship back to the Chenocott boathouse. A hung over Jace slaps my fist on the way out. He's already giving Georgia the cold shoulder, and it just gets worse when he steps down, sees the huge scratch in the yacht's side, and belt's out the world's most panicked, "Shit!"

We spend the rest of the weekend frantically calling

repair places. I'm sure he pays off the family gardener to keep quiet.

Amy Kay – Presh – treats us both like we're radioactive.

Predictably shitty of her, but warranted. I can't avoid the damage my lips did forever.

Sunday, while Jace is still busy racing to hide the damage the Wilkie took on that rock, I ease up to her door and knock. I have to smooth this over, one way or another. "Precious? Let me in."

"No." Her voice is small. Angry. Bitter.

"Listen, what happened yesterday...I fucked up. I'll admit it. I was drunk. You pushed my buttons, but it's no excuse. Didn't mean to lead you on, or worse, make you feel like an idiot. I put you in your place and got carried away. Hoping you'll forgive and forget?" Easier said than done. Even now, I'm craving another taste of her, and that's all I need to know who the idiot really is here.

Silence answers me.

"Presh? Come on!" My fist bangs against the door. I want to pound harder, but I hear Jace pacing upstairs, waiting by the front, swearing and muttering to himself. One more guy is coming to buff out the scratches in the hull, and we're not sure if he'll make it before his folks return by dinner. "Please. Talk to me."

I'm about to give the fuck up when I hear her little feet shuffling on the ground. They're slow, calculated, and when she rips the door open, I get the ultimate kick in the balls.

She can't even hide the hurt. It's written on her face in messy red blotches and shameful, not-so-secret tears.

"You're right about one thing," she hisses.

"Yeah?"

"Forget it. Forget the kiss. Forget everything. There's no other way."

I swallow. It's harder than it should be. "Right. That's all I'm trying to say. Glad we're on the same page. I'm sorry, again. If it wasn't for the beer, the tension, the rain, nothing ever would've –"

"Trent." My name crackles off her lips, silencing the thousand and one excuses wanting to pour out. "Just...go. Go home. I can't have you here. Plus Jace deserves to stew in his own trouble, for once."

She isn't wrong. Stifling a reluctant growl, I turn my back, head past my best friend, and walk the hell out.

Luckily, he's so preoccupied by the Wilkie he doesn't chase me down. I'll text him later.

Mom has a nice steaming pot of chowder ready with fresh baked bread the second I'm through the door. Pops starts cracking jokes right away about my 'fishing trip.'

I feed him fake memories. Happy things that never happened, tell him how we got lucky with a break in the rain, caught some big ones, and spent the evening watching harbor seals.

I lie my ass off. Crafting stories and dunking my bread in that soup is the only thing that keeps me from punching a hole through the fucking wall.

The mountain of homework to catch up on – mine and Jace's – is a welcome distraction.

It'll take time to lick my wounds. To forget I ever flew too close to the precious sun, and walked away humiliated and burned. Maybe it's karma for trashing Amy Kay ten times worse, I don't know.

And I shouldn't fucking care.

That's still the scariest part. I need her to go back to being my wet dream, my best friend's little sister, and nothing else, like yesterday. Because if I can't bleach her from my memory, if we start sharing dirty, secret looks every time I'm over at their place, if we remember how goddamn good that kiss we had really was...

There's no happy ending. It isn't happening. It can't.

I'm not destroying myself obsessing over Amy Kay. I'm not that stupid or desperate or hellbent on leaving my dreams a smoldering wreck.

I'll take my own advice: forget.

Forget her crush. Forget the kiss. Forget fucking everything.

If only I'd been able to follow through.

We wouldn't have wound up with our hearts in tatters, egos drunk on hate, ready to spend our final moments lashing each other to pieces in a broken metal box suspended above the Seattle skyline.

III: THE TWENTY-FIRST FLOOR
(AMY KAY)

Present

I OPEN MY EYES, blinking back a pounding headache. Everything looks dizzy, the entire world flipped on its axis. Probably why it takes an eternity to remember why I'm in this predicament, and *who* I'm in it with.

"Welcome back, Precious. Had me worried. Thought you'd never come out of it." Trent's voice makes me wish I'd never woken up.

I stagger backwards – as best I can with the elevator tilted at a crazy angle. Rubbing my eyes, I try to make this go away. But he's still there, the same beautiful bastard, scary and unbelievable as a ghost.

He stands next to me in the crisp navy suit, a shade that matches his eyes, slightly more rumpled than before. My nose wrinkles.

It's remarkable how gorgeous a man can look and still turn my stomach.

"What's the matter? You ready to talk this out like grown ups?"

Ignoring him, I try to slink away, putting some distance between us, pulling myself up the crooked banister. Of course, it doesn't work.

My heels catch on the slanted angle. They can't hold my weight. I get three or four steps up before my hold on the floor-turned-wall gives way and I go careening right back into the devil's embrace.

He catches me without so much as a curse, pinning me tight in his huge arms. Typical Trent.

Typical and maddening.

God. Were his biceps always this big? I've either forgotten, or he's become an even buffer beast since the day he tried to turn my family to ash.

"Let go!" I snarl, beating at his shoulders, holding back my tears.

For once, I'm grateful for the anger. It stifles the headache and gives me a new reason to fight.

Tears are the last thing I want this animal to see. I can't be weak. Can't be vulnerable.

Can't do anything with him.

"Last warning, Trent. Whatever you're planning, I don't care. The second we're out of here, I'm calling the police. Turning you in."

"Aw, shucks. Must feel pretty goddamn divine to ram that criminal thing home, right? I guess that's the new 'orphan boy' for you. Just like old times, Presh. I missed them."

My heart sinks. The painful throb in my temples instantly doubles.

It's getting hard to see through the pain. Even harder to cling to any hope that I'll ever get a chance to spring the law on this prick.

"I can't believe you!" I whisper, peering through the darkness. It's hard to make out his face. There's nothing but the glittery lights of the city outside streaming through the glass.

A second later, everything is brushed in soft blue light. His phone.

My heartbeat doubles, wondering if it can get us out of this mess. His strong blue eyes hang on mine, silent. "Did you..."

"Sure did. I tried, Presh. Many, many times while you were out cold. Tried to see about getting you an ambulance for that blow to the head. Calls kept bouncing back. No connection. No reception in this shitty old building, or maybe it's just the shaft. So, we've got light, and nothing else. No help." He pauses, cocking his head. "Hard to believe your bro wants to keep doing business here."

I turn away, staring out the window, trying not to get sick staring too long at the Seattle skyline on its side. "Well, keep trying. It's our only chance. I'm sure the line on the emergency intercom got cut when this thing went sideways."

"Brilliant. I'll drain the whole fucking battery so we have no power. Hey, and maybe if a lucky call goes through, you can turn me in like you promised. That's totally what I dragged myself up here for."

I whip around, glaring as hard as I can at his shadowy face.

LAST TIME WE KISSED

"Fuck you." It just comes out, so harsh it scratches my throat.

He smiles, cool and slow. "Have to say, I think I like this sexy spitfire thing, darling. You're meaner than I remember. What the hell you been up to? What made you this way?"

"None of your business," I snap. Every word out of his mouth just thickens the ice wall around my heart. "Why waste your breath? Our chances of touching the ground again in one piece aren't amazing, you know."

"Yeah, you never were much for small talk, except when you wanted to blue ball me. Then you were an expert." He smiles, so broad and knowing I want to send my palm crashing across his cheek.

"If you must know, I've been busy in eastern Washington the last few years. Hotels, inns, tourism." I don't know why I'm telling him anything. It takes about half a second to regret it. "I wanted to get the hell away. Couldn't stay in Seattle. I wasn't as strong as Jace, not after you –"

"You, Amy Kay, an innkeeper?" He shakes his head, wearing a wicked grin. "Serving up breakfast in the morning for guests? Doing mountains of dirty linens? I can't imagine, Presh. Stop screwing around."

"Owner, actually. I wear a lot of hats. It's good honest work that doesn't make me want to rip my hair out. Complete opposite of what I came back here for."

"I've been busy, too. Cryptic Energies, maybe you've heard of it? I'm the CEO and founder." Smugness shines through his eyes. I don't know why he wants my approval.

Maybe he just wants me to admit I gave him a second,

a third, a thousandth thought after he took a sledgehammer to my heart. Well, good fucking luck.

He's not getting an inch from me. Let alone a mile.

"Am I supposed to be impressed? Guess the criminal record doesn't hurt much when you're the one doing the hiring..." I bite my tongue. If he wants to talk, then I'll make this as miserable as possible. "Congratulations, I guess. It's nice knowing you did something with the years you stole from us."

Trent smiles. "You have no clue. I really mean that, Amy Kay. I had to fight like hell for everything I've got since running from this town. I was happy to stay away, keeping my hands and mind busy, but Jace owes me big time. I never forgot, Presh. Karma is a bitch, but sometimes, she needs a little help delivering her sucker punch."

"My brother's an idiot, yeah. But he never torched us. Didn't stab us in the back when we least expected it. That was all you. He went along with *your* crap and almost got ruined!" My voice splinters, shaking. Trying to regain control isn't easy, but the last thing we need up here is a screaming match. "You, Trent Usher. Nobody else. Don't pretend you weren't the mastermind. I want to hear you admit it, just this once."

"Yeah, about that..." He pauses, clears his throat, looking away. His eyes are fixed somewhere in the distance, probably the top of the Space Needle leaning unnaturally on the horizon. "Forget it. I'll leave you to find out the truth soon enough."

"What's *that* supposed to mean?"

He turns, facing me again slowly. A new savage glint in his soft blue eyes makes my blood run cold. "Means I'm amazed how good you still look after all these years. Hell,

Presh, you're like a nice ripe fruit. A forbidden apple that was already too damn tempting for your own good when we were kids."

"And *you're* about to get yourself slapped. Not kidding." Flattening my hands against his chest, I try to use his body for leverage to put a few extra inches between us. It doesn't work.

I'm just forced to feel those muscles I've tried like crazy to avoid. To escape. To forget.

He's all hard edges underneath his suit. Raw masculinity. Powerful and potent.

He's pure madness – all he ever could be – because just putting my hand on his stupid, sexy body eases the rage that should make me want to rip him apart.

This can't be happening. Trent freaking Usher is *not* making my body respond like this after six years hating every chasm of his soul.

"Relax, Presh. There's no time or interest playing catch up naked." The bastard winks. "Hey, if you'd pull your mind out of the gutter for a second and stop groping me, maybe we could put our heads together and plot our way out of here. It's Jace I've got business with. Not you."

"Jesus Christ, Trent. Any business involving you and my brother is mine, and I think you know it. Hell, who do you even think runs the firm now?"

He stares through me, shrugging. "I know who. He's the whole reason I'm here. Anything that's got his name on it is asking for a tactical nuke. I've brought a big one." He nods toward the small briefcase in the corner.

I go quiet, my heartbeat quickening, wondering how insane he really is. "A bomb?"

He gives me a look that stops my heart. Oh, God, he's serious!

"Sure, Presh. Only the very best from Acme, designed by Wile E. Coyote himself. I'm totally about to piss away my reputation and the fortune I've made with the biggest energy company in the Pacific Northwest just to blow up this office. Genius."

God, do I hate him.

So sarcastic. So merciless. So, so prone to bringing a deadly heat straight to my palm, and I'm not sure how much longer I'll be able to control it, listening to his voice stringing me along.

"Can't blame me for wondering. Dad said you were no better than a common thug the day you left for Oregon. He thought long and hard about hiring guys to find you, Trent, especially after his campaign ran off the rails. But he was too afraid of getting Jace tied up in something that'd screw him up for years. You were lucky we left you alone." I wish we hadn't.

He cocks his head, an amused smirk forming on his lips. That's how I know every word I'm speaking is wasted. This asshole *enjoys* my misery.

"You're clueless if you think I ever meant you or Maxwell or Ophelia any harm. Your family was good to me, Presh. Too damn good. So were you, right up to the bitter end. Whenever we get out of here, you have my word I won't let any of this sting your parents. I've done my homework. They were smart enough to disengage from everything before retirement, leaving the firm here in Jace's hands."

"They didn't have a choice," I tell him, slapping at his chest again. His hands fly up, swiftly seizing my wrists. I gasp, shaking off the shock a second later. "You're full of it like you always were. If you knew anything, you'd know mom isn't doing the greatest. Dad threw in the towel early to look after her once her knees gave out."

"Shit." His grip loosens. "That's a real shame, Presh. I'm sorry to hear it. Know how it goes with family. Ma's been dead for three years."

I blink, bat my eyes because the news turns my bones to mush.

Martha Usher, his kindly old adopted mom, dead?

My lips fall open. I don't know what to say.

No words. He's done the impossible with this bomb he just dropped on my head, transforming into the boy he used to be right before my eyes. The one I trusted, who never would have ripped my heart out, until he did.

"I'm...really sorry, Trent. That's sad. She was an amazing woman." I'm not exaggerating that part.

I try not to tear up, thinking how she used to serve us treats, always chasing after the pack of foster dogs she kept for an animal rescue place. It must have broken her to lose them. After they left town so abruptly, packing up their house and taking the dogs to other volunteers.

He lets go, turning away, eyes back on the glass behind my shoulder. "Yeah."

Brutal silence hangs between us. Something hard and bitter forms in my throat. It shouldn't be there, so thick and painful, a blister grown fat off good times I swore I'd torn from my brain a long, long time ago.

"You can quit your crying, or second guessing, or whatever the fuck," Trent says. When he looks at me again, his soft blue eyes are sharp as ice. "I said more than I should. Wasn't asking for sympathy. You've got every right to put walls between me and Jace. Hell, go ahead, waste your energy trying to talk me out of it, Presh. Give me one reason not to nail your brother's balls to his tongue. You won't, but you can try."

I'm shaking my head. He can't be serious. What does he think this is – some twisted modern fairy tale? Where I can just talk my unwilling captor out of...whatever it is he plans to do?

This is a game. A sick one.

"You're insane," I whisper. It's darker again with the sun long gone, the late night restaurants beginning to close up and turn out their lights. I think it's screwing with my body clock. Until now, I hadn't felt tired. Now, it's like lead drifting under my skin. Pulling me under.

We stare at each other across the small gap. My blood heats, even through this exhaustion, wondering how this nightmare ever ends.

I can't talk him out of anything. I won't even bother. Not with this mad man, knowing there's no point.

Only the law can put the brakes on, and it will, the second we're on flat earth again. I watch him turn his back, taking off his suit jacket, giving me a better view of what's underneath.

My hands were right, touching his chest. This Trent is more built than I remember. A mass of pent up muscle and hard angles under his subtle white oxford shirt, begging me to undress him with my eyes.

It ain't happening. Not here, not today, not ever.

"What're you staring at, Presh? See something you like? Something you loved the hell out of once upon a time, maybe?" He puts his hands together below the belt line – stretching, flexing, I'm not sure what.

I just know it can't take the edge off my anger and disgust. I can't let it. Because the second I do, just the tiniest amount, we're in uncharted territory. Wild territory full of wolves.

"Gross. Those times are *so* over." I turn my nose up, releasing an exasperated sigh. "God, you're ridiculous. I'm not sure how we're ever supposed to work together to get off this stupid thing." My hand slaps the wall. My frustration boils over.

Then I hear a sound that shouldn't be there. At first, I think I hit the wall too hard, vibrating my impact through metal.

But steel doesn't ring this sharp, this steady, this loud. My head whirls to the red phone below the control panel. It rings again, the small light under it flashing.

Holy. Freaking. Hell.

Trent's eyes turn mine to stone. The disbelief only lasts a second before we both pounce. He's fast, but I'm quicker, closer. The phone burns like a furnace against my ear.

"Hello? Hello?!" I'm slurring desperate words into the receiver.

The voice on the other end is like tin. Distorted. Small. But it's there. Maintenance or security knows there's been a mishap by now.

"Yes, please, we're stuck in here! Hello? West wing, probably between the fifteenth and twenty fifth floor. Send us help. Send it as soon as you can!" There's no indication if the person on the other end has a clue what I'm saying.

I look at Trent. He's standing there, an eerie calm written on his face, waiting for the hammer to drop.

Jesus, do I want to bring it down. I'm tempted to flat-out tell the man on the phone I'm in danger. Locked in this thing with a creepy stranger, who's bound to do something criminal. But the voice keeps coming back like static, too choppy to make out more than a few syllables.

I hear something like *system outage, emergency, power, on their way.*

"Did you get that? Do you hear me? Hello?!" My voice gets louder. So does the desperation.

But the distortion just gets worse, too, and then there's cold silence. "Hello? Hello? *Hell-o?*"

Trent comes closer, edging in behind me. I feel him against my shoulders. A rich cologne mingling with his scent encircles me. I'd try to hold my breath, but I've been doing that since this shouting match on the phone started, waiting for a clear reply.

"Keep trying. Just because you're getting nothing back doesn't mean they can't hear you," he says, his voice a low earthquake in my ear. His hand falls against my shoulder. I barely hide the flinch. I can't hide the heat pulsing through my skin. "Tell them the truth, why don't you? I know you fucking want to turn me in. Tell them you're in here with a dangerous man. A criminal. A monster. Do it, Precious. Because if you don't hit me first for leaving you, it's gonna be Jace, right between the eyes."

I look him dead in his bastard blue eyes. My hand trembles. The phone suddenly seems so heavy it'll tear my arm off.

Trent isn't kidding. It's a challenge.

Whatever wretched game he's playing, he wants to be done with this chapter involving us. Just as bad as I do.

"Give me one good fucking reason not to burn him down," he growls. "Just one."

Needles dance along my spine. This is it.

If I don't open my mouth and try to save my brother, my family, he'll destroy them. I know what he can do.

I lived it, seven horrid years ago, when I was young and stupid and actually thought I'd marry this man.

IV: BAIT AND HOOK (TRENT)

Why the fuck aren't you taking the bait, Amy Kay? My face hovers over her, watching as she trembles with the phone in her hand, brain on fire.

Hell, maybe I'm the one being baited; hook, line, and sinker.

This woman smells as good as she looks. It's the same barely there beach breeze perfume she wore years ago, pheromones and all. A smell I remember like yesterday.

A flash of our first time – our only – cracks across my memory. Fuck, the way that scent mingled on her skin, especially when I spread her legs and buried my face in her sweetness. Sheer heaven.

I look her up and down, trying not to let my dick get the best of me.

She's all grown up now. The same, but different, and it's screwing with my head because I can't keep it straight in the space of a few scarce seconds. I look her over good and hard, breathe her in, wishing she'd say *something* to my threats.

Then I wouldn't be lost on the details. Then I wouldn't be mired in the past, recalling how good her pussy tasted on my tongue. Then my eyes wouldn't be locked, quenching themselves on her beautiful contrast.

Wouldn't be lost in the past, the present, and who the hell knows about the future. It's all blurred together in her, in one sexy silhouette of raw perfection.

Wavy brown hair. Everywhere hips. Jade green eyes. Devilishly familiar.

But she's got a woman's curves. A woman's fullness now, teasing my cock up and down.

Exactly what shouldn't be happening. What shouldn't be making this so much fucking harder.

"You hear what I said, Presh?" I whisper, running my hand up her shoulder flicking at her hair. "Might be the only chance you'll get. Tell them."

I'm taken aback when she shrugs me off, slamming the phone back in its mount. "No. We need to get out of here alive, Trent. Not settle old scores. Or new ones. Nothing matters if we aren't safe."

Damn. Here I thought I had the control, the calm, the command of this situation.

Instead, my hand hangs loosely at my side, already missing her. My eyes pin hers down, searching, wondering if there isn't just a little hidden regret written on those lips.

"Nothing, huh? Pity. You don't know what safe even is." Turning my back, I suppress a growl, wishing away this reckless hard-on with all my might.

What the fuck is wrong with me?

A second ago, I was begging her for a police escort, whenever the firefighters or whoever get their asses up here to pry this thing open. Now, not only has she decided against skinning me alive while she had the chance, she's got me hot and bothered like I haven't been for years.

My gaze says I'm pissed. Trapped in the moment. Frustrated by a six year itch.

But the past stings more, leaves me drunk on our first kiss. I'm remembering how good she tasted at the Wilkie's helm when I first thought I'd cast off her heart for the only time.

If only I'd known the kick in the face life had in store a few short years later.

She turns away, as if sensing the inferno in my blood. "Whatever. Let's just be done. There's no reason to say another word unless it involves getting help soon."

She's right. Too bad the sudden chill in the pit of my gut hates the silent treatment, though.

It lasts the better part of a half hour before I'm too restless for this crap.

Pacing the crooked space, I reach for the service panel on the elevator. The lock comes apart easy and I'm able to fit my fingers in. It takes all my strength to rip the thing open with my hands, especially after the strain my arms took when this thing went sideways.

I've never seen this crap outside a movie, much less done it, but I have to try. It's our only escape.

"Um, Trent?" She breaks quiet time first.

A smile tugs at my lips. I don't answer, just grunt, continuing to push the panel open until there's almost clearance to fit through.

"What. Are. You. Doing?" She bites off each syllable. "Hey, wait! You don't know if it's stable. We shouldn't. Any movement, any tinkering...what if it brings this thing straight down? Jesus. Do you *want* to wind up plastered on the ground?"

I look down. An evil part of me loves the frenzy nipping at her face.

It's only fair: if I'm being sewn up in stitches, tortured by her presence, then she ought to be, too.

"No. I want to get us the hell out of here by dinner, so you can drag your pretty self home and I can wrap up what I came for." We've still got the night. My plans won't let me leave before morning.

Not even with this massive setback. I'm hellbent on being here bright and early for my old buddy, Jace. Anything that lets me whip out the pretty surprise I've slaved over for months and shove it in his face.

"You're going to get us killed," she hisses, shaking her head, chestnut brown hair falling everywhere over her shoulders.

"Then I guess you'd better poke your head up here before I've got blood on my hands. You're smaller than me. Need to know if there's enough space for me to squeeze out and head to the next floor. Help me out. We'll be off this death trap, and we won't even have to wait for some jackoff night crew to do their job." Her eye twitches. If this wasn't so ridiculous, so dire, I'd laugh. "Truce, Presh? Come the fuck on. Work with me. Just like old times."

She narrows her eyes. I'm expecting defiance when she slips past, edging me aside, but instead I see her standing on her tip-toes, head pushed into the crevice. "Can't believe I'm doing this. For you. Ugh."

She cranes higher, straining every muscle. "Give me a hand, will you?"

I grin. Gladly.

Crouching, I secure her legs, thankfully freed from her heels. They straddle my shoulders while I hoist her up, allowing her to probe the unknown chasm opening into the shaft.

Don't know the first thing about elevators. I suspect she doesn't either. But if it's anything like the movies, then damn, there's *got* to be a backup exit somewhere.

"Well? How does it look?"

She reaches down, her hand flailing by my head. "Let me use your phone. Need more light. It's so dark. Funny, I swore this place had emergency lights..."

Fishing out my phone, I pass it up. The battery is half-drained and we need to make the most of it. I mull how much energy she'll use, but decide it's worth it, if this is our lucky break. "Use the camera, if you're able. A couple flash pics. We can map this out without you breaking my neck."

She makes a sound, head too far up the panel for me to tell if it's a snort or an honest laugh.

I'm teasing. Barely.

Call it payback for the view I get every time she shifts her weight, vying for a better look. Her skirt flows around her knees. There's the faint dark outline of something black and lace between her legs.

I can just make it out in the near darkness. But the faint city lights streaming in through the glass and my own imagination do plenty to fill in what I can't see.

There's that fucking hard-on again. My dick aches.

Mentally, I'm back in bed with her, years ago. Caught

on how she tasted as my tongue dive-bombed her clit, how she used to explode wrapped around every inch of me, whimpering while I pumped into her again and again. I never walked away the next morning more drained, balls sore from the many, many times we fucked.

"Hey, asshole!" Her calves pinch my head, breaking my trance. I'm annoyed, more with myself than anything, wondering how long I've missed what she's saying. "I said, 'ready to come down.' Help!"

Whatever.

My fingers have a mind of their own, sliding further than they really need to up her legs, helping her back to this mess. I'm still gripping her ass when she shoves the phone in my face.

"There's space. I think you'll fit. But it's really dark and tight. Saw a ladder, I think, somewhere off to the side. I couldn't quite make it out the door to the next floor, but I saw a lever, and it seems like it's only a few feet up."

Nodding, I replay the shaky video she captured. It's just as she described. Darkness, messy flashes of metal, but no gaping pits threatening instant death.

She searches my eyes and then looks at the floor. I remember to let her down, eager to get it over with before I run into more distractions.

I give her a look. "All right. Going up. If I'm able to get to the next floor, I'll help you across as soon as I open the door." I drag my briefcase across the floor, using it to help me up.

"Trent?" She calls softly, and I'm halfway to the panel before I look back. What now? "Please, just...be careful."

Shit. I didn't ask for sympathy. Definitely not her concern.

I press on, ignoring her words, trying to blot out that familiar, soft tone hanging on her lips. There's no time for the implications.

Shining my phone into the darkness, I stick my head through the opening and take a good look around.

No obvious dangers. There's a gap, but it should be a straightforward hop to the ladder.

I'm no coward. But fuck, when I look down, my balls try to crawl up my guts. Staring into what seems like a bottomless abyss gives me a second of pause. I can't slip.

I close my eyes and count. Okay, on three.

One.

Two.

Three.

I step off, panting like a cornered animal until my hands are secure in those steel bars. Then, sensing no other obstacles, I scramble up, scouring the shadows with my phone. There isn't much light to work with, but the lever reflects after a minute, the same place it was in the video.

Thank God. It needs a vigorous push, like it hasn't been manually bent for many years, but it does the trick.

The door to the next floor groans open. I push myself the rest of the way up the ladder and fall in. Safety at last. I can't tell where we are, one of the twenty-something floors.

It doesn't really matter. A second later, my jaw hangs open.

Adjusting to the darkness, I see the cable attached to the elevator. It's fucking torn.

Frayed, really. Nearly off its track. Way too fucking likely to send Presh to the next life.

"Presh! Precious, I need you to listen, grab your crap and get the hell up here. The second I say." My heart thuds so fast I think I'm about to pass out. Obviously, I can't. She's depending on me. More than she even knows.

More than she can because the worst thing I can do is panic her.

"What? Trent, what are you –"

"Hang on," I growl, turning to the floor behind me. There's no time.

There has to be something up here I can use to help her.

Easier said than done. I can race back down, try to help her up with just my hands, but there isn't much space between the elevator and the ladder. I'm also worried what having both of us on top of the elevator at once will do.

Could be a fatal, destabilizing mistake.

She yells up to me again, but I'm busy, distracted, frantic. I see a standard wall of office glass and a door, leading to some place called Shaw Financial. I pull on the door.

It's locked. Of course, it is.

It's after hours. If anybody has access, it'd be security or maintenance, the people who've done exactly jack for us.

On the wall, there's a fire extinguisher. I don't even hesitate. Ripping it out of its compartment, I grip it tightly, and then go charging at the door.

The glass panel in the middle shatters. There's an insane shriek and shower of beads.

No alarm. I'll take it. Moving on, I see a row of cubicles, typically spartan, except for the guys who like to make their office space a second home.

Bingo.

It takes no more than a few minutes to navigate the mess of trinkets, plaques, and family photos. A guy named Harold has a workspace that catches my attention. He's got horses everywhere, miniatures and photos of him riding, sandwiched between a mess of DON'T MESS WITH TEXAS kitsch.

There's cowboy boots, a freaking saddle on top of his filing cabinet, and yes – *finally* – a big black rope from some state rodeo tucked behind a frame. "Sorry, Harold," I mutter, breaking the glass with my elbow. "It's my rodeo now."

The rope falls in my hands, dragging on the floor. It's heavy. Sturdy as I hoped.

Another guy, the manager, has an old fashioned gumball machine in the corner of his office. It's solid steel, weighs the same as a small elephant.

I've found my anchor. Even though it's a bitch and a half to move.

Maybe, just maybe, we aren't as screwed as I feared.

When I get back to the elevator opening, I secure the rope to the machine with several knots. Meanwhile, Presh screams up a mess of questions laced with obscenities. Demands. I let her have at it for a second or two, hiding my smile in the darkness while she cusses like a sailor.

It takes me a minute to realize that's the part of this that's missing.

Fuck it. I let loose, laughing, making sure she hears. If she's pissed at me, she'll be too distracted to be scared. And fear is always where the worst mistakes happen.

"What the *hell's* so funny up there, you whacked out

psycho?" I see her little face through the panel, glowing in the light of her phone.

I shine mine toward it, adding to the soft blue luminescence. "Throw me the briefcase. Purse and shoes, too, if you want them. Then I need you to take the end of this rope when I let it down, hold on tight, and don't move until I say. I'll come down the ladder to catch you."

Squinting through the shadows, she blinks, her little mouth falling open. "Are you kidding? You're not getting help? You want me to crawl up and...oh God."

What little color remains in her pale face drains in the flickering light. She knows what's waiting. She's seen it, just like I have. The pit. Far too close to the ladder, which the stockings on her feet won't grip nearly as easy as my shoes.

"Presh...you want out, right? We're almost there. You're gonna have to trust me."

"Been there, done that. Got destroyed. Screw you, Trent. I'm not moving. I'll wait for the firefighters." She turns, steps away from the panel, flattening herself against the wall.

God damn. My eyes flick to the elevator cable. I can't tell if it's worse than it was five minutes ago, but it could go at any time. That's all that matters.

No time for her attitude. Can't waste precious seconds convincing her.

Snarling, I pick up the rope and chuck it toward the panel. Her little cry tells me I hit the mark. It's inside, or near enough. I'm coming for her. I'll drag her out, kicking and screaming, if I have to.

For a split second, I take a look down.

I must be officially crazy doing this shit, swinging in

like Tarzan. As long as I hold on real tight, and avoid the pit...fuck.

Closing my eyes, I let go, ignoring the rope burn exploding across my hands. My ankles catch the crooked edge of the elevator. I drop through the panel a second later, then help feed the rope inside so we have an easy climb back out.

"Help isn't coming, Amy Kay. This is it. We can't wait." I take a deep breath. "You're coming with me now."

"Can't wait? Says who? Trent Usher, I swear to God, I'm not going anywhere with you, much less –" She shuts her mouth once she notices I'm not listening.

Something up above creaks. I don't know shit about elevators, but even I know there's a good chance it's a death rattle.

Move.

I grab everything I can, her purse and my briefcase, scurrying back up the rope. It's just the right angle to hurl our stuff safely to the floor above. My phone blips, a low battery indicator, like a death threat in my ears.

The elevator's creak becomes a groan. Shit.

We're wasting too much time.

We have to go or the next stop will be the grave.

"Presh, *now*. Save your jabs, your doubts, your daggers for later. I'll take them all, after we're off this fucking thing and on solid ground again." She's fighting when I grab her.

I stop just short of telling her the real reason, letting her know I'm trying like hell to save her life. This thing could go any minute, if she doesn't realize it yet.

But I'm not telling her how dire this is. If there's any

chance at getting us out of here, she can't freeze up. I can't let her.

"No, Trent. No. We're *not* doing this again. I'm not following your –"

"You will, Amy Kay." I actually sound resigned as I pull her toward the rope, force her hands around it, and then jump on and hoist myself above her. "Climb," I snarl.

"Not your first choice, I know. Isn't mine either. This sucks, having to fight each other for our lives like this, when all I wanted to do was come here and flatten Jace. It blows all kinds of ways, some that haven't been classified yet. But if we don't do it, we're fucking dead, so get your sweet ass moving."

"Don't you dare lecture me!" Her small white teeth are pinched tight, hate glowing like a scorned panther's from her face.

"Don't make me drag you, darling." My eyes never waver. She does a double take. "I've never been more serious. You know I fucking will."

Finally, she grabs the rope and starts scrambling up behind me.

Confidence boosted, I pull myself through the panel and rest on the elevator, which creaks under my weight. Not creaks, groans. Again.

Damn it all. We have to make this fast, or there's a savagely good chance it won't stand having us both on top for long.

"Take my hand. Let me help," I say, reaching down.

"Coming, coming, and I still hate your frigging guts..."

Let her hate away. If it gets her up faster, I'll take it. The next few minutes melt into each other.

Hell, maybe it's only seconds.

I manage to pull her out, jerk her close, and jump across to the ladder.

She balks at following me, using the rope to swing across. "I'll catch you, don't worry," I tell her a hundred times. "If I'm lying, I'll fly right down that pit and join you. Just listen, Amy Kay. Last fucking time. I promise."

I hope it's one promise I'll keep.

Because I'm as sick of this as her. I should be raising hell for my worst enemy. Not saving my still-too-sexy-for-her-own-good ex.

After endless coaxing, I watch her become one with the rope, edge off the elevator, and swing across the narrow space to the ladder, where I'm hanging. She whimpers, flattening herself against me, damned near throwing us both to sudden death.

We hold.

I'm more thankful than ever for good reflexes. They can't fix everything, though.

She's so paralyzed, so afraid she can't move. Can't climb the four feet up the shaft to safety, and I can't drag her along if I'm going to make it up myself.

"Look at me, Presh. This is hardly the worst it's ever been. Remember that time on the Wilkie? I would've wrecked the fucking boat if you weren't there to help me along. We would've drowned years ago." I tell her, trying to put her mind at ease. "Just a few more feet, darling. I'm saving you. You saved my skin and a whole lot of others that day. It was your advice, your words, that kept us from disaster. You saved our lives then. This time, let me."

"Lives you went and ruined," she snaps, staring up at me, eyes on fire again.

Oh, yeah. That. There's no time for bad memories

because – holy shit – she's right behind me, gripping my leg, and I think we'll actually make it.

I crawl to sweet freedom on the twentieth-whatever floor, spin around, and take both her hands in mine, yanking her to safety.

She only gives her tongue a moment's rest before it's lashing me again. "Jesus. What...what happened up here?"

I turn. There's broken glass everywhere. The gumball machine is closer to the cliff than I thought. We're lucky it held.

The entire floor looks like a war zone from the office I raided, glass shards scattered everywhere. Don't think I've ever been more thankful than now to have a billion dollar net worth to my name. These damages won't break the bank. They're a small price to pay for saving her spitfire ass, and mine.

"Precious, look –" I hold up a hand, press it to her cheek, sarcasm and euphoric affection getting the best of me.

But before I can finish, the elevator gives way. There's a screaming, clanging, bone-chattering chorus of metal-on-metal for the longest twenty seconds of my life as it tumbles down the shaft, pounding the floor with an explosive *wham* so deep it goes straight into my chest.

Presh leaps into my arms. Shaking, scared, shocked, and beautiful.

Yeah, I know. I thought it. *So damn beautiful.*

"Holy shit. Holy hell. Trent –"

"I know," I whisper, cutting her off.

Then I bring her one more shock. Shoving my fingers through her brown locks, I give her a kiss for the books.

The record keepers have to be out there somewhere, chronicling this utter insanity.

* * *

AT SOME POINT, she peels herself away, manages to stand, and looks into the dark chasm of the shaft that almost ended us. "Jesus. Where *are* the police and EMTs? It's like we're the last people on Earth."

I look at her and laugh. "Still a whole city out there, Presh. Plenty of rush hour traffic." I nod toward the nearest window, revealing a perfectly normal Seattle night scene below.

Still, she has a point. If anyone knew we were trapped in the elevator and decided to drag their feet, the elevator's death rattle as it impacted the ground should have sounded like a bomb going off to anyone else in the building.

It doesn't make sense. Where the fuck is everybody?

I reach for my dying phone. When Amy Kay sees me, she does the same.

"Damn, no signal." We blurt it out in unison. It's like this place is reinforced with military grade, or somebody up above really wants to keep us trapped here for their own amusement.

"We'll have to walk. Only way we'll ever get any help at this rate." Or get out of here.

"Trent!" she calls after me, but I'm done listening.

Grabbing my briefcase, I head for the door beneath the neon red EXIT sign.

It's actually a dull brown sign that should be lit bright red, but I don't pause to think about it.

I can't waste more time. I damn sure don't want to hang around revisiting a kiss that shouldn't have happened.

It'll be a long hike downstairs to ground level, more than twenty winding floors. Good thing hiking kept me in top shape, a habit I picked up after running to Oregon. Maxwell Chenocott's favorite past time must have rubbed off, though I'll never admit it.

"Trent, wait –" Presh yells after me again. I hear her shout through the door when I'm halfway down the second flight of stairs.

I don't listen. She won't pursue in her stockinged feet. Her heels were the only casualty when the elevator went down, thank fuck.

Onward.

It's harder than I expect. By the time I'm several floors down, my knees burn like dry brush catching a spark. Every floor seems to have three long flights of winding stairs between it. I could take a break on the landings, but I want to get this over with, or at least figure out what the hell's going on.

It's somewhere around the twelfth floor when I try one of the doors.

Damn thing is locked.

And It's the same with the next floor down.

Security is especially tight around here.

I'm living a bad dream. Worst part is, I can't stop thinking about that impulsive kiss, how her taste hasn't changed in all these years.

It isn't fair. I expected her to be more subtle, more bitter maybe, against my tongue. I expected to taste her anguish, her setbacks, hell, a husband or boyfriend or a long train of guys she's no doubt had in my wake.

I expected to taste the woman I abandoned and not fucking care.

But she was pure. Sunny sweet as the last day I kissed her, before Jace's evil fuckery blew my world apart.

Sweeter, if I'm brutally honest. I won't admit distance has made my heart any fonder, but it's done frightful things to my dick, and my adrenaline.

A need I haven't felt in years to own her little mouth swept through my blood.

"Nostalgia, you idiot," I whisper to myself. I'm clinging to excuses.

Shit. I've never needed them more. Because if I slow down enough to admit how familiar, how natural, how *right* my mouth felt on Presh, and how eagerly she melted into me...

No, damn it. We were drunk on fear. A triumph escaping an early grave, and nothing more.

I know why I'm here. Whatever happens tonight can't change it.

Jace Chenocott *will* pay for fucking me out of Presh years ago, poisoning my family, and savaging my reputation. His life needs gasoline on it, so much fucking gas, poured by my hand.

And I'll be standing there when I strike the match, laughing in his face.

* * *

Joke's on me.

The door to every floor is sealed tighter than Aladdin's

cave. The second floor to the lobby is the darkest yet, and that's when I finally realize the lights are out. Completely.

They're not blown. It's the building that's lost power, keeping these doors shuttered from the outside. A ring of sweat circles my back. My lungs are blazing into ash by the time I reach the lobby.

I grab the handle, say a quiet prayer, and –

"Fuck!" It's closed too. Locked. Sealed.

I bash my fists on the heavy steel fire doors.

Once, twice, a couple dozen times.

As much as I can stand before my pulse warns me I'm working myself toward a heart attack.

But I can't stop here. There must be someone down here who'll hear me beating pits in this thing, right?

That's my working theory. I beat my knuckles raw, until I can't feel my arms, hollering the whole time. I wait a few minutes between breaths. Then I do it again.

Nothing. No sound on the other side. No words. No shrill sirens or raucous emergency crews stomping through the lobby, bleeding commotion I'd hear through these metal slabs.

We're alone.

We're fucked.

It's at least another minute before I tear myself away.

It takes a while to drag my ass back upstairs, disappointment weighing on me more than muscle strain. Presh has shut the door on me in the meantime, leaving it locked.

"Precious, what the hell? Open up!" My fist pounds heavy steel, angrier with every punch.

After a small eternity, I hear her little voice. "Nope. You're cooling your heels out there, Mr. Usher. I'm done playing kiss and run, even if you *did* save my life." It's a hard thing to admit, heavy on her voice.

The fact that I actually did, and she's keeping me out here, is fucking infuriating. "Come on! I just came up from the lobby and guess what? Every damn door's locked. We're stuck here till somebody on the outside finally wants to figure this mess out."

"Hmmm, I'm not so sure, Trent. Seems like you're the one who's 'stuck.' I've got a nice office all to myself with coffee and bathrooms. If you'd just been a little nicer, and hadn't taken off, abandoning me up here, then maybe you'd share it, too."

"Let. Me. In." I ram my fist into the door after every word. Pain arcs up my tendon, leaving my teeth pinched. "Precious, this isn't fucking funny!"

"Exactly," she whispers.

It's the last thing I'm able to hear. Then there's just the soft, almost indecipherable scuff of her feet on the ground, disappearing fast.

"Precious! Amy Kay! You can't leave me stranded. You can't..."

She can. She will.

She's out for punishment after that vicious kiss.

Swallowing a growl, I decide I've had enough. There's nothing more to be gained fracturing my knuckles on this damn door. I shuffle over to the corner, drop down on the cold concrete, clutching my briefcase.

In this commotion, I've barely had a spare second to mull over the contents. I flip the latches and peer inside. It's all there. Three neat little folders.

The treasures inside have already been sent to their targets. I'll catch Jace, sooner or later, just in time for the fireworks. I want to watch the knife twist in his guts when he realizes how unbelievably fucked he is.

That's what this trip to Seattle is. Revenge.

Taking a detour through the ugly past and the awkward present with the girl I wanted to marry wasn't on the itinerary. Too bad. Once this is through, I'm heading back to Portland. I'll do whatever it takes to cleanse Presh from my system.

My fist tightens on the suitcase. The wry smile fades just as weakly as it came, like it was never there. Playing cat and mouse with that delectable, maddening woman behind the door changes nothing.

Nothing.

This body, this heart, this soul are mine. Not hers, damn it.

Not anymore.

V: REMEMBERING EDEN (AMY KAY)

It's bad enough that Trent Usher kissed me.

Worse that he saved my life, and I *let him*.

But the worst part, the thing I can't forgive, is how I forgot everything in the thirty or so seconds his mouth was on mine. Melting into him while his hands and tongue roamed free was a sweet amnesia.

In just a few seconds, he did the impossible. Delivered a peace I've looked for everywhere else the past seven years, never finding more than small bits in Spokane, on long nature walks, forgetting as hard as a woman ever can.

Christ, I hate this man.

Now that I'm on my own two feet again, a safe six inches of hard steel between us, I'm aware. I see, feel, and taste too much.

I remember who brought me to my knees. Once with a foolish smile, and again with a hole in my chest.

I remember because I can't do anything else. Every day

I've tried to forget him, to leave behind our tragedy, is just another savage waste of time.

If the scarring wasn't so bad, maybe this would be the perfect time to move on. He did just save my life, after all.

If he hadn't pulled me off the elevator, kicking and screaming, I'd be an Amy Kay-sized pancake crunched in the building's service basement.

But if he hadn't turned my heat into a dumpster fire – if the self-righteous bastard wasn't *still* doing it – then I might not be here in the first place. Re-living a heartbreak in real time.

If, if, if. Every time I mull the possibilities, they're more sour. They make me want to stare a line of fire through the door, straight at Trent's head, and roast him alive.

I have every right. What the heck does he mean when he says he's back to settle scores with my brother, anyway? It was Trent's idea, the whole dirty money thing.

His mistake when it finally caught up to him, and then brought hell crashing down on the rest of us.

I've got to warn Jace. Somehow, someway.

Flattening myself against the wall, I pull out my phone, holding my breath as the screen illuminates, hoping it'll work.

Except that'd be too easy. Too kind. The same pathetic NO SIGNAL indicator flashes, bright and blinding, draining the battery another bar.

I don't even know if Trent lied about the doors to the other floors being locked. I don't trust a thing from his lips, including the latest stupid kiss where I almost cracked.

Chances are, he's telling the truth. I know it in the pit of my belly.

We're really stuck. Really helpless. Really fighting a war I never asked for.

My stomach turns over, realizing the last seven years were nothing but a truce.

He never let go. Neither did I.

I have to sit, before I pass out or start dry heaving. I can't remember the last time I was this fried. Never, probably, since the day it all went to hell.

Sliding down to the floor, I kick my feet out, staring at my toes through their nylon sheath. They're so naked, so bland. The last time I wore nail polish was for him, a lifetime ago, that summer he came home.

Maybe it's the cold on this floor or the anxiety or knowing the man who ended me is just a few feet away. Leaning my head back, I close my eyes, and try to pinpoint how this all went so wrong.

* * *

Six Years Ago

"Whoa, you mean to tell me *this* is the place, Ames? Talk about worn." Lindsey bangs her heel against the chipped paint on the front step to the Usher place, snorting her disdain.

"Don't be a bitch. They're good people, Linds. Frankly, I think roughing it out a little is good for Jace. He'll have to get used to it if he wants to be Mr. Lean Sigma Entrepreneur soon. His grades certainly aren't getting him there." I shake my head, wishing he'd have to survive his homework, too, but living here with Trent gives him easier access than ever to cheating.

My bestie winces. "He's such an idiot. I'm surprised your dad didn't kick his butt up and down for putting a dent in his boat."

It's my turn to wince. My mind instantly goes back to my first kiss on the Wilkie. Was it really more than two years ago? Feels like half a lifetime.

But that isn't what she's talking about. Not that time.

Jace, genius that he is, decided to take it out on choppy seas last March with another hookup. Dad was upstate at a fundraiser, forming the exploratory committee for his Senate run. Totally unaware his pride and joy nearly took on enough water to send it to the bottom of the Sound.

"Well, at least he found out. Jace didn't have any time for a coverup. Dad was more pissed knowing he had a big liability than paying for the fix. He told him not to come home until after November."

"Harsh!" she grins, enjoying the family schadenfreude. "He made the right move. A kid acting out in the middle of a campaign is a death wish."

"Yeah." I wrinkle my nose, already getting sick of the attention dad fawns over me. With Jace brushed aside, me and mom are his props at the conventions, the meet and greets, the slick glossy pamphlets where we smile for the cameras, looking like one big happy and *electable* family.

"Enough politics." Linds gives me a look, flipping her cherry red hair over her left shoulder. "What about your *other* brother, Ames? Or are you staying pissed at him forever?"

Leave it to Linds to exhume Trent, the delicate subject

I'm trying to forget, even though we're bound to be face-to-face in minutes.

My face overheats. She stifles a laugh, catching my blush.

Thankfully, I'm saved from an awkward answer, because a very nice lady with graying hair and crow's lines appears a second later, throwing the door open for us. "Hi, girls. I'll bring the boys right up. Help yourself to some banana bread in the meantime. Fresh baked this morning!"

I inhale as I step inside, smiling. One thing you never miss in these working class Seattle homes is good food whipped up by women who had to learn those skills the hard way, and always put an original spin on it. My first bite in the tiny kitchen tells me Martha Usher's angle is toasted walnuts. Yum.

Mom likes to fancy herself a baker, too. She does all right, but she'll never have it down like this when it comes to sweet breads. "It's awesome, Martha. How's Dale doing? Bet he's glad to have some time to himself retired."

"Aw, he's off fishing again. Oysters and clamming this time, I think. Says the good ones will turnover real nice in the fish markets. I tell him, we don't need the money, we're doing just fine. But the man just can't let go of his frugal heart, bless him. Fresh air's good for him, at least, gives him something to do."

Linds grins, elbowing me slightly. "Just like grandpa. He's a sweet guy, your hubby."

Even a sheltered snob like her can't deny the Ushers make a dang cute couple. They've had thirty years together. Maybe more since I've lost track.

Trent came along later in life, their only boy. I don't

think Martha was ever able to have kids, but between him and the foster dogs, she's got a heart the size of the Cascades.

We're still soaking in the moment when I hear a crash erupting down the hall. A big black lab runs into the kitchen, tongue hanging out. The beast pounces on Linds, licking at her neck. My bestie's face twists and she lets out an anguished laugh while Martha rushes over to help pry the dog off.

"I'm *so* sorry, ladies! She's a wild one, this pup. Still learning good manners." The lab's full attention goes to her a second later, eyeballing the banana bread. She lets out a puppy whine.

"Sorry, ma! Lucky's turned over her dish again. Guess the appetite for what you've been cooking up all morning got the best of her." Such a deep voice. Its owner turns the corner a second later, plodding into the kitchen.

It's him. Trent looks like he just rolled out of bed, jeans rolled up near his knees, a plain grey t-shirt hugging his shoulders.

Sweet Jesus.

No man should look this good first thing in the morning.

He freezes when he sees us. It's got nothing to do with modesty and everything to do with the icicle looks I've cast his way for the past two years, ever since the Wilkie mishap.

My stupid crush never had a fighting chance. I put it out of its misery after he stomped all over my heart.

Young and inexperienced doesn't mean I'm anybody's fool. Or I'm so desperate I'll go chasing after a man who's made it clear he wants nothing to do with me.

Too bad.

His blue eyes are just as beautiful, just as interesting, just as dangerous as they were the day he stole my first kiss on the boat.

"What brings you two by?" he asks quietly. "Here for Jace?"

"Uh, yeah. What else? Mom sent me to drop off his clothes. She's bought him a few new things to sustain him this summer, more than he deserves." I instantly regret the resting bitch voice in Martha's presence. I look at him again, forcing a fake smile while shame heats my cheeks. "How's the war room? Messy as ever?"

He smiles, looking past me to Linds. Relief mixes with jealousy. "Yeah, sure, Amy Kay. We're busy boys. Companies don't start themselves off nothing but big dreams and endless coffee anymore. Speaking of which..." He reaches past me and pulls out the old drip coffee pot on the edge of the counter, sloshing the contents around. "Care for a cup, Lindsey? Or did you girls swing by Starbucks already?"

"I'm good, thanks." My friend wouldn't be caught dead drinking her coffee black. Or instant. "But you know, I think Ammers here said she didn't get much sleep. I'm *sure* she could totally use the boost."

My mouth falls open while my brow digs into my eyes. *Damn it, Linds. You're supposed to be on my side.*

Martha jumps in before Trent can move a muscle. She fetches a heavy ceramic mug from somewhere. There's a lighthouse stamped on it with a name. It's not anything I recognize from around here.

"Armitage historic site?" I say, looking up.

"Michigan. Some place called Split Harbor, I think,

barely on the map." Trent smirks, pouring me a steaming cup. "They think they're hot stuff out there, Lake Superior and all. Frigging joke, really. They do have a tech billionaire though, that Caspian guy. Crazy story with him, changing identities and coming home years later."

"Oh, son, it's a lovely place. Very romantic. Ryan and Kara's love story will be a movie one of these days. Your father and I enjoyed it. It'd do you good to expand your mind a little."

Trent snorts. "Yeah, ma. Like I don't do that for twenty hours a day already between class and business."

I raise the brew cautiously to my lips. It's actually...not terrible. A far cry from the fancy imported espresso beans dad drinks, and mom's sugary K-cups, but I don't hate it.

"How's the campaign? You sick of spending your summer on the road watching your old man kiss babies, or what?" Trent knows very well I am.

That's why I lie my pants off. "It's very interesting, actually. You meet a lot of people, learn a lot about managing groups. So many moving pieces. It's a shame you're busy, Trent, or I'm sure dad would've loved to take you on as a volunteer."

"Don't trust politicians. Maxwell, yeah, but I wouldn't be caught dead in DC."

"Hell, Usher, he'd have you take my place. You're the *good* kid." Jace announces himself, straddling the entrance to the kitchen, a sour smirk on his face. I can't tell if he's just busting Trent's balls or if he's really dripping resentment.

My brother's sense of humor is too weird. Sometimes it's even a bit creepy.

"Finally. I texted you like five times," I say, walking

over. "Go out to the car. I've got two big bags of clothes for you, with love, from mom. She says you should come visit whenever dad's on the trail."

"Whenever you can hide me away, you mean," my brother says, still smirking. "Nah, sis. I'm not sneaking around like a felon in my own fucking house. You want me back, then I want to hear it from him. Let him be a normal dad for once in his life." Stomping past me, Jace reaches for the banana bread loaf, and rips off a piece, stuffing it in his mouth.

"Hey, man, there's a knife for that," Trent cuts in, blocking him from mangling another piece.

"Yeah, fuck...what time is it? Feels early." Jace rubs his eyes, smacking his lips as he chews

I turn. Linds shifts uncomfortably, giving my asshole brother a stare I hope means disgust. I feel worse for Martha, though, taking in this scene. I flash her an uneasy smile, trying to telegraph how sorry I am.

"You boys holler if you need anything, okay?" she whispers, pale lips pinched tight.

"Don't worry, ma. I'll clean this up and get the dogs watered," Trent says, also doing his part to diffuse the craziness. "Go enjoy your day off."

"Nonsense! We have guests. I'll be right back after I've checked on the pups. Come along, you gremlin." She pulls the lab's collar, motioning her to follow.

"Ma, wait..." Trent rushes after her. I can't hear what they say because Jace – stupid, rude, disgusting Jace – is chewing loud enough to cave the roof in.

I don't say anything. Just step up to him, hand whizzing at his face, patting his cheek angrily until he's pushing me away.

"Whoa, whoa, what the –"

"What's wrong with *you*? Yeah, Jace, because we'd love to know." He staggers back against the cutting board, nearly knocking the bread over. Behind me, Lindsey laughs, either delighted or hiding it really well. "You're high again, aren't you?" I don't have to sniff very hard to catch the pot odor coming through his clothes.

Raising a finger to his lips, he leans forward, eyes big. "*Shhhh*. Are you *trying* to get me kicked out? Martha's not cool with it. She's kinda old fashioned."

"Then maybe you shouldn't be smoking weed like a chimney in her house," I snap, giving him the evil eye. I take a hurried sip of coffee.

"So, did you come by for those clothes, or a lecture, mother?" Jace looks past me, winking at Linds.

If I weren't standing in a kitchen belonging to a family that's way too good for him, I'd smack him so stupid it'd actually knock sense into his brain. Instead, I just give my friend a pleading look. Linds quits laughing.

"Sorry you're friends with this mouth," Jace says, nodding toward me.

Holy hell. It's taking everything not to wipe the mean look off his face. Linds gives a little snort of shock and I walk the hell away, heading for the car, ready to dump his clothes myself and then get the hell gone.

Trent comes barreling to my side as soon as the trunk opens and I'm struggling with the first bag. It's wider than my chest, and heavy, too. "Let me help, Presh."

He lifts it away like it's full of cotton swabs. Normally, I'd be annoyed, getting help from the muscles attached to this man, but right now I don't mind. "Thanks, I guess."

"Least I can do. Jace has been on edge lately, whenever

there's news about home, or Maxwell's campaign. Think it's wearing on him, honestly, all this family feuding."

"Tough. He's brought it on himself, Trent. And it's not getting better anytime in the future when he still hasn't learned decent human manners." Shaking my head, I'm still living the scene in the kitchen, wondering when the hell Linds will come out to console me.

Trent flashes an understanding smile. Summer sun dances in his bright blue eyes, soft and reassuring and oh-so-hard to pull my gaze away from. "Give me a little room. I'll grab the other bag and bring them both downstairs. Sorry for the delay, took forever to talk ma out of playing hostess."

He's so nonchalant. It's like he's in an alternate universe where my brother's crap doesn't matter. Neither does helping a girl who's treated him like a leper the past two years, apparently.

Of course, I'm suspicious. My inner bitch doesn't go to sleep that easy. "Look, if this is about you and me, just stop. I've been camping plenty of times. I can take them."

I pull on the strap slung over his shoulder. He takes a step back, unyielding. His chest is magnificent. He was always hot back in Maynard, but now? I see a man.

Not just a half-grown boy. In two years, everything got bigger, polished, better.

It must be the looks I don't want to admit he has, plus this strange thing between us. That's the real reason I'm staring him down, trying like mad to pretend I'm biting into a juicy lemon. "Trent..."

"Amy Kay, relax. You're letting him get to you. Stay there."

I open my mouth to protest, but he's bounding up the

stairs again. He disappears inside the house with the bags, leaving me to gawk.

Lindsey trots out a second later, a sly flicker in her eye before she pulls her shades down. "Sorry it took so long. I told Jace to lay the hell off. Doing you a favor."

"Not you, too." I turn away from her, fully deflated. Linds makes a confused sigh, wondering what's eating me. "I appreciate the help, Linds, but I'm a big girl. I don't need everybody rushing to my defense. Jace is the same stupid, selfish little boy I grew up with. It's –"

"It's nothing, Ames. And it's not really me, either, is it?" She's practically psychic.

I sigh, folding my arms. "Is it really so obvious?"

"Uh, you drank that battery acid Mrs. Usher served, didn't you? I saw your cup was empty."

"Wasn't half bad, really." I lift an eyebrow, amazed in hindsight it went down so fast without cream or sugar. "I was just distracted when Jace showed up and ruined everything. Story of my life."

"Mm-hmm. You're a bad liar, Amy Kay, but I love ya." She grins, popping the door, sliding into the passenger seat.

I can't walk away after a quip like that. Sliding into the seat next to her, I give her a look, and find my best poker face. "There's nothing going on. I don't even know what you're –"

"Wow. So, you weren't just eye-fucking Trent Usher as he reeled in your brothers' baggage? I think that's the most you've said to him for like two freakin' years." Everybody needs slapping today. Yes, even my ex-best friend, eyes glowing while she aims her *gotcha* grin.

"Whatever. He's still an ass, and you know it. Just not

as up my ass as Jace right now." I reach past her, banging her knee harder than I intend to, riffling around the glove box for my shades.

"He asked us out today, you know, while I was leaving. Said we'd make a good foursome, heavy on the innuendo." Linds laughs, way too in love with her own bad jokes.

"Who, Lindsey? You can't mean –"

"Yup. I think Mr. Usher has the hots for me. Maybe your dumb brother does, too. Figured I'd run it by you, see if it's okay first, before I...you know."

She trails off. Or maybe my brain has just reached its limit for BS today.

"No. Nope. Never." I look her way slowly. Why has it took me this long to realize my friend adores torturing me? "I'm not interested in spending time with either of those clowns."

I nod toward the house. It's quiet for a long second, filled with Lindsey digging through her purse, searching for her phone. "Stanford won't be any easier, Ames. You've got t-minus two months before you'll be two states away, surrounded by brilliant, gorgeous guys who'll jump at their chance to break your heart if you –"

"No! Screw dating." My hands slap the wheel. After her reminder how Trent manages to knot me up, I'm halfway serious about leaving the dating world, too. "Can we just let this go? Please? If you want to date him, fuck him, whatever, then be my guest. I'm done."

"Trent wants to meet us out on Bainbridge. Jace, too," she tells me quietly. "Said he thought it'd be a good way to smooth things over. Apparently, your bro is a lot more relaxed when he's out doing something, or so he says.

Keeps him off the bong hits and beer, too. But if you aren't interested..."

"I'm not." But I am. And just imagining my best friend in Trent's arms, staring into his radioactive eyes, kissing him...it makes me want to drive my brand new hunter green convertible off the nearest bridge. I don't care if it was a present from dad for his little girl turning eighteen.

I'm that pissed.

That run down after doing circles in my own head.

That helplessly stuck on Trent Asshole Usher.

"Hey, Ames, look at me..." Lindsey's voice is softer now, soothing. She reaches over, but I swat her hand away, feeling like a bigger bitch. "I'm sorry for giving you so much crap. I never seriously thought about hooking up with Trent. No drama like that between sisters. No way."

"I'm worried about Jace," I say, deflecting old heartbreak. I'm serious, too. "He's such a little prick. College hasn't changed a thing. Dad was right to kick him out, until he gets his crap together, even if the campaign's his real reason."

"Right. Here's a crazy idea: if you're worried about him, *talk* to him. Brother to sis." Our eyes play tug-of-war, trying to figure out who's crazier, or more stubborn. "He was a total jackass back there in the kitchen, yeah. But he needs some time, and so do you, Amy Kay. I'm worried. It's not healthy, holding all this in, trying to go off to college."

Damn her, she's right. I look down, eyeing my hands on the wheel. If I could just try to set things right with my dumb brother, and find a way to have a normal interaction with Trent, I'd have peace. A clean slate. Probably some secret zen state that'd make me work miracles.

"Screw it. Let's sit here until they come out. I want to get this over with."

Her eyes light up and she sucks in a breath. "Holy shit. You mean?"

I do. I'm so mad, so confused, so screwed up by everything happening in my life that I'm actually taking her advice.

"We'll go out for the day, I'll catch Jace, and we'll talk. You'll join in for moral support. And Trent –"

"I'll help smooth things over with him!" Linds says, cutting me off. She's way too chipper.

I don't know what happens next.

But I'm ready to face the good, bad, and ugly. Everything that's been pointed at my head like a loaded pistol, clenched by a smirking, rage-worthy, sinfully sexy boy who kissed and ran years ago.

* * *

IT'S LESS than two hours since the huge white and green ferry let us off on the island, and I'm already abandoned.

Linds disappears. With Jace.

Jace, of all people. Stranding me outside this darling little fish and chips bar with a lemon-something mocktail in my hand. Alcohol free because I'm too dang young to drink.

Pity.

Jace was all smiles the whole way down. It's the first time in months I've seen him act normal. He got my hopes up, thinking maybe I could have a heart-to-heart talk with my brother somewhere beautiful and remote enough to knock some sense into him.

But he had a different agenda. I wanted to believe he was trying so bad I didn't see it coming.

The hand under the table. The looks behind my back. The way Lindsey laughed at his crude jokes, just a little too hard.

I've been betrayed.

Trent and I finally have something in common after years of estrangement: rolling our eyes at our friends as hard as we possibly can.

Not that I'm on his side. No way.

Hell, I'm glad his ego takes a beating, even if it means Linds just disappeared with my Neanderthal brother. She shot him down. Rejected the self-described genius with the baby blue eyes and rocket hips, which helplessly drew my eyes every time he moved in front of me on the ferry ride here.

There's only one way this ends: savage disappointment. Plus my best friend finding her own way home.

As for Mr. Usher, I'll pretend I'm not this pathetic. Tell him I'm getting drunk whenever he emerges from the town's little streets and kitsch shops surrounded in evergreen.

Totally not nursing a non-alcoholic mocktail. Totally not mourning my broken trust with Linds. Totally not bamboozled into thinking I lost a chance at making my dumb brother act like an adult.

Totally whatever it takes to see Trent with a straight face and ice cold eyes that don't want to – what was the word Linds so eloquently used? – *eye-fuck him?*

Jesus.

No. Nope. Never.

"Looks like you're ready for a drink," a voice rumbles

behind me. Speak of the very suave devil. He's returned too soon.

"Uh, hello?" I hold up my glass with the half-depleted mocktail, rattling the ice.

"No, Presh. I mean a *real* one. Hand it over." He practically rips it out of my hand, fishing around in his pocket. When the small silver flask comes out, I gasp. "Whoa. Here I thought Jace was the drunk in our group..."

He looks up, cocking an eyebrow, stopping after what smells like vodka splashes in my glass. "We came out here to take the edge off, right? Somebody has to help get you young'uns toasted."

He throws two more shots in my glass and slides it back to me. I take a sip through my straw and instantly back off, hacking up a lung. "Blech!"

"Lightweight," Trent growls, his smirk becoming a genuine smile. "Let me get you some water."

He runs into the bar while I pin a new badge of shame to my chest. So much for the tough girl act. While I'm waiting, I force myself to take another swig of the drink.

Up until now, I've only had sickly sweet wine coolers and mimosas snuck from Lindsey's mom.

I smack my lips, adjusting to the acrid taste on my tongue. He isn't kidding about the edge coming off. This stuff sandblasts it away, roaring in my blood, making me giddy and lightheaded in the five minutes it takes him to come back with a dark beer in his hand and a pitcher of water.

"Drink this," Trent says, noticing my glass is a lot lower. "You'll feel like shit if you don't learn to keep your stuff balanced." He pushes a tall glass of water toward me, banging his beer against it. "Here's to science."

I burst out laughing for the first time since this disaster began. "God, you're a dork, Usher. Since when did you study bartending? Thought you were doing physics and engineering or some crap that's way over everybody's heads? No wonder Linds ran off with Jace."

Okay, that was mean. It's supposed to be.

Just once, I want to see his face show a twist of regret. A little sour jealousy. A smudge of regret that he turned me away years ago.

It's the least he deserves for putting the bug in Lindsey's ear, dragging me out here, getting my hopes up for all sorts of stupid things. Also, putting us in a situation where drowning my regrets in long sips from his flask is suddenly way too appealing.

"They're shit out of luck, Amy Kay. All the hotels on the island are maxed out. He'll have to wait for the next ferry if he wants to get his dick wet." Trent leans back in his chair, taking a calm pull off his beer, undaunted by my insults. "I'm sorry for all this. Thought it'd help, coming out here, after the bullshit that went down this morning..."

"Forget it. Don't apologize. It was a mess the second I caught you staring at Lindsey, trying to use my almost-estranged brother to weasel your way between her legs." Wow. Even I'm surprised how scorned I sound. "Sorry. I mean, you're a jerk, but no worse than Jace, really."

Trent's smiley smirk just gets broader. He sets his beer down, leans forward, and cages me in his pristine blue gaze. "She took the bait. It's adorable, though, that you think I want to lay your stuck-up friend so bad."

My mouth falls open, but the words won't come.

My head spins, and not just from vodka. I glance at the liquid in my cup, wondering if I just hallucinated.

Not wanting to screw Linds?

What the *holy hell* is he trying to say?

"I wanted you to hash it out with Jace. Saw how bad you needed it after he waltzed into the kitchen, acting like a fucking idiot, cutting you down in front of us all. A woman needs to give and take with her own kin, darling. He deserves every punch you've got waiting. But that's not the only reason I brought you out here, Presh." His stare only deepens.

Oh God, here it comes, even though I don't know what it really is. My lungs start hyperventilating before he even says the next four words.

"I need one thing."

He leaves me in suspense. Wants me to beg. I try to resist, but the drink and his eyes and the screaming need to know are far too much. My lips move, tasting how much I hate obsessing over this man.

"Tell me," I whisper, throat dry as cotton.

"Exactly, darling. That's what I'm waiting for: you tell me exactly what I need to do so that time we kissed finally stops being a problem. I want to drain the bad blood, Amy Kay." His eyes narrow, blazing blue pinpricks stabbing through me.

"You're crazy. I don't know what you're talking about. That was years ago, Trent. *Years.* Long since over. You think I'm still –"

"Yes. You've treated me like I barely exist for the past couple years, Presh. Like my very presence is pure poison. You've kept your distance no matter how often I came by to see your folks, or how many times Jace got himself in trouble, how many times I tried like hell to get his dumbass back in shape. You're *still* hung up on that time we locked lips alone on the Wilkie."

Face, meet table. That's what I'd love to do, just fall into it.

It'd be a mercy. Being knocked out cold would end this conversation that shouldn't be happening.

But you came out here for your brother and Trent, a small voice in the back of my head reminds me. *Don't chicken out. Don't give him exactly what he wants.*

I swallow, draining the rest of my sour drink, hoping liquid courage is really a thing. "Okay. So, maybe you're right. Maybe a small, teensy part of me never got over how you kissed me, and then brushed it off like it was no big deal. Maybe I didn't like being told to just forget, like I'm just a dumb kid, or that there's no way it ever meant anything. If that's the issue, then maybe I'm guilty, Trent." I pause, hating how the vodka makes my cheeks a brighter red. "Convict me. Will that make you happy?"

"You were too young, Amy Kay. Too *damn* young," he bites off. "Even if there weren't a thousand other reasons why making that thing a repeat would've been stark raving mad."

His logic has a brutal precision. I hate it. I was too young. He was too close. We couldn't do more.

"What choice did I have? You're gonna hold it against me forever, turning you away? Knowing us doing anything, exploring what happened on that ship, would have blown both our lives to kingdom come?"

Too many questions. Too much truth weighing on my battered heart. I twist my face away.

My fingers tighten on my glass, numb from the cool

touch. I want to hurl it at his head, the last distraction I've got left before the pain stinging at my eyes seeps out. "That easy, huh? Just like that, you *finally* give me the truth? God, Trent. What took so long? If you'd just been honest –"

"I was a kid, too. Tried to let you down as easy as I knew how then. It never would've worked, Presh. Not then. Me, you, our family in between, Jace...Christ, especially Jace!" he pauses, staring into his beer, before he takes a swig. "Your brother's got problems. That's the other reason I wanted to get you alone today, so we could talk in private. I'm on your side, Presh. I want to – hey, where do you think you're going?"

I'm standing, every nerve in my body burning. I need oxygen. I also *really* need an escape. Mostly, I need time.

There's only one way out, a narrow path winding around the rocks stretching down to the marina. I stomp past him, so ready to be done.

But Trent Usher has other ideas. A second before I'm out of reach, his hand snatches at my dress and tugs.

"Let me go!"

I whimper. I fight. I'm far too weak for his magnificent hands, and I go down, falling into his grasp.

"What's gotten into you, Precious?" His words are a demanding growl. "Talk to me, Amy Kay. I just bled the fuck all over us."

"Crap I'm not ready to talk about, especially not with you." My eyes pinch shut. I wonder if I'll ever be ready in this lifetime. "Why couldn't you just leave it alone, Trent? If you're worried about my brother, then go to mom and dad. What can I do? I'm not a freaking shrink. Him acting out the way he does, that chip on his shoulder and screw everything attitude...*of course* I worry constantly. Wonder if he'll get himself in too deep and mess up his whole life, and maybe ours, too."

I shake my head, losing the fight. Hating how good, how right, how comforting his big arms feel on mine. Shifting on his lap, I sigh. "You want to help for once? Fine. Get me another drink."

"You've had your fill, Presh. Water's all you're getting next." Non-negotiable, his sharp look says. *Ass.* I wish I could keep believing that's all he's doing, looking out for me. "Fuck. I didn't mean this to go all sideways, honest. Thought we could sit down like grownups, clear the air, try to put this shit to bed."

"Well, I'm sorry, orphan boy. Now you know there're *some* things a big brain and good looks can't fix." I'm biting my tongue, blinking back tears, wishing I had the reflexes to wriggle out of his arms. Wishing *so bad.*

I blink, replaying my words. "Sorry for the orphan thing. Again. Low blow. That's what got us into trouble the first time, right?"

He isn't even mad. His eyes are a sad mix of frustration, warmth, hope. They're beautiful and interesting and so unrelenting.

He lifts me up, but never lets me off his lap. I guess being glued to his rock hard body is part of my punishment for cutting him down.

It's the same with his eyes. I watch every change, every ripple, every small prism of light catching and turning over as his brain shifts, trying to figure out how best to deal with this emotionally strung out baby in his arms. "Presh..."

"Don't bother. Picking words, I mean. Just spit it out. We're talking, aren't we? I'd love for this to be done."

"We're way past that. Fuck words." There's a long, drawn out second where I don't have a clue what he means.

Then his grip tightens, his fingers lock on my upper arms, and he pulls me into those explosive, impatient lips I've dreamed about for two years in the wilderness.

Sweet Jesus.

They're as good as I remember. Better, maybe.

No, definitely.

There's no hesitation. No resistance. His lips take mine on a hypnotic dance I barely match.

I'm melting into him. Flesh going slack, surrender, all while tears steam down my cheeks, whimpering the first time his tongue touches mine.

There's no stopping it then.

I'm kissing him back. Biting his bottom lip. Climbing his tall, lean, hard wrack of shoulders.

Climbing home.

If this asshole, this marvel, meant to condense two years of messed up tension in a sixty second super nova, mission accomplished. I'm wet, trembling, and aching.

I hate him with every fiber of my being. Somehow it makes me want him more.

"Ass-hole. Why?" I whisper, as soon as he breaks the kiss.

"Because I'm done dicking around with the past, Precious. Sick and tired of watching you all tangled up in it, too, never moving on with your life. If this is what it takes to make you forget, then fuck it all. I'm in. I'll throw you against the nearest wall and we'll bang it out till you scratch my back raw."

This isn't even insane anymore. It's toxic.

But I can't stop my lips from colliding with his, once more, this time with so much feeling it leaves my nipples pebbled. Every end of me wants his hands, his mouth, his touch.

A touch that would've been equal parts unbearable and unthinkable mere minutes ago.

"Just...help me up," I whisper, loving how he lifts my body with ease, cradles it for a second, and then sets me back on my feet. "I need to take a walk."

His eyes shift over, lock on, and there's another slap-worthy smirk on his lips. "So, no to the banging part? Really, darling? After how well we fit together?"

"Don't tempt me, Mr. Usher. I'm not sold on one kiss. Not even an amazing, heartfelt, mind-blowing kiss. You'll have to try harder before I let my heart get stuck in places too deep to climb out of."

"Don't I know it, Presh? Don't I want to know *you* like I haven't for two fucking years? Come on." Seizing my hand, he pulls forward, leading us into town.

VI: INTO THE FIRE (TRENT)

I'm outside the guesthouse tucked behind her parents' mansion. It's been tit-for-tat for weeks, ever since Bainbridge, when we started something very fucking dangerous.

I should've known one kiss would lead to...I don't even know.

More kisses, certainly. Hotter, fiercer, tongue lashing kisses, the kind that make her whimper and bring an instant growl up my throat.

The kind that keep me up at night after a cold shower that does nothing, dick sleeved in my fist, beating off to the day she'll take every inch of me.

It led to hands. Fingers. The many times they've driven up her dress or through her shirt, thumbing those pert nipples haunting my wet dreams for fuck only knows how long.

So close to having her naked, owned, marking every inch of her.

Still too damn far.

Just when I think she's giving in, Presh bats my hands away, whispering the reasons why we can't bring this thing home.

It's always the same: Jace is too around, her parents might see, or mine, or even ma's dogs.

We're too public, too pressed for time, but I know deep down it's bullshit.

It comes down to her being afraid, not yet ready to seal the best deal we'll ever make.

She's afraid to let me have her cherry.

Shit. If I'm honest, deep down, then maybe I'm a little scared, too.

Because leaving this – whatever *this* is – a second time would be painful. Brutal, really, after rekindling a fire that should've died years ago. And after fucking, our bodies locked together, tongue thrashing her in places I've wanted to explore forever up close and personal, there's no coming back.

Sanity, gone. And reason with it. And every fucked up reason we shouldn't.

I know deep down there's nothing that'll pull us apart after we go to bed.

Not Jace, not our folks, not even her leaving for Stanford this fall while Jace and me head north again to Bellingham.

Good thing I've spent twenty years throat-punching my fears, and I'm not about to let them get the best of me now. Especially when it's midnight, and I haven't been able to sleep since Amy Kay's last kiss went burning through my brain.

That's what's brought me to the Chenocott place without her parents' knowing. I left Jace passed out with the dogs, confident he'll sleep late into the morning after dragging himself in half-drunk from his latest fuckfest with Lindsey.

They couldn't find a place on Bainbridge a few weeks ago, but of course it hasn't stopped them. There's a wicked irony in Jace getting pussy while I'm just pussy-footing around, letting Presh feed me excuses, my dick turning midnight blue because I'm too afraid to pull her into my arms and leap off the edge.

No more. That ends tonight, I tell myself, parking my beat up F150 under the massive oak tree outside her parents' gate. The back of my truck is still full of solar panels and lab equipment. It's an eyesore in this neighborhood, where median incomes blow past a million dollars easy. Thankfully, it's late, it's dark, and it's the perfect cover to hide the truck and then climb sneakily over the gate.

I'm under her window a second later, tapping at the glass with a spare branch I found. It takes forever for Presh to open up.

More heat throbs through my cock the instant her sweet face appears. "Trent?"

"In the flesh, Rapunzel. Let me up."

She laughs, motioning to the arborvitae tree nearby. It's just thick enough to hold my weight. I scramble the small distance up it, grabbing at her windowsill. Thank God these big houses have huge windows. It's easy to slip inside, and then I'm in her apartment-sized room, eyes going straight to the bed.

"You scared the hell out of me. Thought someone was trying to break in while I'm all alone. They're gone, a spontaneous fundraiser again for dad or something.

Whaaat?" She slurs the last word, staring at the wolfish grin spreading across my lips, eyes searching mine.

"Nothing. Just love how you look when you're surprised. Lucky for you, there's only one thing I'm interested in stealing in this house." Before she can even answer, my lips crash down on hers.

Holy fuck.

I can't decide whose clothes I want to rip off faster – hers or mine.

The harder we kiss, the fiercer the storm in my blood. She's wearing that leaf green nightgown I've seen a few times over the last year. It's practically hanging off her curves, a taunting temptation in the darkness.

Amy Kay's hands flatten against my chest. At first, I think she'll push me away, just like all the other times. But then her little fingers pinch my shirt, pulling it, her nails dragging against the skin underneath.

There's no mistaking horny. She wants me as bad as I do her. Tonight, it's finally happening.

My hands go straight to my belt. At the last second, I hesitate, taking my hands off it and cupping her cheeks. I can't let this happen unless I know. "You're *sure* you're ready for this?"

"Trent, I've been ready. Assuming you'll talk to dad, like we said last week?"

Shit. If she wanted to kill my hard-on mid-rage, mission accomplished.

I tighten my hold on her face, stroking one cheek with my thumb. "Anything, Precious. If we're fucking, I'll have words with the devil himself over drinks."

She smiles, her cheeks going red in her usual bashful way. It's sexy how damn sweet she is, even when she's ready to jump my bones. "I'm serious, Trent Usher. Nothing's happening on that bed unless you promise me this is for real."

"Fine. After you promise me the same, darling. We're off to separate colleges this fall. You'll be on your own for the first time. I've already been at it for several years. You're sure long distance is your thing?"

"I wouldn't even ask if it wasn't. Come on, Trent. You're insane if you think I'd ever do anything to ruin this. I've wanted this forever about as bad as I've wanted you. Ever since that first messed up kiss and the years we wasted. I'm not losing you again. Not losing more precious time."

Heavy words. I grin, press my forehead to hers, brushing her lips with mine. She gives a seductive whimper that brings my dick back, harder than ever.

It isn't that I think she'll cheat, no matter how many strapping young dicks will want a piece of her on campus.

She's so young. Inexperienced. Ripe to trip over her own heart unless I'm man enough to help her.

"I'll talk to Maxwell, Presh. You have my word." I give her face a reassuring squeeze, amazed how even just her cheeks against my palms course lightning through my balls. "Now, much as I like your folks, they're the last fucking thing I want to talk about while I'm getting you naked."

Lust leaves her lungs in a sigh. I bring her face closer, until our next kiss is irresistible. My tongue finds madness on hers, sweet and fierce and wanting. When she kisses me back, a little moan strums against my tongue. I swallow it like fine whiskey.

That's how I know I'm fucked before we've done the deed.

This woman *will* end me. Only way to stop it is if I take full control. If I take everything.

Every trembling inch of her, from the sweetness begging for my tongue underneath her gown, to the secrets, the hopes, the needs woven deep in her soul.

There's no such thing as the one-off fuck I've wanted for years. With Amy Kay Chenocott, it's fucking bodies, minds, and souls. It's a fuck that'll go on in its delectable madness for the rest of my life.

* * *

Present Day

I WAKE up with a manic tension against my trousers and a horrific case of cottonmouth.

It was a dream, of course. A memory. A ghost of happier times.

Same familiar mindfuck I always get under stress.

This time, though, there's good reason. I'm still in the same trap I left behind the minute I closed my eyes and drifted off.

She's behind that door. The heavy, immovable locked door that's pissing me off royal.

I stagger to my feet, grunting because my body aches worse from the ordeal on the elevator after sleep.

Can't say how many hours I've been out. Enough for healing to start, and it always hurts like hell.

Shuffling over, I let my briefcase hit my feet, and slam my sore fists against solid steel. "Precious! It's morning. I still don't have a bathroom out here. Let a man in to drain his bladder, will you?"

Silence. She's ignoring me.

If only I could do that for the weight in my bladder. I need to piss, and I'm not doing it in the middle of a fire exit.

Fuck me.

My hands hurt, but damn if I don't want to beat them against this door until they're raw. If this is a nightmare, maybe the pain will bring me out of it.

Then I hear the sluggish creak of metal, and know this is way too real. "Really? You're going to make me beg?" I snarl.

"You're not getting in. Not until you're ready to promise me you won't hurt my brother."

I stare point-blank into her hunter green eyes. God damn. She's serious.

She doesn't have a clue it's already a done deal. Anytime now, Jace will be waking up to some very nasty surprises.

"Don't do this to me, Precious. I'm *not* making you another promise I can't keep. There are things happening, legally, and I can't put the brakes on them if I want to while I'm stuck up here with you." I manage to force my hand through the door, under hers. If she wants to close this thing again, she'll have to break my fingers.

"Oh well. Sorry, Trent, guess you'll have to find some kitty litter to do your business out there then."

She tries to pull the door shut, but I'm stronger, holding it open. "Wait, wait, wait...wait!"

The door doesn't shut. Not completely. I sigh, growling my next words. "Look, woman, if you let me in now, I'll think about putting the worst on hold. Soon as I can."

It's pure brinksmanship. There's no reason for us to trust the other's word, lifesaving antics and tongue-in-cheek skirmishes about our long-lost romance aside.

At last, she hisses air through her teeth. "Whatever. Just get in here. Do your thing and leave me alone. If you keep pestering me, I'll push you the hell out again, Trent. Mark my words."

"Deal." Pushing past her, I hear the heavy door click shut again. I waste no time heading for the bathroom I saw in the Shaw office earlier.

I remember where I heard that name before while I'm washing my hands. They're a powerful family, three brothers, all married now. They were all over the news last year. Went through drama and bad press aplenty, building empires in real estate, finance, and even Hollywood.

Bad PR makes me smile and cringe simultaneously. It's a big part of the real reason Presh and I are at each other's throats.

The press fucking destroyed Maxwell Chenocott after I took the fall for Jace's idiocy, ruining his bid for Senate. He deserved better. After all these years replaying that hell in my head, it's only fair game I use the same weapon. I've pulled the pin on a few choice grenades meant for my old pal, and they're going to blow him to pieces.

I wash up and grab a couple waters from the cooler on the way out. Amy Kay looks up, frustration wrinkling her pretty face. "I said –"

"Leave you alone. I'm not deaf, Presh. Still, I think last night left us both drained as hell. Drink this, it'll help." I hold out the water and wait a few seconds. She finally snatches it from my hand, lifts it to her lips, sucking it down greedily.

"Still no word?" Her glare answers my question, telling me the obvious. "Right. It's morning, at least. Help has to show up sometime today. It's a Monday, new week, managers won't be pleased to have an elevator out of commission and find out they're locked out of their own offices."

She isn't in the mood for small talk. There isn't much point, especially when getting the hell out of here is totally in the hands of the city's emergency responders. I sit, nursing my water, taking a brief walk before returning to the seat across from her.

"Where did it all go wrong?" Her face is in her hands. So small, so pale, so completely ready to be done with this fuckery.

Her question throws me. "Don't tell me all this crap's given you amnesia? Here's the cliff notes: I did a bad thing, Precious. Your asshole brother did a whole lot worse. Nobody wanted to hear the truth. Seems that hasn't changed."

"You keep saying that, dancing around it like I'm a total fool. I don't need your excuses. We know what happened. Dad was right: we never should've treated you like our own."

Pain digs through my chest. Pain and rage. "He said that?" I pause, waiting for her to look at me again, but she won't. "Fuck, just forget it. There's no use rehashing how the past went up in smoke. What's done is done, Amy Kay."

Technically, it isn't. Not done. Not even close.

Not while Jace Chenocott carries on as a happily married heir to a fortune, without a care in the world except how much money he can squeeze out of the family firm before he runs it into the ground. He would, even without my intervention.

"Trent, just tell me one thing: do you believe in coincidence? Fate?" Her eyes peek out above her fingers, studying me.

I start shaking my head. "What the hell kind of question is that, Presh? You trying to pass the time talking metaphysics? Screw that."

Sighing, her eyes open and shut, long lashes fluttering. "Just fucking answer. Please."

I cock my head, studying her back, shocked she wants an honest answer. "Guess I never thought about it before..."

No, that's not true. All I've done the last six years is think. Search for what explains the vicious path life forced us on. Ask why I lost her.

"If that's what you think this is, why we're here together, forget it. Won't do us any good, thinking we're stuck on this floor because God or the universe wants us to kiss and make up."

Her eyes widen, angry pinpricks dancing in the dim light.

Okay, so I shouldn't have said 'kiss.' Damn if it stops my eyes from landing on her lips. They're pinched in a light pink line.

Fuck.

Whatever else they do, they don't lie. I know they'd still be as sweet as a ripe strawberry if I walked over and decided to shut her up the nice way. If I decided to do more than talk about kissing, and break every last rule stopping us from ripping ourselves to pieces.

"You really want the truth then?" I wait. She nods. "Fuck coincidences, Presh. Fate, too. Haven't bought into fairy tales for years. The times I did when we were young and stupid nearly cost me everything. My fate was ruined a long time ago by your scheming bastard brother."

She bolts up, her little teeth bared for a split second, perfectly straight and white as I remember. "You? No, Trent, you nearly ruined *him*. Or maybe you're the one with amnesia here? Dad could've been the fucking president right now, making this world a better place, if you hadn't derailed everything. He wouldn't have spent years in a drunken stupor, moping around, straining mom to her breaking point. And Jace...Jesus. Jace might've learned to be normal, instead of just acting like it."

"Shit, Presh. Why don't we just cut straight to the chase? If I'd never been born, your life would be roses. The Chenocotts would have their faces chiseled in next to the Kennedys."

Why am I even fighting? Giving her this? I should just head for the steel door, walk the hell out, and wait like a patient man.

It can't be long now. The early morning haze is breaking with the sun coming up over the mountains, giving Seattle another chance to shine. If I had to guess, it's probably after five AM.

"You're pathetic," she snaps. "All these years, and you still won't fess up to it like a man, even though there has to be a reason we wound up here. The odds are astronomical, Trent. And you won't admit it. It's just another day in the life of a reckless blue-eyed asshole who practically got away with murder."

Murder? *I wish.*

Maybe then I wouldn't have had the chance to run. Wouldn't have panicked, taken off with my family, been that scared kid with parents who trashed their retirement to pull him off the firing line.

Maybe I would've been forced to stay. Cornered to fight.

Maybe I would've turned Jace in.

Sure, it would've dragged Amy through the mud, too. Everything I hoped to save her from at the time. But isn't that inevitable?

Coming back here says it is.

Sniping at each other confirms it.

The inevitable, bitter end of life as Jace knows it was always bound to happen every day I got my life together, and owned it.

But shit, if I'd done things differently, maybe it wouldn't be this bad. This painful. This vicious.

Maybe we wouldn't be standing in front of a smashed up office, her with no shoes, and me with the torn button down, hiding the scratches and bruises still throbbing their anger, trying to find out who'll be the first to set the other on fire with just the fury in our wounded souls.

"Congratulations, Presh," I say slowly. "You finally figured it out. I'm just the blue-eyed asshole who fed off your family because he could. I'm that dirty orphan kid who lost his soul, who just wanted to fuck and run after he set everything else on fire. I'm the worst thing that ever happened to you, and totally not the man who saved you twice. I'm the reason your life's shit. I'm your biggest disappointment, smothering all the others – and I can tell you've got plenty."

She drops her eyes. I'm not done. "I'm the fucking scapegoat. All the back-and-forth in the world won't change my mind about giving Jace the kick in the balls he deserves. So back the fuck off, quit trying to get under my skin, and let me do my thing. You believe in fate, then you ought to know it's coming. And nothing, darling, not even *you*, will stop it."

There.

I've said my piece.

Her eyes tell me I'll pay mightily for it. Like that scares me. I'll pay *gladly* if it finally brings this psychotic trip through bad memories to an end.

Her mouth falls open, searching for words through the anger.

Then there's a crash behind her so loud our hearts both rebound in our throats. My eyes shift over to the elevator shaft while my heart slams against my throat.

Is this whole fucking building about to cave? But the sound comes from the door, like there's a charging bull ramming it, and it takes me two more flustered seconds to rush past her paralyzed body and yank on the handle.

About a dozen big men rush in at once.

Police flashing badges, firefighters dressed in long reflective coats, a few more guys and gals and lighter blue uniforms I realize later are paramedics.

Amy Kay's eyes are a soft angry mess as they find mine. I give her a knowing look, suddenly ready to drain the venom left by her barbs. The insults and half-truths don't matter anymore.

Whether we like it or not, the cavalry has arrived.

Suppressing a growl, I rummage through my pocket, searching for the little scrap of paper where I scrawled my room and phone number. Had to do something while she left me locked out in the stairwell. I had plenty of paper in the briefcase and a lot of time to plan for certain scenarios.

Too bad I'm not sure where this one fits. "Take it," I tell her, reaching through the crew swarming us. "You want to hash out the past, this is where you'll find it, and me."

I don't wait for a response after her little fingers close around the scrap of paper. I decide not to look at her again.

It's easier than it should be once five men with badges start barking questions in my face.

Maybe I should've just walked out and cut the cord.

We're clear. Safe. Free. Done.

My only business left is with Jace, and after I've left a crater through his life, I'll blow this town forever. Good chance she's too pissed to ever contact me again.

Maybe that's for the best. Giving her my contact makes no sense, but then, none of this ever did.

It doesn't change what's next: forgetting the last twenty-four hours.

Including the last time I'll ever taste the fallen paradise of our kiss.

VII: SO BARE (AMY KAY)

Are you hurt, ma'am?
Are you alone?
Are you the manager for Shaw Financial?

Questions bombard me from all sides, making the pain in my head ten thousand times worse. For a second, I'd give anything to be back in the frosty silence with Trent.

Just me, him, and a yawning void, broken open only when we can't hold it anymore.

"I'm...fine," I tell the big burly black man in the firefighter uniform with his hands on my shoulders. His grip is strong, sturdy, brings me back to life. "Yes, thank you. Yes, I'm sure. Fine."

Hardly.

I'm actually anything but. My eyes stab through the small crowd, trying to find Trent, aching to deliver one more subtle bombshell: *this isn't over, you prick.*

I had a hundred questions on the tip of my tongue and lost them all the instant our saviors showed up.

How could he say such horrible things after saving my life? Not just insulting, but insane.

Trent Usher is delusional. He's convinced himself the past is wrong. Somehow, someway, he honestly *believes* the nuclear hellfire he unleashed on our lives really isn't his fault.

He thinks he's a victim. Thinks he's in the right to march back in our lives after half a decade and turn everything upside down again.

He's maddeningly set on ruining Jace, blaming him for...I don't even know.

My brother was an idiot. He was up to his neck in their scheme, too dumb to realize he was getting played by Trent's brains.

But Jace isn't malicious. He wasn't steering that mess. I'll never believe it.

He *couldn't* have possibly orchestrated the filth they found in the burned out hulk of my crashed convertible, abandoned on a remote stretch of coast outside Olympia, the car bloody with DNA we never had tested because we decided to show mercy...

No. Hell no.

My brother's not that stupid. He's not an actual criminal. More like a gullible accomplice.

I swallow hard, craning my neck, trying to spot Trent in the crowd. One of the cops is sick of my tight-lipped act. He spins me around, mutters something to an EMT about "checking the lady for a concussion," and reminds us the building's being evacuated.

I'm too dizzy to ask why. I just hear his voice in the corner, incredulous, defiant. "What the hell do you mean?

I'm not going anywhere. I've got a trip to the thirtieth floor to make and I'm not leaving –"

"Sir, whatever business you have will have to wait. Building's closed. Sustained too much damage from the power outage, the elevator crash. It started a fire on the first floor that took us hours to control. Same reason it took so long getting up here."

"Fire?" It's the last word I hear on Trent's lips.

Then there's a flurry of hands around me, grabbing for mine, helping me through the steel door. They treat me like a toddler learning to walk. It takes forever to get downstairs and pass through the door to sweet freedom on the floor above the lobby.

And when I'm on ground level again, waiting outside the yellow emergency tape and cones for a taxi, it's a fight not to rush back inside through the chaos, through the billion cops.

Yes, I'm ground down, dazzled by the fresh morning air, and chilled by the nightmare I just survived.

And I still want to strangle Trent Usher. Right after I find out what happened the past few years to turn him into a self-righteous prick living an alternate reality.

"Don't be stupid," I tell myself, whispering under my breath as a blue and white cab pulls up.

He wants me in stitches. Limping home with questions rattling my brain. Trent would love it if I gave him more rent in my head than he really deserves, and as hard as it is to forget what just happened, I need to try.

The ride to the hotel takes forever in the early morning rush hour traffic. I barely remember to tip the driver. My brain is on fire, begging for sleep. Good, nourishing rest – not the two or three choppy hours that left a kink in my neck, broken by Mr. I-Need-to-Pee pounding on the door.

I don't know why I think I'll win that game where you try *not* to think about something. It never works.

But, I'm trying my damnedest, the whole way up to my room. I take the stairs, skipping out on the elevator. It'll be a good long while before I'm comfortable in a metal box again, even though the climb finishes off my knees.

At last, peace and quiet. The huge king-sized bed in the middle of the room beckons like the world's best chocolate – something I'm sure I'll seek out later to kill the sugar craving pulsing in my stressed out veins. I yank the curtains shut, wash my face, and crash down in the pillows face first, inwardly cursing his name every spare second.

Screw you. This isn't over.

When I have the energy and the heart and the focus to track you down, I will.

Cryptic words won't save you next time.

Two can play at ripping old wounds open.

And it just so happens I've got an arsenal of salt to pour.

* * *

Six Years Ago

"I'll talk to Maxwell. You have my word." His palms sweep across my face and my heart pounds happily in my ears.

Tonight those big hands hold the world, so many promises, only outdone by the gorgeous shine in his eyes.

It's a seductive one, too. The wet, tense heat pools between my legs, fiercer by the second, twisting my belly in knots.

This...this is happening. *Holy hell.*

I shift against him, leaning forward slightly, brushing my lips on his. *Just kiss me again. Please.*

But Trent isn't done talking, no matter how seductively I try to run my fingers up his huge biceps. "Now, much as I like your folks, they're the last fucking thing I want to talk about while I'm breaking you in."

Thunder rumbles in his throat. The next time our lips touch, it's perfection.

Hot and wet and so electric.

Incandescent. The fire in my lower belly flares through me, igniting everything in its wake, plucking every nerve.

My nipples call to him beneath my gown. My thighs pinch shut, seeking sweet friction.

Just a brief flash of relief from this inferno pulsing in my core. His hand sweeps down my back the longer we kiss.

Tongues and hands and bodies unite, finding their natural rhythm.

I need more. Now. A need so potent it's making me delirious.

Trent's knees knock gently against mine. His lips dive bomb mine again, then pull back, making me beg. Then he hauls me up, wraps my legs around his body, and takes us to bed.

I crash down under him with a whimper. His hands

trawl my legs, feeding new flames, a sultry look in his majestic blue eyes that says, *tonight you'll bare your all, Precious, and I will fucking take it.*

No argument here. It's been an insane few weeks.

Ever since the kiss on Bainbridge, the catalyst that never should've followed a volley of insults, we've been inseparable. It's shocking how fast things change.

I'm even more shocked my stupid brother hasn't noticed, but then, he's been busy juggling Lindsey and that skank, Georgia, again. Both at once. Behind each others' back.

No, I'm not letting my ex-best friend know. If she wants to keep hooking up with Jace, she'll learn his faults the hard way.

I'm doing the same with Trent, aren't I? Risking my heart?

Fair is fair.

Oh, but there's nothing *fair* about how my body tingles when his lips stamp a soft line up my throat. His fingers lace through my hair, bringing my face to his again and again. He pauses for breath, pressing his forehead against mine. We share a moment drunk on wanton anticipation, sex and fire mingling in our veins.

"Get this thing off, Presh. Show me every inch of you." He gives my shoulder strap a fierce tug, making room for me to sit, helping me up with his hands.

So, this is it. My teeth dig into my bottom lip while I grab the hem, lift it up, peeling it off my body.

Just panties underneath. Soaked in a way I desperately want to hide.

Nothing escapes his eyes. I'm more naked, more vulnerable, more turned on than I've ever been.

Trent notices the wet heat pooling between my legs. Shoving his hand in my cleft, he toys with me through the drenched fabric, stroking my labia. "Fucking hell, darling. You need it bad. Almost as bad as I do."

I nod. Awestruck that a man like him could be tangled up in the same wild urges ripping through me.

This is wrong on so many levels, and it's never been more right.

I wasn't supposed to go down like this. Not with him.

Dad always hoped I'd find someone richer, softer, probably older and wiser. But no other boy ever would've captured my heart from the very first kiss.

No other boy would've made me wait years, want and hate locking swords in my heart, begging for the day we'd put that all aside and sort our issues out in the flesh.

Today. Tonight. *Now.*

Trent's teasing fingers quicken their strokes while his mouth collides with mine, pushing me into the bed again. A groan spills out of him and his tongue returns to mine. It's my turn to moan when his fingers find my clit.

What sweet hell is this? What agony? It's a delicious torture, a needy pleasure, numbing my senses. Everything dulls except the lightning heat in my nerves screaming *more.*

"Trent!" I whimper, once his fingers find their pace. I'm close to breathless.

Growling, he shoves my panties aside, the better for his fingertips to stroke my naked pussy.

I'm coming apart.

They tease my entrance, but don't quite force their way in.

"Look at me, woman," he rumbles, slowing his frantic

strokes until I meet his eyes. "This is what's haunted my dreams since the first day I laid eyes on you. This is what I've wanted. This is where my dick belongs. This, beautiful, is my pussy now. And after I've had it, neither one of us will ever be the same."

There's a wicked weight in his words. A truth that adds more fuel to my pulse. I reach for his neck, winding my fingers down his skin, loving how strong, how big, how powerful this man actually is.

He wouldn't be here if it were any other way. The bigger question is whether I can handle him.

It's a serious, pointed question, too, just a second later, when he rears up, pulling on his belt. Once it's unclasped, he pauses, a vicious smirk on his lips. "Take a good long look, Amy Kay. You want a peepshow, you'll get it."

His face disappears behind his shirt as it rolls over his head. In the years since I've seen him shirtless, he's become sculpted. All tight muscle packed on manly bones, big and broad enough to end the world. There's a smattering of ink on one shoulder, connecting to the black lightning coursing up one arm. A majestic wolf's face that wasn't there a few summers ago catches my eye.

"What's this for?" I whisper, my fingers gingerly reaching out, marveling at his muscle. The design fits him perfectly, glowing on his skin like a brand for a dark angel.

"It's a reminder, Presh. Tells me I've got the heart, the will, the drive to do anything I set my mind to. Also lets me know I'm a pack animal, however much I wish it weren't true. Wolves defend their kin like nothing you've ever seen. Saw it in a documentary once." Something about that makes me smile, the idea of big, tough, brainy Trent kicking back in a chair, watching a nature show.

"They'll rip the whole world to shit if the people they love are threatened. Call it dumb, I don't care, there's something noble there."

"That's why we're getting naked? So you can talk about your favorite animals?" Teasing, I run my fingers down his chest, suppressing a lustful shudder. I've reached his abs, and oh my God...chiseled isn't even the right word.

They're a coiled six pack. Maybe even *eight*. Just one look, one gentle touch, makes me imagine what they can do, how many different ways they help his godly body twist and fight and fuck.

"You know damn well why I came by tonight," he growls, his blue eyes turning darker. "Next words I hear out of your mouth better be screams, Precious. You've given me plenty of grief with that mouth, and I'd be a liar if I said I haven't imagined all the ways I'll wash that sass right out."

And how.

The bastard kisses me, shutting up my playful tongue. My little fingers haven't lost their fight, though. They hook in his half-open belt and tug. He breaks the kiss, gives me a sexy smile, and then hooks his hands on his jeans, fingering the loops. "Thanks for your patience, ma'am. Special delivery."

"Dork!" Even through the killer heat throbbing in my veins, I push him gently in the ribs, laughing as he rips his jeans down.

Silence reigns the second I see the outline of his cock. "Don't worry. I'll teach you to suck the hell out of this in good time. For now, I've got bigger plans..."

I'm blushing like the excited, scared virgin I truly am as he stands at the edge of the bed, steps up to me, and grabs my hand. He moves it to his boxer's waistband, pinching my fingers tight. "Go ahead. Open your present. It's Christmas morning."

It's mid-July, and we both know it. I'm far too curious to laugh at his ridiculousness this time.

I give it a vicious tug. There's an elastic snap, a helping push from his hands, and then –

"Holy. Shit." I don't know what pops out faster: my words or my eyes. They both want to leave my body the second I see what he's been hiding.

It's thick. It's enormous. It's as hard and determined and maybe a little pissed off as the rest of him.

Trent wraps a fist around the base, gives it a squeeze, and pushes his fingers up to the swollen head. A string of pearly liquid flows out his opening. For a girl who's never seen a penis in the flesh before, I'm stuck on the size. There's no hiding the fact he's *huge*, and I'm forced to wonder all over again if I'm physically ready for this.

But that question seems less relevant by the nanosecond. He pulls my hand to his shaft. New heat screams in my blood the instant I feel his fullness, warm and tense and pulsing.

"Just like that, yeah. Give it a few more pulls before my tongue takes over."

Tongue? I don't get what he's talking about as I give his throbbing, gorgeous cock a few quick pumps.

I don't understand until his lips start at my bare shoulder, arcing down, down, down. Trent palms my right breast, pulling the nipple with his teeth. It's sharp and brusk and oh so warming.

Hello, master. Now, I know.

This tongue knows what it's doing, and so do his lips. Every time he lifts back, encircling my breasts, the sweet tension sends new shocks through my body.

I'm writhing on his hand, helpless for his fingers, pinching my thighs shut. Trent growls, grinding his fingers harder against my pussy, taking my left breast in his stormy mouth.

My pussy aches. My heart beats a firm relentless thud in my temples.

I'm not in Kansas anymore. Or Washington. Or anywhere in the same universe.

The beast on top of me rockets pleasure through my body, bringing me closer to my very first O with a man.

Oh, and *what* an O.

What a brutal, glorious, soul splitting O it will be.

"Presh, spread your legs. Lift your butt. These are coming the hell off *now*." His head slips down and his rough arms pin my legs against his shoulders. His teeth carefully but swiftly hook to my panties and pull.

They saunter down my legs in one quick burst. Raw need roars through me.

There's nothing but his pulse, this heat, this wild, wild fire pining for his touch. His head snaps to the side and I hear the faint sound of my bottoms hitting the floor.

"Please, Trent," I whisper. "Please. Show me what that tongue can do."

My mouth isn't the only one that's been hell for us in the past. The things he's done to me over the years with those piercing eyes, that Herculean body, those whip-sharp lips, and every word they give...

It ends here tonight in a licking, tangled mess. Or does

it ever end?

I can't tell where I begin as soon as his kisses land on my thighs. He moves between them in perfect balance, crawling up my legs, feeding the inner flames.

Trent pauses, lips against my swollen pussy, hot breath wafting a tease. The first flick of his tongue on my clit splits me in two.

He growls into me, holding my legs apart, intoxicated on my scent, my taste, my pleading hips. Every movement, every harsh whimper, every moan urges him on. His tongue quickens, dipping inside me, lashing my inner walls.

It's filthy and delightful and I think – oh, God! – I think I don't have a prayer.

I can't last long.

There's barely time to throw my hands over my head, clench the sheets in angry fistfuls, and suppress a scream.

Hell, screw *suppressing*. Good thing my parents aren't home.

His tongue starts on my clit. I can't even dream of staying muffled. I'm over in a bellow, a flash of legs shaking on his shoulders, a convulsion. The fireball in my lower belly explodes, pouring out, bathing my brain in pleasure.

I come on his face. I come so hard it hurts.

Pinching my teeth together, drowning in his frantic licks, yanked into the undertow by the fiery rings he traces between my legs. They all scream this mantra: *don't fucking stop, Precious. Come for me. Come hard. Come now.*

And I do. I so freaking do.

Pleasure yawns wide with his face working overtime, swallows me up, and seems to go on forever. But even this delicious madness has to end. I come down from my high, white-knuckling the sheets, my vision finally working again.

I'm just in time to see Trent Usher drawing my legs up as he kneels between them, wonderfully naked. He's the pinnacle of *oh, fuck* and *so fucking hot.* His abs draw my eyes, a perfect view between my legs, still shaking as he pins them against his body.

Something soft and metallic glistens in one hand. His teeth tear the corner as he raises it to his lips. A condom, I realize, watching him roll it onto his pulsing length a second later. Then his fullness is against me, hard and thick and ready.

"Any last words as a virgin, Presh? Be quick." He pinches my legs tighter against his rock hard body.

"Just take me," I say, eyes locked on his, amazed how bad my cunt wants him again so soon after coming on his mouth. I stiffen, grinding my wetness against his cock, greedy and impatient. "Fuck me, Trent Usher."

The spark in his eye goes from admiring to feral. Then his hips plow forward, crashing into mine, feeding his hardness into me.

My back arches. Pain and pleasure and a little shred of panic explode in my brain. But I fight through the bad parts, determined to take this, to make my first time something I'll remember on my deathbed.

That part is easy.

How could I forget the glint in his eye as he mounts me for the first time, claiming my flesh?

How could I forget the fierce ripple of muscle in the moonlight, or how the wolf moves on his skin as he digs in to the hilt?

How could I ever forget the slow, powerful thrusts forming my body to his?

They come in a steady wave, fusing us, making my pussy fit him like silk.

"Trent!" I whimper the one word I'm able to remember as he fucks me.

"So tight, Presh. So good. So goddamned mine tonight." He's able to talk because I guess he's done this a thousand times.

But there's a wicked satisfaction when I see his face contort. He's holding back, controlling the full power thrusts, fighting the need to give it to me like I'm just another warm, wet place for his cock to take control.

I'm not just another woman. I'm his, the one he's wanted for years. I'm going to make him come so hard he can't think.

It's another minute of frantic thrusting before I wonder if that's possible. Trent leans in, bowing my legs, grinding in deeper and faster, the better to ignite my clit. His lips fall on mine with a hunger, a groan, a muffled word I never expected.

It sounds like, "finally."

"Fucking finally," he grunts again, breaking the kiss, running our foreheads together. "It's even better than the thousand times I imagined fucking you, Amy Kay. All the nights I beat my dick to you, to us, to having you under me. Fuck!"

"Trent, yes!" His name hangs on my lips. I kiss him again, quick and messy, loving how the friction wrings more pleasure out of him the harder and longer we fuck.

The pain and discomfort in my virgin flesh fades. Our hips collide, faster and faster, and soon I'm in a headlong rush toward my second O, wishing so bad he'd come with me.

I want him losing control. I want him giving up. I want him breaking deep inside me, filling me, surrounding the edgy strongman act so I can see his soul bared for just a few impossible seconds.

"Trent..."

"What did I tell you, Amy Kay?" he growls, slowing his thrusts until I stare into his eyes. "Screams. Only thing I want leaving your mouth when I'm balls deep and damn close to coming."

God, yes. I want it.

Want him to join the frenzy in my veins, my pulse, pinching my legs tight to him to draw him in deeper, harder, closer to the beautiful end.

Come the hell with me, Trent Usher, I beg inside my head, too lost to make words with my lips.

My mouth gives him screams aplenty.

They tell him everything. My pussy betrays my deepest want, my need, every time it convulses around his cock; sucking, pulling, pleading.

Trent. I grab at his arms, hold on tight, and buck my hips into him.

A small gasp escapes his throat. His rhythm changes. Before, a gradual rise in tempo and tension, but now the wall is down.

Trent! He's thrusting harder, doubling his speed, his amazing ass clenched under my ankles. If this is what it is to be power fucked, then I'll never have it any other way.

Trent, Trent, Trent!

Can't think. Can't breathe. Can't do anything except

stare into his fierce eyes offering their conquest, and try to keep up with his rhythm.

I lose the battle I barely knew was happening inside me in an instant. His huge chest swells, I hear him take a guttural breath, and then he goes absolutely ballistic between my legs. Lightning electrifies every nerve, bringing me off.

Bringing me *down*.

I come so hard on his cock I think I lose my vision, my hearing, my tactile sensation all at once. But I can still hear, still feel where we're joined together, and what comes next drives me to places I never knew existed.

There's a rough hand in my hair, tugging like mad, holding me down as he slams his last full measure into me. Then there's a swelling against mine, his cock growing bigger, brandishing new heat against my walls.

"Fuck, Presh. Fuck!" It's the last thing I hear. Then the pleasure becomes so deafening it drowns out everything.

It's just me and him. Trent and Amy Kay, lost in each other, the cord to the universe severed by orgasmic bliss.

We come beautifully. It's a lovely chaos, sweat and flesh and thudding hearts, madness and hoarse screams. I don't even bother to hold mine back, knowing we've got this huge place to ourselves.

Even if we didn't, I'm not sure I'd be able to care or stop.

Trent has officially fucked me into ruin.

And I already want him to do it again and again and *again*.

I don't open my eyes until I feel him pull out of me, sated for now. It won't last long, and I'm looking forward to it.

Trent ties off the condom, leans over the bed, flicks it into my bin. "You sure housekeeping won't squeal?"

"Oh, no. Julia Davis likes me too much to tell mom or dad unless I'm really doing wrong. I'm also eighteen now. Legally obliged to screw your brains out without consequences, Mr. Usher, or did you already forget?" I nuzzle my face against his chest, fingers dancing across his rigid muscle. Reaching up, I pat his cheek, loving the five o'clock shadow there.

More like nine o'clock if I'm being honest. He hasn't shaved in at least a day. Picturing him with a beard just makes me wet all over again.

"I forgot all kinds of things after that," he says, stroking my cheek, then bringing my face up to his. "You fuck like a mad woman, Presh. Or a desperate one. All the years playing good girl must've made you horny as hell. Love it."

The new flush scorches my cheeks, giving me away. It's strange how good he is at making me feel so bare, so honest, especially when I'm completely naked. "Good. Then you'll help a girl make up for lost time," I whisper, brushing my lips against his.

I pull back before he can kiss me. His eyes are narrowed, annoyed, but so turned on. If I look down, I know I'll see him getting hard again, ready for a second round.

"So we're going casual then? Making this all about the sex? Good. No need to talk to Maxwell."

"Idiot!" I play-punch him in the shoulder.

Bad joke. It makes me laugh because I know he'll talk to dad soon. I'm so incredibly lucky to have him. To have this.

He grabs my little wrist, a rich dark chuckle in his throat, and pulls me into another divine kiss.

We thought we'd found paradise that night, and nothing could ever ruin us. If we'd had the faintest hint of the evil waiting the very next day, I wouldn't have been so naïve.

Or so defenseless.

The world would make me pay dearly for ever thinking a Happily Ever After was in our cards.

* * *

Present Day

DREAMS. Nightmares. Memories.

They blur together restlessly in my afternoon sleep. I pull the sheets tighter, hating how I wake up with my heart pounding, and slightly wet.

Dreaming about our first time does that.

Then I remember I hate him, and the new Trent Usher I met downtown is a far bigger asshole than the boy I left behind.

I crash back down into the pillows, hands over my face, hating the pale gray Seattle sun seeping through a crack in the curtains. The sandman easily chases me down a second time and works his magic.

Hate, confusion, frustration, and lost love form a strange geography in my sleeping mind. I hear voices. Remember the morning after our first time.

I woke up to an empty bed, our sex sheets still

wrapped around me. Trent was gone.

But the house wasn't empty. I crept out of my room, following the voices, ears pricked up and heart doing nosedives for no good reason. I couldn't miss the edge, the anger in their words, right away.

"Fuck you, Usher. I don't *need* your brains to bail me out of this one. It's too damn late for second thoughts. You were the one who said we needed to raise capital, remember? Hell, if this money isn't good enough for you, maybe I'll just throw the whole wad at something else. I'm doing this for you, like a good friend and business partner. I listened to what you said. I –"

"Jace? Shut the fuck up. You're doing this for yourself, and you know it. No other reason why you'd even be this stupid, putting yourself and everybody else in danger. We need to get rid of this shit."

There's a brutal pause. They're somewhere near the main door. Whatever touched the fight off, it's serious.

Last time I heard Jace use that wounded tiger tone, he wound up punching poor Michael Bowens. It was after the kid tried to come between him and his fling with Georgia Whats-her-face a couple years ago. I stop by the stairs, just out of sight, too afraid to see their faces.

Too afraid because, Jesus, *what is this?*

"No one's getting caught, Trent. *No one.* A fucking pit behind the boathouse is the last place in the world anybody'd ever look."

"They don't *need* to be looking, asshole. Somebody just needs to find it. All it takes is a nosy person passing by on a boat, or one of your gardeners, or fuck, maybe a rich kid flying a drone. You'll wish it were Amy Kay or your folks. Anybody else will nail your dick to the floor. Same with my folks, and I sure as hell won't blame them after the bullshit you pulled on our property."

Jace stops, snorts, bile in his voice. "You're forgetting one thing: it's *my* house, fucknut. My money. My deal. I'll be by later to get my crap out of your ma's garden. You don't want a piece of this, fine. Here's the fucking door."

"Nice, asshole. Giving me the same courtesy you extended to ma after she put you up, did your laundry, cooked us food all summer." More fury explodes in Trent's voice.

I hear one of the heavy double French doors out front spring open, slapping its safety stopper against the wall. "Shut up. Take your perfect angel act the hell out of here. Don't come back. I'll send somebody by your place for my stuff later. You rat me out, you mess with my shit, I *will* kick your ass, Usher. Hard."

"Hilarious." He draws in a ragged breath, and then whispers in a low growl, like he's right in my brother's face. "To think, I wasted five fucking years trying to tell everybody who insisted that you weren't an impulsive idiot, Jace. Stood by you like a brother. Good luck living under house arrest with Maxwell. If I can't stop you from fucking up your life, dear old dad will before you crash his campaign with no survivors."

I lean forward, straining to hear more, but I can't make out the next few muffled words.

"Stay the fuck away!" Jace roars. "This was your idea, your scheme, your business. I promise, if you go digging any of that shit up and dumping it without my permission, we'll have problems. Don't take matters into your own hands, cock." I wince, hear sneakers screech on tile, like he's lunging for Trent's throat. "You're not family, asshole. Never were. My parents. My house. My sister. You want to keep that perfect goddamn grin of yours intact, you'll keep away from everything. I'll pick up the pieces and we'll be done."

Back in the present, I wake up with Jace's furious words stuck in my head. Ringing.

All these years later, I wish I'd heard Trent give a parting shot, tell my idiot brother he loved me, how he wouldn't walk away for anything.

Oh, but he did. He showed me how little.

We learned the entire truth the next day from a crying, shaken Jace. He showed us who the real wolf was all along, how foolish I'd been to ever trust him.

Speaking of Jace...I look down because the ringing hasn't stopped. It's not just in my head. My phone vibrates, nearly shaking itself off the nightstand.

"What?" I hit the accept call button, pressing the cool screen to my ear.

"Building will be out of commission for at least a week, sis. Christ, can't believe the mess there, I'm glad you weren't hurt." *Is he?* He says it like a footnote, and not the whole reason I'm flat on my back exhausted, every bone in my body aching. "I know you're only out here for a couple weeks. Won't be practical to do much with showing you the floor in person, but if you'll let me send over some pics, I'd love to get your thoughts. We can still hash it out."

"Hmmm." I pretend I'm deep in thought. "Actually, bro, I've got a better idea: find yourself a real interior designer. First chance I get, I'm hopping on the first flight to Spokane, away from this shit show."

"You can't!" He realizes how stupid that sounds as

soon as it's out of his mouth. His next words are cold, but calmer. "Hell, sis, I wish you wouldn't, I mean. My hands are *real* busy here putting out fires. Clients have to meet with our boys and girls at noisy coffee shops and they don't like it. It's hell on confidentiality. We need a place to hang our hats again. Restore trust. Something worthy of a patent firm dad built. I need your help."

He sounds so small, so crushed, almost on the brink of the same suffering I saw that week our lives changed forever. Heat stings my cheeks, angry, unable to shake off the dreams.

"Just send the stupid pictures, Jace. Schematics, too. I'll look them over. But I'm still planning to skip town the second I have a chance."

"Really? Without even a visit to see me, or mom and dad?" He knows my guilt triggers and he pushes them deep. "Seriously a shame, sis. Where are you staying? I'd come down there, convince you stay myself, but I'm in the thick of it. Some really nasty surprises this morning. Not just the stuff with the firm..."

I blink, searching his words, wondering what he's hiding. Nasty surprises, he said. Trent's doing?

It isn't like him to back down so easily. Or hold his cards tight. The Jace I know should be pitching a nonstop fit until I agree to work my butt off fixing up the office, and tell him I'll stay in Seattle.

"What's going on?" I whisper, wondering if I can handle more bad news.

"Nothing, nothing, just Linds jumping down my throat. She's under the weather lately, that's all." He's so tight-lipped every time he mentions my ex-best friend.

The one he married.

"Whatever, you're right, I don't want to know" I tell him, pinching my eyes shut. My temples begin throbbing all over again. "Good luck."

"Yeah. Do me a favor and stay another day, Amy Kay. I'll be out there the second I get a chance to chat over drinks. Sorry, I know I haven't been real sympathetic to the crap that happened. Heard you got stuck in the elevator and all."

"It *crashed*, Jace. Slid right down the shaft and smashed into flames. Less than a minute after I crawled off it. It would've killed me if –" I stop. Just short of praising Trent Usher, who saved my life, and now seems hellbent on ruining my brother's.

"Shit. Didn't know. That's gotta shake a soul up."

He has no freaking clue. None whatsoever.

It's left me in pieces. "No promises. I'll think it over, Jace. I need some time," I tell him, wishing for sweet silence. I almost hang up, but my conscience won't let me. "Oh, yeah, Trent's in town, by the way. Says he's gunning for you. We had a...run-in at the office yesterday. Same elevator." There are no words for what really happened.

"Usher? Fuck me. That explains a whole hell of a lot. It *must* be him. I've gotta go."

He hangs up first. Another surprise. Usually, he'll kill to have the last word.

Whatever he says, I see where his priorities are.

I'm once again stuck helping a man who doesn't want to help himself. I pull up the airline app on my phone, eyes lazily drifting over flight schedules.

I'll think about it, like I told him, but not much.

I'm so done. So ready to get the hell out of here and have a normal night's sleep in my own bed.

Lindsey keeps invading my head with her snake-like smile, too. I can't believe we were ever inseparable, once upon a time.

Things were never the same after the hell that started after the best night of my life.

Lindsey never saw my brother's flaws like I expected. She ran.

Or did she? She was there at the right time, right place, to lend him a shoulder to cry on. She saw money, power, an opening to worm her way in at my family's weakest hour. What started as a hookup became a way to sink her claws in.

Two years later, my frenemy was Mrs. Jace Chenocott. It's just a miracle they haven't had a kid yet. Then there'd be no avoiding the awkward family gatherings, where I try to talk to Linds like a normal human being, without my eyes betraying me. They want to tear her in two for stepping where she never belonged.

I push the uncomfortable thought away and listen to my rowdy stomach. I rummage through the stack of papers on the dresser for a room service menu. A simple burger, medium well, with garlic fries and a giant Butterfinger shake sounds delish. I stop just short of booking flights while I'm waiting for my food.

I decide to clean up instead. A nice hot shower strips the melancholy grease off my heart and the exhaustion from my bones. After, I pad into the room, digging through the messy pile I've left in front of my half-open suitcase, searching for a change of clothes.

There's a scrap of paper tucked into my pocket. It's the stuff from my purse I pulled out and stuffed inside this morning, before I crashed out. An envelope.

I don't remember what's inside until I lift it up, hold it under the lamp, and see the opening sentence.

I hope you go to hell, Trent Usher...

Fitting. And incredibly frustrating.

My hate letter was with me the whole time on that hellish ride. I never showed it to him once.

Crumpling the paper in my hands, I whip it into the waste bin with a snarl. My stomach growls something fierce as I'm pulling my pants up, waiting for the knock at the door a few seconds later.

Dinner. I tip the man wheeling the cart, waiting for him to leave.

Five bites in, I regret my order. My stomach is slowly eating itself alive and I've still got no appetite.

Awesome.

Somehow, I can't get my mind off the stowaway letter I just trashed. Or the insufferable bastard it's addressed to.

It was written years ago. More for my mental health than anything I'd ever seriously mail.

Now, that's different. My feelings haven't changed. Seeing him, hating him, kissing him all over again left bruises on my soul.

He can't get away with it so easy. Especially not while he's trying to ruin Jace!

My eyes drift over to the nightstand where I've tossed my purse. Inside, the small slip of paper he gave me before I gave him hell. It hasn't gone anywhere.

I have his room number.

It wouldn't be hard to fish the letter out, drop it at the front desk, pay the postage, and give Mr. Asshole Usher a parting shot he'll never forget. You can't buy therapy this cheap.

No. Don't be stupid, I tell myself.

I think the same thing again in every sullen bite, trying to enjoy my food. The shake goes down easier, thankfully. I need the sugar rush.

If I'm ever too sick at heart to feed my shameless sweet tooth, then I know for sure it's time to see a doctor. Or a mortician to check my pulse, I guess.

For the moment, I'm safe. I'll wait to book my flight, and ignore the stupid documents I'm expecting Jace to fill my inbox with anytime now. I'm in control, half a city away from Trent, I hope, though it hardly feels like enough distance.

If only I could ignore that damn letter.

Another minute passes, wrestling myself the whole time. Then I drag myself across the room, stoop next to the trash, and rescue the crumpled mess from oblivion. Familiar, shameful outrage storms my blood while I iron the letter smooth again with my elbow.

God, do I hate this.

Hate how I can't get him out of my head.

Hate how he's managed to turn my life upside down. Again.

Probably in ways I don't even notice yet, depending on what's happening to Jace this second.

Hate, hate, *hate* how he makes me feel small and scorned and iced all over. Turning me into a heart-stung, swindled little girl without a clue about the world must be his superpower. And if the kryptonite exists somewhere on this earth to make it stop, I haven't found it.

It took years to find my way back from his desolation.

My twenties are more than half over, the best decade of my life, or so everybody says. What have I done?

Except for dropping out of Stanford my first year and running east of the Cascades, where I used my trust fund to jump start a chain of inns that's a hollow shadow of every business triumph my family ever had.

Some years *still* aren't breaking a healthy profit. I'm throwing my own money into the upkeep.

Trying like hell to forget the man who won't stay forgotten.

If I wasn't so used to disappointment by now, so numb to it, I might've sold the chain off a long time ago. Learned to walk away. I could take my failures as a learning lesson like a normal person, lick my wounds, and move on.

But *he* doesn't let that happen.

Trent fucking Usher condensed a lifetime of killing let downs into a few hazy weeks. He stole my heart and dropped me on my head with no apology, no explanation, and no remorse. He made his smirking memory impossible to bury.

You're not family, asshole. You never were. Jace's furious words echo in my head from the dream, clear as day, like an angry phantom materializing after six dire years.

I wish Trent *were* family. It would've been easier.

I never would've fallen so deep, so hard, so soon.

He never would've trampled my heart in the muck of his lies. All the crap I swallowed. Experienced. Believed.

It wasn't long after the morning that still hurts like hell, when he destroyed my shiny new convertible outside Olympia. But hijacking my car and leaving it a shattered wreck wasn't even the worst part.

Not even when the casualty was us.

It was what they found inside.

VIII: FALSE PROMISES (TRENT)

It's the longest damn day of my life.

Correction: second longest.

Second and worst after the dark day that brought me back here in the first place, obsessed with driving a stake through the heart of the vampire asshole who ruined me.

Jace should dominate my thoughts. If only.

Truth is, I haven't stopped thinking about Amy Kay since the minute the fire crew rushed me out of the stairwell. How could I? There was plenty of time to dwell on everything after I crossed the street, parked myself at a coffee shop, and waited several hours to see if the prick I came to see would show up.

Jace never showed. His sister, on the other hand...

Fuck.

I can't evict her from my mind. Every time I look at the streets, I'm back in that elevator. Locked in a war with my own memory, and it's one I always lose.

There's no way I'll ever win her back.

That's not what I came to do. Everything that happened while we were stranded changes nothing. I want revenge. Same thing I've been after for years.

Too bad a dark, beat up part of me calls 'bullshit.'

A part of me that *knows* if I had another way to make this right, I'd have my mouth on hers again in a single heartbeat. I can't shake her taste, even now.

The kiss we shared before the old venom set in and pulled us away is probably the worst part.

Probably, I say, because her eyes were up there, too.

I'll never forget gazing into them. Bright, green, beautiful.

Never forget how she looked back. Shocked, guarded, hurt.

Did I do that? Bring so much pain?

Is this what Jace fucking made me do?

I don't know. I don't care. If I do what I came here for, it'll be a mute point. One more pile of burning debris gone. Incinerated in the ashes of that asshole's life.

I'm in my hotel room, catching up on business, waiting for a few choice texts to hit my phone. The next phase of vengeance is due anytime.

Just when I start wondering what the fuck is taking so long, I get a call. And not from a name I'm expecting.

"Pops. What's happening? Checking in?" My fingers clench. I hope to holy hell that's the only reason dad's calling.

"You're in Seattle. I'd be insane not to. Son, I'm only asking once: are you really there for business?"

Shit. The old man knows me too well, like any good father should.

He knows when the truth is something else. Always

had a scary ability to read my mind nobody else ever matched except Ma. "Seriously? What do you think it is? Me coming out here to settle an old score and throw away a billion-dollar company? You're too worried. Wish you'd use some of that energy for planning your next fishing trip to Alaska."

"I know you, Trent. It's been six years. I've got a sneaking suspicion you're not up in Seattle again for the – what did you call it?" He snorts lightly into the phone.

"Emerging energies conference. And it's actually about to start up again." I grab the TV remote, flip to the new station were some jackoff politician is giving a speech, and crank up the volume, trying to make it sound like I'm not far from the presenter. "You hear that? Got to go."

There's a long pause. Don't have a clue of who'll buy it until he finally talks to me again. "I'm warning you, son. For the love of your Ma, for me, tell me you haven't gone up there to get yourself in trouble. It'd break her heart to know everything we did couldn't keep you away. We gave up everything, son."

I know.

That blinding, brutal fact hits me in the gut every day.

So does the fact that she's gone. The exile killed her. Being away from this city she loved, her dogs, the fresh air of the Cascades.

And all because of me.

All because of *Jace.*

I don't say anything. We both know his atrocities broke mom's heart years ago.

A broken heart technically isn't why her health gave out, and she went to an early grave, but I know.

We both do.

She never settled in Portland. Shit, the cost of living wouldn't even let her buy fast food off their pensions and a little Social Security.

"That's not what I'm here for, Pops. Hope you know it. It's business. Serious cutting edge business. Didn't come up here to play vigilante." I hope like hell I sound convincing.

"Last warning, son. If I didn't care so damn much, I'd leave you to make your own mistakes. You're a grown man. But if anything happens again, those blue blooded bastards won't let you off a second time so easy. Sure, you can probably buy yourself a lawyer as good as theirs now, but that won't matter if they decide to dredge up old dirt." He takes a deep breath, probably saying a quiet prayer that some of this will get through to me. "You promised me you'd let it go, Trent. Keep your word. No visits to old friends. No detours. Especially no Chenocott girl. Tell me when you're home in one piece."

"Pops, pops, calm the hell down. I'll be back in a couple days and you'll be the first to –" I'm talking to dead air. He's said his piece and ended the call like he always does in his wise-ass way.

I throw the phone down, feeling like shit for the second time in twenty-four hours.

My lies are catching up with me. The trickle becoming an acid drip.

I said just enough to Presh, leaving her pissed and confused. Didn't have a better option.

I hope it'll make her back off and let me do what I need to with Jace. As for my old man, it's just a fucking tragedy.

Having to BS the man who gave me everything. Who sacrificed so much to keep me away from here, away from this suicide run that might torch everything I've built since leaving Seattle the first time.

But I can't walk away. Can't give up on payback. Not now.

Can't forget Ma, God rest her soul. Lost too young because I loved the wrong woman.

Because I made friends with the wrong backstabbing fuck.

Nothing changes my resolve. Not even her big green eyes, stuck in my head on loop.

The suffering in her sweet face is just another reason Jace Chenocott deserves hell.

My phone pings again. This time, it's one of the texts I've been waiting for – the first of many arrows meant to bleed the snake dry.

Smiling, I rub the drowsiness from my eyes. I probably haven't nodded off for more than a few hours since the incident on the elevator.

Now, I wouldn't dream of it. The wheels are turning.

I force myself up, shake off my exhaustion, and grab my briefcase.

However this thing ends, it starts with paying my old pal a visit.

* * *

THERE IT IS. I've only seen my tormenter's house in pictures before.

It's one of the new gated communities that's sprung up

on the city outskirts. A grand old house he's probably leveraged himself to the hilt to buy, dwarfing the luxury condo I keep back home even though I'm certain my fortune could crush his.

Irony churns in my guts. The place screams Jace.

It's ugly, all manufactured finishes and sterile looking windows big enough to drive a car through. A rich person's idea of what they think they've earned. Better for impressing company like a fancy museum piece, rather than a real home to live in.

Pathetic. Still doesn't do anything to lessen the hellfire in my fists now that they're almost in striking range.

Six years ago, the asshole threatened to knock my teeth out. We came close to blows that day so many times. I wish to hell we had. Wish I'd knocked him out cold. Wish I'd pounded some permanent sense through his skull.

Maybe it would've stopped the insanity that came later.

Whatever happens here, I can't get physical. Assaulting this prick is the surest way to buy myself a cell behind bars, plus a whole lot of grief for Pops.

"Wait here," I tell the driver, popping the door and stepping out.

I'm sure he wonders what I'm doing, sneaking around the back of the house, carefully avoiding the motion lights. Good thing I'm paying him plenty not to ask questions. My briefcase suddenly weighs a ton, swaying against my leg while I try to find a good entry point.

People in neighborhoods like this are sloppier than most would think with locking their doors. The private security guards and gates keep common vandals away. For most situations, that's enough.

Street thugs can't buy my appearance – the right one.

No one gave us a second thought when I told the man at the guard shack we were here for a dinner party. He was bored out of his mind and knows you don't delay a man who shows up in a polished Lincoln with the chauffeur, asking for ID.

There's a side door leading into the seven car garage. I try the handle, and it gives way automatically.

I'm in, slipping to the front door, which is also unlocked just like I hoped.

I'm expecting icy silence, I need to be very careful with what I say and do if I don't want to give myself away too soon.

That might be easier than I'd hoped, judging by the screams assaulting my ears the second I press the door shut behind me.

"Baby, baby, baby, sit down! For the last fucking time, this *isn't* what it looks like." Even after years away, I know he's lying. Incredible he hasn't gotten better at it.

"I'm not stupid, Jace. I saw the texts, the photos. You, with her. And the other one. Hell, how many were there? I couldn't force myself to flip through the rest of the file. Too many photos – all sick! So many women, you lying prick." I can't tell whether Lindsey sounds defeated or if she's gearing up to explode.

A nasty guilt roils my blood. This is the part I hate, dragging her into this, but doesn't a woman deserve to know what her shit of a husband gets up to when he's 'working late?'

There's another roar from Jace, louder and incoherent.

Several fists smashing against a door, eager to knock it down. A quick look at the woodwork tells me it's expensive and Brazilian. A little more resilient than the flimsy doors in most homes.

Good. He'll risk a fracture if he really wants to get to her.

Fuck.

I expected fireworks, but I don't want this getting dangerous. The cops are a phone call away, if this domestic dispute turns into death threats, but I'm hoping it won't.

The fists ramming the door half a house away are already running out of steam. Even if he's pissed, he can't keep this up forever.

"Come the fuck out so we can talk about this! Please, Linds. I love you. You've got to believe –"

"Love? Don't you *dare* lie to me again. I'm not opening this door. Go tell Amy Kay where to stick the load of crap you said she fed you. If only *you* hadn't made it up! Trent Usher, back in town, back to hurt you. Jesus. What kind of idiot do you think I am?"

Fists ball at my sides. I can't help joining in the fury, hearing Presh sold me out. *Goddamn, what did she tell him?*

"He hates me like nobody else, Linds. He's loaded. They can do anything with computers today, fabricate all kinds of fucking baloney. Those pictures aren't real. I swear. I'm telling you, I never did a thing. Nothing you didn't already know about." His panicked denial puts a tiny dent in my rage.

I have to settle down. See how this plays out. There's a scraping sound in the corner. My heart beats a thousand miles per hour. Is there a dog I don't know about?

No. It's just a robo-vacuum, skimming across the floor to clean. I shake my fist at the Roomba, cursing underneath my breath.

Don't be so fucking jumpy. This is what you wanted, I tell myself, nodding.

"Linds? Jesus Christ, open this door!" His fists bash the door again when she doesn't answer. "What are you gonna do about this then? Walk away? Divorce? Suck me dry so you can keep yourself in heels and imported wine? Shit. You'll probably drive me right back to the bottle, when I was doing so well –"

"You were hiding that, too, asshole. Don't even try to deny it. And don't you ever blame your demons on me." I'm waiting for another explosion from Jace, but he says nothing. "I found your bottles out back, buried by the fire pit, just a couple weeks ago. You've been drunk or high ever since you started screwing up the firm."

"I was working. Bitch."

"You were in over your head. We both know it. You should've just sold the place, lived off the trust fund you keep burning through like crazy, and let me go a long, long time ago." Sensible advice.

Not something I expected to find in this house.

The breath she drags in is so ragged I can almost hear it. "Amy tried to warn me. Years ago. Jesus, if I'd just taken off with Trent on Bainbridge that day, none of this would've happened. Whatever he did, it can't be worse than you."

Icicles hit my blood. She's pushing buttons that will get somebody killed, dredging up the past, taunting the unpredictable Satan who's probably gearing up to kick down the door.

Ignoring my own gut-wrenching worry, I dig for my phone, ready in an instant to skip out the door and call the damn cops. Or fuck, rush up there myself as a last resort, and knock him out before he can do any damage.

But there's a sound I don't expect. Like something heavy and wet hitting the floor, followed by the most horrific sobs I've ever heard.

The kind of shit I've only heard in nightmares. Whenever I think how Amy Kay and her parents reacted after they found her car and the filth inside.

"Just get it the fuck over with, then. Just fucking leave. Do it." I don't realize Jace is the one bawling his eyes out until I hear him straining to speak through his shredded grief. "Walk out and ruin me like I know you always wanted! You'll get your piece of my ass, gold digger, and I hope you *choke!*"

"Jace...Jace?" Lindsey has to call him several times, her voice like stone. "If you've got any sense, sell your stake in the firm. Alimony won't be kind. I'm taking the house, the car, the boat, and then whatever else I can get my hands on. Only fair. I can't believe I wasted so many years on you."

Brutal. And well deserved.

My breath stops. Feels like an eternity of icy silence passes. I push forward, peering around the corner. It's clear. I walk to the edge of the other massive sitting room, stand on the stonework of the massive fireplace, just to get a better look.

I see a crumpled form at the end of the hall upstairs, next to a shuttered door. Several gouges are in the wood, probably left by his watch when he tried to beat it down.

LAST TIME WE KISSED

He's slumped over, twitching like somebody kicked him in the ribs, face in his hands.

Is this what poor Maxwell felt when he thought I'd kicked him in the balls, after his concession?

Is it how Amy Kay cried the night she knew I wasn't coming back?

I don't fucking know, but it's a dagger through my ribs. I'm still afraid for Lindsey, however destroyed Jace looks.

That's why I hang around for five, maybe ten more minutes, waiting to get the hell away from his misery.

Brutal fucking misery I inflicted. Awful as it is, there's no regret. Some confusion, some uncertainty, maybe, which causes me to react too slow.

Jace springs up off the floor and beats his feet down the winding stairs like a soldier who's been licked. He takes each step two at a time, too fast for me to go anywhere.

Shit.

I hold my breath, waiting to be charged by a very mad bull. We're roughly the same size, broad shouldered, and whatever he's been up to since we turned into enemies, he hasn't stopped lifting. There's a rare unease, imagining how I'll take this asshole down.

But there's no rage, no scream, no ambush.

He tears down the hall as soon as he's on this floor, not even stopping to give the fireplace a second glance. I hear a vehicle start and then one of the huge garage doors open. Tires screech down the long driveway and a powerful engine growls, rocketing the car down the road.

This is what I came here to do. Annihilation is in progress, with many more tricks to come, but I'm slow to leave the house, bounding out the front door to my waiting ride.

There's one more vicious thing I can't get out of my head.

The whole reason I'm dragging myself out feeling strangely hollow, despite the crushing victory. It has everything to do with the other presence here tonight, which wouldn't leave my thoughts while Jace was dragged kicking and screaming to justice.

Amy Kay. Precious.

The reason there isn't a wicked grin contorting my face. No matter how much I hurt him, it won't get her out of my head.

I return to my room and sleep like the dead. Tossing and turning becomes second nature in long, dark dreams.

I wake up to a voicemail on the landline tied to the room. A man from the front desk, telling me something about a message. I sit up, panic surging through my veins, wondering if something went wrong with the next round of fun waiting for my enemy. But I never gave the guys putting it in motion this number.

I tell them to bring it up, waiting. It's a huge let down when I see the faded envelope, my name scrawled on the front in a small, wavy blue script. *Or is it?*

Tearing it open, the first line hits me square in the gut.

I hope you go to hell, Trent Usher.

Buy yourself a nice long ticket and enjoy your stay...

My eyes devour every word.

I'm grinning like a man with a hard-on for punishment by the end because I can just imagine her saying every word, and only half-meaning it.

How could I have forgotten? It's obvious why leaving

Jace a shaken mess left me so hollow. Why giving him hell won't save me from my own.

Vengeance can't be satisfying alone. Not with the loose ends we left hanging in a wrecked elevator.

Just like Pops said, what could one more detour hurt?

IX: HOMECOMING (AMY KAY)

The autumn rain pounds the window next to the little nook where I'm reading my book. Seattle's infamously rainy season has started with a bang, and an unusually violent one. Several heavy storms cause such a commotion at the airport I don't bother listing myself on any flights.

I'm a nervous flier. Always have been. Also despise being stuck in one place, helpless and waiting.

Kind of like where I am right now.

I've spent two days in my room walled off from the world.

The hotel will never feel like home. I never thought I'd be here and feel so homesick for Spokane. It's an older city without Seattle's sleekness and ocean side charm, but it's where I've staked my life after Trent, after Jace, after my parents' retirement.

Speaking of which – a text loudly announces itself on my phone. Annoyed, I fold a page in the Cormac

McCarthy book to hold my place, tapping the button next to my screen.

I'm relieved it's not an unfamiliar number. I've blocked Jace, ever since he kept hounding me. Can't put it past him to use another line to keep pestering me, but he's been weirdly silent for the past thirty or so hours.

There's another name: DAD. Asking when I'm coming for dinner.

I swallow. Then sigh. There's no escape, is there?

As much as I'd love to exit this huge mistake of a trip without the awkward pleasantries or seeing the monolith of bad memories where I grew up, I know I'm screwed. A good daughter doesn't pop into town without seeing her parents once.

Firing off a quick message, I let him know I'll be here at least a couple more days.

God. *At least.*

We'll set something up soon, I promise. Don't worry about anything fancy, I say. Life at the Chenocott homestead is the irrational exuberance I've tried like hell to get away from, almost by default.

Nothing fancy still means catering, or else something cooked to perfection by our maid, right out of a Blue Apron kit. Or whatever the multi-millionaire equivalent of gourmet-by-mail order food is. Right now, I could really go for another burger, fries, and shake from the room service menu. But if I don't get some greens today, I'm afraid I'll start mooing.

I'm flipping through an app on my phone for food delivery, searching for delis with salads, when the landline in the room goes off. I walk over, press the receiver to my ear, and hear a tin voice from the front desk.

"Visitor for you, Ms. Chenocott. Would you like me to send him up?"

"Him?" My stomach knots.

It's got to be Jace. My brother has *some* nerve, thinking he's entitled to bully me in person over the stupid decorating job after I've cut communications. "No. Please, just...let him know I'll be right down."

I hang up, grabbing my coat. I'm already hangry.

I'm sure I'll be ravenous by the time I've made it clear where he's welcome. It takes me a while to get down the stairs from several floors up, but it's too soon for elevators.

I'm slightly winded once I hit the main floor, annoyed how out of shape I've gotten. The inn business takes up too much time, and I haven't wanted much to do with long walks since leaving the coast behind. They remind me too much of dad, which sends my mind to very dark places.

Like the one I'm staring at up ahead. *It can't be!*

But it is. After what happened before, it's time to stop doubting and just believe my own eyes. They wouldn't hallucinate the smirking hell that's in front of me.

I almost whip my heels around and head for the elevator. I think I'd rather face the trauma than deal with Trent. But he's too fast, on me before my reflexes kick in.

"Aw, Presh, are you really so surprised?"

I sigh. No, of course not.

Leaving this city and the mess my brother wants to throw me into without encountering my ex would be too easy. "How'd you find me, anyway?"

"Cashing in a few of the many favors I'm owed." He speaks without a shred of hesitation. "Should've given the front desk an alias after you checked in if you wanted to be left alone."

"Oh, that's totally not suspicious. No thanks. I'm not interested in being looked at like a criminal." Not like you, I want to say, but I hold my tongue. *Barely.*

"Ah, yes. None of that 'dirty, evil stuff,' I'd gotten into, right? It'll have to...how did you put it? Just 'play itself out?'" He's using my own words against me.

It's hard not to cringe, hearing lines from the hate note quoted.

If I have to face this hell, it's worth remembering I invited it.

"You read it," I say numbly.

No question. I'm standing red-cheeked beneath his hawkish blue eyes, stating the obvious. Owning up to what I wrote, or trying to.

"Devoured every word, Precious. Deserved it, too."

He – *what?* Deserved it? That's not what I expect.

Nor the shifty glint in his eye, holding the envelope up, eclipsing his strong jawline.

I take a step backward, unsure what new game he's playing. "After what you did to us, I only wish I was harsher."

"Me, too. You've got yourself a lovely way with words, woman. Weren't you trying to be a writer before things went to shit?"

My stomach cramps, another broken dream clubbing my hunger to death. "What's it to you? We both know how things played out. Reality's what counts." Merciless reality, like being trapped together the other day. "There's no time for dreams when you're living disaster."

"Do I look dead to you, Presh?" He cocks his head like

it's a serious question. I shake my head, hating this more by the second. "That's what I thought. Because if I recall right, we both walked off that damn elevator breathing, no thanks to me. Not my definition of disaster, darling."

My breath lodges in my lungs. "So, that's what this is. You wanted to torment me a little while longer with your guilt trip. Go ahead. I'll give you five minutes." I spread my arms.

"You asked me if I believed in coincidences. Fate, remember?" Like I could ever forget.

He comes closer, backing me into the marble wall by the potted fern. "Nothing's changed. But our little reunion the other day got me thinking...and then this letter made me think some more. We've got history, you and me. A long, dark shadow that just won't fade, no matter how hard we try dragging ourselves to the light. It's the reason we both came home. Same reason why we hit each other head-on. It's why we're standing in this lobby, me holding in the roughest hate fuck I'm ever likely to get with my clothes still on, and you with that wide-eyed stare, begging me to wipe it off your pretty face."

Don't you dare! My hand twitches.

He's not doing this again.

If he tries kissing me this time, there'll be consequences. I won't be caught off guard a second time, especially when he's eyeing me like this, like –

"It's too late for love." Damn. Like magic, he says the very thing I'm fighting with my all to ignore. "I'm not stupid, Amy Kay. That's not why I'm here. A little truth, though, that shit never hurt anybody. While we were busy arguing over consequences, fate, life, I forgot the one thing we've both got in reach."

Shaking my head, I look away, ignoring his withering gaze. Without much success. "If you came here to talk, forget it. I said everything I'll ever need to in that letter, Trent."

"You told me to 'move on.' That's all I've ever tried to do and it's the reason I'm back here, making your brother's life miserable. But what about you? Wasn't time for many pleasantries on the elevator. I've done my homework since – looks like your whole life's the travel biz. No husband. No kids. No *alma mater*. You quit Stanford due to Jace, and that's far more fucked up than anything."

"I quit because of *you*." Catching my voice going up an octave, I look around, a reminder we're in public. Even if this is a secluded spot. Good thing, too, or I might just slap him without any provocative kiss. "You, Trent. And the asshole moves you made, which I've spent the better part of a decade trying to forget."

"Regardless, that hasn't gone very well, has it?" He touches the rumpled envelope's edge to my cheek, curls it to my chin, and applies a soft pressure. "Look the fuck up, Presh."

Jesus.

I didn't have a nasty thought in my brain, but he's making me feel like I just got caught looking at him the way I did as a kid. "Get to the point," I warn.

"Reason I'm here, basking in your eyes, not caring if they're full of murder, is because you deserve the truth. And so do I, Amy Kay. I'm here to tell you what really happened that night." There's a soft, honest waver in his tone, like he's about to dredge up something brutal.

Too honest. I can't fall for this again, whatever it is.

"Not interested," I say, tearing myself away from him,

staggering back a few feet. "I'm not in the mood for more lies, Trent. No more games. Just turn around and go."

He stiffens, straight and broad shouldered and painfully gorgeous. "You *still* think I'm lying? Ridiculous. I'm giving you exactly what you've waited for. What you wanted me to say when we were stuck together, not knowing if we'd live or die or –"

"I didn't ask for anything – none of this! You're sure you read the letter?" I swallow, hating how bad the rock forming in my throat hurts. "Because if you did, you missed the important part: *don't come calling.*"

His mouth opens, ready to twist me up all over again, but I don't give him the chance.

I'm on the offensive, in his face, trying not to shout, banging my hand against my thigh to keep from lashing his *very* deserving cheek. "We're *not* doing this. You want to talk truth? Fine. Time to listen: I'm done with the past. Done getting between battles. Done telling Jace you're here, trying to screw him over. That's all I told him, and all I really care about. Because as soon as this rain stops splattering itself all over this city, I'm on the first flight for Spokane. Going home. Leaving this behind. Everything, Trent, once and for all. Especially *you.*"

He reaches for my wrists. Smart move because both palms are so, so ready to strike fire on his smug, hatefully sexy face. "You can't fight your way out of this with words. Be honest: we've had enough of those, Presh, and I've only got room for a few more. I want to sit down and tell you everything so we can finally walk the hell away. Exactly what you want. Or is it?"

Bad enough his vile eyes strip me naked. Worse because they cut through the bullshit, straight to my soul.

Of course I want to know his version.

I want the full story.

I want to sit here like a teary-eyed fool with my mouth trembling, heart racing so violently I'm almost passing out. So fucking ready to hear the sorry excuse that should've come out six years ago.

"I want peace. I want a life again. And to find either one of those, I really need you gone." His grip relaxes, letting me yank my hands away.

"That's fucking anticlimactic. I'm not leaving till you listen. Don't you get it? I came to clear the air, Precious, not poison it more. If you'll just calm down and –"

"Just leave? Right. You haven't left me a better option."

The next few minutes are the first time in years I've felt this alive.

I slip away before he can strike back, rush up the stairs. He's left speechless, for once, and he's still standing there when I march past him ten minutes later, luggage rolling behind me. I head for the front desk to check out.

I feel his eyes on my back. Wanting to approach, wanting to chase, but the steely-eyed guards in the front of this place would give anybody pause. A place this expensive has a direct line to the Seattle Police Department.

I'm a little disappointed he doesn't try once my business is done and I'm outside, an Uber summoned on my phone. It would be *so* satisfying watching Trent Usher hauled away in handcuffs.

Too bad. I'll just have to settle for the stormy look he gives me through the hotel's window, it's spotless perfection tainted by his fingerprints as he raises his arms, like he's trying to keep me there, prisoner for his mind games.

It doesn't hit me until I'm halfway through the ride where I've seen that look before: only in my dreams.

They're not the playful, all powerful eyes of the bastard who broke my heart.

They're haunted. Tortured, even.

They're exactly how I want to imagine he looked that night he left Washington, and knew he'd never be coming back.

They're guilt gone nuclear, but they can't change my mind. I'll suffer endlessly if it finally ends this.

If it just rips me away from Trent long enough to finally heal.

* * *

THIS ROOM. This house. This *look*.

I wish I'd just checked into another place downtown. Coming home tells me I traded one pit of emotional quicksand for another.

I expect mom and dad, but Jace is a surprise. An unpleasant one.

No sooner than I'm through the door, he's in my face. Shouting about the screw up with the firm, how none of this would've happened if I'd just shown up three weeks ago like a good little sister.

Good little servant is what he really means.

"What the hell did you tell him, sis? Where I lived? Where I spent my off hours? Where Lindsey and I had trouble? Shit, did you hand him the keys to the company's fucking tax returns and charge accounts?" Jace backs me against the glass door overlooking the old boathouse, belting out question after question.

Then I remember.

I'm way too old for his crap. I slap him against the chest, so hard I hope it reverberates in his ribs. "Get off me! I didn't *do* anything. Trent found this stuff out on his own. I'm sure it wasn't hard. And what do you mean trouble with Linds?"

He winces, like my blow did more damage than it did. "Asshole knew how to hit me where it hurts, and how. He had to learn that somewhere. Fuck."

He staggers backwards, rubbing his face. At last, he stops, stands his ground, and looks at me. "I'm sorry. Maybe I was too quick to point fingers."

"Far too quick, asshole." I sigh. "I'm on your side, Jace, as big a dick as you've been."

Something sour hangs in the air around him. I smell an acrid stink on his breath and wrinkle my nose. Whiskey. He's been drinking again.

Drinking a lot.

No wonder he's so off balance, slurring his words.

"Then how?" He stumbles backwards after I whack him again. I don't like the nasty look shining in his eyes.

"How? He already knew everything, Jace. He's been planning this for a long time. Probably watching you – watching us – for weeks, months, years. I don't know. It just so happens we ran into each other while he was on his way to spring the trap. I spent God knows how many hours with that man, stuck in the elevator, and I hated every second. I didn't feed him anything."

That isn't really true. I didn't hate how his lips crashed into mine, but my brother is the last man on Earth I'd ever spill the complexities of Trent Usher to. Also no point in telling him our latest encounter is what drove me here.

"You had a chance to stop him and you didn't?" He tilts his head. Light catches his eyes, revealing the dark circles around them.

A thin sympathy runs through me, but I know it'll be short-lived as soon as he opens his mouth. "Christ, sis. Why didn't you call the cops? If you'd done the right thing, I wouldn't be staring into a black hole. He'd be in jail. Maybe my life wouldn't be shot to fuck."

He rips himself away from me, staggers to the breakfast bar. I don't notice the bottle until he sits down, overflowing his glass with amber whiskey.

"This isn't the end," I tell him, laying a hand gently on his shoulder. "Look, I don't know the details. Don't know what he's done to you or why. But he really believes what happened years ago is your fault."

"Fuck Usher. Fuck him straight to hell! It's been a long time. Nothing's changed. Dad should've sent detectives down to Oregon years ago to nail his prick to the wall." He knocks back another shot, muffling a belch in his elbow. Then he slumps. "Forget it, Amy Kay. None of this matters now. It's already lost. Way past fucked."

"Wrong. It matters if he's coming after family." I gingerly reach for the bottle, wrap my fingers around the long neck, and slide it away. "And you need to lay off this stuff. It's no good, especially now."

Jace glares, his green eyes soft, pale, drained. I whisper in his ear. "We have to fight. All of us. I'm not letting Trent waltz in and smash everything dad worked for. What you should've had a chance at making yours."

"The firm survives one way or another...just without me, sis. I'm boned. The shit legal coughed up this morning makes that very clear." A rough chuckle leaves his dry lips and turns into a hiccup.

I frown, walking the half-drained pint to the opposite side of the kitchen. When I look back, Jace is hunched over, chin on his palms, staring into his glass.

Freaking out is his standard M.O. He's self-destructive.

I'm used to it by now, the angry, flustered crap he gave me the second I walked in. But this dejected thing...it's new. Defeat doesn't really suit him.

What *did* Trent do to him this week? *What the hell happened to my brother?*

"Talk to me," I say, retrieving a couple mineral water bottles from the fridge and sliding one across the counter. "He hasn't been in town more than a couple days. He can't be twisting your balls that bad."

"Sis, he's fucking ruined me." Jace looks up, cheeks red, defiantly ignoring the water in front of him. "You got any idea where he's gone?"

I open my mouth to answer, recalling the hate letter I sent to his room number scrawled on the slip that's still in my purse, and then our encounter, but I think better of mentioning it. However we fix this, it has to be legal. Clean. No guns or knives or fists.

"No. I'm not sure what good finding him will do. You need a lawyer, Jace. A good one."

"You mean like the dozen or so I was all set to manage before Mr. Vigilante pissed away my chance? Yeah, sis, they helped *a ton*. Trent came here to take justice into his own hands, or whatever the fuck. Only one thing he'll understand."

"Jace," I say quietly, not liking how his arms tremble a

couple times on the counter. Just like frustrated rattlesnakes. "Don't do anything illegal. Whatever's happening, we've got mom and dad to –"

"Oh, fuck you, Amy Kay! I wouldn't dream of dragging them into this, upsetting their peace and quiet. I'm a grown man, sis. You think I want daddy fighting my battles for me? Taking my hits? If I hadn't let him take over years ago, fuck, then Usher would've spent time in a cell like he deserved, instead of running back here to start fires years later."

There's a violent edge in his voice. A chill runs up my spine. "Protecting yourself isn't what worries me." I wait to catch his furious eyes. "We were lucky Trent leaving town and ruining dad's campaign was the worst thing that happened last time. You get yourself into trouble again, next time, nobody might be able to bail you out."

His left eye twitches. I'm expecting him to fly up and get in my face again, but he just stays glued to his chair. Like he's too tired for more than stewing quietly in his drunken fury.

I really hope he'll drink that water. I leave the kitchen with a sigh. His nasty eyes burn a hole in my back until I'm out of sight.

* * *

"Peanut! Why didn't you say you were heading over?" Dad pulls me into his arms a second after I knock on his library door.

"Getting a little too old for the nickname, dad. And formal dinners. Don't worry about it, I'm not even hungry." I hug him hard, frowning a bit as my hands brush his shoulders.

He looks a little rougher every year since retirement. New lines on his face, his hair grayer and more mottled, and is that a wispy goatee? Never thought I'd see the day my clean-shaven, buckled down father decided to beard it up.

"I trust that has nothing to do with the sorry display upstairs?" Dad keeps his hands on me as I pull away, a sadness in his familiar green eyes.

Oh, no. Wrangling with Jace still would've left me an appetite, but taking crap from him *and* Trent... "I had a big lunch, that's all." I smile through the white lie. "How long has he been here?"

"Since last night. Stormed in without a warning. I didn't have the heart to tell your mother. God, I knew things were strained, but divorce?"

I rock backward, pressing my toes into the floor. "Wait...divorce?"

Dad nods. "Almost all but certain, I'm afraid. She's a proud woman, his Lindsey. I've warned him too many times to get serious and fix it if he wants to keep his marriage. Seems he tossed my advice and did the opposite."

Dad won't list his sins. They aren't hard to guess.

My jaw tightens when I picture Jace laughing, drinking, partying like a kid with girls easily impressed by his make-believe money. I'm no friend of Lindsey's anymore, but she doesn't deserve a cheater.

"Of course, I told him he could stay as long as he wanted," dad says. "Sometimes, I think if I hadn't turned him out that summer, before everything went wrong, maybe none of this would be happening."

"Dad, no. You had to protect your image." I close my eyes, suddenly back in my eighteen year old self, remembering how phony and forced his political career seemed. But he'd had good intentions. "We can't keep second guessing the past. That's what's got Jace so riled up. That and –"

"I know. Mr. Usher." Dad holds up a hand. He rounds to the leather chair behind his huge ash colored wooden desk, gesturing me to take the empty chair across from it. "I always knew he'd turn up again, much as I'd hoped he wouldn't."

His voice isn't just sad. It's downright hurt, like he's talking about an estranged son.

My stomach flips sourly. "You couldn't have known. We couldn't. We hoped he'd just go, stay away, let bygones be bygones. But he's back to make us suffer. I just don't get it. He's doing so well dad, he's got that energy company...why here? Why now?"

"I've read all about it, Amy Kay." His sharp look tells me there's no need to go on. Of course he knows. Probably before this latest blowup, when none of us could resist wondering what became of the boy we loved who betrayed us. "Truly amazing he'd sacrifice so much to hurt us all over again. If I'd taken losing that election like a man, got my head together, gone after him –"

"Dad, no." I watch his hands on the desk tighten into fists. "It's too late. Don't beat yourself up. We'll figure this out. Is there anything else to worry over besides the divorce?"

"Oh, yeah. Jace and the firm, the embezzlement...goddamn. If I'd only known, I *never* would've trusted him. I never, ever would've turned over my company, the one your great grandfather started, to a child who wants a money tree with none of the responsibilities." Dad shakes his head, his eyes pinched shut. "I'll have to talk to Meade come Monday. See if there's any way we can get Jace's trust fund loan disentangled from the corporate accounts."

"Wait, wait, embezzlement? Don't tell me..." I trail off. It's hard, resisting the urge to race upstairs and thrash my drunken, reckless brother. "Jesus. Was he even managing things for a solid month?"

"Long enough," dad growls. "That fool thought the accounts were his to raid the second he'd put his skin in the game. I never should've let him buy my stake, even ceremonially. The rest of the board thinks Usher did us a favor, shining the light on his untoward withdrawals so quickly."

He pauses, sighs, digesting the terrible news. "God. If we hadn't caught him for months, he might have cashed out *millions* before accounting caught up to it."

I hang my head, unsure whether rage or disappointment will get the best of me. "Make him give it back. Every damn penny," I snap.

Dad lifts another hand. "Of course, he says he will. Whatever he's able to prove was wrapped up with the company. I'm just hoping our lovely daughter-in-law will wait before her lawyers pounce. This could get *very* messy. Already is, honestly. As it stands, we'll never have a Chenocott in charge of the company again."

Guilt spasms through my heart. If life tread a different path, it could've been me in Jace's place.

But I would've gone to law school. Would've taken it seriously. Would've let myself be groomed for the career I know dad secretly hoped I'd always want.

Regrets do nothing. I might as well wish Trent hadn't made us ground zero for his dirty, destructive secrets.

"How much does mom know?" There's no point ignoring the other elephant in the room.

Dad blinks, leans in his chair, stroking his short beard. "Very little. That's how I'd like to keep it, just between you and me, peanut. She doesn't need the grief. I'm more worried about the divorce than the business with the firm, honestly. It'll be a terrible shock. When she finds out her only chance at grandkids is gone –"

He stops. We lock eyes.

Shame heats my blood.

So does a steady anger.

It's no secret he gave up on me having a normal family life since leaving Washington. Still, it stings to have it brought out openly.

"Forgive me," he says, averting his eyes to the huge bookcases on the wall. "Your mother's as lovely as ever these days, but her state of mind can be...difficult. Always focused on the future. Oh, how can I blame her? Our best years are behind us. We desperately hoped for something more. Jace's woes are just one more blow."

"Jeez, it's not a funeral, dad. I get it. There's a lot to worry about, but Trent isn't controlling our lives. Whatever he does to Jace, it only ruins us if we let it."

"I hope you're right," he says in a hushed way. "Now, enough ugliness. That's not the homecoming my daughter deserves."

Dad pulls his flannel shirt tight, as if putting himself

back together. "Make yourself at home. Haven't touched your old room upstairs except for the routine cleanings. Dinner is...anything you'd like."

"Dad, forget it. I'll feed myself. It's getting late, anyway. We'll talk through this more tomorrow, okay?"

Smiling, he nods once. "I'm glad you're home, Amy Kay, however briefly. Lord knows we need you."

I hate feeling like the golden child again as I step out of his huge makeshift office and close the door. It's a burden I never wanted. Jace never gave us another choice. His screw ups are the reason running off to Spokane and doing my own thing hurt my parents even more.

They'd tried to get over it, too. Tried to make a life here with their son, who led them to believe he was finally getting his crap together. He was the one who got married, after all.

Pretended he'd twisted himself in knots trying to be better. Cleaned up his act. Convinced dad he was worthy of a seat at the firm and it's big financial rewards.

Now, we know everything was a lie.

We know no thanks to Trent freaking Usher.

My lips purse together in a tight, painful line every time I think about what only happened hours ago in the hotel downtown. I still don't understand how my back-stabbing ex put our entire family on the run.

But I do know one thing: next time he shows up – and he will – I'm not turning tail.

If Trent Usher comes after me again, if he's so hellbent on smashing Jace he hurts us, there'll be no backing down. I'll fight.

Whatever it takes to put him in prison. Exactly what he deserved the first time.

* * *

I FLOP over in my PJs, staring at the clock. It's after midnight and I'm wide awake, using my inner cheek as a surrogate to chew on my own anxiety.

I don't know how I ever slept in this room. There are too many memories in this old double bed, these spartan walls, even in an old teddy bear I left years ago. It peeks out at me through the crack in the closet door, as if to say, *I saw everything. You and him. Happy.*

The best of times were here. So were the worst.

Everything, under this vaulted ceiling, and the old Victorian lamp that makes everything glow like an oil painting.

Memories are incredible things. They make ghosts real. They make us cry. Sometimes they drive us completely insane.

Then I hear the noise, and I *know* there's something very wrong in my head. I'm losing it, aren't I?

It sounds like a short, staccato tapping on my big bay window. Almost identical to the night six years ago when I gave him my virginity.

I wonder if I'm dreaming when I throw my legs to the floor, grab my robe, and step up to the window holding my breath. *You've got to be kidding.*

Oh, but if this is a joke, my own sadistic eyes playing tricks on me, then it looks *exactly* like the man who chased me out of the hotel today.

Trent. Here. In the flesh.

He stands just a few feet away, a long branch in one hand, methodically scratching at the glass. At least he isn't smirking – he looks about as excited as a man waiting for the bus.

Like this is routine, and totally not a monstrous invasion of my privacy.

Swallowing my shock, I unlock the window and throw it open. "What the holy hell are you doing here?"

"Waiting. Not leaving till you listen, darling. Same thing I told you this evening." There's the smirk I want to wipe off his face forever. "Let me up for old time's sake? Bet I can climb this tree faster than I did then."

"I'm not your darling and you're *not* coming up here. You're going home, or I'm calling the cops."

"Then we'll have a lot of explaining for the boys in blue. Like why you've got your asshole brother here. He's lucky there isn't a warrant out yet for his arrest with all the white collar crimes he's had a hand in. Sure is a shame some things never change." He shrugs his broad, damningly sexy shoulders. "Oh, wait. Except, this time, I'm not the dumb kid being framed. And I've got plenty more ways to make him suffer."

A scowl replaces his sharp smirk. Those blue eyes are almost scary. So full of moonlight. So much like the wolf I remember stamped on his chest, feral and dangerous.

For a second, I think what it'll do to mom, having the cops show up here. I stare into his baby blues, beaming hatred, wishing I could magically open a pit to hell in the ground under him.

Trent's taunting eyes go huge a split second after I slam the window shut.

I can't do this. No negotiations.

There's no use in talking to him, I decide. Or in

making demands I know he'd love to throw back in my face.

There's nothing to do but throw myself on the bed, bury my head in a pillow, and try very hard not to scream bloody murder.

X: OUT WITH IT (TRENT)

I'm impressed.

The old Amy Kay would've caved. Would've jumped at a chance to reason our way out of this.

This new woman I'm dealing with is feisty. A fighter. Sick and tired of being flattened by life to the point where she's immune to its utter bullshit.

And right now, that bullshit is me.

She's in a familiar place. Familiar because none of us know where this is going. This uncharted territory is full of sharks.

I see it instantly. She's in there, re-living the same hole I've squatted in for years, building Cryptic into an empire, planning for this day.

It's finally come. I'm using the time and money and will to make my darkest dreams a hellish reality for one deserving fuck: Jace Chenocott.

I planned so carefully. Spent so many long nights probing underworld classifieds for guys willing to dig, get their hands dirty, and not ask questions. I made my hires, I put plans into motion, and I bided my time.

But fuck, I *never* planned for this.

Never factored in an elevator mishap from hell.

Never imagined running into her, face-to-face, igniting a fury in my blood I hoped I'd never feel again.

It's in her, too. The same rush. Same frightening, magnetic, self-destructive pull roping our hearts together. And I'm afraid those ropes are a whole lot stronger than any hate, any fear, or any common sense.

Shit.

The fact that I'm standing here, risking everything just to see her, says how much I've changed since the last time I was here to fuck the love of my life.

That love hates me now. The cold warrior I thought I'd become, replacing the stupid kid, is telling me to walk the hell away while the going is good.

Finish it. Finish Jace. Finish everything and fucking leave before there's collateral damage strewn all over our lives.

I'd be a fool not to listen. But a deeper, darker part of me says I'd be an even bigger fool to let this go.

I step up, closer to the house. Lifting my branch again, I tap-tap-tap at regular intervals. Just like a damn woodpecker, drumming in the night.

I *need* to talk to her.

Just destroying Jace isn't enough.

Not while I know Amy Kay, Maxwell, and Ophelia are standing by, thinking I've lost my mind. Thinking the worst of me – pretty much the norm for years.

Why the fuck do I suddenly care? Why the need to

clear my name when I told myself it'd be enough just to watch Jace fall face-down in flames?

Why isn't hit and run good enough anymore?

One answer: Precious.

The only way I'll ever figure this out, and un-fuck myself, is hidden behind the same thick glass she once threw open for me, surrendering her sweetness. I keep tapping that branch on the glass for what seems like forever.

Don't even stop for rest. If I annoy her enough, she'll have to let me in.

Or she'll finally bring down the hell I probably deserve.

It's already loose in my blood: the rage I feel every time I pinch my jaw, the hard-on I keep wishing wasn't there, the maelstrom in my head that's blown my cold, calculating master plan to Jupiter and back.

I focus my thoughts, the same thing over and over.

Come the hell on, Amy Kay. Open up.

Open up!

Let's talk this stupid shit out.

Open the fuck up. Let's get this out of our systems.

Out of mine.

Open –

I can't feel my arms through the numbing burn. Maybe another reason I'm shocked for the second time tonight when her window pops open. I throw the branch down and wait for the screaming threats.

She never sticks her head out. The window hangs open, the world inside silent and waiting.

I scamper up the tree like a monkey, carefully stepping into her room. Can't stop my jaw from hanging open.

Fuck.

Her room hasn't changed a bit. Same décor. Same little desk in the corner. Same bed where we quietly tangled bodies, working young flesh to ecstasy.

Fuck again.

I remember how her moans poured into me. How they choked down my own guttural pleasure. How hard I came, her clenched to every inch of me, pulling pure fire from my balls.

That was us, an eternity ago, before everything went hurling to hell.

Tonight, there's just me. She's gone.

"Amy?" Her name comes out in a harsh whisper.

A second later, the world goes blinding red. It's like my skull explodes from the inside out, motion and pain blurring together. Then everything spins and my knees give out.

I go down. Hit the floor, too messed up to even swear, or remember what a stupid desperate asshole I am for coming up here.

* * *

"Trent? Trent?! Oh my God." There's an angel whispering my name.

I wonder if I'm dead or dreaming, staring up at her face, soft and pink and panicked. Also, suddenly looking at me like my presence isn't akin to finding dog crap in her slippers.

I think she's shaking me. Lightly. Somehow, it takes longer than it should for my arm to register the weight of her touch.

"What..." I stagger up in a sitting position, and instantly regret it. My temple throbs.

There's something hard and wrong on the side of my head. My senses work again. Reaching up, I touch my fingers against the tender lump rising on my skin and whistle softly. "Goddamn, Amy Kay. What'd you...oh."

My eyes adjust to the darkness. I see her fall back against the bed, those green eyes so bright, fingers cupped around a dense ceramic mug.

"I didn't mean to hurt you, I swear. Just wanted to scare you away, is all. I thought you'd leave after a good whack. Maybe you'd just jump back down the tree and beat it."

"You thought a little bump on the noggin would make me think twice about bleeding the truth?" Pretty fucked up I'm smiling. Even worse I won't consider leaving. Not without releasing the words I've worked so hard to put in her ear.

She shakes her head. I can't tell if she's impressed or disgusted.

Both, maybe.

"You're insane. If there's no concussion, here's what'll happen: I'll help you up, lead you down the stairs, and send you out the front door before anybody else wakes up. Surely, you've got a car parked out there, or a driver or something? I'll call you a taxi if you don't. Or if that won't do, an ambulance."

"You assaulted me, Presh, and now you're giving orders?" A vicious laugh sticks in my throat. "Who the hell are you? Sometimes I wonder if I'm looking at the same beautiful woman with big dreams and bigger sass I had years ago. Or if you're her evil twin."

Her face sours. "Things change. After what you did to Jace, to dad, I ought to just keep you here until the police show up. Maybe you'd drop this crap you're pulling so we don't press charges."

Dad? Frowning, I try to stand up, but it's too soon.

"What's wrong with Maxwell?" I ask. A split second later, my ass crashes back on the floor, winning a sympathetic look I'm not sure I want.

"The usual. He's worried to death. Sick to his stomach, finding out the truth about my stupid fucking brother." She blinks. It lasts a little longer than it should, like she doesn't want to wake up and face the cold reality. "Don't fight me on this, Trent. Please. You've done enough damage. Knowing the why, hearing it from your lips, won't change a thing. It's too late."

"Wrong." Soon as I say the word, strength flows back in my body. I'm able to reach out, grab her hand, fish the mug away from her.

Once it's a safe distance away, I put my other hand on hers, grateful she isn't fighting. "Just hear me out, Precious. That's all I'll ever want. Hell, if I'm still the bad guy to you, then here's what I'll do: turn around, leave for Oregon, and call off my dogs. I'll let that bastard-prick stumble through his divorce a free man. His pride won't be the same, or his future. Still, if you'll just listen, I might think twice about bringing down the house. Throw me a damn bone."

Her eyes go wide, and then narrow. "You're telling me there's more? Like you haven't already done enough?"

It sounds ludicrous. But Jace is the man who won't have his life completely ruined hemorrhaging money, a career, his woman. He can still slink away with a few million to his name, locked up in a trust nobody else can touch, plus a few toys, unless I set them on fire, too.

"I'm a total fool for not dumping it sooner, Amy Kay. Like when we were stuck that long, hellish night." It seems like the elevator malfunction happened a hundred years ago rather than just last week. "I have to get this out. If I do, you'll finally understand. You'll know why I put my life on the line a second time to help mother karma find her target. You'll get why I want to skin him alive."

She slumps against the bed, jerking her hand out of mine. "If I say no again, I know you'll never leave. Fine. Let's get this over with, asshole. Out with it."

* * *

Six Years Ago

I wake up in Heaven.

Seeing my green-eyed sleeping beauty curled next to me, naked as the day she was born, is the best damn sight in the universe.

My dick goes hard, ready for a proper wake up call. Even after we fucked five times, late into the night, it's still not enough.

I haven't begun to own this woman, to make every inch of her mine.

Perfectly, completely, unforgettably *mine.*

There's a small mark from a hickey above her left breast. A vicious pride puts a smile on my face, remembering how hard, how deep, how good we went at it the night before.

So fucking good.

I've barely begun to have her all the ways I will. Still know I'll never get sick of her.

Not after years sharing the same bed.

Not after thousands of times ending in her screaming my name.

Not after walking through hell for one more piece of her.

I hold her close, loving how she sighs, still lost in hazy dreams. Pressing my lips to her ear, I let it come out. All of it and then some.

"You're so fucking beautiful, darling. And I was an idiot to run, even if I had a good reason. I'm never leaving you again. Not after seeing you naked and perfect and peaceful like this. You're the only woman I'll ever love, Presh. You were made for me. Only girl I'll stand to wear my name, my ring, my everything. Watch me wife the hell out of you." My cheeks go red hot as the scalding words slip out.

Am I really doing this? Pouring my heart out? I am. While she's asleep.

Don't know if she hears a single word. Doesn't matter. I've made my confession and someday soon I'll say it to her face. After we're engaged, without another care in the world except how happy we'll be.

Now, it's time. I roll away with one more kiss on her neck. I stagger into the bathroom attached to her room.

My stomach growls while I take a leak. The thirst isn't far behind.

We've got this place to ourselves. What will it hurt to

walk down there, brew some coffee, and then scrounge us up breakfast?

I march into the kitchen and start pawing through cabinets like a starving bear. Maxwell's stash of fancy coffee beans teases my nose through the bag.

No sooner than I'm reaching for the grinder, I see movement outside the huge window overlooking the Chenocott's slice of the Seattle shore.

A figure. He – at least I think it's a he – stoops down by the rocky crop of beach adjacent to the boathouse. There's a shovel in his hand, methodically smoothing a rough patch of dirt, patting it even. His boot kicks several more heavy black rocks over the top, head twisting side to side.

Weird is an understatement.

My stomach rolls. Adrenaline spikes my blood. My pulse quickens.

Something very wrong is happening here.

I briefly wonder if it's a servant, a gardener, some contractor doing late season landscaping before summer melts into autumn. But no one should be creeping around like this, suspicious as hell in that oversized black hoodie.

"Fuck," I whisper, wondering if this is the price for such an incredible night.

I drop the bag of beans on the counter and stomp to the wall, ready to grab the phone and call the police. Then the figure turns, showing me the back of his hoodie, and I see familiar white letters.

It's a local band, some post-grunge Nirvana throwback popular in the clubs downtown and on campus.

Jace.

Pursing my lips, I slam the phone back in its cradle,

and open the door. Seems like it takes forever to cross the massive expanse of their three level deck, tethering the staircase to ground level. Then I'm off, bolting across the acres stretching to the coast.

I catch Jace mid-way while he's walking toward the house. He immediately looks startled, knowing I'm not supposed to be here.

Too bad. I don't intend to start on why, and I definitely don't want to disturb my beautiful, naked Presh upstairs, still dreaming sweetly in the sheets.

"Usher? What the fuck?" There's something else on his face.

Alarm. Suspicion. Worry.

"Took the words right out of my mouth, bro. What're you doing here? Dropping by while Maxwell's preoccupied in the woods?"

I don't like how his eyes shift around.

It's the look of a guilty man, pretending to make eye contact but actually avoiding it. "Yeah. Mom missed a few shirts I really like when she had Amy Kay bring my clothes out to your place a while back."

Total lie. Ophelia's a meticulous woman. And there's nothing truthful in his weak-ass tone. "You lose your shirts out back then? Were they floating down the coast or something?" I nod toward the spot where I saw him digging.

Not sure what he's done with the shovel. It's gone, along with any sign he was out there digging, except for the sand stuck to his rubber boots. It's an oversized pair of fisherman's wear he must've borrowed from the boathouse.

"Well?" I press him through the silence.

Jace's eyes bug out. I've never seen anyone honestly lost for words before.

His head drops, but only for a second. When he looks up, there's an odd excitement in his eyes.

"Shit. Listen, man...what if I told you we don't have to spend the next year holding our dicks, begging angel investors or writing congressman for research grants?"

I cock my head, not saying a word.

"I've found an awesome way to give our company a huge shot in the arm by Christmas. I wasn't sure if you'd like it at first, but since you're out here...come on."

"Jace!" I call after him, but there's no slowing him down.

Fuck. He turns, takes off, urging me to follow.

I expect him to lead us to the stretch of shore where I caught him digging. Instead, he turns into the boathouse, giving me a sly wink as he unlocks the door. "Need to shake these things off, anyway," he says, stomping grey sand off his boots.

We step inside, stopping next to the hulking Wilkie. It's a little older, more worn than when we took it out years ago. Still brings a smile to my face, remembering my first kiss with Amy Kay at the controls. Plus last night's many hotter kisses.

"Give me a sec," Jace says. Shaking his boots off and throwing them against the wall noisily reminds me why we're here, and I don't fucking like it.

There's a large chest in the corner, probably stuffed with life jackets and spare boating gear. He slips back into his shoes and then walks over, undoes the lock, and throws it open. Whatever I expected inside, it's not a briefcase.

My guts knot. He's coming toward me, the mystery briefcase slapping his thigh, a shit-eating grin plastered on his face. "Just so you know, I was waiting for the right time to let the cat out of the bag. And this cat's a fucking tiger, bro. Check it out."

I can't help but stiffen, standing over his shoulder, while he stoops down and undoes the clasp. The thing pops. My eyeballs almost burst from my head.

It's full of cash. More than I've seen in my life. Bright, crisp, forest green money.

Everywhere.

"This is...how much...Jace...what the fuck?" I clutch his shoulder, demanding answers as much as I need support so I don't fall over.

He turns, shooting me a devilish grin. "Four hundred thousand, or pretty damn close. Been scrounging it up since May. All those long nights where I'm sleeping till two or three in the evening? It's not just shaking off pussy and beer. Been working like a fiend."

Working? It can't be a normal summer job.

Millionaire family with deep connections or not, no ordinary trade pays a hundred thousand a month in cash.

"Jace..." I want to nail him with a hundred questions.

I'm still speechless when he stands, and slaps me on the shoulder. "Impressed? I thought so. Bet you've got that big brain going, figuring out all the ways we'll turn this shit into millions. Our own empire, Usher. Rich as sin before we're twenty-five. Think of the world class ass hanging out limos that'll buy."

My eyes jerk to his. Shaking my head, I finally growl it out, "Tell me what, and how. Right the fuck now, Jace. You're freaking me out."

I desperately want him to say it's not something illegal, as unlikely as that seems.

His chin tilts, no doubt studying my horrified expression. I can't even hide it because wherever this money came from, I know I won't like the answer.

"Oh, yeah. That part. Kinda the reason I didn't tell you from the get-go. Look, before I say anything, you've got to know what would've happened if I hadn't decided to strike out on my own."

My stare is pure ice.

"I'm not as stupid as you think," he continues. "Let me spell it out for you: we'd have muddled through our last couple years in college, working our balls off, lucky to land more than a few measly thousand. Hardly enough. We'd take on huge fucking loans, or else we'd go to dad with our tails tucked between our legs. My old man might've given us the money, sure. Then we'd owe him every penny, but that's under normal circumstances."

"Normal?" God help me, I can't stop growling.

"Yeah. Normal, that's what dad would do. I don't know how *Senator Maxwell Chenocott* would treat us. Hell, there might be a law or something stopping him from investing in our company." His voice drips sarcasm, wrinkling his nose. "Hey, dude, quit looking at me like I've lost my mind. You know every word I'm saying is true."

True or not, it changes nothing. "Where'd you get the money, Jace? Where?"

"Shit, Trent, give me some fucking credit," he says, ignoring my question. "I'm looking out for us, our company, our future. Because as loaded as I am, politics changes everything. So does having a straight edge prick for a father who'd rather throw me under the bus than believe I'll ever claw my ass up to his level."

"Jesus, dude. That's what this is about? Your ego?" There's no use hitting below the belt line, but my filter is off. "You still haven't answered my question. Jace, where?"

His dark green eyes look like pond scum in the dim light. "I'm getting there. You really want to know where this miracle came from, or are you just gonna execute me without a trial, too?"

Too. Just like his old man, or so he thinks. That stings, and it shouldn't, but god damn.

We're too close, him and I. Brothers in all but blood.

I don't like it, but how the hell can I judge? He went behind my back making money doing God knows what.

And I went behind his with Amy Kay – who might wake up any second, wondering if I've ghosted her after one unforgettable night. Not in a million years. I want this shit over and done.

"Show me," I say coldly. "I'll try to hold my fire."

I hope that's not a lie. Jace doesn't say another word. He turns, rips the boathouse door open, and holds it until I'm right behind him. Then it's the world's longest walk across the property, to the very end, not far from where the boat launches into the water.

"Shit, I forgot the shovel," he mutters, stooping down. "Help me dig."

I get down in the sandy dirt next to him, dreading what we're about to unearth. It's wet soil, waterlogged from the sea. Safe on high ground from all but the highest tides. Nobody would ever come digging around in this barren soil unless Maxwell and Ophelia decide to build something here, and they've got bigger worries.

We're several feet in, scraping the soft sand with our fingers, when I feel something heavy, cold, metal.

"Bingo," Jace whispers, crowding in front of me to clear the rest.

He yanks another key from his pocket, sticks it in the padlock, and after a few choppy seconds, the big metal box pops open.

It takes several tense seconds to process what I'm looking at. There's several neat rows of a green leafy substance tucked in what almost looks like plastic wrap. When it hits me, I don't want to stand, but I bolt up anyway.

"You're dealing weed?" I choke out. I hold the last bit in, something along the lines of *you fucking idiot*.

He turns, still stooped over his cache, wearing a strained smile. "That's my stash, bro. Just a little extra kickback. We'd be at least 50K richer if I wanted all cash, but a man deserves a bonus, doesn't he?"

I have no words. Jace digs through the top layer, lifting a fatter bag stuffed to the brim with what looks like milky hard pebbles.

"Here's what's earning us a fortune. Catch," he whispers, tossing it neatly over his shoulder.

My hand flies out, plucking it into my palm before it hits the ground. I swallow, wondering what kind of mess we'd have to clean up if this bag bursts.

The rocks, crystals, whatever the hell they are, feel sharp through the plastic. They stab at my fingers like little knives, nasty secrets begging to get out.

Whatever the hell I'm holding, it can't be good.

"Got a few more pounds stashed away. Met a guy at the club last spring who was in our chem lab. Snowball, remember him?" Jace stands in front of me now, staring at the bag clenched in my hands like it's his first born.

"Yeah. Stupid asshole flunked out completely last semester, I heard." Can't hide the venom in my voice. He was a pudgy older kid in a leather jacket and devil tattoos. Too grungy to fit in with the clean, chic aesthetic on Bellingham's campus, but somehow, he always showed up at every frat party. "Didn't much like him."

"Thought you'd be smarter, Usher. Don't judge a book by its cover." Jace gives me the side-eye. "Turns out, Snowball left school loaded. Hell, maybe he always was, I'm not really sure. While we were off chasing citations and internships, this glorious motherfucker was making bank. We were his market. Kids love to experiment like hell on campus these days."

My throat goes dry. The saltwater ocean breeze in the air wafting up my nostrils only makes it worse. "Market for what? Ecstasy? Weed? Heroin?" I cough on the last one, dreading the answer.

"Think a little more salt of the earth, Usher. A little cheaper. That crap you're holding isn't just for rednecks and biker pricks anymore. *Breaking Bad* did wonders for marketing this shit to a new crowd."

Methamphetamine.

My face dips down in disgust at the poison I'm holding. It isn't sky blue like it was in the TV show. It's dirtier, in just about every sense. My hand slips, subtly shaking, and the bag hits a rock tucked in front of my toe.

"Hey, asshole, careful with that!" Jace growls, snatching it up, bringing it to his chest. "There's at least another ten grand in here, and plenty more where it came from." His eyes shift to the pit, which might as well be a smoking crater, threatening to open wide and bring my whole world into hell.

"You're fucking crazy!" I bite down on every word, ramming my palms in his chest. He rocks back, throwing the bag into his spider hole when he's steady again. "Goddamn, dude. A drug dealer? Don't tell me you've thought this through!"

"If you'd lay off the kick in the balls for two seconds, ass-wipe, you'd know I'm not *selling* anything." He talks like it's plain as day, written on his forehead or something. "I'm more like...a middleman, let's say. Giving these babies a nice home until it's time to send them down the distribution chain. Snowball has some wicked friends across several state lines, Usher. He's paying me big money for storage – nobody would ever suspect any of the places I've picked out. They're practically invisible."

"Places?" I growl, shaking my head. "You're telling me there's *more?*"

"No shit. I told you, it'd be dumb to put all my eggs in one basket. Your ma's dogs have been sleeping right next to one." His smile darkens, as if to say, *fuck you, you're in this whether you like it or not.*

"Get a damn grip. I was real careful every time," he whispers. "Made sure your ma and pops didn't see anything. Kept it away from the dogs, too, at the edge of the garden, so nobody'd ever –"

I don't let him finish.

My fist plows into his face.

First time in my life I've ever hit another man and meant to do damage. *Serious fucking damage.*

Crunched bones and bruises. Ruptured blood vessels.

Whimpers. Tears. Heartbreak.

Everything a shady, backstabbing, sociopath cock like my soon-to-be-ex-best-friend deserves.

"Leave my parents the hell alone. You're not welcome in our house anymore." Thunder ripples in my throat. I stare through him, wishing my eyes could burn a hole through this asshole's chest.

"Usher, you fucking coward...should've known you weren't man enough for this." He stands up taller. "If you're kicking me out of your parents' house for the summer, then you're not showing your face around here either. Go home. Pretend I never showed you anything today. You rat me out, you're a dead man."

Pain stabs at my chest. It's not his threat that bothers me. My thoughts go to Amy Kay, blissfully oblivious to this shit flinging. This nightmare on her doorstep.

Fuck, I need to leave, but I also need to say goodbye. "Whatever you say, asshole. I'm going."

I'm not thinking straight. Turning my back on this traitor, without growing eyes in the back of my head, is a huge mistake.

I've only taken a few steps toward the house when he rushes forward, shoving me face first into the ground as hard as he can.

I roll, so pissed my blood burns, ready to kill him and throw his body into that pit on the beach.

"That's for putting your hands on me," Jace growls. "I'm warning you, Usher, you're not as fucking brilliant as you think. Let me stop by your place one more time to get my stuff. If I find out you've touched it, wrecked it, thrown it away before I get there, you've got a guaranteed ass kicking coming."

I nod, standing, retreating toward the house and this

time looking over my shoulder. Of course, I'm planning to rip his filth out of ma's garden first chance I get.

Shit. As bad as I need to talk to Presh, I need to get home more.

My parents could have their lives ruined by a DEA raid every second his crap sits on our property. There's no telling how sloppy he's been. For all I know, this house is under surveillance right now, Federal agents waiting for the right second to swoop down like hawks.

I practically punch the door open, stepping into the kitchen. This time, my stomach growls, but it's all rage fueling it.

I find a pen, tear a page off the notepad stuck to the fridge, and start writing frantically underneath the Chenocott and Morse Legal header.

I keep it short and sweet.

What fucking choice do I have?

I can't just tell Presh her brother is a meth slinging halfwit. Not like this.

I say there's urgent family business – true.

Tell her last night meant the world – true.

Swear I'll be back to explain everything – almost true.

I don't know when, or how, or if I'll go for the jugular and make sure the Chenocotts find out the danger this asshole put them in.

I hesitate on the last part, but only for a second.

Love you Presh, I write, because I'm not sure I'll ever be in the mood for games again. I'd rather have her know and think I've lost my mind, saying it too soon, versus risking her never hearing it at all.

Hell, now that it's on the page staring back at me, I know it's something I should have said a lot sooner. Jace's bullshit changes nothing. After this is sorted out and things are fixed at home, I'm heading back here, having that talk with Maxwell.

I look up, ready to storm out to my car. Jace is waiting by the door, blocking an easy escape.

Fuck him.

I'm so on edge, it's hard not to run him down like a screaming bull. I stomp toward him, hating the thought of tearing up the Chenocott's lovely home if he throws another punch.

There's no choice – it's on him.

Despite the urge to knock his teeth out, if I squint carefully, I still see a brother. His twisted flip to the dark side can't change what we were: friends, fighters, wing men, endless bawdy laughs.

Students, partners, inseparable as twins.

We balanced each other's soft points. Made ourselves better together. Now, that's gone forever.

"What's wrong? Too big a baby to walk past the guy you're about to screw over?" His words are a slow poison drip on my soul.

"It's not too late to fix this." We both know it is. I don't know why I'm bothering to give him wishful thinking, but I do. "Dig the crap up. Destroy it. Dump it back on Snowball. Pay him every cent you owe, and extra for the weed, too. Call it good. I'll go to the police with you."

Jace's face goes red and he scratches at the ten o'clock scruff on his cheek. "Fuck you, Usher. I don't need your brains to bail me out of this one. Too late for second thoughts. You were the one who said we needed capital, remember? I did this for us. Hell, if my money isn't good enough, then maybe I'll just throw the whole wad at something else. I see what I get now for ever listening to you. I –"

I cut him off. We go back and forth, slinging accusations, getting absolutely nowhere.

If Presh isn't awake by now, goddamn, she will be if we get much louder.

It's past time to go.

Last time we lock eyes, I can't believe how soulless he looks. His anger comes out mechanically, reactionary, without apology. My best friend is gone forever.

He's too wrapped up in his own shitty excuses, his daddy issues, his own twisted ego. He can't see why housing meth to get ahead is the biggest mistake of his life.

Jace's nostrils flare, and the last words I ever want to hear from his evil mouth sour the air. "You're not family, asshole. Never were. My parents. My house. My sister. You want to keep that perfect goddamn grin, you'll keep away from everything. I'll pick up the pieces and we'll be done."

There's nothing left to say.

I wheel around, slamming the door shut so hard behind me I think I damage the roof.

* * *

HE'S FASTER than I think. It's a late summer night and I'm working like a maniac. I'm dirty, exhausted, in a mad rush to fix ma's garden. All so I can get the leather duffel bag unearthed and in my truck.

Amy Kay's texts rattle my phone all day. I'm forced to ignore them.

Haven't decided what to say back. There's nothing *to* say while I'm still struggling to get several pounds of drugs in plastic wrap off my property.

I'm cleaning up, carrying the bag to my truck, when I hear another vehicle roar onto the curb next to our driveway. Stopping cold, I peep through the window, hoping Pops doesn't notice the sound.

He's slumped peacefully in his recliner, the TV going. Right where he should stay for a few more hours until he lumbers to the other side of our rambler and crawls in bed for the night.

Good. Means there's a chance I'll be able to deal with the asshole on our doorstep without anybody being the wiser, if I can keep my voice down.

If we don't rip each other to pieces, I tell myself.

Seems like the likeliest outcome after Jace climbs out of his convertible.

Wait. Convertible?

My eyes narrow. A coolness creeps into my veins. Jace drives an Escalade. Same black luxury beast he got for his eighteenth birthday.

This is Amy Kay's car, and I can't imagine an excuse for him driving it that doesn't make me want to cave his face in.

"Hold it right there with the bag, Usher," Jace snarls, slamming the car's door. He stands, fists at his side, ready for a brawl. I'm not close enough to tell if he's drunk, but there's a good possibility.

"Just hand it the fuck over and I'll be on my way. Don't care about my clothes. I *need* what's in that bag."

"Finders, keepers. Asshole," I add.

He snorts. "What, so you can sell it off behind my

back?" Jace creeps closer, the moonlight turning pale in his eyes. "Or maybe I ought to be worried you'll just snort it up yourself and burn your smarts out, Usher. A boring, two-timing orphan piece of dog shit like you probably can't wait to have a little excitement."

My fingers white-knuckle the bag. It suddenly weighs a hundred pounds.

Not so heavy I won't hesitate to throw it into his criminal face. "Fuck your excitement. I already get plenty of that with your lovely sister, thank you very much."

His eyes go big and he bares his teeth. I don't regret pissing him off.

Amy Kay's too sweet to kiss and tell – I'm not that kind of asshole – but I knew it'd be the perfect way to bait him. Even better because it's true.

I never take my eyes off her car behind him as he lets out a few more muffled curses and charges forward. We're roughly matched with strength. My reflexes are better.

He's too enraged, and I'm eerily calm. I step aside just before he grabs my throat, throwing my full weight into his side. Jace never knows what hits him before he goes head-first into my tailgate.

There's a savage echo through the metal after his head impacts it. He goes down groaning, clutching at his neck with both hands.

"Move, asshole, so I know there's nothing broken." I'm not so cold I'll leave him suffering out here if he's done real damage.

It takes my shoe pressed into his ribs to turn him over.

"Fuck...you..." he grunts, every syllable on fire.

Smiling, I grab his arms, pull him onto the lawn. The

vicious looks never stop while I dig in his pocket for his phone, finding her keys. "Can't have you messing around with this. You know the gas station up the street? The guy there'll probably let you use his to call for help. Whenever you're able to walk again. Rest here as long as you need to, buddy." I slap him on the shoulder.

He takes a swing at me, but it's way too slow and sloppy, sending him into the grass again. "Don't work too hard. I'll put this dirty laundry where it'll never bother you again. I'm sure Snowball won't be happy your little hiding spots weren't as secure as you said, but hey, at least you've got four hundred grand to pay the damages – and you won't even have to worry about laundering it."

A parting kick to the ribs leaves him breathless. That's how I want it.

He gives me the finger as I throw the bag in the backseat, burying it under an umbrella and a blanket from a picnic we had a few weeks ago.

Fuck, it was so much simpler then. How did everything get this complicated so fast?

It's a question I keep asking as I turn onto the highway and drive south to Olympia. The gas tank is low, so I stop for fuel and a coffee after twenty minutes on the road. I want to go at least an hour or two down the Olympic peninsula, where the touristy places turn into the boonies.

Something's been rattling around in the trunk since I squealed out of the neighborhood. I open it on my way back to the car and freeze. It's got nothing to do with the loud thunder booming overhead, a storm cracking through the atmosphere.

"Oh, Jesus." Words can't do justice when I see a familiar, dirty metal box.

My fist bangs against it lightly before I remember I'm not alone here. I slam the trunk shut and jump back in the driver's seat, trying not to have a fucking panic attack.

Jace must have come looking for all his drugs. He knew he couldn't trust me to stay quiet after our fallout, and hell, maybe it's the smartest thing he's done. If I'd managed to dispose of crap he buried by ma's flowers, I damn sure would've figured out a way to clear the Chenocott's place next.

Looks like I don't have to. That's the only good in this. Amy's little car is stuffed with what I'm pretty sure is his entire very illegal stash.

Of course, it also means I'm driving through the night with enough drugs to get a twenty year prison sentence. Fuck, maybe life.

"Just breathe," I tell myself, fusing my hands to the wheel, driving more careful than I ever have in my life.

It's harder once the sky rips open. Hard rain pelts the road in a thick ocean deluge. Somebody pissed off Poseidon *bad*.

But I follow the dark twisting highway as it narrows past Olympia. Into the night. Into the icy silence cut by wind and rain and nerves. Into my only chance to fix this shit for me, my folks, and the woman I love.

It's an ugly miracle. I should be thankful. I keep telling myself I just need to find a ravine, somewhere with tall trees and water flowing back into the sea, where I can make this disgusting secret disappear forever.

Lightning knifes the sky the further I drive. I'm somewhere near the edge of the Olympic forest, searching through the darkness for an isolated campground I can try, when it happens.

Another shriek of blue howls through the darkness. I hear the wind whistling through the trees, but no thunder. It's too soon.

There's no warning whatsoever before the top of the huge cedar slams into the road in front of me.

No time to skid around it. No time to hit the brakes. No time to save myself or the car or my whole fucking future.

There's a crunch of metal, a split second vertigo, and then I'm out.

I don't wake up until morning, when I run miles, torn and bleeding to the nearest gas station.

I tell Pops everything. He picks me up a couple hours later, brings me back, and we spend the next twenty-four hours in a mad rush to pack everything. The police were already picking through the wreck when we drove past it. What was left of its fire-blackened husk, anyway.

Jace will never admit to his shit. He'll throw me under the bus and the Chenocotts will hire the best lawyers in Washington to save his skin.

I see my only chance, and my parents agree: we have to leave Seattle forever.

XI: LOVE UNBLINDED (AMY KAY)

Present Day

MY LUNGS WORK SO HARD they shake my whole body.

Still not enough to stop the world from spinning while I press my back into the bed, knees trembling together, staring at the haunted man in front of me.

"Presh? You okay? That's the long and short of it. You can pretty much guess what happened next, and fill in the gaps on your end."

Oh, I can fill in the blanks, all right.

My heartbeat quickens to a sickly thump against my ribs, dark memories coming in threes.

It started with the visit from the cops the next morning, not long after my parents came home. They questioned all of us, except for Jace. Dad wouldn't let him talk without a lawyer.

I knew he was guilty. Knew it the instant I saw him

with his busted lip and bloodshot eyes, not to mention the huge scratch across his head he tried to hide, angling his face up unnaturally.

He also did the unexpected. He poured his heart out.

My rock solid asshole brother actually broke down in a whimpering mess.

How could I not believe him? Show him no sympathy?

I'd never seen anything like it, him regressing to a little boy. A *scared* little boy at that.

Usher's fault, he said.

Two words I've staked the last six years of my life on. Two words I never wanted to believe.

Two words I now know were planted by a liar, a hypocrite, and a coward.

I press my face into my hands, wishing I could make Trent go away. It's not his fault the truth hurts so bad, sure. But him watching it sink in, seeing my misery...what the *holy hell* took him so long?

My mind scatters in a dozen directions, stuck in the past.

I see Jace shaking, walking with dad's lawyer, after he delivered his statement where he called Trent a drug dealer, a mastermind, a schemer who needed a dim-witted accomplice. He told the district judge it was Trent who hijacked my car, filled it full of the drugs he tried to bring to the police, and then crashed it on an isolated stretch through the woods just south of Olympia.

We believed him.

Even though the car burned too badly to positively ID any drugs, all the signs were there.

We believed.

Oh my God, we believed.

Then the media blowup three days later, when my poor totaled convertible became the talk of the Seattle press. A 'troubling' incident involving the daughter of a frontrunner for US Senate, they said. Dad huddled with his lawyer. Donors pulled their money. Local party hacks backed off.

He dropped out of the primary the next day, giving a quick, tearful concession speech.

We sat in the library that night, just him and I. Mom was too sick to even get out of bed after the speech. I asked him what he'd do to Trent, secretly wondered if I'd have to watch the man who raised me annihilate the man I loved, however much he might deserve it.

Dad surprised me then. He refused to release the hounds.

"Move on," he said. We had to. He said Usher, wherever he is, would pay for this hell in his own way.

Now I know he did.

He paid for a crime he never fucking did, trying to save me.

I look up through bleary eyes, studying the eerily cool, older face of the boy I knew I wanted to marry after our night in this very room so many years ago. One word hangs on my lips, so heavy it hurts. "Trent, why?"

Why? His blue eyes pierce my soul, his head tilts slightly, almost like he doesn't understand what I'm asking.

"Isn't it obvious, Precious?" he says softly. "I didn't have a clue what your old man had in store if I ever popped up again. Neither did my parents. Ma, it ripped her heart out walking away from her dogs, her garden. She couldn't bear to lose me, too. Neither could Pops. He gave up his home, his late night TV, his fucking fly fishing for me...and it tore me up, you want to know the truth. This clusterfuck was Jace's mistake. No one else's. I got caught in the middle and panicked like the scared, clueless kid I was. Couldn't breathe a word to you. If I'd written, if I'd called, if I'd shown up on your doorstep, we'd have lost it all. Your family would've suffered more. DEA raids and six figure legal bills. And I'd be in jail. I *had* to stay fucking mum."

"Wrong, Trent. You chose to. Dad never would've had you arrested. You left me alone to suffer, to wonder, to think I was losing my mind!" The last words slur together. "What else is a lie? Was it the note you left that morning, where you said..."

I can't even force the words. I just remember his messy signature beneath three crabbed words: *love you, Presh.*

"You sent me a letter, too," he says, a wry smile on his handsome lips. "Real life's not always like it is on paper. Never easy. We say shit we don't mean all the time."

My eyebrows bore into my head. His gaze intensifies. "Other times, we mean it more than our own life. But the crap that happens off the pages doesn't care, does it? The script keeps moving, Presh. Always. No matter what we say or how we say it or who we say it to."

I quietly chew on his words. They're as smooth as ever, quintessentially Trent Usher, but this isn't the time for platitudes.

Tears can't be quelled forever.

"You're an asshole! This whole time, if you'd just come back, if you'd just written, if you'd just –" I leap toward him, slapping his face. Trying.

He catches my wrists, grips them tight, pulls me into

him almost effortlessly. My forehead crumples into the nook below his chin. Every breath is a sweet torture, inhaling this gorgeous man who lied to me by omission, and damn it, I want to forgive him.

"Presh," he whispers, a low rumble in his throat. "When you think you'll behave, look at me."

I look up, glaring. His eyes are soft blue stars. Whirlpools drawing me into the same dark memories he's made me re-live, no thanks to a truth that's just as ruthless. "No. I can't just let this go, pretend it never happened. You came here for freaking closure, Trent?"

He nods sagely.

"What the *hell* were you thinking? Spilling this, ripping open old wounds, showing me who Jace really is...God. It's too much." Okay, so he can't be blamed for the last part. Nothing about the lows my brother stooped to are surprising after seeing his recent screw ups.

But that was Trent too, wasn't it? Exposing him?

Jesus.

If he'd never come to Seattle, and just stayed in Portland...

I close my eyes, seeing a blissful ignorance. Jace was bound to do something stupid in the clear light of day sooner or later. Embezzling money, screwing around on Lindsey, finding more friends in the underworld, even.

Trent may have just saved our family again. As sickeningly hard as that is to admit.

"Gave you what you needed, Presh. What *I* needed. Don't you see? Once I'm done settling scores, we can move the fuck on. Finally." He speaks like he's so sure. Madness. "We've got something valuable, darling: closure. When you fly home to Spokane, leaving this mess behind, you won't have to wonder what might've been anymore, or why it couldn't be."

He's trying to console me in his own clueless asshole way. It just sends my fists into his chest. I swallow a muffled whimper.

How can a man so intelligent, so calculating, completely miss the point?

These aren't the words I want. Everything spoken in the past tense, one eye on the future, and nothing in the present. I'm an emotional wreck.

"Hey, Presh? Amy Kay?" He shakes me gently, and then a little harder after a solid twenty seconds not responding.

I'm limp in his arms. Defeated. So fucking done.

Growling slightly, he stands, lifting me gently with him. I'm in his arms, being put to bed like some kind of messed up sleeping beauty. He calls to me a few more times, but I can't handle more. If he won't face the demons he's turned loose head-on, I just want him to leave.

That's what I'm expecting when he turns his back. Can't say I blame him, considering every second spent in this house risks a whole new shit storm if my parents or Jace find out I'm not alone.

It seems like minutes pass. I lay crumpled up on the bed, my eyes only opening when I feel a huge, heavy weight next to me.

"You're too tired. This'll all make more sense in the morning. Promise." His arm hugs my waist. His body eclipses mine, big and Herculean and weirdly reassuring through the confusion.

There's a warmth from his sleepy breath against my neck. It's nothing compared to the heat of his flesh on mine, or near enough. A snug, calming sea telling me it's okay to let go. Drift away.

That's what I do. Eventually.

But before I let the sandman stake his claim, I remember Trent's last words, and know this is just one more reassuring lie.

How can anything about this *ever* make sense?

I'm sleeping in the same bed with my ex, where he deflowered me years ago. I'm so ruined I let him.

Hell, maybe I encouraged it, settling back against him.

There's sanctuary in his heat, his strength, his wicked familiarity.

He knows it, too.

Trent's breathing picks up, his lungs work a little harder, every time I shift against him ever so slightly. There's a hardness against my butt. One more artifact from a time gone by, ruined by everything that's happened since, but I can't deny how good, how right, how nice it feels.

I shift against him harder. His breath catches in his tired throat. My core ignites, rushing heat to my thighs, my nipples, my pussy. My hand tightens on the edge of the pillow, clutching for dear life, considering whether or not I have the energy and the courage to turn around and stare into his eyes.

But I'm no fool.

We've faced too many hard truths tonight. Too many roller coaster rides down that unforgiving bitch called Memory Lane.

I can't. I won't throw my body at his. I'm not inviting more heartbreak, more hell, more agony.

Animal lust is an easier thing to suppress than other emotions. When sleep finds me, it's peaceful.

I'm not even surprised when I wake up the next morning and find him gone.

* * *

A QUICK SHOWER gives me the strength to face the day. My stomach growls. Amazingly, I have an appetite, which I didn't expect after last night's insanity.

I head downstairs, wondering if mom still picks up duck eggs, even if her arthritis doesn't let her get out as much as she used to. I'm half-expecting my parents at the breakfast table, even though it's late, but they're already in the sunken living area adjacent to the kitchen.

Sighing, I decide to go simple, fixing myself some toast and tea. The locally sourced strawberry jam has the perfect sweetness. I chew a few crisp mouthfuls before joining them.

"It's so good to see you again, Amy Kay." Mom holds her arms out for a hug. I set my food down on the tray and walk over, minimizing any need for her to hobble over.

"Sorry I didn't come sooner. Important business."

"Oh, I heard. You're so kind to help out, dearie. I'm sure Jace appreciates it even more, considering his tough times." Her smile fades.

I feel a knife in my chest. Looking across the room, I see dad, a strained expression on his face.

He hasn't told her anything. Not about the embezzlement, or the divorce, or *oh my God* I hope he isn't planning to dump it all at once. She won't take it well.

"That's what family's for, right?"

"Eat your breakfast and then let's plan a night out. It's been so long since we've had both our kids at the same table." She beams at dad. "A nice dinner downtown, perhaps. A movie. If we can get Jace to join us –"

Dad clears his throat, trying to brush aside the question. "He's very sensitive at the moment."

Mom shakes her head. "Of course. How silly. We'd best handle him gently, then, until he's able to sort out his woes with our lovely daughter-in-law. I just know they'll patch things up. Time works miracles."

Not in this lifetime. I crunch my toast, trying not to make my anger obvious.

Hearing my poor, innocent mother still talking about Jace like he's her lost little boy sends hellfire through my veins. Even dad doesn't know the truth, about why he was humiliated in front of the entire state, and who's really responsible.

"Sis?" Hello, Satan. I turn, facing my brother, an equally cold look on his face. "Sorry to intrude. I need to talk to Amy Kay."

I don't answer. Not until mom gives me a worried look and opens her mouth. "You don't need my permission!" she says cheerfully. "You two catch up. I'm sure we'll lock down a nice place for tonight, won't we, Maxwell?"

Dad nods. I feel his eyes on me as I sigh, leaving a bread crust and my almost empty plate on the counter, before I let Jace lead us out the front.

He keeps going, past the trees, their buds just peaking out for spring. I wait until we're a comfortable distance at the side of the house. Then I stand my ground, folding my arms, digging my feet into the soggy ground. "What? Why are you looking at me like that?"

"Had a visitor last night, didn't you, bitch?" His eyes seethe, never wavering as my mouth drops, wondering how he could possibly know.

Then he holds up a sheet of paper covered in a familiar hurried writing.

Another note.

Does Trent have a death wish? I really wonder as I reach for it, but my brother snatches it away at the last second, balling it up in his hand, then letting it fall. "You were in on it the whole fucking time, weren't you?"

"In on...what, exactly?" The words taste sour because I can't believe what's happening. I'm standing here being accused of ruining his life, after what he did... "Your drug deal? Setting up Trent to save your own skin? Screwing over dad, mom, and then the whole company years later?"

He doesn't want to hear it. Predictable. But I don't expect him to lunge forward, slam me into the wall, push his thumbs into my clavicles.

"Shut. Up." His eyes are insane. "You fucking did this to me, Amy? With him? I thought as much, but goddamn, to hear it from your own mouth."

"I didn't do *anything*. Trent came here on his own. I tried to ignore him. But he wanted to talk, wanted to give the truth, told me everything that happened years ago." Tears come fast and searing. I'm starting to miss the days I didn't cry. "Drugs, Jace? Were you out of your goddamn mind?"

His grip loosens, freeing a subtler pain that makes me wince. "That was a long time ago, Amy Kay. Should I be punished for the rest of my life?" Growling, he turns his back, kicking angrily at a dead branch on the ground. The *snap* is like a gunshot.

"No, idiot. But after finding out why Trent wants to bring you down, maybe you deserve it. Some of it, I mean. It's not like you were an angel to Lindsey, or the firm. You clearly didn't learn a damn thing from what happened years ago. A situation *you* caused, Jace."

He turns, new daggers in his eyes. "What's it to you, little miss perfect? Fuck, I wish dad had found out you were fucking that prick years back. He'd have turned you both out on your asses, rather than let that orphan piece of shit drag down this family. I *never* would've hooked up doing dirty deals in the first place if he hadn't busted my balls so hard over how bad we needed money."

I gasp and stop rubbing my aching shoulder. "You're serious? Jesus Christ. Can't you man up and take responsibility just this once? If I heard an apology, a confession, a little honesty, maybe I'd still think there's hope."

"You don't anymore, do you?" he says quietly. He steps on the crunched up note on the ground. "I wouldn't believe this shit if I wasn't seeing it with my own eyes. This turncoat fucking family..." He pauses, closes his eyes, exhaling a long breath. "Even when I told you what happened, it wasn't enough. You still fucking blame me."

The fabricated story, he means. I try not to grit my teeth.

"Dad let him off with a slap on the wrist. You couldn't keep your hands off him, all ready to throw me under the goddamn bus and let him take my place. Shit, maybe you still want it, after everything that's happened. You're that much of a desperate little whore, trapped in yesterday."

No more.

It's my turn to catch him off guard. I jerk forward,

reach up, and lay a satisfying palm-burning smack across his cheek.

"Shut the hell up. This is your fault, Jace. All of it. I'm just clearing the air with mom and dad, whatever else you think is happening. That's what this is, isn't it? Clearing the air," I say, tapping the mystery letter with my toe. "Trent didn't just come by to spill the beans to me. He wanted everyone to know, to find out who you really are."

I think I get it now. He's more interested in clearing his conscience, his name, than precision revenge.

I'm ready to throw my hands up defensively. Finding out what a huge creep my brother is makes me feel less secure than ever. If he hurts me, if he puts his hands on me again, I'll fight him with everything I've got, and then I'll scream and scream until the servants hear. I saw old Jorge this morning, the longtime gardener, and on a nice spring day like this he'll surely keep making the rounds.

I think Jace knows the same thing. It doesn't stop an eerie chill from sweeping up my back, wondering if the only reason he doesn't throw his hands around my throat is because he's afraid of getting caught.

"You've had your chances, Jace. So many." It hurts to count the litany of second chances he's had in my head. Worse when I open my eyes, and see a brief flicker of that scared, lying young man who scorched Trent years ago, and seemingly never thought twice about it. "I love you, even after all this, but you're a disgrace."

Anger lights up his eyes.

He opens his mouth, but I cut him off, raising a hand. "I'm not finished, Jace. You can fix this, own up to your mistakes, and start to undo them. Easier said than done. I know. It'll take years, probably. You'll do a lot of explaining. You'll have to make a lot of apologies. But it's the right thing. If you want more chances, this time you have to work for them."

There's a long silence.

I hold my breath, hoping he'll come back with something sane. Something reasonable.

"Fuck you, sis," he snarls, putting more distance between us like a cougar losing a fight.

I should've known.

"Didn't waste my time with you to get a lecture. Just do whatever the hell you want. I knew as soon as I read the bullshit that asshole left behind there's only one solution. He wants to demolish what's left of my life? Fine. I won't make it easy."

He stomps away, leaving me biting my lip, dreading whatever he's planning. I reach for the crumpled note, unfold it, wiping away the dirt. It's addressed to my parents.

Maxwell and Ophelia,

It's been forever. I should have written this years ago. It's taken an odd reunion of sorts with Amy Kay to convince me to stop dragging my feet, but here goes. My version of everything that's damaged our lives...

My eyes skim the next half quickly. It's the same nightmare he whispered last night, a blow-by-blow recount. I know how it ends with the frantic car ride through the woods, the crash, the painful retreat. I can't bear to read the end.

What do I do?

I could just carry this in the house, show it to dad, and let him decide where we go from here. But is he ready to find out what a wretched worm his own son really is? Ready to learn Trent didn't actually screw us?

It's just a matter of time, I suppose. Also, sooner or later, there'll be no hiding any of this from mom. And Jace's very present screw ups are a mystery to her.

I hang my head, wracking my brain for answers. The soft Seattle sun retreats behind the clouds.

A car's engine roars, banishing my funk. I cross the path to the house quickly, careful to avoid the freshly tilled soil for the ornamental flowers Jorge has probably just planted this morning. I'm just in time to see Jace's polished black Tesla darting out of the garage like an ugly eel leaving its cave.

He gives me the finger, tearing down the long path leading to the gate without stopping. I want to say *good riddance.*

But I can't shake the persistent, ugly promise in my brother's eyes.

Jace is a loose cannon. He lost his morals a long time ago, if he ever had them.

Breaking my paralysis, I head to my room, stuff the note under a book on my dresser, and high tail it to my car. Later, I'll deal with the truth, my parents, and the massive fallout it's bound to bring. Right now, there's something more important.

I can't let him go after Trent.

* * *

I'm driving like a crazy woman through rush hour traffic downtown. I'm in such a rush I don't even care about crashing the rental.

Jace could be anywhere. He might even beat me to the tall posh hotel. I've got the local news on the radio, and so far, I haven't heard any disturbances, brawls, or shootings. Small comfort.

After an eternity fighting traffic, I pull the car to the curb by the entrance and shove an eye popping wad of cash at the valet. "Just park. I won't be long."

I hope, I add mentally, running through the circular doors.

The well manicured man at the front desk looks at me suspiciously. I know how out of place I look: badly out of breath, hair tossed everywhere, fist in my purse digging for that stupid piece of paper.

"Miss, can I assist you?" he asks for the third time.

Finally. I slap the paper on the marble counter, looking for the tidbit I've forgotten. "Trent Usher. Room 313. Will you let him know we need to talk?" I also want to ask if there's anyone else who's come by looking for Trent, but I hold it at the tip of my tongue.

"One moment," he says, professionalism winning out, fingers working the keyboards. "Ah. It appears Mr. Usher checked out early this morning."

Damn! On second thought, I'm not sure whether I'm upset or relieved.

If he's gone virtually anywhere else, he's probably safe from Jace. But if he left without a goodbye...

"Did he leave a contact? A message? A destination?"

The man strokes his chin. "I recall helping him myself, yes. Believe he said he's heading home. Portland, if I recall. Had one of our drivers collect his luggage for the airport."

"Thanks." I grab the slip of paper with his room and number, wheeling around, a little less urgency in my step than before. But before I do, I turn one last time. "This might sound weird...hope I'm not overstepping any bounds...but can you tell me if anyone else was here looking for him?"

The man pauses, hardens his eyes, wondering if he should tell me anything. My heart sinks because I think I already know the answer. "As a matter of fact, there was a visitor. A tall, rather flustered man who, frankly, left a very unpleasant impression. About an hour ago, well after Mr. Usher had checked out."

"Thank you!" I don't give him any time to cross-interrogate. I almost crash headfirst into the valet, asking for my car.

I need to get home.

While I'm waiting, I dial the only number I have for Trent. Predictably, it belongs to the room, redirecting my call to the same bewildered man at the front desk I just left in the dust.

Hanging up, my heart sinks. Wherever he's gone, I still need to warn him.

There's a decent chance my brother isn't so insane he'll do anything in an airport. Still, it would take him no time to book a flight to Portland, or God forbid, drive.

The ride to my parents place is a little less insane. Too bad I can't shake the sick feeling in my stomach this is far from over.

Then I see Jace's car in the driveway. He hasn't bothered pulling into the garage. I hold my breath all the way inside the house.

Just because he has no immediate plans to follow up on chasing Trent doesn't calm my nerves.

I close the door behind me and hear...laughter?

Steeling myself, I push through the door, into the house. I can't stand what I see next.

Jace is in the living room with mom. They're reminiscing over some mundane thing from the past I hear in quick bursts. I'm so livid my ears blaze red.

My brother isn't just screwed up and out for revenge. He's a complete sociopath. Nobody else would go after a man in broad daylight looking for a fight, and then laugh it off over tea in less than an hour.

There's a dull, painful roar in my head. I barely make it past without them noticing.

I don't breathe again until I'm in my room, hoping to God almighty she's forgotten her dinner plans.

* * *

IT'S LATER, after dusk, when I finally creep downstairs. I didn't mean to sleep so long, but the past twenty-four hours has left me drained.

The house is weirdly quiet. So still I think I'm alone when I step into the kitchen.

Then I see his dark silhouette reclining in dad's favorite chair, inert in the darkness. It's too soon. A half-muffled scream bellows out before I get my hands over my mouth.

Jace just chuckles, long and low and nasty. He's been expecting me.

"Calm the fuck down, sis. Our folks are downstairs, working out last minute reservations." He smiles, stands up, and crosses the space between us, stopping on the other side of the counter. It's hard not to jump again as his hands slap the surface.

"Listen." He leans toward me, leering. "I've thought an awful lot about our little disagreement this afternoon. Decided we're still family. Everybody in this house, including you. My beef isn't with my baby sister."

Shaking my head, I feel the anger hit my blood. "Leave him alone, Jace. I went to the hotel, heard you went looking."

"And what if I did?" he bites out. "That's my fucking business, Amy Kay. Whether he was justified or not, Usher threw the first punch, dragging my skeletons out of the closet. Then the bastard scuttled like a rat when I came to settle like a man."

He's delusional.

That isn't at all why I think he left. But of course I don't say it. "Jace –"

"Amy Kay." He nods curtly. "Listen to your big brother for once – stay the fuck out of this and we won't have problems. It's not your fight. Judging by the warm welcome our folks gave me this afternoon, I'm guessing you didn't drop this bomb on them?"

"You went in *my* room?" One more crime shouldn't shock me. Doesn't change the need to stare him down as he holds up the crumpled note I tucked away, and lets it hit the counter with a crisp *plop*.

"You'll get over it. Same thing you'll do after I burn this

fucking thing tonight, and we try to put this whole ugly fever behind us." I lunge for the ball of paper, but he's too fast, snatching it up and stuffing it back in his pocket. "Rude. Finders, keepers, Amy Kay."

"Asshole," I whisper back. "Why the game, Jace? You're crazier than I thought if you think this is something I'll just forget. Not after you went after Trent, trying to do God only knows."

He smiles. "Usher's a sad little man if he needs your protection. I'm not psychotic, sis." He pauses, as if he can sense how much I don't believe it. "I just wanted to convince my old buddy. Get him to see things my way, or at least lay off springing any other fun surprises."

My lips thin. He deserves what's coming, and probably more, but I don't like the idea of Trent running around with more hit-and-run attacks. Cooler heads have to prevail eventually, right?

"That's my sis," he says, patting my arm twice before I rip it away. "Fine. Be that way. Rest assured, whatever beef I have with Usher won't get violent or out of hand."

"I don't know why I should believe anything you say."

"Because, sis, I've got nothing left to lose. If I'm so fucked up, so crazy, I decide to jack a flight to Portland and pay him a visit on his home turf, what will you do? Squeal to dad? Break mom's heart? Force our parents to lock me up like a mad fucking dog?"

I don't say anything. He's got me there.

Of course, I'll consider it if I think my brother could be a murderer, but Jesus, I don't want to.

"Exactly." His eyes brighten, making my skin crawl. "I know being under the same roof's fucking torture for us both. Don't you worry, sis. I'll be out of your hair real soon. I was already planning to tell everybody I've got a new place lined up over dinner tonight. Need some time to myself to think about this, how I'll un-fuck my life. Lindsey's lawyer's already up my ass, and dad wants me with his guy on Monday. Won't have much time for retaliation against the asshole who did this. Not for a while."

I say nothing. We stare at each other for a minute longer. Then he turns, marches past me, and disappears into the next room.

I can't trust a word from this chronic liar, but one word wasn't lost on me: *time.*

Trent, in all his wisdom, didn't leave me a Portland contact. Every hour Jace stays here buys precious time for a proper warning.

Sighing, I know what's ahead: I'll play this cat and mouse game as long as it takes to make things less crazy. I'll warn Trent. And the second Jace steps out of line, I'll make sure mom and dad know everything.

Then, sometime in the next century, I'll wash my hands of this nightmare circus and figure out how to live a normal life.

XII: PESKY CONSCIENCE (TRENT)

Two weeks back in Portland and I'm bored out of my skull.

Another seven figures in the bank as Cryptic's stock hit the moon. More meetings, more offers, more hobnobbing with bald headed billionaires who treat this as nothing but a cash cow for their pet projects. I spend ten hours one week discussing experimental batteries with a man who says he'll have a hotel orbiting the moon in five years.

Smells suspicious. Too bad the scent is eerily similar to cold hard money. A lot of money.

If only money had the same charm it used to. Since Seattle, it's been hard to give a shit about anything and even harder to focus.

I've had exactly one thing on my mind since I slipped out of bed early that final morning.

It was dark. Presh was peacefully asleep. I'm still not sure if I spent more time stepping on my own dick or my heart.

I couldn't go on with the rest of my master plan. Not after spilling my confession, fighting her calm, and laying next to her sweetness, face-to-face with a vicious truth: I'm human.

Felt it for the first time in years with Amy Kay nestled in my arms. Her warm, soft flesh plush on mine kicked up the other memories we didn't discuss that night. And I don't just mean the obvious fuck-her-through-the-floor urges leaving me hard as a brick.

I mean the kiss. How familiar, how irresistibly her lips brushed mine. She turned in her sleep, brushing her hair on my skin, and my eyes opened to her siren mouth. I think I stared at them a minute, or was it ten?

Again, I'm human. Fuck yes, I took my last opportunity to taste that sweetness. I brought my lips down on hers while she slept, stirring gently, a soft whimper-moan melting on my tongue.

It was goodbye. Had to be.

Because if I didn't sit up, straighten my clothes, and creep through the house like a bandit to the front door, I knew I'd have too many reasons to stay. The kiss made another decision for me, too.

I lost the heart to bury that fucking prick. Jace Chenocott deserves hell's seventh circle, and probably several more not yet charted, but I couldn't swing the hammer again.

Not after telling her the truth. Hell, not after re-living it with every supple curve of her body molded to mine.

What else could I do? There's a time when every man's mercy is bigger than his bite. He lays down his arms and picks up the pen.

Stopping in the kitchen, I found her ma's old notepad,

a pen, and scratched out a message to her folks. Writing those words wiped whatever howling need for vengeance I came here with. They just wanted the truth, no different than when I sat across from her upstairs, cut my soul, and bled the darkness I'd held in for so many years.

It isn't supposed to be so simple. But it is.

I walked back to my napping driver and slid into the leather seat a whole new man. By the time I checked out, got to the airport, and sat in my first class seat bound for home, I couldn't tell who the fuck I was.

No longer bent on destruction.

No longer driven by vengeance.

No longer sated on violence, humiliation, and tears.

Honest to God, our last kiss did something indescribable.

The something I thought only happened in movies.

Something otherworldly.

Something miraculous.

Tasting Precious restored my soul. Like some kind of warped inversion of Sleeping Beauty, or maybe that kid's tale where the hot princess sucks face with the frog.

Shit. I am that frog, aren't I? And if I've reverted back to Prince Charming, all the more reason to leave.

Because the only reason this one way non-aggression pact with Jace works is if I stay far, far away from Seattle.

Sure, I can't rule out retaliation. I've been watching, waiting, expecting Jace to attack me directly or the empire I've built. That fallout, I'm ready for.

As for the rest...I can't let the new Trent Usher get anywhere near Amy Kay.

If I let my lips wander back to hers again, this quest to

finally let go of the past and move on becomes impossible. Then there's no keeping this haunted peace I've found.

* * *

It's weird being back in Pops' old truck. He's had the same F-150 for twelve years. I suppose it's fitting. Touching, even. This truck has seen us through so many times: good, bad, and heartbreaking.

This was the truck I rode in the day we buried ma. It was raining like hell, a long ride out to the cemetery past the city limits. She wanted to be surrounded by nature.

Pops would've rather died a thousand times himself than fail her dying wish.

I try like hell to push the dark memory aside. We're almost to my place after eating an early dinner, where he'll let me off before driving home. There'll be plenty more time to settle into my high back leather chair with a drink, staring at the lights dancing on the other side of the Columbia.

"Glad you kept yourself out of trouble, son," Pops says, when he knows I won't have much time to protest.

"Yeah, well...you were right. I'd be lying if I said I didn't go up there without the Chenocotts heavy on my mind." I bite my tongue, hating how I'm still lying to him now.

Pops gives me the side-eye, his grey mustache twitching. If he knew what I'd done to that asshole, and then to Amy...fuck. No good will come of more confessions, though.

"How many times did you see her?" he sighs.

I turn, shaking my head, wondering where I slipped. "How many *what?*"

"How many times, Trent? You're not fooling me, coming home with your nose cleaner than I expected. Too clean, matter of fact. Did you call her? Do dinner? Sleep together?"

What the hell? Pops and I have never been shy discussing anything, but this is the first time he's asked about my sex life.

Then again, this is the first time bedroom happenings could have vile consequences.

"Christ," I growl, tapping my fingers lightly on my temple to check if this is a dream. "If you *must* know, we met briefly. Not far from their old building downtown. It was tense and awkward and nothing happened." Technically true, as far as the sex goes. It's still a goddamn lie. "You'll be happy to know she helped keep me out of bigger trouble, Pops. If we hadn't met to hash out the past —"

"You could've gotten yourself in too deep. But you didn't. If that's the long and short of it, then it's good enough for me." I hope to fuck he's right. His grip on the wheel tightens and I see his knuckles turning white. "You're *sure* you didn't upset her again?"

"Nah. We won't be looking forward to any surprise visits from the cops or the FBI soon, if that's what's got you up in arms." I'm praying this ends soon. The traffic couldn't be slower winding up the hilly road.

"Not what I mean. I stopped fearing men in black on my doorstep a long time ago, Trent." He talks like it's so obvious. "Asked if you *upset* her, son. Because I think that poor girl's been through enough, having *him* as her brother, and you in her rear-view mirror."

"Shit, are you listening? I told you. We sat down a

couple times to bury the hatchet. Not swing for anybody's throats again."

"That so? A *couple* times?" There's amusement in his thin smile. "You're no angel, son, but you've got a thing or two to learn about women outside sleeping with 'em."

Again, my sex life.

When does this torture end?

Wrinkling my nose, I stare at the road, mentally counting the last few minutes to my place and sweet freedom.

"She never would've wanted to see you again if a part of her ain't interested." He lets it out after a long pause, like he's been holding in a movie spoiler.

I do a slow turn. "No. Amy Kay wanted peace of mind and a few free dinners with a lonely billionaire. That's it. Thank you, Pops. How would I ever see what's right in front of my face without you?"

My sarcasm meter is so broke it's spinning off its track. Pops guns the last few miles to my place. The truck chugs up my long driveway and stops outside my door. "All I'm saying, dear boy, is get ready for trouble if she comes calling. And she will."

I grit my teeth. "Wrong. I left without much of a good-bye. She'll get the message. We're more done now than we ever were. She's got her happy ending and I've got mine. Sweet closure." His engine chugs through the silence, a beast on its last legs. "By the way, whenever you're in the market, let me buy you something that runs."

Pops' face darkens. He taps the wheel with his fingers like he's stroking an old horse. "Needs a little work, is all. She's got a few more good years in her, same as me."

I'm annoyed how predictably stubborn he is, but I

don't dig. "Thanks for doing dinner. I'll call you next week."

I'm out of the truck and inside before he sees the sad weight on my face. The old man has a remarkable way of being right without a lot of words.

That used to be ma's thing, but it's rubbed off on him since she left us.

Tonight, it's hard to figure out what frustrates me more: him refusing to admit he's hanging onto that old truck because he's heartsick missing ma, or me pretending I won't cross paths with Amy Kay again – even if it means treading dangerous ground.

That last kiss is part of my blood.

I taste her in every breath. Feel her heat every night I'm under the sheets. Let her sweet madness take too much of my headspace with too little fight.

I'm fucked, is what I am. Thoroughly, completely, madly. Thrashed to my very soul.

I decide to skip the drink because the hot, prickly alcohol rush in my system only makes this worse.

I head for the big black admiral's desk in my home office, grab a new sheet of paper, and begin writing like a man possessed.

* * *

UNLIKE EVERYBODY else on this planet, I loathe weekends.

Sundays are a special kind of hell, far too quiet, impossible to find distractions. Even the prospect of a good meal downtown and a walk along the Columbia's banks with spring in full bloom can't fill the vacancy in my soul.

When I wake up, have my coffee, and pick up where I

left off writing at my desk, I ought to know this won't last forever.

But I never expect the end of my funk to come that evening with the steady, shocking thump at my door. I sit up, throw my pen down, and stop for a second in the hall.

Probably something benign, I tell myself.

An Amazon package I forgot or a kid raising money. A kid with balls the size of Saturn, maybe, who's come knocking at a mansion tucked in the northwest's finest natural shade and NO TRESPASSING signs on every corner of my wrought iron fence.

Hell, I'll buy a couple thousand of whatever he's selling. Just to show him risks *sometimes* pay off. That thought's a thousand times happier than thinking asshole Jace has finally found his way to my home, and he might be armed.

There's a gun I keep in a safe under my kitchen sink, but I've never fired the damn thing once outside the range. I briefly pause between the kitchen and the door, wondering if today it wouldn't hurt to tuck it into my belt...but whoever's at the door is persistent.

They're knocking again. Louder. Harder.

I rip the door open, half-ready to throw a punch. I'm the one who takes it on the chin.

"Precious?" I try not to let my jaw hit the floor.

It's her. In the supple flesh. Here. On my damn doorstep.

She steps past me without waiting for an invite. "I had to see you. Hope you'll forgive the short notice."

Like I've got any choice. "Let's sit," I say, grabbing her hand. "Let me get you a drink."

She gasps when she sees the view. Downtown Portland reigns majestic as ever in the distance, tucked between the trees, the city's lights shimmering like tinsel along the stretch of river.

It's my turn to stifle a noise. A deep, guttural sound in my throat trying to work its way out, remembering that sound oozing out of her. How familiar it is to another noise I used to taste.

Fuck, this is bad. I tell myself to play it cool, ignore the anxious hard-on already tenting my pants. I walk to the corner table, pull out a small bottle of good wine I keep for these occasions, and pour two glasses.

Then, wine in hand, I sit on the ottoman across from her. I'm lost in those big bright green eyes, denser and richer than any cedar forest. Lost and waiting.

"You're not here to shoot the breeze. Why?"

She takes a sip and gently clears her throat. "So, I'm sorry for blowing in like this again, but –"

"You didn't have a choice," I finish for her. If we're able to keep this brief, maybe there's a chance being alone with this woman in my own house won't end in a fucking disaster. Or a disastrous fuck.

"What's Jace done this time?"

She blinks, turns away, as if she can't believe we're hung up on her idiot brother again. "He's coming after you. I think."

I soften my stare. "You don't sound very sure. Long trip here on guesswork, Precious."

"No. I mean, we've lost track of him, Trent. He spent a solid week trying to put out the fires you'd set. He moved out of our parents' house, said he'd found a place near Tacoma, but dad told me that's BS. I waited a few days, tried to find your number, but you're not exactly the world's most accessible."

I smile, swallowing a sip of burgundy sweetness. "True. I like my privacy. It's also more than a little necessary when your net worth's as big as small countries. You know how many lotto winners and celebrities hire permanent body guards?" She shakes her head, tempting my eyes down to the subtle low cut in her purple sweater. "You should've taken the hint, Presh. We did what we had to in Seattle: move on. Remember?"

Her lips twist sourly. "Sure, about as well as *you* recall how to stop being a dick when I'm trying to help."

Touche. "Well, I'm touched you'd come all the way out here just to check in on me." I cross my heart, smirking the whole time. That wins me a green-eyed glare. Good. "But in case you hadn't noticed, I'm a big boy. I've built billion dollar companies. Kept myself out of prison, framed for the shit I never did, and came crawling back to the scene of the crime years later to set it right. If I'd wanted, I could've buried your fuck of a brother alive."

She's not impressed. Even if she knows it's true.

Presh shifts on the couch, draining half her wine, searching for words. Her legs uncross and then merge together again, hounding my gaze to her thighs.

Don't look. Don't let her tempt you. Don't be an idiot.

"Yet you didn't," she says matter-of-factly. "You let him go without a knockout. You hit him with scandals that were bound to blow up sooner or later on their own. Why didn't you finish the job?"

Goddamn, her mouth. Legs, too. She just had to show up in a secretary skirt, didn't she?

She's dressed like something out of Alice in Wonderland, if Lewis Carroll did erotica. Shy low heels, pale long legs crawling up her skirt, Cheshire cat colored sweater. My cock throbs, drunk on need and the wine's warmth flooding my veins.

I shake my head, trying to find my senses.

"Way you're talking, almost sounds like you *want* me to put him away." I try to look her in the eye without lust clouding my judgment. What the ever living fuck is she actually doing here if she hasn't come to torture me? "That can't be right. That's not the Amy Kay I know. She'd never flip on kin."

"I want him out of trouble, Trent. For good. If that means prison, hopefully something light..." She sighs, looking down at her wine. Then she closes her eyes, opening them again, sadder than before.

"No, forget it. I don't want him behind bars, either. Unless it's all that keeps him from hurting himself or others. I got my hopes up after I figured out what you were really doing." She sighs, flipping her hair.

"Wish he'd listened. Hoped like hell he'd *finally* get the message after the bloody nose you gave him. But he read your note the morning you left. He barely missed you at the hotel, after you'd checked out. Every day he's not here messing with you is just a delay. Not because he's changed his mind. He's out there, scheming, drunk on bad blood."

Speaking of drunk...I can't handle this shit sober. Especially not this subject, while every inch of her teases my cock.

Standing, I take her glass, and walk over for refills, mulling the wolf who's coming after me. Hiding my anger and the bulge in my pants are top priority, too.

I'm also pissed the rat bastard found the note I'd left

for her parents' eyes only. I push down the urge to smash the almost empty bottle against the wall.

"Look, you can't control a coward prick. Whatever he decides is on him. Not you. Not your family. You tried, Presh, like any sister should." I pass her a fresh glass, downing half of mine in one gulp.

"You've also got a life. The night I paid you a visit through your window, I meant to put this behind us for good. Meant it so fucking much a funny thing happened the next morning – I decided to let Jace go, Amy Kay."

She blinks, surprise on her face. "You...what?"

"That's why I left. Why I came home. Decided I'd forget screwing with Jace, and get on with life. I did what I needed all along: got it off my chest. Told you and your folks what really happened, who Jace is, and that's enough. Confession should be plenty. Even if the prick managed to burn mine before it reached your parents."

"Yeah, about that..." She sighs, setting her glass on the end table before she looks up. "Jace dirtied it up, but I kept your note. I just...couldn't bring myself to break the news. Not yet. Dad doesn't need the stress. And mom? It could kill her."

Fuck. Who's side is she really on?

I take the last of my wine in one sip, then slam my glass down next to hers on the wooden surface so loud the crystal squeals. "Bad move, Presh. I wrote that thing to put this to bed. Thought we had an understanding."

"Oh?" Her eyes are bigger, brighter, worried. They don't deter the need to spell out what the hell I wanted, what I *needed* to happen in Seattle.

"Don't you get it? I needed to come clean, woman. Don't tell me you're perfectly okay with your folks thinking I'm the drug slinging prick who crashed your car and cost your old man a Senate seat?" My words are hoarse, angry.

I step closer, take her chin with two fingers, making her look at me. Then I see the storm in her eyes and my asshole rage withers.

"He's my brother, Trent. My screwed up, impulsive, morally bankrupt, pants-on-head stupid brother." Her eyes are defiant, unflinching. "I want the truth to come out just as bad as you do. But it needs to be timed right. We've all suffered enough. And right now, I'm hoping we won't just suffer more. I'm scared Jace will make us."

She's not lying. Or wrong. Or numb to this hell.

The tremor on her lips barely hides the fear, her heart splayed wide, weeping for me and Jace alike.

I pace across the room, fists like boulders at my sides, turning around again once I reach the mantle.

"He's family. I get it, Presh. Hell, I was done hurting him the second I left, just like I told you. Jace was like family to me once, too, forever ago. Setting his life on fire didn't give me half the satisfaction I found just sitting on the floor next to you, telling my story." I stand taller, watching her slide off the couch and do the same. She studies me, wanting to come closer, but not knowing if she should.

"Trent..."

"No. This crap's partly my fault, but I'll always pin the biggest blame on the reckless fuck who used to be my friend." Our eyes are magnets and I hate it.

Longer I stare, losing myself in her soft green madness all over again, the harder it is not to make this about us, rather than the threat hanging over our heads. "All this time, after he screwed me over, I thought I'd sleep easy just watching him burn."

A cold smile pulls at her lips. She sees the crack in my armor, the way I try to look away, poison spilling out and thickening the atmosphere. Her heels click across amber Brazil wood until she's so close every part of me goes rigid – especially the last part in the world I should obey. "But that wasn't what you needed. Not deep down."

"No," I admit.

Don't fucking look at her, I tell myself, a last ditch warning.

Who am I kidding?

Next time we lock eyes, I take her hands, clasping them to my chest.

She's all kinds of beautiful here. All kinds of wrong.

Invading a world that was always meant to be Precious-free. Maybe that's why her chestnut hair glows with the same seductive sheen in her eyes. She's already taking the fuck over, occupying the very air I'm breathing.

"Trent?" she whispers my name, forcing my eyes to her small pink lips.

My dick hammers so hard I think it'll make me pass the fuck out.

"I needed to clear my name. Needed the truth. Needed..." I stop just short of the obvious, what's right in front of me. "You're killing me, Precious. Fair warning. Last chance to call another cab and walk your sweet ass out."

She doesn't move an inch. I can't either.

There's nothing else to say. Not with any words.

Not when I wrap my arms around her waist, pull her body to mine, and give in to the only thing that makes sense tonight. Only thing we've ached for since this psycho universe reunited us on a broken down elevator.

My lips attack hers like a starving animal. That's what she's made me. I've become the wolf branded on my skin. A desperate, battered, single-minded beast.

My sole purpose isn't to talk this out or stop her brother. That's a million miles away.

Tonight, it's to strip her naked and cart her off to bed.

To let fencing tongues and swinging hips figure out what our brains can't.

To let flesh speak what souls keep trying to get out, and can't through our lips.

Not without them falling all over each other, unchained, free to suck and kiss and lick until we scream.

What we've started here can't be stopped.

My hands snake down the small of her back, hug her hips, and then strike lower. I cup her ass and squeeze, swallowing the moan she purrs in my mouth.

Fire floods my balls. My legs move automatically and I sweep her up, ferrying us across the room until she's against the wall.

Our mouths speak in silent kisses. No more words. Just teeth that pull, tongues that chase, half-hooded eyes that meld whenever we stop for a second to breathe.

Oh, fuck, her breath.

It's shaky, intense, and tells me she's beyond ready to have her hair in my fist and my full cock buried to the hilt. I'm rock hard, pulsing in my pants, my balls promising hell every second I'm not in her.

"Not yet," I bite off, shoving her skirt up her legs, giving the bulge in my trousers the perfect access to her soaked panties. My hips roll against hers, a vicious friction, so damn ready to be in her but not before she begs. "You come for me first. You come hard like I remember. Like I've wanted for six fucking years, Amy Kay, and then we'll move upstairs. You come beautiful with your lips on fire, leaking all over me, lungs pumping overdrive. You come so fucking hard you lose your mind. You come so fucking hard your pussy feels this dick before I'm even in you."

She lets out a wicked groan. Poor girl.

She doesn't understand how serious I am until I dry hump her again, this time harder, pinning her to the wall. I know her clit catches somewhere because this time she whimpers, folds in on herself, too lost for words. Drowning in the same insanity that's consumed me.

"Trent, shit. You want me to – *ohh! Oh.*"

Oh, yes.

O.

I sandwich her more against the wall, thrusting harder, a manic grunting need steaming through my teeth. She eases into me, pushing back. We dry fuck just like that for God only knows how long. I snarl my satisfaction once I see her sweet eyes roll.

It doesn't take long.

Her body gives up without a fight that can't last more than a few scorching minutes.

Amy Kay digs her fingernails into my back so fucking hard it hurts. Just makes me go faster, harder, bringing her over the edge. She gives me a shrill, whiny scream as her pussy convulses.

"Do it!" I throw one hand between her legs, shoving aside her panties, hearing something rip. I'll buy her whatever the fuck she wants in the morning. Something lacy and delicate and just as ready to be destroyed.

Tonight, she won't need a fresh pair. Everything between her legs belongs to me.

Her body knows it. That's why it thrashes, seizes deliciously against mine.

I find her clit and press hard while she starts coming. It brings her off hard, makes her swiftly, completely, furiously mine.

"Don't. Fucking. Stop." I tell her, frigging her swollen nub.

She whimpers louder. I feel her nipples through several layers, aching to be sucked soft. We'll get to that in a bit.

Right now, I shove my fingers in her, finding the trigger point that makes her come more.

Sweet fuck, I missed this pussy. This tight silk clenching my fingers, teasing my dick without even touching it.

Missed her teeth digging into my lip. Missed her trying like hell to stay conscious while her body jerks and twitches. Missed owning her into the next life with my fingers.

Missed this beautiful woman.

I let her feet touch the ground again after she fully opens her eyes. She's lost both heels – heard them hitting the floor behind me more than a minute ago – and I'm glad. One less thing to remove.

I don't give her time to speak, to have any second thoughts. I need to get every molten drop in my balls into her, and I need to do it soon.

She watches my fingers, still drenched in her sweetness, rising to my lips. I suck them slow, then we kiss again. My tongue reminds her the night's young, and she's still very wet.

She practically leaps into my arms the second I throw her over my shoulder.

Upstairs we go, my dick pounding like mad in my trousers. Her pussy so ready for more she grinds on my thigh. I'm barely up the staircase before more greedy kisses hit my lips, every little movement of her tongue screaming *fuck me.*

Six years. That's not a dry spell, it's a goddamn desert. Half a hellacious decade without the only woman in my bed who's left me wanting her there in the morning.

Oh, Precious.

Presh.

Fuck.

So much time to make up. So few hours in the night. So many we'll make count.

We'll kindle fire in every breathless whimper between feral kisses.

Every slap of my body on hers.

Every savage O I pull out of her.

Every bearish load she wrings from my balls.

I practically cave in the door to my bedroom, kicking it aside, throwing her on the bed.

My hands go to work on her clothes. Every time I imagined this moment, waking up hard in a cold sweat, I thought I'd take my sweet time.

Now, I know I'd be insane losing another second without her naked perfection.

"Precious," I whisper, devouring her mouth again, touching my forehead to hers.

My hand slides up her sweater, jerks it over her head, revealing her black lace bra. Her tits are magnets for my hands. She gives me a sly look, pops the clasp, freeing them.

One look at her nipples, aching for my mouth, and I'm gone.

Her back arches, a moan escapes her mouth, and her tits meet my mouth. Tasting her pink after all these years makes me more animal than man.

I suck. Lick. Pull. Stroke every tender end of her in growls, teasing as I go, enjoying it now before I can't resist the urge to suck her hard.

When I do, her moans deepen. She goes down squirming, grinding her hips into mine, but I'm in control.

I yank off her skirt as I kiss trails down her soft, sweet skin. I know her pussy's pulsing and wet before my face even reaches it. I take my time, breathing hot and deep against her folds, sweeping a single lick through them.

"Trent!" My name. Again.

A curse and an object of worship in one.

My tongue flicks, this time harder, pulling her tight cunt open. Her taste, her scent, her everything leaves scorch marks on my brain.

She's burning me the fuck down and all I can do is grab onto her hips, shove her legs apart, and eat her like no tomorrow.

Like the last six years never happened.

Like I always knew I'd fuck her velvet with my tongue and leave her shuddering, still attached to my face, whining and begging and desperate for more.

Like this pussy is divine, and divine because it's mine, and mine because it's so close to coming on my face.

Pleasure hits fast once I go to work. Her clit smolders against my tongue. Twitches, throbs, and stiffens, a willing prisoner. I move my head, adding my stubble's friction, a low thunder in my throat that vibrates to her core.

"Trent. Oh. Jesus."

Come for me, darling girl. Come like you haven't for years. Come on the face you can't decide if you want to smash to pieces, or kiss like it's the end of the world.

"Trent!" Her little cry rings shriller.

My cue to bring her over.

So I do.

Her fingers scratch, dig, try to mark my shoulders through my shirt. Fuck, I hope she does it again later, puts lines down my back while I'm fucking her ten times harder than this tongue can.

Her hips go insane against my face. I have to hold her down, licking harder, kissing and tongue-fucking her to Heaven and then guiding her back again.

Perfection.

She's still gasping for air as I let her drift into the pillows again. If she didn't need to stop for breath and recover her wits, once the maelstrom I've kicked up in her body is done, I'd shove my cock inside her. Make her scream twice as loud.

Finish with a rogue message my tongue can never say, not in full, and then fuck her like we've been apart for a thousand years.

But she needs a minute. Maybe I do, too.

I let up. Relent. Crawl backwards off the bed, and start freeing my body from the prison of these clothes.

Presh opens her eyes halfway through me undressing.

I turn, pumping my cock in my fist. Once is all it takes to see the sexiest sight ever.

That's my woman, sprawled out and naked and waiting to be ravished.

That's the excitement in her lush green eyes.

That's her plush lips falling open, drunk on the memory of our first and only time, plus six years of waiting for *this.*

"Legs open, darling," I tell her, climbing onto the bed again.

Presh complies. I take an ankle in each hand, press them against my shoulders, laying my throbbing length against her opening.

She squirms beautifully the instant my swollen head taps her clit. I do it a few more times, forcing the sweetness from her lungs, the soft gasp that lets me know how bad she wants this.

"All those fucking years," I whisper, stopping to taste her lips. We're eye to eye and I'm so fucking ready to be in her it physically hurts. "We lost a lot of time, Amy Kay."

"Don't remind me," she whimpers. Her little eyes shimmer as I tease her cunt again, grinding my dick into her. "God, Trent. I need –"

"You need more than this wild cock and the man attached to it, darling," I say, forehead burning against hers. "You need to fuck exactly like you've thought about for the last six years. Fucked so hard you forget the bad, the past, and the reason we're even here, tangled up together."

"Yes!"

"Baby, I'm not done," I growl, crushing my lips on hers. My balls are about to go up in flames any second, but damn, I need to get this out. "Tonight, we're fucking like our very lives depend on it because maybe they do. Maybe if I fuck you hard enough and long enough and deep enough, Presh, knowing your pussy's tight as the last time we did this and wet for me, wet because it's *mine*, then maybe we'll finally figure out how we move the fuck on. Maybe we figure out a lot. Because just between you and me, no matter how much I say it, I still don't know how to do that."

I hear her swallow. Hard. Lust soaked heavy with tears.

"I just know one thing: I want you like the air in my lungs and the ache in my pulse. Want you like I've never wanted anyone or anything, Precious, because nothing ever did compare to Amy Kay. And once you come on me a few times and I pour myself in you, I've got a real wicked feeling more of this, more of us, is all I'll ever want."

She opens her mouth to say something, but what comes out is a gasp.

Perfectly timed. I push into her, baring my teeth, electric pleasure igniting across my brain.

Fuck, she feels good. She feels amazing. She feels better than anything I guiltily pulled myself off to these last six years apart.

"Trent," she whimpers, still trying to talk.

I don't let her.

We've both said too much. So I just take her mouth instead, driving into her harder, shaking her from head-to-toe.

Her tight little pussy sucks me in so deep, so sweet, it'll be hard as hell not to blow.

Maybe that's what causes me to fuck her harder. Faster. But I think I'd have my whole soul in this fuck anyway because it's *her*.

Truly, beautifully, finally Amy Kay Chenocott.

I throw my hips into hers, holding her legs to my waist for leverage. Her sharp moans become a fevered whimper. Her pussy constricts, tighter and wetter and so damn maddening on all of me.

I send her over the edge, savoring every scream, marveling how hot she comes for me.

Amazed because it's even better than that first time an eternity ago.

Her body hitches, shaking harder as she comes down from it. Her O leaves her in a ruin that turns my dick to diamond. I bore into her, a growl coming unstuck in my throat, fucking my darkest dreams into every inch of her flesh.

"Hurry the hell up," I whisper, running my hand up her leg, throwing my balls against her ass, doubling my speed. "Presh, come with me."

"It's too soon. I don't know if –"

"Presh! Come on this cock. I know you've got it in you, and I want your pussy sucking me dry when I go." The sparkle in her eyes tells me there's another O in her.

I'll find it. Fuck it right out of her. Bring her crashing over the edge even sweeter than before because she'll see I'm right about her body.

I know her too well. Know how to make her flesh do miracles.

Leaning, I press my mouth to hers, chasing her tongue. When I catch it, the way we stroke tells her how serious I am.

How much, how serious, how fucking soon I need this.
Come, Precious.

My hips glide back and impact hers, all my might thrown in my hips. I deepen my strokes, making sure my pubic bone hits her clit. I swallow every moan spilling out of her and growl my need back.

Then the fever rises in her body: the ache, the desire, the need she swore wasn't there. Her little hands curl around my neck, nails drag down my back, and her breath catches like she's kissed paradise.

No more.

"Precious, fuck, coming!" I bite down on her shoulder, kissing and teething her skin while I slam myself deep.

Her legs buckle against me. Her eyes fly open. And then she's just gone.

Two of us melting into one.

Hearts, minds, bodies, souls.

Hot magma pumps up my shaft and fire bathes my spine. I'm in a cauldron of ecstasy and she's there with me, her pussy milking every inch of me.

Too much.

Too fast.

Too. Fucking. Good.

And that's the understatement of my lifetime because I've never – ever – felt anything like this.

My whole body buckles. Still thrusting. Still flooding her womb.

My eyes grind shut, softly opening after my raging dick finally weakens. I release her shoulder, kissing trails away from the place where I've marked her, not yet going soft.

"Look at me, darling," I say, tipping her face up with a finger under her chin.

"That was –"

"Earth shattering." I finish for her, but what I'm really interested in are her eyes.

They're bright. On fire.

So completely stuck on me, I think the worst really is behind us.

But fuck thinking, too.

This the moment I start believing.

Next time I dip my face to hers, I take her mouth nice and slow. Savoring her taste, her tongue, the subtle tremor in her lips.

I have her completely, without worrying about the psycho who might be after me or the mess we're still in.

I take her like the man I've always been – her lover – and I'm finally home.

"You're stunning as hell when you come, Presh." I smile.

She smiles back like it's no big surprise. Little minx.

Damn, my dick twitches inside her, hard as it was a few minutes ago, before I came my brains out.

"Beautiful, you said. Just like before. We came beautiful. Remember?"

I do. But it's also not quite right.

"Sure, Precious. That's not the reason why I'm about to flip you over and go at it again, though." I pause, watching the surprise light her eyes. "We were too young then. Too innocent. Too soft to appreciate this kind of rapture. We didn't have to fight for it before. We had each other, but we didn't. Not like now."

She's beaming, pulling herself into me, cutting me off

with a kiss. I know a woman who can't stand waiting another hot second. Especially when her lips work mine like *this* delicious torture.

My cock stiffens inside her again. I might be serious about the second round, without even taking a breather.

"Don't say it," she says softly, brushing her lips against mine once more, as if to stop me from jinxing the spell. "I just want to enjoy tonight. You, me, us."

My eyes bore through hers. There's too much bleeding out of her and it's too damn obvious. It's too much hurt, too much fear. Too many questions, wondering if I'll fade as the sun comes up, leaving her heart in tatters with a sore ache between her legs.

"You're so wrong," I growl, bringing my lips to hers, fisting her hair, pulling her into me. "This time it's different, Amy Kay. You'll see. Won't even let you see different. Right after your vision gets over the next three Os I burn through that sweet pussy tonight."

If this wasn't the time to shut up, I don't think I'd have much choice. The blinding fury building in my balls peaks, calling me to shift her over. I put her on all fours, loving how she moans, taking my time to admire her ass.

It's just as full and lush as I remember. Perfectly shaped. Dangerously inviting.

It's been years since I had an ass like this to grab. Far too fucking many.

That's the only coherent thought on my mind once I'm in her, crashing in from behind, swinging my balls smack at her clit. I fill her with a growl in my throat, loving how she shakes, ripples, comes apart.

Sweet chaos.

Just like this delicate, unspeakable thing between us.

Like the promise I just made, to make this time different, something I never thought I'd admit before she showed up on my doorstep.

But that's not quite true.

It was something I was already working on, bleeding on the paper in my office, using the same silver pen I used to sign every multimillion dollar deal for Cryptic.

This chaos is ours to embrace. Ours, and nobody else's.

Clean, orderly love never stood a chance.

Not with how I'm fucking her now, driving to the hilt, my fingers digging into her ass. I reach up, grabbing her hair again, jerking it a little tighter as her body arches, gasps, and falls so closer to –

Fuck!

For a second, I think Portland's being hammered with a moody spring storm. What seems like rain is actually my own pulse.

Her pussy convulses, my thrusts hitch faster, and I'm matching her O, pouring myself in her all over again. I come deep and hard and feral, roaring my pleasure through pinched teeth, hammering her to the mattress like the imaginary storm behind my eyes.

So, this is what it's like to fuck with my all.

I don't know what comes tomorrow. Neither of us do. I mean to leave us so spent when I'm finally done we both hit the pillows face first and don't move till morning.

Whatever it is, it's got to be right and it's got to be heavy.

If this is what moving on looks like, feels like, tastes like, then I might just move the whole damn universe to keep this woman forever.

XIII: THE OTHER SIDE (AMY KAY)

I wake up with the mellow sun in my eyes. It filters softly through the venetian blinds, landing on the empty spot next to me on this enormous bed.

I sit up, heart pounding. Am I actually awake? Or is this another nightmare?

No, not this time.

Trent hasn't left me. I hear water hissing in the bathroom attached. A shower running. Probably him cleaning up after last night.

Jesus, and what a night.

The instant I stand up, I feel it in my bones, and smile. I haven't had sex like that since...well, ever.

I'd also be a fool to pretend it's just the dull throb he's left between my legs. Or the soreness in muscles that haven't had that kind of workout for a good long while. It's the passion, the heat, the way he held me to his chest after we'd finished, kissing me to sleep.

Mud runs have nothing on sex with this man.

It's him, the boy I told myself for half a decade I'd lost, and that I had to get over.

Move on, just like he said.

If moving on looks like this, then I'm ready to run at it head-on.

My stomach growls. Breakfast sounds nice. Even better if I'm able to find something in the kitchen to whip up for us both.

I throw on my robe and creep quietly out of the bedroom while he's still busy cleaning up.

His home is predictably enormous. A penthouse, supposedly, the kind of sleek, ultra-modern place a powerful CEO who's short on time and long on obligations ought to have. The size rivals my parents' house, though, even if it doesn't have all the custom amenities or the acreage.

Downtown Portland's view over the Columbia stops my heart. I catch it walking past his office, all sprawling bookshelves and windows, vast skylights overhead bringing in the light. I stop, turn, and look around.

At first, my eyes are fixed on the amazing landscape behind the glass, but then I see something on his desk. A black leather journal, still open, a thick silver pen thrown across it.

My feet move faster than my brain. I really shouldn't be in here, snooping, but when I see my name in black ink, there's no stopping it.

I pick up the journal and read:

Precious Amy Kay,

I'M IN HELL. Congratulations. You put me there six years ago when I couldn't come back.

Spent them all torturing myself.

I tried to deny it. Tried to blame you. Then I tried pinning it all on fucked up circumstance.

That elevator ride changed everything. More than when we smoothed things over later, even, that night in your room.

Lying was like gouging out my eyes, cutting out my tongue, stuffing my soul in a permanent hell.

Back in it, I should say.

I've tried to convince myself the worst was over for six fucking years. Swore up and down if it wasn't, then I'd make damn sure that changed after coming back, carpet bombing Jace, settling accounts.

I did all that.

It didn't do shit.

Pouring my heart out to you convinced me I didn't need to spend another night in Seattle to finish driving my vendetta through your brother's heart. I made my confession to you and left the note for your folks. I walked away.

I moved on one more time.

Trouble is, that trip showed me what I was really missing all these years, the reason I tried so hard to convince myself I wasn't stuck in a sea of flames.

You, Presh.

Entirely you.

You damned me to hell a long time ago. And I went just like you wanted. You put me there.

That's the lie I told myself, anyway, but I know the real reason why I've been there for so long.

Me, Presh.

All me.

I did it the second I walked away, all those years ago, and took too many fucking years to make things right.

I still haven't finished. Not like I want.

"Move on," I keep saying.

Now I know they're the emptiest words in the universe.

You proved it. You showed me how worthless those two words really are.

Because I can't walk away a second time.

Because I haven't been able to pry you out of my head the past two weeks I've been home.

Because maybe moving on is pure bullshit.

Maybe there's no moving on, no walking away, no going anywhere.

Not without you.

T

"Found what you need?"

I look up and almost jump out of my skin. Trent stands there in nothing but a towel, his gorgeous inked arms plush at his sides, eyeing me up and down.

"Oh, crap. I didn't mean...I mean I..."

"Precious, relax." He steps closer and then just keeps coming. Not stopping until I'm enveloped in his broad shoulders, where everything always seems to be okay. "Should've put that damn thing away. Shouldn't have left it out in the open."

"Trent, no. I read every word. It's beautiful."

"It's something that was never meant for your eyes. Therapy, really." His blue eyes flash like lightning.

He tries to kiss me, but I move my head away. "Come on. You're telling me you wouldn't have sent it?"

"No," he barks. His grip on me tightens and amusement lights his gorgeous face. "I'd have delivered it in person. Probably next weekend, if you hadn't made your way here."

"Ass!" He certainly is, but it doesn't keep my mouth off him.

I kiss him with the full might and fury of a woman thoroughly confused.

Not wanting to admit the same dormant love in my heart is alive again, singing in my soul, bending my lips to his today and forever, if we really can *move on* together.

"I'm sorry for last night. The other week, actually. I need to call dad, tell him exactly what was in that note Jace crumpled up, which I stupidly hid."

"Not yet." He pulls me closer. "Wait, Presh. If Jace thinks he's safe at home, he just might give up his hypothetical chase and show up there again."

I bite my bottom lip. "I hope you're right." *But I doubt it.*

"Bullshit. Let this play itself out," he says, as if he can read my mind. "After we've talked your brother down from trying to screw us over, or fuck his own life even harder, we'll have all the time in the world to come clean. Your folks think I'm a monster, don't forget. In their eyes, I did a lot of fucking damage, and I'm still doing it to their son."

My heart sinks. Hearing it like that spells out just how complicated this really is.

"Look at me," he says, as soon as my eyes drop. Then his hand is on my face and excitement flaps in my heart and there's no choice but to listen. There never really is once his eyes devour mine. "We'll sort this shit out if it's the last thing we do."

"We?"

He gives a solemn nod. I think I'm floating. I wanted so badly to believe him last night, when he said it'd be different this time. Now, hearing it, seeing it, I'm starting to.

"You and me, Presh. Just like it should be." He pushes his forehead to mine, bathing my lips with his soft, warm breath. "But first, I have to say, I'm not exactly a fan of waiting around and letting your crazy-ass brother show up here." He waits for me to look up. "I was planning to get away before I sent that letter. Head out to Lincoln City for a few days and clear my head. I'd still love to, matter of fact, the second I hear you're coming with."

My heart stops. I want to so bad, but the frown tugging at my lips says different.

"Precious, what's wrong?" his hand captures my cheek.

"It's just...my business. I need to be back in Spokane sometime this century. We'll be into planning for the third quarter soon. Also, I think my phone will die next time I open my corporate inbox. There's a billion messages I haven't answered."

"What you need, Amy Kay, is to do that shit some place you can breathe. Preferably after I've fucked that stress right out of you."

I let go of the sigh I'm holding in. This gorgeous devil knows my every weakness way too well. "Okay, fine. But I'm bringing my work. We *can't* spend all day on the beaches. And the second I hear Jace is home, crazy or sober, I'm giving mom and dad a full briefing."

Grabbing my hand, he pulls it to his chest, and then drops it lower to his waist. I gasp as the towel falls.

It's incredible, really, how easily this man makes me feel like a lust-struck schoolgirl again.

"Wouldn't have it any other way, darling. Remember that *we* part? And remember how Trent Usher doesn't fuck around?" I do.

God, do I ever.

"Seems we've also got ourselves a nice hard desk here. I know these robes get awfully claustrophobic the longer you wear them. Let me help."

His hand swats mine away, pulls on my belt, and soon my robe joins his towel on the floor.

Trent helps all kinds of things then with his fingers, his tongue, and the rock hard part of him that's very good at making me forget every adult responsibility I'm supposed to have as a business owner in her mid-twenties.

Beneath him, being fucked into this desk, I'm just Amy Kay.

I'm Precious.

I'm alive.

Folding my hands around his inked shoulders, I dig my legs into his magnificent ass, enjoying the storm he thrusts into me.

It's not long – barely a few minutes – before I cry out and feel his searing heat filling me again.

* * *

"Holy shit – out *here*?" I'm trying to bat his hand away

for the third time in the last hour. "Not the beach! I told you –"

"Darling, it's mine. Got more than a mile going up and down the shore the whole weekend. Money rents a lot of privacy. Plus I think I'd really like to ruin this awesome view with your tits in my face."

So far, he's been patient. But there's only so much self-control a man like Trent Usher can grasp on an isolated stretch of pristine Oregon beach. Alone. With me.

Especially after we've had a few drinks and I've been curled up on his lap for the better part of an hour.

He isn't the only one fighting for composure. I've let my mouth wander to his neck a few times, shamefully tempted by the evil heat between my thighs.

"I've never done anything like this. Out in the open. With you." Why can't I speak in normal sentences? The second I shift on his lap, feeling the massive bulge against my thigh, it all makes sense. "You're *sure* there's nobody else around?"

"Certain, Presh," he rumbles, squeezing my hips, pulling me closer. "And if I'm wrong, so the fuck what? I'm way past caring if the whole world hears us. Time to live a little. Make up for all the living we lost apart."

He's insane.

But I can't even protest as he pushes his face to mine, melting my lips on his, winning a moan from my throat. It's evening, the sun slipping behind the Pacific. The breeze blows off the waves, serenading our skin just on the right side of chilly.

If not now, when?

When will it ever be this perfect?

I don't know, but perfect is starting to feel like the norm for the three days we've been out here. The little house he's rented next to the shore is simpler than I expect considering his billions and his sophisticated tastes.

But it does seem isolated, like he said.

It's also got everything we need. Which isn't much when we spend our days hiking, taking in the view of the rocky coasts and winding through the soft sands, me pretending to work while he whips up some honestly impressive dinners.

I don't know where Trent learned to cook, but it's one more arrow in my heart. And right now, with his hands busy stripping me naked, there are *plenty* of those making me a fool. A happy, thankful, full-hearted fool.

He lifts me off him gently, a vicious glint in his eye, pushing me down to his knees. He pulls my hands to his swimming trunks, the only scrap of clothing between me and every awesome inch of him.

"Know how you said you wanted to suck me to the stars the other night? And I wouldn't let you because I was too busy buried in your sweet cunt?"

Relentless heat reddens my cheeks. I nod slowly. I do.

"Here's your chance, Presh. Suck. Suck me as long and hard as you want." That's the only warning I get before his hands move mine, freeing his gorgeous cock in its fury.

"Suck," he says again, winding his fingers through my hair.

It's an order I'm happy to follow. But not before I have my fun.

My tongue flicks out, teasing his tip, then melts into a rush of air. His eyes sharpen, fury igniting, and his fingers nest my hair in a fist. "Fuck, Amy Kay, you're killing me."

"Not yet." I run my hand up his cock, admiring his strength, his warmth, flicking my tongue at the end of him again.

He groans, tries to grind into me, but I'm able to crane my head back, just out of reach.

Trent's eyes are delirious now. It's the same look I saw on the Wilkie. The same in the elevator.

The very same when he's on top of me, driving me into the mattress. The same raging, wanting, *shut up and let me love you* beast-gaze.

My pussy tingles. Every second, every tease, it's harder to resist plunging my mouth down, taking his fullness.

Somehow, I try.

"Presh," he growls again, an edge in his voice.

I flatten my hands against his muscular thighs, pinning him down in vain, then flash my sweetest smile. "What's the rush? This is our private beach. Nice and isolated. Remember?"

"Precious, fuck." No more, the anger in his face says.

I suppose he's suffered enough.

I give his cock another squeeze near the base, loving how his pre-come spills over his fullness, and then he's engulfed in my lips. His rigid cock fills my mouth.

His hips arch, lifting into me. A sound escapes his throat like a growl trying to mask a helpless curse, and I smile, even while I'm full of him.

It's so on.

I run my tongue down his gorgeous length. Deep as I can without gagging, then up again, ringing my lips together. Tighter.

This is how I get Trent Usher back for the last six years apart.

This is how I say, never again.

This is how I make him let go of his control, his strongman balance, his relentless need to remind me how easily I'm brought to my knees.

So, I'm addicted to him. I won't deny it.

But if that's the scary truth, there's no way he's getting off without being an equal slave. Drawn to my flesh and all the beautiful, filthy things it can do to him.

My tongue goes to work, loving his taste, his heat, how he seethes in my mouth. I find the spot underneath his cock – the one that makes him twitch – and give it a furious licking.

"Precious!" he growls again, adding his second hand to the side of my face.

I'm caught between two big paws, rhythmically scaling him with my mouth. His whole body tenses, pulls at my hair, lifts off the cabana chair. I rear up, sucking at his head, begging him to blow.

"Presh, fuck, I'm gonna –"

It's my final warning. Like he doesn't know I won't swallow.

His cock erupts a second later, filling my mouth with rich fire. I wring his shaft with my tongue, taking as good as he gives.

It's hot, it's intense, and he's so mine.

There's a steady fever in my extremities as I swallow him down. My nipples, my fingers, my toes, my pussy...a dull throb owns them. It's darker by the second as the sun slips beneath the horizon, but my skin knows a heat like the sun.

Even when I'm full of him, I still want more.

His head falls back. He's groaning, snarling my name

between his teeth, lost in the storm I've kissed into his body from the cock up.

He comes for what seems like forever, pouring his essence into me. I suck him until his cock stops jerking against my tongue and softens ever-so-slightly.

"All better?" I kiss his tip again.

"Halfway there. Give me another thirty seconds with that mouth, darling. Then it's you on my lap, riding me for all you're worth."

Oh. My. God.

I didn't know men like him really existed. Men who can just keep going several times, barely getting soft between rounds, but then there's never been a man like Trent in my life.

And there'll never be another.

His want mirrors mine. Precise and perfect.

I recognize his growl like the beat of my own heart once my mouth pulls at him again. It's familiar because it ripples, vibrating the same raw heat that clashes through my veins at every glance. I know *that* look when he tilts his head, staring through half-hooded blue eyes, a beautifully perfect mirror of how I've seen my own eyes reflected back in his shining pools.

This is where we belong. Entranced in each other. In this love that's been aged by a whirling, heart-dizzy madness.

"Presh?" he calls to me and I open my eyes. His hand pulls at my hair, harder than before, lifting me up. "Come the fuck here."

Then his hands are on me. A powerful Goliath hoisting me high, swinging my legs neatly across his. I'm in his lap. My pussy slides onto his cock and I choke out a moan.

I was so damn ready, the line between pleasure and agony blurring the second I'm on him.

Then it's just gone as his hands clench my ass, pulling me lower, another animal sound escaping his throat. "You want that O bad, precious girl?"

I can't speak. I just whine a close approximation of *yes*, moving my hips into his, drawing him deep inside me every time. His bastard force holds back, letting me work, shifting on top of him faster and faster. I put my hands on his shoulders, lean down, until we're eye-to-eye.

"Fuck me, Trent. Please."

His fingers dig into my ass. "You ride this cock. Give me your first O if you want to keep screaming real sweet through your second."

God.

Yes.

Please.

My eyelids shudder. Every conscious thought melts in the blinding speed I throttle my body into his, impaled on his cock, fucking and grinding and hurling myself toward unholy release.

"Harder, woman," he growls, white-knuckling my ass. "I know you can fuck faster, harder, better than this. Give it to me real fucking good, and you'll get it like a god."

His body stiffens against mine. His stubble rakes the nook between my neck and my cleavage. One more tantalizing sensation my burning brain can't process.

He knows what he's doing.

Overloading. Overwhelming. Overtaking.

Tearing me in two, a human wall, giving as good as I

give. Making me work for it like a mad woman. He's my rock, my mountain to climb.

I'm panting as the realization hits me. Not for long. The pleasure cresting in my core destroys my ability to realize anything at all.

Except the shrill mewl escaping my throat.

Except my fingernails raking at his skin. Clawing, tearing, holding on for dear life before I'm swept away.

Except for the roar of the ocean behind me, devouring the sun, plunging us into an ecstasy indistinguishable from a storm-front forged in flesh.

"Give it, Presh. Give it to me now." He reaches with one hand, grabs at my hair, pulling my face to his. "Right. The. Fuck. *Now.*"

I don't know if it's the princely look in his eyes or the way he slams his cock into me a second later.

I don't know anything.

I just go crashing over, screaming, pinching his shoulders so hard it hurts.

I'm coming harder than I ever have in my life.

Every nerve, every muscle, every sea-kissed stretch of my being turns to lightning. It turns to the sun, the moon, and the stars, and then to things I can't even describe.

A feral woman. Lost and broke and helplessly addicted to this man slamming into me, a guttural breath on his lips, a curse every few thrusts as my pussy convulses on his thrusts.

He fucks me straight through my first O without missing a beat.

Never stopping until we both feel the strange, sticky heat between us. For a second, I wonder if he came, but

I've felt his glorious heat in me too many times to know this is something else.

"Trent, what..." I whisper. I still can't form full sentences. "What's –"

"You just squirted on my dick for the first time, Presh. That's what," he says, pushing his hips to mine, going deeper again. Shame and confusion heats my cheeks. "Relax, Precious. It's fucking hot. And I've got a terrible need to find out how many times you'll do it tonight."

His arms bend around me. This time, he fucks me good and proper, holding my body like a life-sized toy while he crashes into me.

Deeper. Harder. Faster.

Deeper again. Oh, holy hell, *so freaking deep.*

He's using this angle to do something marvelous. *Extra* marvelous, I should say, because this man hasn't shown me a night where he doesn't fuck like he wants to bring down the sky.

Trent throws his body into mine and meshes us together all over again.

Grunting. Thrusting. Growling.

There's no bucking this storm, no fighting it, so I just let go. I give in. I let him have me in my entirety. I let him use me. Full submission to his awesome power and frantic hips, driving me up toward the stars beginning to pepper the sky before he jerks me back to him again.

The friction, the frenzy, the look in his eye – it's irresistible.

There's no fight because I've lost.

I'm going over again before I even know what hit me.

This time, it's not my heat alone, consuming me from head-to-toe. Halfway through my first breathless spasm,

Trent rams himself deep, holds his cock against the edge of my womb, and his whole body quakes.

There's a manic growl as he comes. Pleasure swallows me whole.

* * *

Later, I step out of the cabin's tiny outdoor sauna and throw my clothes on. I pick an outfit that's nice, loose, and easy. I'll need it since we're thoroughly spent and happily sated.

At least until we both turn in for good tonight.

Back in the house, I smile, eyes drawn to the delectable spread on the small circular dining table. My stomach growls. Sex works up an appetite under any conditions, but our sex, specifically, leaves me drained and ravenous.

"Steak and lobster coming up, just the way you like it." He pushes a full plate into my spot as I sit down, taking his seat across from me.

Might be the best thing I've ever smelled. I'm sure it'll taste just as lovely because he's a damn good cook.

I sip my wine, clearing my head, and then turn my knife and fork on the feast in front of us. It's buttery, medium well done, and divine. Even the asparagus has the perfect crispness, and the garlic mash does crazy things to my taste buds.

"Save that look for later," he says, a jokingly serious prickle in his eyes. "Can't enjoy my dinner when you're ready to jump my bones all over again."

"Your fault for making it too good." I swallow and stick my tongue out quickly. "This is amazing, Trent. You're handling dinner from now on."

Slowing my chewing on the next bite, I study him across the table.

Was that last part too much? Too hopeful?

Too obviously pointed at a future I hadn't even consciously known I was hinting at?

Crap. I swallow hard, second guesses flying in my head.

"Sorry. That came out kinda wrong. Didn't mean to imply I'd be expecting you to fix dinner every night. Or any night. Or like, we'd be moving in or anything crazy, I just –"

"Presh."

"I'm babbling. Clearly." I'm also flushed.

I shake my head slightly, embarrassed at the direction this is going. How deep can a girl fit her foot in her mouth?

"Presh, stop apologizing," he says firmly, letting his fork fall against the plate.

He wipes his hands roughly before they disappear beneath the table. "I'm glad you brought it up. I've given it some thought. Hell of *a lot* of thought, actually, ever since you showed up on my doorstep, needing to confess your little heart out. Longer than that, really. Ever since I got home from Seattle and tried to stay sane. Since I sat down and started writing that letter you came across the other day."

"Trent?" I cock my head. There's an invisible boulder hanging on his shoulders.

"That letter, fuck, I meant to deliver it in person. Like I told you before. No do-over there, but this, what I've got to say next, *has* to happen in person."

I'm waiting. On pins and needles. Heart lodged in my throat.

But then my phone vibrates itself off the nightstand next to the dining room, clattering on the floor so loud it makes me jump. I'm red faced, hand over my mouth, aghast at ruining whatever he's trying to get out.

Okay, so maybe I'm also laughing. Just a little, knowing how ridiculous this is.

"Jesus. Sorry, I think it's done, go ahead."

He leans back in his chair, his eyebrow quirked.

Before he can utter one syllable, the phone goes off again, vibrating across the hardwood floor, a jittery howl breaking our silence. "Go for it, Presh. You'll give me your full attention later."

I stand, still flustered, annoyed at the interruption.

So is he, I think, but he said that last part in a caring way. Like, he truly wants my undivided focus, and damn do I want to give it to him to find out what kind of surprise he's hyping.

But I also *really* want to smack whoever's dialing me off the hook. I hope it's not related to Jace.

Probably just my regional manager in Spokane, I bet. Probably calling to tell me she's locked herself out of the corporate account, or there's some furious group of high strung tourists demanding to speak with the owner over a broken ice machine.

"Be right back," I mutter, racing across the cabin.

I'm just in time to yank my phone off the ground before it blows up again. It's dad's number on the screen, and the little pull down in the corner says I've had about ten missed calls and just as many texts.

Shit. So it's Jace, after all.

"What's wrong?" I answer the phone with the question already torturing me.

"Peanut, it's mom."

Three little words. That's all he gets out before my world goes darker, crushed under the ten ton tragedy that wasn't supposed to happen.

He's still talking. Says something about a fall, a bad head injury, critical condition.

I can't even hear him over the welt in my throat.

I'm choking on my fear, grief that's coming like blood from an open wound, no matter what he says next.

"Dad...just...I..."

I'm struggling to find words when the phone leaps out of my hand. I look up and see Trent, a cold understanding in his eyes. His other hand lands on my shoulder. "She's hurt right now, Maxwell. Give me the details. No, you can't trust me, at least not yet, but damn it let's put that aside. Let me get her on a plane home. I'll have her right back to you."

He squeezes my arm. Tears burst from my eyes, falling for too many conflicting reasons I couldn't cite to save my life.

"Got it. We'll be there soon," he says, killing the call.

By the time he sinks to the floor, I'm shaking my head, his words finally sinking in. "Wait, you said –"

"We. I know, darling. Don't care what kind of shit's in store for me. You're not facing this down by your lonesome."

The last thing I remember that night in our spoiled paradise is crashing into his chest. Then he lifts me gently, walks me to the corner with our suitcases, and starts barking orders into his phone.

* * *

A SOGGY, mournful rain pelts the Randolph Medical Center. It's newly renovated, state of the art, a facility staffed by world class doctors recruited thanks to the generous donor pressures of another billionaire Maynard classmate slightly before our time.

It doesn't make me feel the least bit better.

What does is how he ferries us to the airport and drags me on a private jet.

What helps is how he holds me the entire flight, and then again once we're in the back of a sleek black town car.

What saves me from having a complete fucking breakdown is how he kisses every tear, growls out the unthinkable, tells me, "Enough, Precious. You'll be okay. Won't let you do anything else."

I'm barely able to whimper out the same phrase every hour, heartfelt as it is lame. "I love you."

And the thing that makes this better, that stops it from eviscerating me, is how he always tips my face to his, caresses my cheek, and echoes every word.

"Love you, too, Presh." His voice drops an octave. "Love you so fucking much."

How did I get this lucky? I don't know, but I'm praying it'll continue the whole disorienting journey to the waiting room. I can't stop holding my breath in brutal bursts until we see mom.

Dad's eyes go huge the second we walk in and he sees Trent. In the flesh. The man he thinks wrecked his future, his reputation, and left gaping holes in our family that might never heal.

I rush to his embrace, throw my arms around him, and hold on so tight I think it winds us both. For a second, I think it'll be okay, now that his attention is off Trent.

"Thank God you're here," he whispers. "She's in recovery. Stable for now. Should let you see her at the top of the hour, before they cut visiting hours for the night."

"I was so scared, dad. Tell me she'll be okay?" I look up, searching his eyes.

I know that look. Dad wants to lie. Reassure me the entire world isn't caving in. It's like a horrible living memory from the night everything went wrong, after Jace got done talking to the police.

And speaking of my idiot brother...there's another awful question in my throat, sour as it is necessary.

"Jace?" I whisper. "Does he know?"

Dad just clears his throat, pulls his mocha cardigan tighter, and beams daggers out his eyes over my shoulder. If looks could kill, he would have torn Trent up several times over.

"Let's step into the phone room first, peanut. Family business *only*."

XIV: RAIN, RAIN (TRENT)

I watch Maxwell Chenocott usher her away, shooting me the dirtiest look I think I've seen since a conference a few years ago, when I outbid a major competitor who needed the solar battery start up I stole under his nose.

Can't blame the old man. Fuck knows I'd do the same if I had to watch my daughter depending on the bastard who ripped his family's life to bits.

Maybe I should have let her have the talk about Jace after all. But that's the thing about wishes: they're dirt cheap.

Utterly worthless until they come true, and time always makes some forever stillborn.

I take a seat in the waiting room, listening to a fierce Seattle rain hammering the windows. Despite the evil eye her dad's giving me, I regret nothing being back here.

Didn't even stop to think the second I found her on the floor at our Lincoln City cabin, phone hanging limply against her cheek. I just acted. Picked her up and carried her home with all my might.

We, I'd told her. Now, she's learning what it means.

Means I've come home to deal with my demons once and for all.

Means I'll do anything to protect her heart, knowing I'm the luckiest SOB on Earth to have a second crack at it.

Means I'll work my balls off making her life picture perfect – no matter how rough or painful or messy it'll be.

And it's guaranteed to be all that and then some, knowing her asshole brother's out there.

Because I haven't let go of the secret in my pocket. My hand brushes against it even now, the box controlling the tip of my tongue, begging to come out. If only my words hadn't stuck in my throat while we were in Oregon.

Deep down, I'm glad fate intervened at the last second and kept me from getting down on one knee. I'd have needed one hell of a do-over if I'd asked Presh to be my wife a split second before she heard the tragic news.

Next time, I'll wait until the storm's over. I have to. Even if every minute I don't get it out makes me want to bury my fist through the nicely painted wall of this floor.

I don't see Amy Kay or her dad for the better part of the next hour. She comes out again, shutting the door gently behind her, walking toward me with a nurse. The woman peels away from her before we're together again, me on my feet, waiting for her with open arms.

"What's the word?"

"She'll live. More scans coming in the morning. Her eyes were open. She remembered me, knew who I was, thank God, but didn't say much else. I'm worried. They don't really know how bad it is, Trent. Not yet. Maybe by tomorrow –"

"Come the hell here." I stop her mid-sentence, jerk her to me, refusing to let more hot pain stream down her cheeks. "How'd it happen?"

I hold her, wait for her breathing to stabilize, her body stilling in my arms. When she looks up with the glossy pain in her eyes, I know before his name leaves her lips.

"Jace. He was gone for so long mom knew something was up. She confronted dad. Demanded answers. He told her about the divorce, the money problems, stealing from the firm. All his dirt."

I don't say anything. Just squeeze her tighter.

"Well, mom lost it, bolted upstairs, trying to run away to their room. God, the arthritis – one of her knees locked. She was too choked up to stop herself, to grab onto the banister before..."

"I've heard plenty. No more tonight, darling. You'll tell me the rest once she's doing better again." I don't give her any choice, pressing her face to my shoulder, stroking her chestnut hair.

It's velvet in my fingers.

Fuck. She's too amazing for life, this woman.

Even when her heart's imploding, she's an angel. Velvet heart and silk skin. So rare and beautiful.

Makes me want to find Jace and break every bone in his evil fucking body. Maybe his pain will buy an end to hers.

"How's Maxwell? Still pissed I'm here?" I give her a few more seconds, then lift her face gently to mine, smiling as wide as I can with my eyes.

"He'll get over it. Dad's just glad I'm back. Says it

doesn't matter, if you stay out of the way...but he doesn't want mom to see you anytime soon. We don't know how she is. It might upset her all over again."

"She'll get all the space she needs. I'll make myself a ghost, Presh. You need family time, just say the word." Her little hands fold to my arm, seeking my strength, tighter than before. I give it my all, so past ready to make this right. "Let's get the hell out of here. I can take you home to your parents' place, if you prefer, or a hotel –"

"Nah. The house will do fine. Just wish we could be together, tonight, but I should be there for dad. Don't know when he'll be home. Or if." She blinks, her eyes big, as if she's working through the hot mess of her thoughts. "This sounds really bitchy doesn't it? After everything you've done for me..."

"Precious." I stop, wait until she looks at me, lifting her face by the chin. "Not bitchy. Not anything. You just keep your family's spirits up."

"Trent –"

"No," I growl in her ear, then silence her with a heavy kiss.

No more excuses. No more apologies. No more worries over me.

Whatever's got her freaked out and ashamed doesn't fucking matter. Not tonight. Not ever.

"Quiet," I whisper, bringing my mouth to hers one more time. "Let's get you home. Left the driver waiting out front. He'll be happy to drop you, and I'll find some place to stay. I'll be by my phone. You call, you need me, I'm there. Won't even sleep till I hear your voice again."

"Trent." She tilts her head.

"Let's move, Amy Kay. Right the hell now." I pull her

gently by the wrist, leading her down the hall, trying to remember how we found our way to parking.

She falls into me. I throw an arm around her shoulder and march her toward the elevator, loving how good she feels against me. Why the fuck did it take so long to get *here?*

I tap the button for the elevator. She turns her little face up. "Haven't been on one of these since last time with you."

"Shit, you're right. How about the stairs then, darling?"

"No." Her grip tightens on my arm and her little hand slides down it. "No sense running from my fears. That's how we got ourselves into this mess. If you're by my side, we'll survive anything."

She's finally starting to get it. *Good.*

Damn good. I can't even hold the growl that slips out as I press my lips to hers. Our lips are still locked together as the door swings open, and the universe flips us the middle finger. Laughing.

Jace stands stiff as a board the instant he sees us. His eyes go big and his fists fly from his pockets, braced at his sides, fully ready to put me through the wall.

Shit!

I put myself in front of my woman, still staring in disbelief. "Jace, what the –"

"Fuck, Usher? Fuck you." He lunges, too fast, catching me off guard.

The situation's too surreal and I'm wearing the wrong shoes for this. They slip on the polished floor and send me spinning back into the wall.

My balance returns the instant I catch myself and look up again. His filthy paws are on Precious.

"Have you lost your fucking mind, sis? Him? Here? With you? The fucking animal who put mom *under?*" He's shaking too bad to hurt her, but he's got her shook up, too. All it takes to make my blood storm.

"Let her go!" I snarl, grabbing at his neck. He tries to whirl around and knock an elbow in my guts, but this time I'm ready.

I block his swing. Grab the back of his wrist. Pull until tendons creak.

Drop him to the floor, still bending his hand back. It's been a couple years since I did that crash course in martial arts for a company health initiative, but I've kept practicing a few times per month, and it all comes flooding back.

"Ah, fuck you!" he spits again, undaunted, teeth bared like a wild beast.

Giving no fucks, I keep bending his wrist.

"You're lucky we're in a hospital, asshole. They can fix this right up if I have to make you behave."

Amy Kay rushes to my side, lays her hands on my shoulders, and squeezes imploringly. "He didn't hurt me. Go easy, Trent. Please. For mom."

Damn.

I can't deny the tremor in her voice, no matter how much the manic fuck on the floor deserves a kick to the throat, too. I'll have to settle for answers instead.

"Why'd you come here, Jace? Start talking." I stop bending, just short of breaking his wrist.

"Why. The. Fuck. You. Think?" He spits every word, pain crushing his throat. "Mom, asshole. Have to see her. All I'm here to do."

"Whatever. First, I think I'll have your sister search

you for everybody's safety. You'll tell us exactly where you've been the last few weeks. And then, maybe, I'll let you touch base with your folks."

"Trent..." Amy's voice breezes my ear, pleading and knowing at once.

"You heard me, Presh. Check his pockets. Make sure he hasn't brought any surprises." If this prick walked into a hospital armed, I will break his wrist. No question.

"You're fucking crazy. Both of you!" The hate stamped on my ex-best friend's face could scare the devil himself.

Slowly, Amy Kay drops off me, stoops on the ground next to her brother, and begins patting him down. His hateful eyes stay trained on me the whole time.

A nurse walks by and does a double take. Probably wondering what the hell's happening on this floor.

Part of me feels guilty, making a scene. Too bad this jackoff didn't leave me any choice.

Any slip up here could cost us and her entire family. We've given him too many passes. I gave him the last he'll ever get the second I decided not to finish hacking his reputation to pieces.

"You're a psycho bastard for doing this," he snarls, shaking his head as Amy Kay sifts through the pockets in his trousers. "I'm here for her. Ma. Nothing else."

"Interesting. Next I suppose you'll tell us Portland wasn't on your itinerary the last few weeks."

"Pacific coast, asshole. Ocean Shores, Coos Bay, Tillamook...got as far as that on highway 101, clearing my head, before I decided not to show up on your doorstep and blow your fucking brains out." His voice is too harsh to be a bluff. He's telling me the truth.

How kind.

Takes everything I've got not to break his wrist like a twig. "Appreciate your honesty, but something tells me you're not over it that easy. You only stopped after you got the call from Maxwell, didn't you?"

He doesn't answer. Just looks at the ground, staring into his own vicious reflection mirrored on my shoes.

"He's clean." Amy Kay stands, saunters up to me, her eyes big and green and sweeping. "Let him up. We can always call security."

Snorting reluctantly, I release him. Jace stands, dusts himself off, maintains an icy distance a few feet away.

"You're both sick." His finger flies out, stabs me in the chest, but it's Amy Kay he's beaming daggers at. "Especially *you*, sis. You and everything you've done to this family, running off with him."

He looks past us, craning his neck to see down the hall. "Where the fuck's dad? Has everybody just *lost* it? He should've had Usher hauled the fuck out of here the second he walked through the door."

She shakes her head, tears brimming in her eyes. I'm ready to get in front of her again, but she steps out before I can do anything. Presh sends a crisp slap across her brother's face. "Shut the hell up already. You're an idiot, Jace."

She's shaking. Equal parts fierce and adorable when she's pissed. "Without this man, you'd probably be in jail. He dragged your demons into the light of day before they consumed you. It's not too late, if you'll grow a pair and stop blaming everybody else just this once."

I don't like the look on his face one bit. Rather than taking her tough love like a man, the bastard sneers.

My fist tightens, ready and so willing to wipe his face clean.

Asshole's mouth opens, but before he says anything, there's another voice behind us. "What's going on here, peanut?"

Shit. Maxwell.

I turn, unclenching my white-knuckle fist, gazing on the elder Chenocott.

"Finally," Jace rumbles, turning toward his father. "You see who's here, dad? With her?"

He nods without hesitation. "I'm well aware. Mr. Usher brought your sister home. There's another question I'm more interested in: where in God's name were you, son? I've spent the last twenty-four hours calling."

Jace slaps his hands against his thighs, doing an exasperated turn. "Jesus Christ, here it comes. Dad, I came the second I heard. Checked out of my shitty little hotel and came running like a good boy. I'm here. Isn't that enough? Or maybe I should've wasted precious time yammering on the phone, not knowing you were both having a fucking pow-wow with the asshole who put my life in ruins, waiting to ambush me the second I came back."

"Jace?" Amy Kay cuts between them, her voice a soft whisper. She waits for her brother's eyes. "Shut *up*. This is about mom. Not you, as difficult as that is to believe."

His eyes widen, then turn sharp enough to cut diamond. *Give me one reason. One excuse to pound this fuck through the floor.*

"Enough crap. I'm going to see mom." He brushes past us, closer to Maxwell, who gives his son a look like he's sizing up a dangerous animal he's crossed unexpectedly in the woods.

"Jace, no," Maxwell says sternly, quick-stepping after him down the hall. "Visiting hours are over for the night. They have to run more tests early tomorrow. She needs rest. I promise, first thing in the morning you'll –"

"You're insane, too, aren't you?" Jace snaps, whirling around. He reaches out, as if he's ready to put his hands on his own father.

Thankfully I'm not far behind. The look I give him makes him think better of it.

"Get out of my way, old man," he warns again. "Not waiting for tomorrow. Shit, you think I'm the reason she's here, don't you? Her own fucking son?"

Maxwell says nothing. Just reaches out, grabs Jace's shoulder, and pulls with all his might. The force stuns all of us. Especially Jace, who rocks backward, has to do a quick dance to regain his footing. "I said *tomorrow*, son. Don't make me say it again. What do you think this is? Rules are rules. I don't write them here."

Jace blinks once. "Rules? *Now* you care about rules? Even though there's a wanted fucking criminal next to us with his hands all over Amy Kay? The same criminal prick who actually busted mom up this bad, screwing with my life..." I see his teeth again, chewing words like something vile in his mouth. "Just unbelievable. Where the fuck's security? If you won't get them involved to put a stop to this crap, I will."

"You'll do nothing!" Maxwell bellows. There's always something shocking about a clean, civilized man hitting his limit, becoming unhinged. "Jace Calhoun Chenocott, if you take another step toward her room, I swear to God almighty I'll call the police. For you. There's only one person in this hall sowing chaos. Whatever wrongs Trent did us all those years ago, it's not him."

My eyes digest the grisly scene. Amy Kay gasps, clings to me so hard her fingers bruise my bicep. I don't even care.

I'm waiting for Jace to freak out, get nasty, get violent. It's bound to happen. Any second. And it'll be on me to step in. Stop the uproar before anybody gets hurt.

It never happens.

Jace's shoulders slump, his head hangs for the longest second, and then he looks up. Hatred seethes in his eyes. It's the first time I've seen him look at his own flesh and blood the same way he does me. "I hate you," he snarls.

"Jace, if you'll –" Maxwell cuts in, tries to get closer, but Jace throws his hand off.

"Stay the fuck away! You're dead to me. All of you." His eyes flit from his father to Amy Kay, so much darkness spilling out. Then they land on me. "And you, Usher, this isn't over. Not by fucking half."

My fists are up. I'm expecting him to lash out as he walks by, but he just keeps going. Slams his fist on the elevator button so hard a night nurse walking by gives him a dirty look.

"Jace...where are you going?" Presh asks softly.

He turns, looks up, a second before the elevator's steel doors slam shut, hiding his nasty face. "Home."

He's gone for more than a minute before we move. Before anyone speaks.

"I should go after him," Amy Kay whispers quietly, releasing her death grip on my arm. "He's crazy. Confused. He might do anything."

"Bad idea." Maxwell steps up, pulls his daughter from

me, holds her to his chest. "Let me handle this. It's my fault I didn't lay down the law a long time ago."

"No. Dad, no way, you can't blame yourself for anything he's doing. He's out of his flipping gourd."

"Amy Kay, listen. He's going to the house. I'll head back there and find him in an hour or so. After I wrap up one last check with your mom's nurses. Stay here. Stay with Trent. Until I call, and let you know the coast is clear."

Her eyes go huge. Terrified. "You shouldn't. Dad, don't go after him alone. You can't know what he'll –"

"He's a disturbed young man. Not a monster. I stopped believing in those some time ago," he says, turning to me on the last part. "I'll talk your brother down like always. He's capable of hurting himself. Capable of incredibly stupid, destructive decisions, sure. But he'd never lift a hand against us. That, I'm certain."

I'm not. Neither is Presh.

Know it by the way her little mouth falls open. The words, the bitter truth we've had to face, the full hellish extent of what Jace can do hangs on the tip of her tongue.

I give her a look, speaking with my eyes. *Not now, darling. There'll be a better time. Don't smash his heart to pieces all over again.*

As if sensing what I'm trying to say, she gives a subtle nod, then looks at Maxwell again. "Call us, dad. The very second you're home. We'll wait."

"Understood, peanut." He pushes his wry smile to her forehead, planting a firm kiss. Before he turns, heading back into the hall, he lets out a sigh, locking eyes with me one last time. "I'm sorry you got caught in the middle of this. Though that's how it always was, I suppose."

"That's how it always is with family," I say, extending a hand.

Maxwell Chenocott takes it, gives it a vigorous shake, and then he's gone.

By the time I turn, Amy Kay is on me again, whispering in my ear. "Let's go. While he's busy. We should get to the house, scope things out. We'll wait for dad to do whatever he needs to, but I'm not leaving him alone. We'll be close behind if Jace tries anything crazy. Anything more, I mean." Her voice sours, strain creeping in.

She still doesn't want to believe it. None of us do. But fuck, I'll never forget his crazy eyes, or the raw venom seeping out between his teeth.

It wasn't just the usual idle threats from an edgy fuck who's gotten himself in too deep.

He's pissed off. Wounded. Backed into a corner.

I grab her hand, give it a squeeze, wait for her to look at me.

"I'll scout your place out ahead of him."

"You? Hey wait a second–"

"Precious, listen: he looked like he was ready to kill somebody. He's fighting crazy. Mad as hell. That energy *will* go somewhere if he doesn't drink himself in a stupor. If he doesn't turn it on himself first, it'll be on someone else, and I'm not letting that be Maxwell. Or you. Understand?"

"Trent, if it's dangerous, we'll do this together. Only option. I *have* to come with." She pushes her fingers against mine, harder and harder, lines splitting her face. "If he's fighting crazy, like you say, what do you think he'll do if you show up unannounced?"

Exactly what I hope to fuck he'll do.

Lash out. Charge. Use me as a shock absorber, a buffer, a shield so nobody else gets hurt.

I'm also confident he'll go down easy. If he hasn't snorted or drunk or blazed himself into a blinding stupor by the time I'm there, then I'm willing to give up every penny I own.

But I see Presh won't give up. Not this time. Not after I've admitted how dangerous this is.

"Fine," I bite off, a reluctant sigh trapped in my lungs. "You're staying in the car."

"Whoa, that's not –"

"It's the *only* thing I'll agree to, Precious. We have the driver bring us out there. You stay put while I go over the gate, see what the situation is. Once I know he's not ready to tear anybody limb-from-limb, then you'll see him. If all goes well, he'll be tucked in for the night, and I'll be gone before your dad shows up and catches himself in the middle of more shit."

She bites her lip, face strained, not liking anything I'm saying. But she knows this is as far as I'll bend.

"All right. Let's go. Dad said an hour."

It's a wicked irony there's almost as much tension in the air the second time we climb onto an elevator together.

* * *

An hour later, the driver pulls up to the house. I get out, run to the usual vine-covered spot on the wall where I always climb over, looking back one more time to make sure Amy Kay's sweet butt stays in the car.

She does. Told her it wouldn't be long.

I move, clambering onto the property, looking for signs of Jace. There's a stillness in the air. The electric, foreboding kind that's there before a storm.

The keys Presh handed over clink in my hand. I'm gripping them tight so there's no movement, no jingle in my pocket.

I do it because I need the silence. If I'm brutally honest, though, it's also stress relief.

There's something here I can't pin down that scares the shit out of me.

Lights twinkle, giving every window a dirty golden glow. Only, it's the ultra-lit configuration I've seen too many times in high society. It's the lights left on by the servants heading home for the evening.

Too vacant looking. Too quiet. Too fucking eerie.

His car is in the driveway. Parked crooked. First sign the asshole's alive, here, and probably as insane as ever.

Also means I can't go through the front.

I round the backside of the house, brushing past the tree I always used to get to Presh's room.

Perfect timing, too.

The sky opens up in a near-monsoon. The angry showers sweeping through Seattle earlier deepen, a royally pissed off Zeus throwing a flood at the world.

"Lovely," I growl under my breath. Only silver lining is the sudden burst giving extra cover, helping obscure my advance.

Back of the house, I remember. Service door. The one that comes out by storage, where the servants keep most of the yard supplies, next to the second mud room. I remember the layout of the house like yesterday. Easier tonight, maybe, when I don't have the luxury of a beautiful woman up in her room, waiting to invite me in.

Said beautiful woman is stuck in the car with baited breath. Depending on me. Silently mouthing prayers to whatever powers in this universe will keep me and Jace from murdering each other.

I slide the key in the lock and turn, reaching for the knob. I'm in.

Inside the house, I press myself against the wall, straining my eardrums. It's freakishly quiet in here, too. My heartbeat pounds in my throat.

Okay, quick scan. Get in, get out.

Find him. If you can't, move on.

The first sign of life is the kitchen. It's a fucking war zone. I blink several times, trying to process the full disaster in front of me.

Glass shards everywhere. Ceramic pieces mingling with diamond cut knives, broken crystal catching the dull light, priceless China pulverized to specks barely bigger than gravel.

It's like a raging bull came through, but at least a bull only charges after it's provoked for good reason.

The dining room was spared, thank God. And there's nothing worse than a broken mirror in one of the bathrooms on the main floor. I head upstairs, quickly scan the rooms, see them in order.

Downstairs, though...downstairs is a fucking mess. Just dirty, destructive chaos.

Maxwell's beautiful library has holes through it. Literal *gunshots.*

I see the prize hunting rifle he used to have hanging in the corner on the floor, a heavy dent in its barrel. A family heirloom Jace somehow found ammunition for, it's blown out the windows, annihilated several shelves of books, torn out their wood support.

Like civilization itself spilling its guts.

Before, I was stunned. Now, looking around, taking it in, I'm completely *pissed.*

Asshole Jace has to pay. *If I can find him.*

I don't think he's in the house. Not after his violent binge. He's got to be outside.

I'm halfway to the service door, swinging around Ophelia's custom solarium, which remains mercifully intact, when I see it from the window.

A light on in the boathouse. *Fuck.*

My heart pounds like mad, picturing the havoc he'll wreak on the Wilkie.

I stare at the light, streaming through the open door. Then grit my teeth, swallow my fear, and wheel around.

He's in there. I fucking know he is. Irony stabs my intestines, adding weight to the portal to hell in front of me.

The place where this started years ago is where it has to end.

I push my way outside and try not to shiver. The cold rain runs down my already numb spine in rivulets.

Closing my eyes, I picture the one thing that keeps me sane. Amy Kay's beautiful face. Hopeful. Patient. Counting on me.

I hide my phone beneath the cover of my hand, typing out a quick message. I can't lie to her again, but I also can't bring her face-to-face with this horror. It isn't even over. So, I just tell her the truth.

Trent: Precious, stay put. Coast is almost clear but it's not good. NOT GOOD. Stall your father. Don't move until I say.

I ALSO SEND a text to my driver, ordering him to switch to Plan B: keep Presh in the car by any means possible. Unless I say otherwise.

Then I shut my phone completely off. She'll be sending me a flurry of texts, no doubt, and I can't have them going off. Not even silently.

I'm too busy, planting my boot up a psychotic backstabber's ass, and discovering how far it reaches until it finds some common sense.

XV: ORDERS (AMY KAY)

I'm stabbing furiously at my screen again.

It's been *twenty five and a half minutes*. Hell yes, I'm counting.

"Damn it, Trent. Why aren't you answering?" I'm grateful for the privacy visor, but only a little.

His driver isn't paid to judge or ask probing questions. He's a chauffeur. Tonight, maybe one part glorified babysitter. I haven't even jumped on Trent's command to stall dad.

Like it's so freaking easy.

Like I even know *how*.

Like there isn't something seriously messed up happening inside the only home I've ever truly known, and it's driving me insane.

Face twisted in disgust, I reach for the door, and pull for the second time. *Locked.*

I tap the button on the intercom and start talking. "Hello, sir? I need to get out. If you could please flip the switch for my door, that'd be stellar."

There's a long pause on the other end. *Too long.*

"I'm sorry, Ms. Chenocott, I'm afraid I can't. Client's orders. He says you're to remain in the car while there's a situation." His voice sounds deep, robotic, not even a shred of fear or doubt in it. Strictly professional.

Totally infuriating.

"*What* situation?" I run my finger over the plastic beneath the intercom, holding the driver's name and credentials. "Listen – Jason – I don't want to get between you and your job, or your pay, but damn it, you're *not* making it easy. If you don't let me out this instant, the first thing I'll do is scream bloody murder and find out how many kicks it takes to break one of these fancy shaded windows. Then I'll be calling up your boss and finding out exactly how much your company would enjoy a big, fat lawsuit for holding a woman hostage. We clear?"

I'm not used to being this big a bitch. My knee shakes.

"Perfectly, miss. I sincerely hope you'll choose not to damage my private property. I'm a small time operator with one car – this one. My not-so-little-boy, Robbie, he's a straight A student in his first semester. Trying for architectural engineering at Purdue. It's a very expensive program and I'm the only parent he has, I'm afraid. Tuition's due next week and I'm counting like hell on this job from Mr. Usher. He's paying me a mighty fine premium to watch over you just for a little bit. So, obviously, I'd *really* appreciate it if you'd calm down, find some patience, and –"

The sound of my fist impacting the seat cuts him off. It's a blow of frustration more than anything. I couldn't do much damage punching leather if I tried, and after his

SOB story, what kind of demon would I be if I robbed his kid?

Not everyone lives in the luxury I've known for most of my life.

"Thanks, miss. You've made the right choice. Now, I'd be happy to play music, put on a show, take you anywhere, let you roam wherever you'd like. Just not here. Not until Mr. Usher gives the okay. Thanks for your patience. I mean it."

"And I mean someone's getting it tonight," I snarl to myself, slumping backward in my seat.

I run through my options. None are very appealing.

I could go ahead, ignore my conscience, and beat my way out of this fancy car. I'd probably be restrained real fast by Mr. Driver.

I could have him take me across town, let me off at a gas station, and sneak a block away to call another ride to bring me right back here. But then I wouldn't know what I'm walking into. And that could take an hour or more.

I could just listen to Trent – as bad as it scalds my blood – and save all this ugly energy for later, when I'll throw a well deserved slap across his face.

Maybe him and Jace both.

If they both leave the place alive.

It disturbs me to no end that I don't know what I'm dealing with. I stare through the tinted window, trying to see signs of...well, anything.

It's brutally quiet. Just a sea of hazy orange light shifting in the rain, which hammers the car plenty loudly, drowning out any sound.

Fifteen minutes. That's all I'll give him. In the meantime, I have to call dad.

* * *

A QUICK PHONE CALL LATER, and I know dad hasn't left the hospital. Not yet.

Mom had a terrible nightmare and woke up screaming. She wouldn't stop until they let him see her. They've agreed to let him spend the night in her room and he's asked me to check on things at home – but in the morning, after he's spoken to Jace.

I tell him I'll find somewhere else to stay for the night. I lie through my teeth.

Pretend I'm his ever trustworthy peanut, who'd do anything for her family. Okay, so the second half is true, but the fact that I'm stuck in this car, instead of at the hospital with him, consoling mom...

This can't be happening again. I close my eyes, fighting back the bitter tears.

No.

Hell no.

I can't just sit on my hands while the people I love are in crisis. Nothing and nobody – not even this damn determined driver – will stop me.

There's too much at stake to have a nervous breakdown now. I shove my phone in my pocket, staring at my weary reflection in the limo's privacy visor.

What did Trent mean? Those two words in his message?

Not good? *NOT GOOD.*

He'd said it twice. Without elaborating. Making me wonder if he found Jace disemboweled in the dining room.

My mind runs rampant, a thousand hellish scenarios

exploding in my psyche. I see them both up close and bloodied, throwing punches, kicking, biting, dragging each other to death's doorstep. I see my sadistic brother cornering the man I love, pulling a gun. He turns it on Trent once and fires. Then he turns it on himself.

I gnaw my lip, more anxious than ever. Glance at my phone.

Another fifteen minutes. Seventeen, to be precise. Jesus Christ.

I can't wait any longer.

Stabbing at the button for the visor, I angrily lower it, waiting for the driver's dark eyes to look back in the mirror. "Tell me how much Robbie's program costs. I bet I can cough up all four years and tell my bank to wire it over right now if you'll just let me out of here."

I hear a sharp intake of breath. Jason's eyes go wide. If I could see his hands, I'm sure they'd have a steely grip on the wheel. "Miss, that's incredibly gracious, but –"

"No buts. How much is he paying you? I'll double it. Triple it. You see that place out there? It belongs to my parents. They left me pretty well off, I'm happy to say, and your boy deserves a fighting chance. Let's get ourselves a deal."

His eyes turn over a few times in the mirror, staring at the house, then back at me. He's considering my crazy offer.

Come the hell on, Jason, I think to myself. *Let me give you money.*

Figure it out.

If you don't, two men I love are as good as dead.

XVI: THE ZEN OF GASOLINE
(TRENT)

I try my damnedest to stare into the boathouse from several feet away. It's too dark, too dim to see anything inside, and I'm far too short on time.

Clock's ticking.

Maxwell could be rolling through the gate any minute. It's almost been an hour. Presh has to be getting restless, too, especially after I told Jason to hold her.

Hopefully she's not throwing herself at the door, making him restrain her. The very notion makes me see red. Mostly at myself for giving the order.

This is majorly fucked up and down.

Every sweet second I'm wasting isn't doing us any favors. I have to find out what the hell he's up to.

I dig in my pocket, searching for a weapon that isn't there. My jaw clenches.

Fuck. I'd been in such a rush to get Amy Kay home I hadn't given a second thought to my nine millimeter, safely locked away in my Portland mansion. Hadn't given a third thought to Jace showing up in the hospital tonight, making me wish I had a backup weapon like never before.

Whatever, it can't hold me back. I creep forward, panther-like through the rain, grateful the wet tears pouring from the sky silence my footsteps squelching the mud.

He's in there. Waiting. Scheming something awful.

All five senses tell me it's true.

I stop when I get next to the door, take a deep breath, and look inside. I see the usual mess of boating equipment sitting on the shelves. A few blunt objects I can grab if I'm quick, and things get ugly, or even if they don't. *Here we fucking go.*

Rushing into the boathouse, I reach for the first object I see. It's a steel pole almost as big as a baseball bat. I manage to grip it a split second before something punches me in the face.

Not physically.

It's the smell, a familiar strong scent racing up my nostrils, dark and strong and dirty.

Gasoline. Fuck!

My heart starts slamming my ribs. I see the shape shifting around in the corner, the dark spot closest to the Wilkie, which sits perched in its dock and ready to sail through the open hanger door.

There's no time to think. I drop the makeshift weapon and start running, quick as I can toward him, eyeing the glint of something metal in Jace's hand. "Don't fucking do it, asshole! You're not *this* crazy and I'm here. The one you really want."

He looks up, an ugly light in his eyes. We share an

understanding. Both know how fucked up and precarious this situation is.

One wrong move. That's what he's waiting for.

One flick of his finger could ignite the lighter. A single toss of fire, a lick of flame on gas, and then the boathouse goes up in an inferno. Hell, maybe more than just the building, considering the reeking trail he's left toward the back of the house, through the gardens. It's even soaked into him.

I know because the closer we get, the worse he stinks. This insane bastard might be suicidal.

"Jace," I try again, wishing I hadn't tossed aside my club after all. "Don't. You're better than this."

"'Bout time you showed up, Usher. I waited half the fucking night for you, Amy Kay, dad...somebody who actually gives a shit. I was almost ready to let my thirsty little friend here drink her fill." Smiling, he flicks the lighter on, lifting a bright red gas can in his other hand.

I've lost my pulse. I have to get this crap away from him somehow. No fucking choice.

He sees my eyes darting around, desperate and searching, and staggers to his feet. "Whatever you're thinking, don't fucking bother. You're too late. Won't walk out of here without watching this place burn to the ground. Shit, since you always loved it so much, there's plenty of fire to go around. Maybe you can go down with the ship."

"Ship's not going anywhere," I growl, banging the Wilkie's hull with my fist. The noise reverberates like God's fist, a distraction I hope will do something.

Jace staggers toward it, clumsy as ever. He's drunk, no surprise.

His eyes have trouble following me for more than a

few seconds. But shit, that lighter in his hand...I don't know if I can overpower him, fish it away, before he does something incredibly stupid.

"Don't fucking do this," I warn him again. "Just put it down. Hand it over. We'll talk this out. There has to be a way to make this right, end the hell you've put yourself in. Damn it, Jace, if you'll just get help..." I can't go on. I'm suddenly a twenty-one year old kid again, staring at my drug dealing friend in disbelief, wondering how something so deranged can hide in a human skin.

"Blame on, Usher. Shout it to the sky. I don't give a piss anymore about your holy-poly act. You've wrecked my life. Even after I convinced them for years *you* were the one who landed them in hell, just look how quick they come crawling back. Look!" He ignites the lighter again, holds it under his face. It'd be a bad parody of a Halloween scare, except there's a real monster behind the flame.

"I'm looking," I whisper.

It's hard to only look and not send my fists crashing through his psycho face.

"Yeah? Then you see how fucked I am? You see the reason: you, you, always, *you.*"

I shake my head. If there's a logic somewhere in there, it's just as twisted as the rest of him. Still, I have to reason with this prick, as long as he's holding that burning Ace in his hand.

"Damn it, Jace, it's not like that. This isn't a pissing contest. Never should've been. We were friends. We –"

"Shut up. You were the perfect son mom and dad always wanted. You're too fucking right for Amy Kay, and I fucking knew it, the second I found out you were after her pussy all those years ago." He holds up his flame again, urging me back.

"It pissed me the hell off, knowing you'd be part of this family. *Always* better than me. I spent years trying to give dad what he wanted, you know? *Years*. I married that bitch, Lindsey, knowing she never wanted shit beyond my money. Cleaned up my act. Got myself nice and neat and ready to act like a fucking adult, for once. One who could've done amazing things for the family business. Sure, I took some kickbacks I shouldn't have, but isn't that what always happens at these multimillion firms? Dad sure as shit wasn't shy, funneling money from his business into his goddamn campaign. I saw the books!"

"Jace, look –"

"No, Usher! Not this time. Not ever. You do the fucking looking!" He stumbles forward, flashing flame in my face, almost close enough to scorch my chin. I crane my head back slowly, wait for him to give me space, looking for an opportunity to end this. "This is how it ends. Tonight. You're the fuck who brought us here, coming back and sticking your shit-rubbed nose in places where it doesn't belong. And never will. You burned me, Usher. Ruined my marriage. Broke my family. I've fucking had it. You keep burning, then I'll burn you and burn them and burn everything right to the motherfucking ground."

"Jace!" I scream his name again.

It's not enough.

We're way beyond talk. Beyond reason. Beyond ending this peacefully.

He flicks the flame, stoops over, tries to plant it in the thick gas puddle reflecting on the wooden dock. I ram my shoulder into him as hard as I can, send him falling backward.

The lighter bounces out of his hand.

I'm quick, chasing after it. He's faster and luckier, even in his drunken bloodlust.

I crash down on top of him, slam his wrist to the floor. Trying to pry the lighter out of his hand.

Trying and failing. The angle is all wrong.

His grip is a vice. He won't let go. His thumb flicks the button for the flame again, pushes it to my fingers. I rip my hand back with a roar, but I don't drop his wrist. "Asshole, let go!"

"Hurts, doesn't it?" Jace's voice is ice.

"That's what this is about?" I growl into his face, my heart beating a dull roar in my temples. "Making us feel your pain? One last big 'fuck you' to the world because you couldn't hack it? Shit, man. The Jace I grew up with would've at least been original."

My words cut deep. Snarling, his smirk disappears, and he swings at my head.

Swings and misses.

I crawl up his chest, smash myself into him, trying to knock the wind from his lungs. Jace struggles underneath me, losing the battle by the second. Still, I can't give up, knowing what's at stake.

"Fuck. You." He grunts each syllable, my weight a boulder on top of him. "Go ahead, prick. Rub your superiority in the black sheep's face one last time. Where'd I go wrong, Usher? Enlighten me."

I blink, unsure why his eyes are suddenly so sad in the darkness. "You can't see your ego? How much it's cost you?"

"I see it! Crystal fucking clear. Not what I'm asking," he snarls, rolls under me again, trying to throw me off in vain. Then he just goes limp, holding the lighter over his head, barely out of my reach.

Shit. If I can just –

"Tell me, Usher. Tell me when my entire life went down in shit?" His words slur.

I narrow my eyes. Maybe the booze, the drugs, whatever he's on is soaking deeper in his brain. Giving me a chance to end this.

"When you abandoned your friends, asshole. When you went lone wolf. When you stabbed me in the back and ripped the only woman I ever gave a damn about away."

His face scrunches, as if he's in pain. An act I'd be a fool to believe. Or is it?

Something hot and unexpected hits my hand. The one that isn't trying to crawl up his arm and fish the lighter away, trying to pin him against the ground by his ear. Tears. Rolling off his cheek, splashing my skin, hot and thick and vile. "Christ. I fucked up real bad, didn't I? Then. Now. Tonight."

More bleary, scalding tears. He can't be serious. This can't be happening.

I gaze through his bewildered pain, watching his wrist tremble. Just a little more, and he'll either drop that thing, or push it close enough so I can grab it. *Don't let up. Talk him down. Save Presh. Save her family.*

"You did, asshole. But you're never out for good. Not unless you bury yourself. Took me years to claw my way back from the damage you did. I managed. I fixed my life. I did amazing things." I watch him scowling through the darkness, defeated but still so dangerous. Drawing in a huge breath, I decide to let the hammer fall. "It's not too late, Jace. Let go. If you're willing to calm the fuck down and hand the lighter over, then you've still got a friend."

"Bullshit!" he snaps, his thumb struggling for the switch, trying to light the flame. "Nice trick. We both know the second I hand this thing over, you'll knock me on my ass. You'll call the cops. I'll be put away for good. It's too fucking late."

I cock my head, smiling, shaking my head. "Amazing. You still don't know shit."

There's a brutal pause. Anger bleeds confusion in his soiled eyes. "You're fucking with me. You're –"

"I'm the only chance you've got at a normal life. No joke. No trick. No bull. Give me your hand. Let me help."

He can't believe it as I lift off him, pulling at his fingers.

Hell, neither can I.

The asshole stands, sniffing through his tears, trying to comprehend this lunatic mercy. It doesn't make sense to me either, but it's the only way I'm able to peel him off the floor.

My one chance at preventing this from ending in two scorched bodies.

I can't tell who's acting anymore. Who's leading who. Or where.

I take the biggest risk of my life slapping his back, throwing an arm around his shoulder, pulling him into me. "I'm a man of my word, Jace. Always was."

"Right...that's why this *kills* me, I guess." His eyes fall to the lighter in his hand.

I stiffen, horror rampaging through my brains.

Don't fucking do this. Not after we've made so much progress. Goddamn it, Jace!

I try taking a step forward. If he's about to bring a world of fire, then I delay him a few seconds, dragging him toward the boathouse door. Then another minute.

Then he's leaning against me, fighting more sobs, his whole screwed up body wracked with poison. I reach for his hand, holding my breath. "Let me. Please, Jace. We're almost there. Just a few more steps and –"

"Fuck this!" he screams. "You win."

Warm metal slides into my palm. His hand falls from mine. I'm holding a fucking miracle.

We're outside and I shove the lighter in my pocket, staring at this beaten, worn out man I still want to kill.

Cold logic says I should seize my chance, throw him to the ground, knock him out.

Just to be sure.

I wish I could be a monster just once in my life. But fuck, it's just not in my makeup.

I can't punch out a defenseless man I've just offered a second chance to. No matter how many times over he deserves it.

Plans clash together like lightning in my mind. It's not over until he's somewhere he can't do more damage.

I see it so clearly I don't dwell on the danger. I have to get him in his car, the passenger seat, drive him to the nearest mental health facility.

Then I'll call Presh, brief her on the damages, her brother's condition. She'll tell Maxwell.

And holy shit, this whole nightmare *might* finally have a happy ending.

A strange euphoria fills my blood. I feel like I can fly, even though I'm very much grounded, stumbling through the rain with this drugged, crying brute against my shoulder. I'm slow to realize when he falls a few steps behind me, unmoving, rooted to the ground.

Shit. What now? We were just a few steps from the service door, where the gas trail begins.

Tearing my eyes off him, I look dead ahead.

I see a ghost, the teary face of a woman I love, who shouldn't fucking be here.

Precious.

* * *

SHE'S HOLDING HER PHONE. I think the death grip is where the tremor begins, the one that's shaking her entire body as she holds it up, presses it to her ear, someone else already on the line. Her mouth opens, almost in slow motion. My ears don't want to believe what they're hearing.

"Emergency in Mount Sutton, gated community, Chenocott residence. Please hurry. Please come now. My brother's gone insane and he's trying to hurt us."

My heart jumps into my throat and starts crashing, so hard and fast and ruthless I can hardly speak. Somehow, I scream two words. "Precious, no!"

Her eyes go huge. I don't know whether she finally smells the gas, or if she still doesn't understand.

She can't know what happened out here. She can't know it was almost – *fucking almost* – under control.

Not anymore. The second I feel a rough, furious hand

in my pocket, ripping out the lighter before I can react, I know how screwed we are.

By the time I've turned around, Jace is on the ground, his lips peeled back in a chaotic smile.

He's past pain, past betrayal, and *way* past sanity.

The look on his face is almost calm, in an evil way, like he knew somehow this was coming.

I start screaming again, "Presh, phone down! You have to put the fucking phone –"

Too late.

Jace touches the flame to his gas-soaked arm. Orange ignites his body in the blink of an eye.

In a matter of seconds, I'm rushing to Presh, lost in a hellscape of lashing fire blistering up the mansion's backside, streaking toward the boathouse.

Rings and rings of fire, surrounding us, just like a scalding noose. It's weirdly silent for the first thirty seconds, like Jace is too drunk or drugged or numb to feel the devastation he's unleashed.

I open my mouth to speak again, to holler, to tell her we have to get our asses out of here.

The roar around us drowns me out. Jace's unholy screams fill the night.

XVII: BEFORE NIGHT CLOSES IN
(AMY KAY)

I think the last thing I'll always remember before I blacked out is the smell.

Not the demon screams. Not the panicked weight of Trent's awesome arms around me. Not him dragging both of us to safety, then rushing back through the rain, toward the sputtering flames, ripping his shirt off and trying so, so *hard* to beat the flames lashing my brother's body.

Not even the rapid-fire chaos that came later: the flashing sirens, the platoons of firefighters, medics, and police. Not dad's contorted face at the hospital, the same place the ambulance leads us, where my mother is supposed to be recovering in a room upstairs. Not the way his knees crunch when he hits the floor, followed by his fist, followed by his curses.

Not the flurry of nurses and doctors battering us with questions through a long, sleepless night. Or Trent's gentle giant weight against me, comforting as the morning sun that's still MIA behind the clouds come rainy morning, the entire reason I'm somehow still sane. Or sane enough.

I think I'll remember the smell because the stink of gasoline has a mysterious way of drowning everything else out, even the horrible stench of burning flesh, wood and plants and glass on fire.

But there's another smell I'll remember, too, behind the hideous odors erupting from a home I'll never look at the same way again: Trent's scent.

I breathed the fear steaming from his pores. I also breathed his strength. I breathed his hurt, his hope, his prayers. And he prayed hard – harder than anybody ever has – for me.

For us.

Even for my fucked up brother.

That rich, deep, earthy masculine scent drifting off him in waves grounded me. Kept me from screaming my throat completely raw.

If I just pressed my face to him and breathed his love – and I did more times than I could count – I knew it'd be all right. Somehow, this wouldn't be the end.

The night would never close in.

Not while I had this man holding my world together, preventing it from scattering to the wind like blackened leaves.

* * *

"It's funny, Presh. First time I got over the gate and felt the rain, I thought it'd be my biggest problem tracking him down, making any headway. Can't believe it's the one thing that kept all this from being more fucked up."

I can't believe it either.

I push my head into his shoulder while his arm wraps tighter. We sit together, under a soft pink umbrella, parked on a bench in the hospital's brilliant green courtyard. It's still raining, sometimes in waves. Nothing like the deluge that came only seconds after Jace lit himself on fire.

"Yeah. It saved his life. The house, too. Those firefighters wouldn't have been able to do much if they'd shown up a few minutes later with everything in flames. God, Trent. We're *lucky*." It hurts to even say it.

It should sound absurd.

On the surface, there's nothing remotely lucky or pleasant or thankful about this. Mom lays in a bed broken and bruised, barely upgraded to stable.

Dad's beyond shattered. It'll take six figures easy to repair the damage to the house, more for the beating the boathouse took.

As for Jace...he's lucky to be alive. Relatively undamaged, considering the flames that torched his clothes to blackened scraps.

If it hadn't been for an act of God, the sky opening up when it did, and Trent's relentless efforts to beat out the fire...

No. I won't let myself think about it.

I close my eyes, a lump in my throat, struggling to understand why I still care.

It's my brother's fault. Everything.

If anyone should suffer, it's him. But when I think of him in the burn ward, under police escort, certain to face arson charges, I just lose it. And Trent gets to bask in the millionth tears I've shed the past twenty-four hours.

"You know, Precious, Lady Luck shafted me more times in life than I care to count, but damn, I think I could kiss her for coming through for us when it counted." He's wearing his trademark smirk when I look up, scorn in my eyes. He pats my cheek. "Don't worry. She's a homely looking broad. Nothing for you to ever worry over."

"Jerk," I grunt, shaking my head. It's impossible to hide the wry smile pulling at my lips. "You know, you don't have to stay. I know you're a busy man, running a billion dollar empire, and you've got work. Ugh, *I* have work. Don't think I'll profit much this year paying out the bonuses I will to the ladies keeping the inns afloat during...all this."

All this. I don't know what else to call it.

The end of life as I knew it. And the rough beginning of something new.

"Quiet, Presh, because now you're talking crazy." He runs his fingers lower down my arm, holding me close. I swear I hear his heart beating softly behind the steady rain. "Business will take care of itself for a few more days. Weeks, maybe, however long you need. I'm not planning to go home to Portland by myself. Not ever again."

"Huh?" I look up, my eyes big with wonder. "You *sure* I'm the one talking crazy?"

His blue eyes land on mine, intense and all conquering. I try not to shudder. "Certain. It's my fault I couldn't stop this from getting more fucked up. I'd be a royal bastard to walk away now. If only I'd punched him out, called you first, or paid Jason *more* to make sure you never left the car..."

I tilt my face. I'm still a little salty over being taken

hostage and having to pay a king's ransom to his driver just to stumble into a freaking mess.

Of course, Jason was good about it, seeing what happened next. His panicked calls to 9-11 are probably what got the emergency crew out to the house faster. He also settled for a year of his son's tuition, but I insisted on two.

"Next time, nobody else gets caught in the middle of our business. And no more special arrangements with drivers," I say, scratching at his chest.

"Fuck next time. It's over, Presh. I swear to you, with this pink umbrella as our witness," he motions, a silly, sly joke that makes me laugh, "I'll never let this happen to you again. Once Jace is out of the burn ward, he'll get the help he needs. I'll see to it if your parents can't. I've got the connections."

My smile fades. My stomach slowly folds in on itself, souring, thinking about how Jace won't be the only one who'll need serious mental help. Sooner or later, once she's recovered, mom will find out. It's bound to pulverize what's still left of her shattered heart.

"What now?" Trent whispers softly, squeezing my hand.

"Nothing. Getting too far ahead of myself, that's all. There's a lot to sort out. But we'll do it, I guess, little by little. What choice do we have?"

"You will," he growls. Such feral confidence it almost makes me believe it's that easy. "Wish to hell you didn't have so much stacked up on your plate, Precious. If I'd been a little quicker, if I hadn't let Jace ever leave this place...I'm here for you and your folks. Even your damn worm of a brother. Just rips me up inside knowing I wasn't able to stop this from becoming the worst night of your life."

He doesn't continue. He knows better. Especially with the conflicted look I'm giving him.

I shake my head, truly amazed. He's so wrong about one crucial part.

This wonderful man still doesn't get it.

"Trent, stop. It wasn't the worst."

He blinks, cocks his head, a quiet look on his face like I've lost my mind. "You're serious?"

"Because you saved me and you're not allowed to beat yourself up. Because without you, I don't know where we'd be. Mom, Dad, Jace, the house, me...this whole ordeal was far from the worst night of my life. Just give it a few years. After the pain goes, and we're not raging pissed at Jace – if he ever gets his crap together – I just might look back on this as one of the best. Best, I said, as twisted as that sounds. You saved us. You saved me. You saved us all."

He turns, stares into the rain for several seconds, rolling over my words in his mind. When he looks at me again, there's a heartwarming smile on his face. I can't resist lacing my fingers through his a little harder.

"Hold the umbrella for a second, darling," he says, pushing it into my other hand.

"Why?" I bat my eyes, wondering what he's doing stepping off the bench, into the rain, which has thankfully softened just enough not to leave him drenched.

"This is the most fucked up time in the world to do this. At least, that's what I thought until you told me different. Presh, I talked to your dad this morning. You were in there with your ma, and he was in the waiting room alone. I didn't press him, he struck up the conversation. Thanked me for doing what I did. Then I filled him in on everything that happened. Everything six years ago that got us into this mess."

My jaw drops. Something starts to wet my cheek, far too warm to be rain. "How...how'd he take it?"

Trent smiles, takes my hand, clasps it between his huge palms. "Not happily, of course, but Maxwell's no fool. The holes in Jace's story bothered him for years. He did the same thing anyone would do staring into a hurricane: left it the hell alone."

Shock shoots through me. So does a little bit of rage. Dad doubted, and he'd never said anything?

"Don't pin too much on him," Trent says, reading my mind. "He tried to get on with his life. Tried like hell to move the whole family forward. He even figured I'd be back someday, one way or another, and then maybe he'd get the truth."

I slowly release the sigh I'm holding in. Whatever. Fine.

There's too much hurt in my heart to hold more grudges.

Trent pauses, his blue eyes heavy, almost sparkling in the dull grey morning light hiding behind the clouds. "I gave him that truth. Finally. Then I apologized up and down for taking so long to figure this shit out and do the right thing, just like I did with you."

I can't believe what I'm hearing.

I think I start shaking just a little, but I force my nerves calm again, because everything he's telling me suggests it's not just talk. This ugliness might actually be over.

"Trent..."

"Hold up. I'm not done yet, Precious. I also asked your old man something else." He pauses, reaching into his pocket. A second later, I'm face-to-face with a cube wrapped in burgundy. "Had this with me since we were in Lincoln City, darling. I was about to do it the night everything went to hell, but you got that call. Nothing else mattered except getting our asses back here. Getting it fixed. Now that it's said and done, I'm fixing us."

Oh. My. God.

Now, I'm *definitely* shaking. I'm delirious as his thumb flicks the box open, revealing a ring cast in white gold, studded with more diamonds than I think there are stars in the sky. I've grown up around enough wealthy women to know it cost him a pretty penny, even with his enormous resources, but that's not what shocks new tears from my eyes.

It's the cost to him in hearts. The price we both paid.

The horror, the nightmare, the tragedy, the wait.

All so we could finally have this moment.

"I asked Maxwell for his approval to marry you. Just between you and me, he almost fell over, at first. But the more he chewed on it, the faster he came around. He knew. Just like I did, and just like you reminded me of the one thing I've ever been good at, darling." He stumbles over the last word, then pauses, drawing in a massive breath.

Holy crap. Is Trent freaking Usher actually *nervous?*

For the tenth time today, my heart bleeds wonder. Wonder, awe, and love.

"I know this is crazy, Presh. Pure insanity. It's crazy all I've ever been good at is putting the light in your life when we've had so much darkness. Crazy I've never been prouder of anything I've done more than loving you. Not my billions. Not my brains. Not my biz, or my charity, or all the lives I've changed. And yeah, it's also crazy I'm asking this with everything gone to pieces, so much unknown, so many ugly things still ahead...but fuck, I'd be a fool to wait a second longer. I'd be truly crazy putting this off. Not claiming you now. Not vowing I'll protect you and your family till my last dying breath. Not asking you to be my wife." His eyes are huge and twinkling as he brushes the ring box against my hand. "Marry me, Amy Kay. Give me forever."

It's my turn to stare into the rain.

Brain on fire. Cheeks warm and wet.

Approximately thirty seconds from totally falling to pieces.

I don't wait for him to utter another word before I answer.

I throw myself on the ground, next to him. Throwing my arms around this gorgeous, brilliant, mystical man, I hold on for dear life before I look him in the eye, open my lips, and answer with all my might.

"Yes! Of course, Trent. It couldn't be more perfect." Oh, but it could, a thousand different ways.

Then again, did morning ever look like anything without the sun devouring the night?

"Let's get married, darling," he growls, a big grin stretching across his face. His forehead presses into mine and we share a kiss that seems to last forever.

"Married," I echo the word, still trying to believe it, squeezing his fingers in mine. "I love you. So much it hurts sometimes."

He grabs my hand, pushes on the ring, and it's a magnificent fit.

I don't have time to look down and admire the new mark he's left on my hand before I hear his voice, half-whisper and half-growl. "Darling woman, you have no idea. Love you so much it's made me fucking crazy. Made me hurt. Made me bleed. And I wouldn't have it any other way."

* * *

Three Months Later

IT'S HIGH SUMMER. The rainy season long behind us.

We spent our last night engaged on the Space Needle, a private viewing Trent arranged just for us and must've spent a fortune on, watching America celebrate her independence with fireworks exploding across the Puget Sound in messy circles.

The colors glowed so beautifully on the waters. Even prettier reflected off the urban granite, steel, and glass. I'm thankful the Fourth was on a Friday this year, one day before the biggest day of my life.

Now, it's here.

The dress makes me look like royalty. Layers of lily white lace with cream-gold flourishes, sparkling Keds with ribbons for shoelaces, and no freaking veil.

That's intentional. I want to see every beautiful nanosecond of our wedding.

I also want Trent to see my face. No matter how much

I'm bawling like a baby.

His blue eyes burn the second they're on me, stepping out as the music swells. I walk down the aisle, taking in the scene, dad leading me gently by the arm. He can't stop looking over, and every time I do there's a teary smile nipping at my cheeks. I know he's overwhelmed to see me this happy, and mom, too.

She follows our every step from her perch near the front. It's the biggest I've seen her smiling in months, dressed to stun with her dark green dress and silver cane. She's next to my soon-to-be-father-in-law, Dale, who looks rather dapper in his checkerboard jacket. There's a woman's hairpin tucked in his lapel – Martha's – a piece of Trent's mother here with us today. I've caught my love looking at it a couple times, as soon as I watched his father arrive out the window this morning.

Right now, though, his eyes are on me. *Glued* to me.

"Almost there, peanut," dad says in a low whisper, guiding us forward, closer to the altar and through the throngs on both sides. It's a mixed crowd, a little of his side and mine, since his family isn't nearly as large.

There's even a dour looking Lindsey, who's been friendly to me lately. She came out of respect for my parents, and for me, I suppose. So far, no sign of my brother, but for better or worse, that's what I expect.

I look ahead, focused on the moment, ever closer to the sharp dressed God at the altar ready to take us to Elysium. Trent looks damn good on any normal day.

But today, for our wedding? If looks could kill, this would be a funeral.

Mine.

His suit is navy, a shade darker than his eyes. There's a

burgundy tie, flat and delicate against his chest, a stark contrast to the hard valleys and rolling hills swathed in dark ink underneath.

A wicked heat burns between my thighs, imagining all the things running through his head as he sees me in this dress. Imagining later, once we're alone, and he peels it off...

It's been two weeks since we've had sex – a record.

I made him wait, just to make the honeymoon sweeter, but he made it crystal clear fourteen days was the upper limit. I'm still a little dizzy when dad releases me with one last kiss on the cheek, then takes his seat next to mom.

"Dearly beloved," our officiant begins, speaking into the mic, a lovely woman with gold hair. "We're gathered here today to celebrate the joining of two hearts denied for too long. Trent Usher and Amy Kay Chenocott..."

I hear his words, but I don't.

I'm too busy trying to keep my balance once his hands take mine, releasing a swarm of butterflies.

I'm too busy trying – and failing – not to lose myself in a sea of manly blue. His crisp suit contrasts wonderfully with my blue. And nothing will ever hold a candle to his eyes, sharp and bright and soul-piercing as ever.

Oh, and I'm definitely too impatient. Waiting for my line, when I'm finally able to choke out a mushy "I do" between muffled sobs.

I told myself a thousand times the past three months I wouldn't cry. But here I am.

Here. We. Are.

The place I thought we'd never be.

It hits me then. I grip his hand tighter, so fierce it makes him tilt his head, questions in his eyes.

Damn you, Trent Usher, you'd better stick to script. If you've got something up your sleeve besides the basic vows we decided we'd stick to...

Of course he does. He wouldn't be the man I'm marrying without doing this his way.

The officiant nods to him. He smiles, tightens his grip on my hand, and we both know in our gut what's coming.

"I do, Amy Kay. I do because I didn't know it was possible for a man to love a woman this much and be denied for so long. Didn't know we'd ever have a second chance – a forever – and now that it's here I'm holding on for life. Didn't even know how happy we could be, how lucky, how certain it only gets better every day you're in my life. I do, Precious, and I always will. I'll be by your side in sickness, in health, in dust. I'll be there to catch you when you fall, and when you really need a midnight ice cream thanks to our baby growing in you..." He pauses, eyes drifting to my lower belly. I flush, tearing up again. "I'll be there for all of it, darling. Because after the years we've missed, I'd rather die than miss another second. Love you like the sun in this soggy ass city, and because we're too good at lighting up each other's worlds. I do. Today, tomorrow, forever."

Is he done? *Is he through pulling my heart out of my chest in slow motion and replacing it with mush?* I don't think the happiest woman on Earth stays human after this man has screwed up her pulse. Knotted up her inner rhythm in all the best ways.

"Then by the power vested in me by Washington, I hereby pronounce you –"

Torch the script. Trent Usher, my amazing husband,

isn't the only one here who gets to stray off it and do whatever the hell he wants.

The crowd gasps as I throw myself at him, push my lips to his, and drink him in so hard it hurts my face. It doesn't even take a second before he catches on.

We kiss ourselves into bliss. We synchronize souls. We fall into forever with the sunlight leaking through the church's tinted glass, a kaleidoscope of colors bursting onto us. It's a spotlight that cuts straight to our hearts.

They're huge. Happy. Drunk on love.

* * *

"You two look amazing together."

"Dad! Are you trying to break a record today, seeing how many times you can say it?" I'm trying to give my dad an annoyed look, but I can't help but smile. We're saying goodbye to our parents – or trying to – but they're way too good at talking our ears off.

It's the last stop. Incredible we're not completely exhausted, too, after the dinner, the dance, and endless conversations with distant family I haven't seen for years, plus more of Trent's business associates than I can remember.

"Because I mean it, peanut. Long, hard road getting here. A few months ago, I'd have never believed it, but now...my God. Can't see anything else."

"Neither can I," mom cuts in, sipping her champagne. "You know, this is the first day I've roamed around without noticing the pain? They said that wouldn't happen for a few more months."

"As long as you hydrate, dear," dad says softly, giving a

knowing look at her glass. She shoots him a dirty look back. "Only because I love you. Don't want you paying for this lovely day in the morning."

She opens her mouth to snap back, but then closes it. Instead, she presses her arms around Trent one more time, whispering in his ear, loud enough so I can hear. "We couldn't be happier for you both. Except, I don't think anything will ever make us smile more than having our family together again."

He pats her hands and looks at dad. My father nods, a rare smile creeping out behind his salt and pepper goatee. "Ditto. It's good to have you back, Mr. Usher."

The four of us trade hugs one more time and then we turn. Trent gives me a knowing look. I smile back, shaking my head, suddenly blushing like I did years ago, when we were just two stupid kids afraid to admit our crushes. "Okay, out with it. You've been looking at me like that all night. What's up?"

He wrinkles his nose, leaning in. "A little sympathy, Presh. Much as I've loved all this talk and pressing hands, there's something I've waited very patiently for. It involves you, me, and a horizontal surface sturdy enough not to break. But for simplicity's sake, let's make that last part optional."

Laughing, I push against him. He growls, grabs my hand, and leads me on faster, toward the back entrance of the huge historic mansion where we've had our reception. There's a private marina down in the docks and a familiar ship waiting, illuminated by the soft lamps on the shore.

"I can't believe you want to take the Wilkie out. We're lucky dad was even able to salvage her after the fire. The kitchenette still smells a little like smoke, last I checked."

"She's aged like a fine wine, Presh. Look, we both know I could easily afford to buy my own fleet of yachts. Thing is, if we really want to sail up to the Orcas and onto Victoria in style – and we do – there's nothing better. We'll never find another ship where we began."

My heart overrides the soft roll of my eyes. "You're right. I'm just...do you want me to keep crying? Because this is how it happens, Mr. Usher." I'm blotting at my face again. Even after so much emotion today, I'm still overwhelmed. I don't know if it'll ever end.

"Mrs. Usher," he growls, taking great delight in the Mrs. part, "I'm very good at taking your mind off tears, if you'll give me a chance."

The hand he's kept on my low back drifts down, grazing my ass through the dress. Smiling, I shoot him a knowing look, trying to control the goosebumps peppering my helpless skin. "Not until we're out of here and in port. Privacy, Trent. You're lucky I remember how to drive this thing after all these years."

He opens his mouth to say something, but it's not the reason I jump again. This time, much higher, my heart in my throat. An arm reaches out of the bushes, grabs his shoulders, and he whirls around, ready to put his fist through the intruder's face.

"Jace? Holy shit." I'm covering my mouth, heart pounding, fearing the worst.

He looks rough. He's wearing a white shirt with the top three buttons undone, his curly dark hair is a mess. The freshly grafted skin on his neck glows unnaturally pink in the light.

"There's my lovebirds. Relax, sis, I'm not here to –"

"What the hell do you want?" Trent snarls, hooking me around the waist, using his hard body as a shield.

"I came out here because I had to. It's been too long. Yeah, yeah, I know dad said I should stay in treatment. Rest assured I'll be marching my ass back to the reservation right after this. Go talk to my driver if you don't believe me. I also came to say...fuck, this is difficult...I'm sorry." His eyes hit mine. I relax and tense simultaneously. They're not crazy eyes, but my brother with a conscience? I can't even. "Trent, I fucked you over hard. Then I kept doing it. I lost my shit when I should've been a man and learned to straighten it out. I'm doing that now. I swear."

"Jace, you're sweet, but I'm not sure this the best time –"

"No, sis. No." He pivots, drilling his eyes into mine. "It's the *only* time. Only one that makes sense. Now that our family's changing, merging like it was always supposed to. We've finally got a chance to put this crap behind us." He looks away, over the sea, and then sighs. "I came out here to bury the damn dagger."

"Hatchet," Trent corrects. I think we both expect my brother to get pissy over that, but he just laughs.

"Right, Usher. Got it. Listen, I won't keep you much longer. I've said what I needed to, and in case it didn't sink in yet, here it is one more time: I'm really, *really* fucking sorry. Sorry for everything. And I'm working like hell to make sure it never happens again."

Trent cranes his face, studying my brother. At last, he nods firmly. "Then you deserve nothing but my best, Jace. Thanks."

His hand stays in mine while I lean forward, yet another round of tears fighting to get out, and give my brother a bear hug. "You'll be better soon. I know you will."

He's smiling when I pull away. We watch him turn away quickly, wiping something from his eye, and then kick gently at a couple loose rocks at the edge of the dock.

"Should be fully done with rehab by October. Maybe we'll catch up then?"

"Count on it," Trent says, preempting me. He pushes his fingers through mine and gives his reassuring pressure. "We'll probably be back in Seattle around then. Or if you ever come out toward Spokane –"

"That'd be amazing. I'll see what my schedule looks like. Got a new internship lined up with one of dad's old partners. Heavily supervised," he says with a wink. "See you soon, sis. In case you both wondered, I'm heading straight home – against my better instinct to start working on Linds tonight. I'll win her back, one way or another."

He turns, pacing up the hill. Trent glances further ahead, making sure the driver is really there like he said, and then we both share a confused look.

I don't think Lindsey will ever forgive him for the horrible things he did. But if there's anything I know, bracing my head for a second against the man who's given me so much, it's that change is inevitable.

And sometimes it's pretty shocking.

Sometimes change branches out in strange, beautiful, awesome directions.

* * *

"Easy, hubby!" I'm surprised how feral I sound.

He's not the only one trying to practically tear my dress off as soon as we're anchored for the night after a steady cruise north, somewhere near Bellingham.

"Fuck no. I've waited all night. Dress off now if you want to keep it looking pretty." His words come rough, through his teeth, a split second before he's on me again, dive-bombing kisses at my neck. His five o'clock shadow rakes heat through my blood.

His hand finds my right breast through the fabric, squeezes, and my heat becomes fire. I toss my head back, giving in. So completely gone and loving it.

"Trent!" I'm gasping quite possibly the one name I can comprehend.

"You heard me, Presh. Dress. Off. Now."

I don't know who's faster. I'm grateful for how he puts his lust on pause, barely long enough to help me shed my dress without any crazy damage. It falls to the floor, a heap next to the massive bed, and then I'm on him, pulling at his tie, leveling my mouth against his.

His hand reaches between my thighs. A knuckle goes against my clit, pushing hard through soaked fabric, tortuously enticing. I whimper.

"Fuck this," he says, hurling off his jacket, working on his buttons like mad. "I'm not just stripping down like a sailor on drill because I'm eager to be in my wife – though that's *very* much part of it. I've waited all damn day for you to see your surprise, Presh."

"Surprise?" I think I blink twice, the only time his prowling hands allow, tearing at his shirt.

His chest is the same broad masculine mass of steel muscle and dizzying ink I've loved forever. I bring my face close, stamping kisses, wondering what he's getting at. "Found it yet?" he says, sifting his fingers through my hair.

When I do, I stop. Reaching up, I run my fingers across the new tattoo on his shoulder.

It's today's date next to a ring of black fire, intricate and beautiful. Our names are stamped around the flames in a circle, but that's not what makes me grin and shake my head.

Apparently, I'm not just the happiest woman alive anymore. I'm also the luckiest.

"This lifetime and the next. Forever." I read aloud, a strange shock gnawing at my stomach. Why is this familiar?

Wait. How could I ever forget where I wrote those words before? My throat tightens.

"You...Jesus. You used the words from my hate letter?"

Trent smiles, big and knowing. He grabs my hand, lays it over the tattoo, dragging my nails into it, into him. "Seemed fitting. That's what we did here, didn't we? Turned hate into love. Hell into forever. Figured that belongs on my skin just like your name, darling. Why the hell not? We both know it's already branded thick on my soul."

"Trent..."

"No, woman. No more tears. Not while the night's young and you're so hot and wet, begging for every inch of me."

I'm still in disbelief, my heart drumming out of my chest, but my body can't lie. It responds automatically to his touch as he drops to his knees, and then sinks lower.

He spreads my legs, rips my panties off with his teeth.

Whatever soft, tender, bedazzled thoughts I had banish once his tongue goes to work.

Oh, and *how.*

Long restless licks up my folds. Measured heat against my clit. Two fingers slip deep inside me as I arch my back, powerful and in control, holding back their sweetness until I push my hips into him.

He pauses just for a second, looks up, and gives me my marching orders. "Fuck my fingers, Precious. Fuck my mouth. Fuck my all. Come for me a little harder than you ever have before. It's easy...you're my wife."

I can't breathe. Can't think. Can't do anything except lose myself in this amazing man, melting down, down, *down.*

It doesn't take long. His tongue attacks my pussy in long, deep strokes. Once it finds my clit, he's relentless.

I come, trying to yell his name.

Trying and failing because all that comes out is a sharp, breathless gasp. Two weeks without coming on his face and a lifetime of wanting to. Years of dreaming about our wedding night, and finally – *finally!* – living it.

He growls into my pussy, pulling my ass into him, tongue lashing at my clit. I come so hard even my bones tense, joining my flesh, my heart, my soul in the storm he forces through me.

"Fuck," I hear him say, flat on my back, desperately replenishing spent breath. "Legs around my waist. Hold on *tight.* We're not stopping, darling. We're making this count. I'm not fucking pulling out till I've had my wife's pussy thoroughly drenched, fucked, and marked by this dick."

Like what's coming next needs any introduction.

Trent does everything he promises and then some. Our first fuck as a married couple is sharp, intense, and frantic.

The fire in his body can't wait to spill itself in mine. I come again just thinking about it, no more than a few dozen strokes in, his hips slamming mine into the mattress.

I swear, we might be screwing each other so hard the entire boat rocks.

For once in my life, I don't care.

Don't care about anything except holding this man, pushing my hands and feet into his walls of muscle.

Riding out the love, the lust, the passion of us.

"Need to feel your pussy go again, darling," he growls, pressing his forehead to mine.

One rough hand reaches up, tugs at my nipple, sends more electricity through my blood. Then it's in my hair, flattening me against the bed, giving him more leverage between my legs. All the better to give me longer, deeper, unbelievable strokes.

"Trent! Oh, hell. Yes." My eyes roll as his cock does something wonderful inside me.

He catches just the right angle. Just the right speed. Just the right –

"Oh my God. It's good – so good – but hubby, I don't...I don't know if..."

"Presh, you hear me? Fuck me like you mean it. Your married pussy feels so good and I'm so close. Give it to me *now*." He silences my next denial with a vicious kiss, sinking his teeth into my bottom lip. "Come the fuck with me."

Just when I think my body has hard limits, he smashes

them.

My eyes roll back after a few more rough strokes and I'm so gone.

Coming!

So hard, so swift, so blindingly hot on his cock I lose my whole weight and just fly.

"Precious, fuck! Coming."

And he does. Violent spasms rip through him. Every muscle on his huge, magnificent body becomes hot stone, a slab of man pouring himself into me. His cock plunges deep and he roars his release, the heat of his seed floods into me sharper than sin.

Coming. Together.

Coming. So good.

Coming. Forever.

He holds his cock in me as we slowly drift out of our stupor. Then he buries his lips on mine again, a softer, saner kiss, one that settles deep in my heart.

"Amazing, Presh. Just like you. Must be the luckiest asshole anywhere, knowing I've got a lifetime of that ahead."

"This lifetime. And the next," I say, smiling into another kiss. I nip at his bottom lip, catch it, and then give back a bite as good as he gave.

Only trouble with life is, it spins by so fast, especially after you've found the man you're meant to have forever.

I pause, loving how he laughs, rubbing at his lips, and then attacks mine all over again.

Our next kiss, I savor. Because as fast as our new happy lives are rocketing by, they'll never catch forever.

Lucky me, lucky us, forever with Trent Usher is a very long, very sweet, very perfect eternity.

XVIII: EXTENDED EPILOGUE: TWO YEARS LATER (TRENT)

I'm standing over the crib, utterly lost in how beautiful she is.

How beautiful they *both* are.

My perfect little girl came from the perfect woman. She's a small, pink, very sleepy reminder how blessed I'll always be.

Katie Usher smacks her tiny lips, rolling on her side. Barely a year old and she's already got her ma's habits. When her eyelids open, there's no mistaking what she's inherited from me.

"Come here, baby blue. With eyes like that, you're gonna make some man lose his mind one fine day." I hoist her up, sliding a palm under her weight as she wriggles in my arms.

"Just like her father," a voice says behind me.

Two seconds later, Presh slides her soft hands around my waist. The sun cuts the rain, streaming in through the blinds.

They say timing is everything, but today it's divine. I

never thought I'd appreciate such simple things. But then I never thought I'd be a family man, smiling like a fool.

"Morning, darling," I say, turning to face her. "You're up early. Thought you'd want to sleep while I got her some breakfast."

"And miss the big day? Her Uncle Jace might throw a fit if we're not the first ones there. He's counting on us."

I stiffen at those two words. *Uncle Jace.*

Fuck.

I'm not sure I'll ever get used to it.

It's been two years since her brother lost his mind, set himself on fire, and then spent months between rehab and a white collar prison sentence. Maxwell's lawyers were able to cut the best deal they could with his arson charges. One year in minimal security prison, with visitor privileges. Twenty hours per week doing supervised community service around Seattle. He paid the toll, and now he's a free man again.

Shaking my head, I slide our daughter into Presh's arms, strolling across the baby's room to open the blinds. "He's changing, it seems, I'll give him that. Thought for sure he'd slip back into his old habits after he got out."

Presh shoots me a dirty look, her soft brown hair a bobbing bun on her head. It's a new look for her and it teases my blood. Too much like a hot school teacher, or maybe a naughty librarian, not to tarnish my brain with some very wicked urges.

"Well, he hasn't. Amazingly, he's getting his crap together, thank you very much." She sighs. "Really, though, I wasn't sure we'd see the day either. But I think it's here. My reckless brother's growing a heart."

"Maybe." I nod, hoping she's right. Then I see them in

the sun beam again and smile. Crossing the room, I throw my arms around them both. A lingering kiss melts the chill in her lips. "Skeptic in me thinks this orphan thing is a ploy to win back Linds, but hell, so what? He's doing good for the world. That's enough."

Precious twists her head away, smiling at my kiss even though she doesn't want my cynicism. Still, she can't deny it.

"He's raising money. Potentially *a lot* of money for those kids. Ulterior motives can't change that," I say. I reach over, sliding a couple fingers through our sleepy daughter's light hair. "I know one thing: I'll take our Katie knowing the reformed Uncle Jace any day over the jackoff he used to be."

Presh sighs, lines forming in her face as she scrunches her forehead, then smooths them again. "Yeah. Let's just try not to jinx this, okay? There's kind of a lot riding on it. If this doesn't go right, I'm afraid he'll start heading down a different road again."

"Enough," I growl, silencing my wife with another kiss.

I'm not letting my own doubts about Jace turn infectious. She deserves better. Hell, maybe we all do.

My thumb flicks her ring lightly, loving how it feels on her skin, even after it's been a fixture for years. "We'll think positive today, darling. Good goddamn vibes. Now, let's get her cleaned up, fed, and go."

Next time I look into her eyes, she's smiling. Her worries temporarily erased.

Sweet perfection.

Soon, we'll find out if Jace Chenocott manages to keep the beautiful start to our day rolling, or if his 'new man' act ends in a blaze of monumental stupidity.

*　*　*

THE AUCTION IS SILENT. The crowd is huge. The kids are so adorable even I crack a smile.

I have to hand it to the crazy bastard, he's done a solid job. The silent auction for two Seattle orphanages has already raised over half a million dollars. A new record, or so the founder says.

Of course, it helps having high society greasing the wheels. My in-laws drop a check for fifty thousand in the donation bowl right away. I double it, hiding my check from Maxwell so this doesn't turn into a family pissing contest.

We've all got another goal on our minds besides raising money, unlike everybody else here.

I'm standing next to my father-in-law, watching Amy Kay saunter across the room, toward the man who's brought us together. The man who wronged us. The man who made me hate. The man who once upon a time, in a galaxy far, far away, used to be my closest friend.

She's holding our daughter, fast asleep in her arms.

Jace wears the same high-necked sweater he usually does. Even though it's still late summer, attracting a couple odd looks. I think he's self-conscious about the burns that have haunted him since that vicious night.

My frenemy leans over, kissing Katie's precious forehead. My fist tightens in my pocket, then relaxes.

Shit.

I have to remember that particular frenemy is my brother-in-law. Also a man who's seemingly changed his colors, but is it for real?

I want to believe.

"They're so sweet together. She brings out a side in Jace the boy desperately needs. Say, any chance you'll let grandpa have her for the weekend? You should've seen her little face last week! The dear thing practically *begged* me to read her the next part, after the Cyclops." Maxwell claps me on the shoulder, his well groomed hair showing more salt than pepper all the time.

"Only if you don't scare her with the *Odyssey*. She's too young," I growl, remembering the crazier parts the Greeks came up with. Maynard forced us to memorize plenty my first year in early literature.

"Nonsense! Children are never too young for the classics." He pauses, giving me a reluctant nod. "However, if you insist, I suppose we can settle for cartoons. Always was partial to Looney Tunes, just between us gents."

I hide my grin behind a sip of coffee, trying to imagine the tight-laced old man watching cartoons and enjoying them. "Well, looks like you've got your chance to practice."

Maxwell follows my gesture to the big TV screen in the corner. A newer kids' movie starts playing, less than a minute before the orphans come storming in.

They've bused them over for the day. I try not to chew my lip, remembering when that was me.

Thankfully, my parents saved me from too many memories.

Modern charities like this try to get kids placed with good foster homes as quick as they can. Still, a dark part of me remembers how fucked up it was without a home, surrounded by other kids, endless smiles and hand-me-down toys trying to keep our spirits up.

A familiar whine draws my eyes. Katie wakes up in Presh's arms. She beams like the sun, seeing the cartoon show and the other children. I walk over, lifting her out of my wife's arms, smiling.

Hard to do anything else when I'm holding the best thing our love ever created.

The joy doesn't last long. Next time I look up, both Chenocotts are next to me, Ophelia holding out her arms anxiously.

"Go see grandma and grandpa," I whisper, laying another kiss on Katie's head, before I pass her off. "Ought to take her out for a stroll. Clear weather out there today. Did you see the grounds? Just beautiful."

"Simply marvelous, my dear!" Ophelia does her best movie star impression and gets a laugh from my little girl.

Presh sits next to me, patting my knee, a spark in her eyes that says more than just she's happy to see me again. *Damn, what now?*

I say goodbye to her folks one more time while my brain goes a hundred miles an hour. Jace is nowhere to be seen, suddenly. Weird with all the orphans here, either glued to the TV or running around the room, some with juice in their hands.

I take her hand, my grip tightening, knees so tense I want like hell to stand. "Everything okay, darling? Where's he gone?"

"Jace?" she cocks her head, amusement in her eyes.

I nod like my head weighs fifty pounds. Who else?

Fuck, I can't take it. We have to find him. Make sure he's truly on the up-and-up, and not relapsing into bad habits.

Before she even finishes, I pull her up, impatiently darting away from our seats.

"Trent, whoa, you need to –"

Calm down? Like hell I do.

There's lightning in my blood.

It won't shut up. Not till I've seen he's fine, we're fine, everything's *fine*.

Fine. Not a bad re-run of Jace the Destroyer. Or getting himself into some stupid trouble that'll take the family another solid year to pull his chestnuts out of.

"Trent!"

I hope I'm not pulling her hand too hard. I throw my gaze around the room, looking for her brother, not seeing him. My pulse becomes a jackhammer.

"Slow down!" she hisses again, flashing me a stern look.

I can't. I just yank her forward, sending us around the corner, down the long corridor, toward the gardens out back. If Ophelia and Maxwell took my advice, they're out here.

With Jace, maybe. And our little girl. Plus an equal chance that means disaster or something so mundane it'll make me feel like a complete fool.

"Trent, Jesus, what's gotten into –"

Me? Who the fuck knows.

When we barge outside through the glassy French doors, everything I expect blows itself to pieces. We both come to a screeching halt, looking at a very pissed off woman with her back turned.

Even from behind, it's clear her arms are folded. Jace stands in front of her, next to a tall tree, one of several fountains running off to the side, their waters sparkling wonderfully in the sun.

"See? Nothing. Congratulations, Captain Freakout."

Presh rips her hand out of mine, curiosity melting the anger in her emerald eyes.

"Quiet, darling," I whisper. "Let's just make sure."

She gives me the evil eye, but doesn't protest as I take her hand again. I lead us around the crop of bushes, where Jace hopefully won't see, taking us in earshot. We sit on the bench behind them, obscured by the trees, and listen.

"Dinner, babe. On me. Just name the time and place. One hour of your life and I'll never ask for anything again." Jace's voice has an eerie calm.

"Jace..." Lindsey sounds a lot more flustered.

"How does next Friday sound? Or would a weekday work better? Don't know what your schedule's like, Linds. Don't know much of anything since we've been separated for so long. I hate not knowing."

"Jace..." The tremor in her pitch only rises.

"How 'bout Elliott's? Remember the good times there? Think I won you over there with forty oysters and the perfect champagne. You loved how I paired them. Just a few weeks after we went out on Bainbridge, two kids going at it like crazy, right under Amy Kay and Usher's nose. Hell, we –"

"Jace!"

Presh and me both cringe. He's relentless. She's had it with his bullshit.

"You're disgusting. And ridiculous. And sad. Don't you get it?" The air curdles during the five seconds before she starts speaking again. "It's over, Jace. So completely over. I've moved on. I've had to put my life back together from almost nothing thanks to you. I came out here today as a courtesy to your parents, your sister. Not you. And because I thought we'd all be better off if I gave a little of your alimony to those poor kids. Look, maybe you've done some good here, there's no denying that. But Jace, Jesus..."

"But babe..."

"You did me so much wrong. So fucking much." Lindsey sighs, as if letting the sadness and contempt she's been holding in takes a hundred pounds off her shoulders.

I'm on the edge of my seat. Hoping he'll do the sane thing: leave her the fuck alone.

Sensing how bad I want to stand, Presh pushes her little fingers through mine. Squeezes my hand so hard it must hurt her knuckles.

"Don't. Just give them another minute. Please. One more minute." She's mouthing the words.

I lean back, plant my spine against the bench, even though it kills me.

Whatever. One more minute.

Or until Lindsey screams.

Then, I'm done. I'm ending this insanity the hard way.

But Jace's next words aren't the furious, ego-damaged outpouring from a dejected limpdick. Not the sour show I expect.

"Lindsey, babe...I know. I treated you like shit. I drank too much. Screwed around with too many skanks. Gave up too many pieces of my soul. Fuck, didn't even feel how everything I took from you came back on me while I was busted up and crazy. Not till I got my mind back, after that fire...after rehab. Spent every night thinking hard. Thinking like I should've years ago, rather than hammering myself out cold. Rather than fucking you over." He pauses for breath before he continues.

"I finally understood. Saw what I did. Swore I'd never,

ever fuck anybody else over. I haven't been on a date for two years. You know that? Haven't even paid to get my dick wet."

"Wow, such sacrifice!" she bites off. "I guess you'll tell me you're about to join a monastery, too. I mean, why not? You've always been awesome at playing martyr."

It's torture listening to this. Presh buries her sweet face in her palms, shaking her head. Her brother is blowing it big time, though I'm wondering if there was ever anything to blow.

She's not giving him a second chance. She'd be crazy to, after everything he did.

Hell, after everything they did to each other.

She married him for money. He married her for...fuck knows. She treated him like a prop, and he treated her like hell.

Is there any coming back for an honest to God sociopath? Seeing this charity thing today, for some things, maybe the answer is yes.

But for love? For two people who never should've been together? For a man who savaged the woman he swore his heart to?

"Babe..." He pauses. I hold my breath, wondering if old Jace is about to come roaring back. "You're right. Fuck, I'm still doing it, aren't I? Making this all about me."

"Damn right, you are," she snaps.

"You know what? Screw it. Since we're here today, banging our hearts together again, I'd might as well spit out the rest. Make a full confession." He turns, brushing his elbow against the bushes, which shake like mad. "I wanted to help those kids. Really, I did. But I wanted to help myself, too. I hoped you'd come out here, see how different things are, see for yourself the man I've become. Not who I used to be."

Lindsey doesn't say anything. Presh gives me a look. I think we both wonder if we're about to hear her palm flying across his cheek.

"Trouble is, I haven't changed enough. I'm still the same selfish prick with zero self-awareness. Still the same asshole who's in it for me, and nobody else."

He sniffs. Jace frigging Chenocott actually *sniffs back tears.*

"So, you know what? Fuck it. You're more right than you know. You've been right about everything. I don't deserve the time of day from you till I get my shit together. So together, so tight, I don't need gimmicks anymore. Because you'll see I'm different, then, and I'll spend the rest of my life being sorry for the evil shit I did to you. All of it, Linds. Every bit of pain I've ever left in your bones."

"Jace..."

"No." He starts walking, his polished shoes scraping the stone path. "Just...take care of yourself. Till you find a man who treats you right, take care. Don't ever put up with any of the same bullshit, even an inkling, ever again. Not for anybody, or for me. You're too damn good for that."

We don't move a muscle until his footsteps fade to nothing. Then we hear Lindsey crashing down on the edge of the fountain, her purse jingling, and muffled sobs.

Presh gives me a look, gets up, and turns the corner.

That's my cue to go. Whatever these old friends have to say to each other, they deserve a little privacy.

* * *

"Gotta hand it to you, Jace. You did the right thing." I catch him near the parking lot later, alone, after he's said his goodbyes to the big patrons who contributed the most. The kids are gone too and the place is clearing out for the day.

"Right thing?" he cocks his head, realization swelling his eyes. "Shit. You mean you heard...?"

"Everything." I slap him on the shoulder before he's able to twist away, hiding his humiliation. "Listen, walking away from her, after I know how bad you wanted it to go different...that took balls."

"Yeah, well, fuck. I'm just as surprised as anybody. Living clean, trying to do the right thing. Not having a drink or a hot piece of –" He shuts his yap and smiles at an older couple passing by just in time. "It's hard as hell. Jesus, Usher, I think sometimes it *is* hell. But you know, like I told her, that's what I deserve. After everything I did, it's too kind."

He doesn't finish. Just sighs. And that's all he needs.

"You've got yourself a heart. Congratulations." I wink, trying not to bust his balls too hard. "Actually, I've got a confession, too. When I couldn't find you inside, after your speech, while the auction was wrapping up...I grabbed Amy Kay. I kind of freaked out."

He doesn't understand. His eyes pierce through me. He reaches up, scratching the patchy flesh under his shirt, a scarred reminder where his life went wrong he'll carry forever.

"I mean, I was worried. Over nothing. Thinking you'd turn into the old Jace again." I pause, releasing my hold, standing up taller. "And that, I've got to admit, was a real shitty thing to do. You're not the same guy anymore. Maybe you're not perfect and maybe you never will be – welcome to the club – but shit. If you can't win back Lindsey, you deserve a second chance. Long as you fly right, you're family."

He looks at the hand I extend. At last, he takes it, and gives it a hardy shake.

"Thanks, Usher. You're a real dick sometimes, but hell, you're family, too. No denying. You always were, even when I was out of my gourd."

We both break our little moment just in time for Maxwell and Ophelia. They trot up, holding my little girl. Katie slumps over her grandpa's shoulder, secure and snoozing, too heavy for grandma to carry for long when her knees start acting up.

"There's our girl!" Jace says excitedly, patting her little back. "Where's sis? Anybody see her?"

"Present!" Precious chirps a minute later, coming up behind us.

Maxwell gives his granddaughter another kiss, passing her back to mama. I give her a look, nervous as hell to find out what Lindsey said. She'll tell me everything on the way home. "Look at her, tuckered out. Hard to get her afternoon nap here. We'd better be going."

"This weekend!" Maxwell reminds us, gently wagging a finger.

"Saturday, dad. Good timing, honestly. We're flying out to Spokane again anyway to wrap up some business. Wish you'd told me selling a company was so much work."

The three of us beam. Fuck, she isn't kidding about the work, though.

Presh decided to sell off her inn business a few months ago. It's as profitable as ever, a dramatic turnaround. She insists the next few years should have travel and mothering our kids on the itinerary.

Kids. Plural.

I try not to think about it too much, working on baby number two. Or the instant hard-on knocking her up means.

We'll be trying soon. But fuck, soon isn't fast enough.

"Worst will be over in no time, peanut," Maxwell says. "Run along. We'll be ready, bright and early, to take the little angel off your hands."

I slip my hand into Amy Kay's and turn, heading for the car.

"Usher, wait!" I stop, several steps into the parking lot, while Jace runs after me. "Have to say, I really appreciate what you did for me again. Only person I shit on more than Lindsey was you. If you're seeing something besides the prick who screwed you over, and screwed away your chance with marrying my sis years earlier then...it means a lot. An awful fucking lot. I'm not squandering your trust a second time. I love you, man."

He grabs me in a bear hug, pounding my back. My eyes go wide. I hear my in-laws laughing.

Just like that, the world goes insane.

For once, though, it's a good madness. I give him a brotherly squeeze and then I'm gone.

Whatever I thought today would bring, it wasn't *this*.

I've gone through hell thanks to him, heaven thanks to my beautiful wife, and all kinds of craziness since I became a father.

Soon as I'm in the car, I'm thankful. Turns out life still has a few surprises.

* * *

LATER, at home, we're flat on our backs, resting after putting little Katie down for her late nap.

"Thanks for turning it around today," she whispers, sunbeams in her eyes.

"Turning? What're you –"

"Jace. You were *so* worried, Trent. Thought you were gearing up for a fistfight. But I heard bits and pieces. What you said meant a lot to him. That's what I've been telling you he needs – support. Forgiveness. It's hard, after how bad he hurt us, but as sappy as it sounds, that's all it takes. I finally have a brother again. All thanks to you."

Fuck me. She's right.

Isn't she?

I don't know, but that heartfelt purr in her throat does miraculous things to my pulse. It runs higher, harder, faster when I bring my lips to hers. Then it does wicked things to my dick.

It's not long before our lips take over. My tongue chases hers. Our fingers lock together. I'm holding her just a little harder, seeking the one rhythm, finding it in record time as I get on top, pressing her into the mattress.

A moan slips in my mouth. Soft, delicious, dangerously addictive.

Some people go their whole lives trying to define heaven.

I know where it starts and ends: Amy Kay Usher under me.

Whimpering.

Grinding her hips into mine.

"Off, darling," I rumble, reaching up her skirt, between her legs. I find her panties and start pulling.

I'm too hard, too desperate, too dead set on being in her to bother removing anything else.

That'll happen later.

She bites her lip, one last tease that makes me throb like hell.

I go in hot, attacking her lips, her forehead's warmth on mine. It happens in a blur about three seconds before her phone blows up.

It vibrates. Pings. Chirps like an annoying bug I want to grab and throw at the nearest wall.

Our gazes meet. We're both thinking it.

Both holding our breath, remembering what it meant the last time this happened.

"Answer it," I say, reluctantly drawing my fingers off the wet heat between her legs.

She snatches her phone off the nightstand with a sigh. "Looks like...texts. From Jace? Oh, God."

I sit at the edge of the bed, hand on her back, and wait.

Fuck, I swear, if that crazy SOB did something stupid after our heart-to-heart talk today, *and* cheated me out of screwing my wife's brains out...

"Whew. Close call. I think." She turns my way with a smile sweeter than her eyes.

"You think?"

"Who knows," she says, trying not to laugh, passing the phone. "See for yourself. I can't see this going anywhere, but...you never know."

No one ever does.

I see the hundred texts he's blasted her way for the last few minutes. And I'm only exaggerating a little.

She said yes to dinner! Holy shit, sis. Holy fuck.

Help me not be stupid. Help me more, I mean...

Should I play it cool? Or go in for the kill?

Run it by Trent if he's around?

There's at least a dozen more like it. God help me, I break down and release the mad chuckle building in my throat. Feels good when it finally rolls out.

Also signals her turn to lay a hand on my back. "Hon, are you okay?"

"Better," I say, pushing the phone back into her palm. "Jace Chenocott finally has something else to worry about besides making mischief."

"Trent!" she elbows me gently in the side. "I think it's sweet. Never expected Lindsey to come around so soon. Heck, I thought she'd be a lost cause for sure. That's...amazingly big of her, to hear him out at all. Just hope they're ready."

I stop laughing slowly, rubbing my face. "Maybe. Tell him to calm the hell down and play it cool, when you get a chance. And no, he didn't hear that from me."

Still grinning, I grab her phone again, and silence it. She's shaking her head after I reach over, laying it on her stand.

"Really, Mr. Usher? You don't want me to tell him now?"

"It's not like they're going out for a few more days. He'll have plenty of time to figure out how to not spill his spaghetti before then. Most important part when a man gets a second chance."

"Oh? So confident. Almost like you're speaking from

experience..." Presh smiles, tracing her pointer finger up my chest, fingering the top button of my shirt.

Growling, I grab her, pin her wrists to the mattress, shifting the raging hard-on in my pants neatly between her legs. "Darling, please. Think we both know the only experience I'm interested in right now involves Mrs. Usher blowing up on every inch of this dick."

I don't even let her respond. Just bury my lips in her sweet kiss, find her tongue, and own it into silence.

Jace is a lucky man, staring down the mouth of something that'll be his biggest disaster or a massive triumph.

Once, that was me.

That was us.

That was where we found our real beginning.

I don't know where we'll end. Just know I'll be taking this woman on one hell of a journey in the meantime.

Starting right now. I pull her lip gently with my teeth. Her nails rake my back. I reach between us, furiously undoing my belt, shoving my pants down. Her skirt goes up and I breathe her scent.

"There. Trent. *Yeah.*"

"Yeah, darling. Keep your legs open while I fuck you." I push my cock into her sweetness, growling at how tight, how warm, how fucking perfect she is.

We've done this hundreds, probably thousands of times, and it never gets old. I crawled through broken glass on fire just to have her forever, and there's no better time I feel it than now, engulfed in her pink.

Presh throws her head back. Her hips begin moving with mine.

And she's gone.

We're past words. Too deep in souls. Our bodies collide with a frantic, animal lust.

Her delectable cunt pinches my dick. Sweat beads on my brow, focus overwhelming me, the need to bring her off a few times before I lose my ropes inside her.

"God, Trent! Yeah, baby, yeah." Every sound steaming out of her mouth comes shriller. Breathless whispers more than words.

A perfect background track while I fuck her to nirvana and back. My strokes come harder, deeper. They grind against her, adding that extra delicious friction, right against her clit. I shove my lips to hers, taking everything, as she goes over into O-land.

Dear. Fucking. Mercy.

She's on fire. Inferno in her kiss, in the explosive moans I dip my tongue into, in how her pussy convulses, pulling at my dick.

Just makes me fuck her harder still.

Just ends time and space and everything between her and me.

Just puts us in one body. One fuck. One rhythm.

Whole minutes scream by in thrusting bliss. Lose track of how many times she goes off on me.

Too many, and not enough.

The magma building in my balls slowly short circuits my brain, tensing every muscle, winding me up until I have to blow.

"Precious, fuck, come with me. Come with me again! Come, darling, come."

My hips don't give her any choice. Neither do my strokes. Neither do my feral lips, stealing every soft whine she gives, every filthy word and tender plea.

My spine electrifies as her little cunt twists around me again.

Tighter. Hotter. Needier.

Beautifully desperate fuckery.

We come together just like that. Lashed by our madness, our ecstasy, our hearts striking head-on.

I come so fucking hard I see stars, balls on fire, pumping and seething like mad in the cauldron of her womb.

I own her.

She owns me.

We own things I can't even pin down, much less describe.

It doesn't even matter. Because it's one more moment when I know, when every part just knows, how damn madly I love this woman. How much I need her. How right we are in every trembling breath.

And there are a lot of those before we give it up. Before I'm soft enough to leave her perfection.

"Love you, darling. Love you like hell because we've got our days like this, and so many more ahead. So fucking many, Precious."

For almost a full minute, she barely says anything, her words hidden behind her exhausted smile. Then she opens her eyes, sweeps me up in emerald, and I hear the four most perfect words in any language.

"Love you, Trent. Forever."

Second chances are the ultimate gamble. Sometimes they're easy because they were always meant to be. Other times, like ours, they make you pay in blood, sweat, and fire.

I'm too lost in our next volley of kisses to think too deep. Just know one thing: I'd do it all again for us.

I'd do it a million times.

I'll keep on doing it every day I'm not pushing daisies.

My wife is too Precious, too perfect, too generous for anything less.

Amy Kay Usher and the many children we'll have after our Katie deserves all my will, all my heart, and all my soul.

THANKS!

Want more Nicole Snow? Sign up for my newsletter to hear about new releases, exclusive subscriber giveaways, and more fun stuff!

JOIN THE NICOLE SNOW NEWSLETTER! - **http://eepurl.com/HwFW1**

Thank you so much for buying this book. I hope my romances sweeten your days with pleasure, drama, and all the feels! I tell the stories you want to hear.

If you liked this book, please consider leaving a review and checking out my other romance tales.

THANKS!

Got a comment on my work? Email me at nicole@nicolesnowbooks.com. I love hearing from fans!

Nicole Snow

More Intense Romance by Nicole Snow

CINDERELLA UNDONE

MAN ENOUGH

SURPRISE DADDY

PRINCE WITH BENEFITS: A BILLIONAIRE ROYAL ROMANCE

MARRY ME AGAIN: A BILLIONAIRE SECOND CHANCE ROMANCE

LOVE SCARS: BAD BOY'S BRIDE

MERCILESS LOVE: A DARK ROMANCE

RECKLESSLY HIS: A BAD BOY MAFIA ROMANCE

STEPBROTHER CHARMING: A BILLIONAIRE BAD BOY ROMANCE

STEPBROTHER UNSEALED: A BAD BOY MILITARY ROMANCE

Prairie Devils MC Books

OUTLAW KIND OF LOVE

NOMAD KIND OF LOVE

SAVAGE KIND OF LOVE

WICKED KIND OF LOVE

BITTER KIND OF LOVE

Grizzlies MC Books

OUTLAW'S KISS

OUTLAW'S OBSESSION

OUTLAW'S BRIDE

OUTLAW'S VOW

Deadly Pistols MC Books

NEVER LOVE AN OUTLAW

NEVER KISS AN OUTLAW

NEVER HAVE AN OUTLAW'S BABY

NEVER WED AN OUTLAW

Baby Fever Books

BABY FEVER BRIDE

BABY FEVER PROMISE

BABY FEVER SECRETS

Only Pretend Books

FIANCÉ ON PAPER

ONE NIGHT BRIDE

SEXY SAMPLES: FIANCÉ ON PAPER

I: Look Who's Back (Maddie)

Something in his makeup made him an utter bastard, but I owed him my life.

It's my heart I refused to give up without a fight. If only I'd known from the very start Calvin Randolph never backs down.

Not in love. Not in business. Not in any corner of his battered existence.

I'll never understand it.

Maybe he's missing the gene that stops a normal man from sinking his hands into the earth and ripping it to messy, screaming shreds until he gets his way.

Perhaps defeat just never made sense in his head.

Or possibly it's because this was just meant to be. There's a natural mischief in every heart that loves bringing together what's complicated, dangerous, and totally incompatible in a blinding impact.

Oh, but I still wish I'd *known*, before our blind collision became love.

We would have prevented so much suffering.

* * *

I'm in no mood to pull a jet black envelope out of my mailbox. Not after an exhausting day dealing with corporate legalese and a language barrier that's like a migraine prescription. Especially when said legalese is a hodgepodge of English and Mandarin bullet points outlining bewildering trade concepts that make me want to pop aspirin like Junior Mints.

But the coal colored envelope isn't what ends me. It's a single word, the one and only scrawled on the front in bright pink, without so much as a return address or a stamp to accompany it.

DOLL.

No one's called me that in years. Seven, to be precise.

I have to steady myself against the mailbox when my heartbeat goes into my ears. For a second I'm afraid I'll faint.

It's incredible how the only man who'd ever call me a name I haven't heard since high school still has a freakish ability to reduce me to a knee-shaking, cement lunged mess so many years later.

My fingernail slides across the seal, digs in, and splits it open. I tear gingerly, like I'm expecting a snake or a tarantula to jump out. There isn't enough room for creepy crawlies, I suppose, though I wonder about the hard lump in the corner, rubbing it against my palm.

The constant noise in the hall of my cramped Beijing flat has faded from a roar to a whisper. It's hard to focus on the slim white note I pluck out when I'm trying to remember how to breathe. There's no mistaking the handwriting.

They're his words. I'd recognize them anywhere, even after so long.

Blunt, mysterious, and taunting as ever. He keeps it short and sweet – assuming there's anything sweet about reaching down inside me, and yanking out a dozen painful memories at once.

It's been too long.
    You still owe me that favor, doll, and I'm cashing in.
    Marry me.

-Cal

"Marry me?" I read it again, shaking my head.

If this is a joke, it isn't funny. And I already know it isn't. Cal wouldn't break a seven year silence for a stupid laugh. It's serious, and it's a brand new kind of terrifying.

My eyes trace his three insane sentences four times before my knees give out.

I go down hard, banging my legs on the scuffed tile, dropping the envelope. The object anchored in the corner bounces out with a clatter as loud as a crashing symbol, leaving a haunting echo in my ears.

I look down and mentally start planning my goodbyes. It's a gold ring with a huge rock in the middle, set into a flourish designed to mimic a small rose. I don't need to try it on to know it's probably my size.

I flip the note over in my hands before I lose it. There's a number scrawled on the backside in the same firm, demanding script. CALL ME, says the two words next to it in bold, as if it's the most natural thing in the world to ask for a mail order bride in less than ten words.

As if it hasn't stopped my heart several times over.

I can't believe he's back.

I can't believe he's found me here, on the other side of the Earth, and decided to drag me back to the hell we both left behind.

I really, *really* can't believe what he's asking me to do.

But it's my fault, isn't it? I'm the one who said I'd do *anything*, if he ever needed it.

Without him, I wouldn't have my dream career working trade contracts in China for a prestigious Seattle company. I'd be lucky serving tables with the criminal stain on my record if he hadn't stepped in, and saved me when it seemed hopeless.

There's a lot I don't know.

Like why he's gone emergency bride hunting, for one. Or what he's been doing since the last dark day I saw him, crying while they hauled him off in handcuffs. I don't even know what kind of devils are in the details if I actually agree to this madness – and it's not like I have a choice.

Small town guilt will gnaw at my soul forever if I turn him down.

Oh, but he'll catch up with me again soon, and let me know exactly what new hell awaits. That much, I'm certain.

It won't be long before I'm face-to-face again with the sharp blue eyes that used to make my blood run hot. Twisted up in knots like a gullible seventeen year old with a bad crush and a blind spot for bad people before I know what's hit me. And yes, revisiting every horrible thing that happened at Maynard Academy in ways I haven't since my therapist discharged me with flying colors.

He's right about one thing, the only thing that matters in any of this: I owe him. Big time.

All the unknowns in the world are worthless stacked up against this simple truth.

So I'll wait, I'll shrivel up inside, and I'll chew on the same nagging question some more.

Jesus, Cal. What the hell have you gotten yourself into?

* * *

Seven Years Ago

The beautiful boy with the constant entourage ignored me until my seventh day at the new school.

How my parents thought I'd ever fit into this place, I don't know. They just saw the school's shiny academic track record and absorbed its prestige from Seattle socialites several leagues higher than we'd ever be. A fast track scholarship I won in an essay contest sealed the deal. My old English teacher in Everett submitted it behind my back when I was ready to throw it in the trash, and the rest is history.

Who could blame them for leaping at the chance? They want the absolute best for me. I'm ready to make my family proud, even if it means trading a huge piece of my seventeen year old social life for the best education several states over.

It's not like Maynard Academy has a welcome wagon. The other kids keep their awkward distance since the first day I show up on the seating charts next to them. Almost like they smell the stink of my missing trust fund, or the Mercedes that didn't materialize as soon as I got my license.

I still take the bus. And I'm not sure my parents could ever afford a trust lawyer on their seventy thousand combined income, raising two girls. Their struggle to keep up rent and bills reminds me how lucky I am to get a scholarship to this place.

Turns out the benefactor behind the money at Sterner Corp shares my love for John Steinbeck.

Ever since we moved down to south Seattle, uprooting lives and careers just for this special chance, I'm in another world.

If the black lacquered study desks, the library with the crystal chandeliers and the skylights, or the marble fountain out front hadn't tipped me off the first week, the natural pecking order here certainly does.

My face is stuck in a German textbook when he comes up to me. He doesn't bother with introductions, just pushes his fingers into my book, and rips it out of my hands.

"Do you ever speak?" His voice is smooth as ice, a rogue smirk tugging at his lips.

"Hey!" I stand up, dropping the rest of my small book stack on the floor, arms folded. "I don't know, don't *you* have any manners?"

"There's never been much point," he tells me, sizing me up with his sky blue eyes.

I hate it, but he isn't wrong. It took all of three days here to notice how everyone hangs on his every word. There are always a couple grinning jocks and puppy-eyed cheerleaders at his shoulder. I think the teachers would love to knock 'Mr. Randolph' down a few marks, if only he didn't keep acing all his tests.

He's too good a student and too big a dick to be worth the trouble.

I've seen the summary sheets tacked to the boards. Every time, every class, Calvin Randolph ranks infuriatingly high. I've heard the gossip going around, too. Just because I like to keep my nose buried in my books doesn't mean I'm deaf.

He's a straight A jerk with money, good looks, and brains behind his predictable God complex.

"Seen you around, Maddie, and you haven't said shit. That's a first for me, being ignored like I'm not worth your time." Oh, he also has a filthy mouth, which makes it doubly ridiculous every woman in our class would kill to have it on hers. "I'd love to know why. Everybody, new or old, wants on my good side if they want off Scourge's bad."

For such cool, calming eyes, they burn like the sun. My

cheeks go red, flustered and hot when I jerk my eyes off his. "I don't know who that is," I say. "It's only been a week."

"Interesting. Thought a girl who goes for the librarian look would be a lot more observant than that." I stick out my hand, going for my language book, but he jerks it away like I'm a helpless kitten. His smirk blooms into a cruel smile. "It's okay if you're a slow learner, doll. I'd have my eyes glued to this boring crap all the time too if I didn't have a photographic memory."

He's so full of it he's overflowing.

"Give it back," I snap, looking around to see if there are any teachers walking by. I'm not sure I'd have the courage to ask them to step in. This school isn't any different from an ordinary high school when it comes to attitudes, despite the family income level. Nobody wants to be the class runt who goes crying for help, and suffers the outcast consequences.

"Cal, I'm not playing around. I need to get to class."

The second to last bell of the day sounds over the speaker, adding its emphasis to my words. He clucks his tongue once, his strong jaw tightening. "So, you do know my name."

"What do you *want?*" I whine, trying to keep it together. "I don't have time for games."

I try to snatch my book again. Too slow. He lifts it higher, far above my head. I'm barely up to the neck attached to his broad, vast shoulders. He towers over me, one more way his body tells me how small I am next to him. Even physiology rubs in his superiority.

"I want you to crack a damned smile first," he says, laying a patronizing hand on my shoulder. "Show me something human. I've seen two expressions on your face since the day you showed up, doll. Tell me there's more."

"What happens on my face is *my* business, jerk. Not yours." By some miracle, he relents, letting my German book swing down with my hand the next time I grab it. I stumble a few steps back toward the bench to collect my mess of things.

I've got maybe sixty seconds to make it to class before the next bell if I don't want a tardy slip.

"Jerk? You're adorable." He steps closer, swallowing me in his shadow. A few of the kids racing down the halls slow, watching the tension unfolding between us. "On second thought, fuck the smile. I'd love to see those lips say something nasty a whole lot more than I'd like them right-side up. Fact that you're blushing at the mere suggestion tells me I'm on the right track, doll."

His tone is creeping me out. I stuff a few loose books into my backpack, sling it over my shoulder, and start moving down the hall. Sighing, I decide to waste a few more precious seconds asking him the only question that really interests me.

"Why do you keep calling me that – 'doll?'"

"Christ, do I have to explain *everything?*" His smirk is back, and I decide I don't like it, no matter how much light it adds to his gorgeous face. "Button nose, brown eyes, chestnut hair that looks like it's never seen a real salon. You don't fit the Maynard mold. Must be smart if you made it here in the first place without money, but I can't say I'm impressed. Brains don't matter here. It's my job to make sure you find out how this school works the easy way. You don't want hard."

Hard? I have to stop my brain from going into the

gutter, especially when he's looking at me like that. I'm also confused. *What in God's name is he talking about?*

I don't remember being so insulted, and never by a man who uses his good looks like a concealed weapon. "I'm perfectly capable of figuring it out myself. Thanks very much, ass," I yell back over my shoulder, moving my feet to put as much distance between us as quickly as I can.

"Thanks for giving me exactly what I want," he growls back, hands on his hips, his strong arms bulging at his sides. They look more like they belong to a weight lifter in his twenties than a boy who's just a year older than me.

The last class of the day, chemistry, is just a blur. It's one of the few I don't share with Cal this semester, thank God.

He's the lucky one, though. Not me. If I had to sit with his smug, searing blue eyes locked on me for more than another minute, I think I'd rush to find the easiest recipe for a test tube stink bomb that would teach him not to stick his nose where it doesn't belong.

* * *

Okay, so, maybe he's not the biggest dickweed at Maynard after all. It's a couple more weeks before I find out why everyone dreads Scourge. He's gone for my first weeks thanks to a long suspension. Meanwhile, I've aced my language studies, made a few loose friends, and even settled into a study routine blissfully free from Cal's attention.

That changes when the human storm blows in.

There's a commotion in front of our lockers at noon,

near lunch, when the kid in the leather jacket rolls in late. He wears mostly black, just like every other coward in a tough guy shell since time began. Chains hang off his sleeves, looking like they were designed for whipping anyone in his path. I don't understand how he gets away with it at first, seeing how it violates every part of the school dress code.

He's every bad school bully stereotype rolled in a cliché. Shaggy dark hair with a black widow red stripe running through the middle, piercings out the wazoo, and a sour scowl dominating his face that makes Cal's smirk look downright angelic. He also has tattoos peaking out his neckline and crawling along his wrists. Screaming skulls, shooting fire, blood dipped daggers – the scary trifecta for a troubled young man trying his best to look hard.

I've also wondered why there's never anyone using the locker on my left side. I wrongly concluded it might be a spare.

Oh, sweet Jesus, if only I'd been so lucky.

Alex "Scourge" Palkovich Jr. shows me he means business without uttering a word. The boys and girls in front of him who don't clear a path fast enough get pushed out of his way. I get my first shot of panic when he's still ten feet away, after everybody between us slams their lockers shut and scurries across the hall.

"You." He points. I freeze in my tracks. "Where the fuck's Hugo? You his new girl, or what?"

"Hugo?" I don't know that name.

The psycho has his hands on my shoulders, shaking me like a ragdoll, before I'm able to remember why it sounds so familiar.

I inherited my locker from another student. There's a worn label stuck inside my locker with that name. *Hugo.*

"Don't play dumb with me," he snarls.

"Jeez, look, I don't know him. Honest. I'm not who you're looking –"

"Shut up! Stop covering for his fucking ass, little girl. He put me out for three weeks when his sorry ass got caught smoking what I sold. Nobody does business and then fucks me over, understand? No one!"

My nerves are on needles. His nostrils flare, and the muscular fingers digging into my arms are starting to hurt. "Sorry, I'm new here. I don't think I can help you," I try to tell him, cool as I can manage. "I really don't know Hugo."

He sucks in a long, ragged breath and then shoves me away. He pushes me hard. My shoulder impacts the locker with an *oomph*, and I'm left leaning against it, wide-eyed and staring at the mess of a boy fuming next to me.

Scourge twists the knob on his locker for the combo, nearly rips the door off when he opens it, and slams it with a deafening bang after staring inside for a few breathless seconds. He looks at me. "Consider this your only warning. I find out you lied to me, I'll spend coin getting even, bitch. Already had two suspensions this year. Not afraid of a third, and you look like you're dying for someone to pull up that skirt and throw you against the nearest wall, teach you some fucking respect."

I can't breathe. I can't think. I can't stop my thumping heart from making me light-headed.

"Maddie, come on," Chelle says, tugging at my arm. "Get away from him."

I let her numbly lead me away to the school cafeteria.

As soon as we've grabbed lunch and sat down, I start asking questions. It's the best way not to breakdown and cry after one of the scariest encounters of my life.

"What's his deal? Why do they let him stay?" I can't stop thinking how Cal used that name – doll –

as if I'm the misfit at this school. My chicken tenders and chocolate milk comfort me with the slightly-better-than-average charm school cafeteria food has. The academy's selection is nothing amazing, but it's filling and just tasty enough.

"Special protection. Principal Ross wants to run for school council next year, haven't you heard?" Chelle smiles sadly. I shake my head. "Well, guess whose father just happens to be a major shaker in Seattle politics? Ever heard of Alex Palkovich Sr., the councilman?"

"Oh, God." I wrinkle my nose. "You mean *he's* Scourge's dad? He used to show up for fundraisers and inspirational speeches at my dad's company."

"Yep, the apple falls pretty far from the tree this time. It's banged up and rotten."

"Who does he think he's convincing, anyway? I mean, the scary ink, the piercings, the punk bomber jacket...amazing he doesn't get called out for breaking dress code." I look down at my own soft blue blouse and plaid skirt, frowning.

Chelle just laughs. "Girl, you've got a lot to learn about how backs are scratched at Maynard. He's gotten in trouble tons of times. Scourge never gets suspended unless he's done *really* bad. Hugo got caught by his pastor smoking the roaches he bought off that kid. Gave up his source pretty quick, and they had to do something this time because the police were involved."

"Yeah, Hugo, I keep hearing that name. Where the heck is he?"

"You don't get on Scourge's bad side and get away without catching hell," Chelle says, wagging a finger. "Hugo's folks were smart. They pulled him out and transferred to Jackson High the next county over. Heard he *begged* them for it. It's not as good, of course, but it's better than spending the rest of his high school career waiting for the knife in his back."

I'm worried she means it literally. Could it be *that* bad? I knew this boy was bad news, but I didn't know he was a total loon.

"And what's with the name? Scourge?"

Chelle opens her mouth to answer, but another voice cuts her off behind me. "Scourge of God, doll. It's from one of those dumb death metal bands he listens to. He only says it about ten times a week to remind us what hot shit he thinks he is. And don't you know he's got an Uncle in the *fucking Grizzlies?*"

When I spin my chair around, Cal stands there with a twinkle in his blue eyes, his hair tossed in a subtle, delicious mess. He's just come from gym, still wearing his black lacrosse shorts and grey jersey with the school's royal crested M.

"I wasn't asking you." I turn, pointing my nose in the air. I'm not in any mood for his games after what just went down.

"Heard you had a little run in with our pal. Move over, Emily." He takes her seat without even acknowledging the blonde sophomore next to me who looks like she's just been kissed because he remembers her name.

"I thought the Grizzlies cleaned up their act. That's

what mom says, anyway. She used to ride with them sometimes in her wilder days, before she settled down with dad." I'm frowning, trying to figure out why he's decided to give me his precious attention today if it's not for his own amusement.

"They did. The uncle he makes sure everybody knows about has been in jail for years. One of the turds they flushed before the club started making money off clubs and bars from what I hear."

"Always so eloquent," Chelle says, sticking her tongue out.

"Did I invite you to this conversation?" he asks, scorning her with a glance, before turning back to me. "Shame about your mom, though. Good times are underrated. Sure hope the wild streak is hereditary. You look like you could use some fun and take your mind off this crap, doll."

I'm blushing, and I hate it. Especially because it's all too easy to imagine the good times he has in mind.

There's no hope. I'm more like every other girl in my class than I care to admit: smitten, shaken, and yes, completely fascinated by this tactless jerk with an angel's looks. He's bad, thoughtless, and more than a little annoying. But he's safe in a way Scourge isn't, despite how easy his teasing becomes insults.

He also gives everyone on his side a certain amount of protection from what I've gathered. Hugo never got close to Cal, and he became easy prey.

"Seriously, don't be scared of him, doll. *Do* stay out of his way. Tried to warn you when you got here. I can help."

Great. So he's come to impress me by playing hero. No thanks.

I'm also done being a doormat for anyone today. Walking out and giving him the cold shoulder feels like an easy way to replenish the self-esteem I've hemorrhaged with the bully.

"Tell me if you change your mind, doll. We'll work something out." His eyes aren't moving when they lock on, and the flush invading my skin just keeps growing.

I have to get out of here.

It's my turn to do the eye roll. Without saying anything, I pick my tray up, and pause just long enough to share another look with him before the blood rushes to my cheeks. "I'm old enough to take care of myself, thanks. If I ever need your advice, Cal, I'll ask."

He doesn't say a word. But he watches me the entire time as I throw my trash away, drop the tray off, and head out for my evening classes. I resist the urge to turn around until the very end.

Of course, I do. How could I resist?

I'm just in time to see Chelle kick him under the table. He gives her a dirty look, stands, and heads back to his crew of jocks across the cafeteria.

Like I need this weirdo treating me like a damsel in distress, I think to myself, smiling for reasons I can't pin down as I head off to Pre-Calc.

I wish I'd taken more time then to appreciate the smiles we shared, however small. Months later, after the train wreck everyone took to calling 'the incident,' it's a miracle I ever learned to fake smile again.

II: Backup Son (Cal)

If I still had it in me to give a fuck, I'd mourn my father.

I've watched the surly, balls-to-the-walls lion who raised me waste away into a hyena for months. Today, he barely lifts his head when I step into his room, fighting the burning sensation in my nostrils from a hundred medications in the air.

"What do you want?" he snaps, once his dimming eyes focus, and his drug blasted brain remembers who I am.

"Came to keep you company, dad. It's Sunday." I round the space to the front of his bed, taking the chair next to it. I run my fingertips along his nightstand. There's a ghostly dust coating on my hand when I hold it up to the light. "You've been telling the staff to stay the hell out again, I see."

"No point in wasting precious resources on a dead man," he growls, grunting as he lifts himself up with his hands, finding his back support in the headboard. "What'll it be today, Calvin? Hoping for a deathbed confession? The last minute change of heart where I crack, tell you what a good son you are, how it's finally high time we put the bad behind us?"

No. I've stopped expecting miracles a long time ago.

"Or maybe you're just here to taunt me?" he says, giving me a sideways glance.

"Wrong." A wry smile pulls on my lips. "I've met someone, dad. Wanted you to be the first to know. The doctor says you've got a few weeks left, yeah? Should be plenty of time to introduce you to my new fiancée."

His eyes widen, and then he scoffs. "You, married? I'm not going to my grave a fool, kiddo. Forget it. Spare me a meeting with whatever sugar baby escort you've hired to confuse an old man into thinking you give a damn about anything except getting my money."

He's got me there, minus the escort part. Hell, even after all these years, I can't imagine doll fucking anyone else.

My cock is the only one she's ever had in the stroke fantasies sustaining me for years. Naive, sure, but mental masturbation always is.

I didn't mention those thoughts when I sent her the note in the little black envelope last week, but now I wish I had. Just for fun.

That piece of paper and the twenty carat rock had to travel halfway around the globe. Almost a shame I decided to keep it short, sweet, and boring. I can't believe she's in China. Easily the biggest sign yet the Maddie Middleton I'm dealing with today is a far cry from the scared, helpless little girl I took a bullet for seven awful years ago.

I haven't even heard from her yet. I'll be calling the number I dug up with a lot of connections and detective work tonight if I don't get an answer.

I won't be disappointed. Because if there's one thing I know, despite what's changed on her end, she won't let me down. She'll wear the ring, by God, pretending she cares about her loving fiancé every time we make eyes.

A nurse comes in and walks to my dad's IV while the icy silence between us stretches on. The grandmother clock in the corner ticks on. I fold my hands, watching as she adjusts the dose of whatever painkiller keeps him from screaming in mortal agony. We're both quiet until the woman smiles gently, and finds her way out.

I have to try this again. As much as I don't fucking want to.

"I'm a changed man," I say. "It's hard as hell for you to see, I get it. You're too sick to read about the extra billion in revenue my marketing strategy brought the firm, and you don't take calls from Mr. Turnbladt anymore –"

"I don't *care* if Turnbladt thinks you can turn water into wine. I'm out of RET forever," he says, turning over. He stops turning propped on a pillow, his back to me, a human manifestation of the proverbial wall I talk to every time I'm stupid enough to come here. "Keep raking in the money, though. It'll do the charities getting it some good once I'm gone. Or else the partners, whenever they decide to stop fucking around and buy your share out, I suppose."

It's my stake in Randolph-Emerson-Turnbladt he's talking about. Mine, which he controls. He has it set up in his trust to cockblock me from ever truly owning it, the dividends going to feel good groups he hasn't even bothered to vet.

"That's all you really care about, old man? Making sure I get jack squat while working my fingers to the bone, dragging your company kicking and screaming into the twenty-first century?"

He's quiet for several seconds. Then I hear his low, infuriating voice, a poison whisper. "Things don't always go according to plan, Calvin. Make your fortune elsewhere, like your grandfather did, or settle for your measly $200K salary like an ordinary corporate grunt. You're never getting my share. I'll lose it all before I let you become the public face of anything at RET after what you did. The board feels the same way."

I'm ready to spit nails. "Then why include the amendment in the trust at all? Your lawyer slipped over too many drinks at the last Christmas party. Told me everything. He said there's a section for rehabilitation. If I prove myself I'm worthy with good deeds, family, a woman –"

"I had to give you some kind of carrot to shape up, didn't I? The offer stands, son, but we both know the clock is running out fast. You've got a better chance of making a miracle before my eyes than proving me wrong. Show me a woman worth marrying, one you aren't bribing to lie to my face, and anything is possible. Until then, we both know what's in the cards doesn't include you controlling my firm. Not since John –"

My hand shoots up, and I hold it in the air. "We both know what happened. Why waste more words?" I pull out my phone to check the time. It's getting late. "I have to go. Get some rest."

"You always were the backup son after everything that happened. It should've been John filling your shoes, and we both know it." Dad isn't backing down from his parting shot. "This isn't personal anymore, Cal. It's circumstance. Stop thinking I don't care."

Care? The asshole has a funny way of showing it.

He's only stealing my future, killing my career before it goes anywhere. I have to get out of here *now.*

I'm able to resist punching holes through the brittle old walls of the seaside mansion I grew up in until I'm in my car. My fist bangs the steering wheel once before I start the engine.

My black Tesla screeches down the long driveway to the front gate, which the servant in the guard shack has already opened for me. I make it home to my condo in record time, loading my car onto the ferry waiting to take us across the Puget Sound. It's a nice place worth seven figures where downtown Seattle meets the waterfront.

Nice, yeah, but it'll never morph into an unfathomably posh estate surrounded by the mountains, the sea, and centuries old forests. I won't be building any castles I choose while I'm being robbed of my birthright because I'm nothing more than a reluctant Plan B in my father's eyes. A 'backup son' he won't even trust to earn a full partner's stake because that means media, which in turn means reminding every client, fat cat, and blue blood our illustrious company deals with that I have a felony record.

Backup? Where the fuck does he get off?

I don't know, and I try to forget my rage when I'm home. I head for the balcony, pouring myself a glass of good wine. For a second, I slow when I pass by the photos on the mantle, staring into John's long dead smiling face.

My older brother is still the favorite, despite being gone for almost six years. Paid the ultimate sacrifice for his country somewhere outside Kandahar, where an ambush by the Taliban ended him.

It seems like a lifetime ago.

When I'm in my ivory chair outside, overlooking the evening lights beginning to twinkle on in the hills across the water, I check the calendar on my phone.

It's been six days since I sent my little package to Doll.

She's taking her sweet time getting back to me. I decided when I sent it off I'd give her a few days, roughly a full week after it reached Beijing. It's the least she deserves for the hand grenade I just threw into her life, commanding her in not so many words to bring her sweet ass home to Seattle, and pretend she's my blushing bride.

Desperation does evil things to a man. If I could've let her go without another word, I would.

Hell, I did for all these years, seven and counting. I stayed away.

It was the humane choice. Never forgot how bad she hurt just looking into my eyes the last time I saw her, when she was down on the ground in tears, slapping the pavement like she wanted to drum up mercy for me from God himself.

Her words are branded in my brain.

Wait, wait! Don't take him away. Please, you can't this is wrong.

It's not over, Cal. It can't end like this. I'll be here. I'll do anything to help.

Anything!

I close my eyes, stuck on how loaded the last word she ever said to me was when it came out, hoarse and true. Sometimes, the emotional bomb planted in my memory goes off. Everything returns, rushing through me like the lava replacing my blood whenever those memories hit.

The sacrifice, the humiliation, the dirty mistake I made for her because I didn't have a fucking choice. Because it was the right thing to do.

It went further than any act of chivalry ever should.

I'm lost in the past when my phone rings. There's an international area code on the screen. A smile tugs at my lips before I punch the accept button.

"Took you long enough, doll."

"Cal...how are you?" Her voice is soft, slightly huskier than I remember, warm honey to my ears.

"Alive. Making money. Doing whatever and whoever the fuck I want, when I want them," I say, taking a pull off my wine. "All the best in life. What are you doing in Beijing?"

"Contracts for Sterner Corp," she says, ignoring my edgy introduction. "My Mandarin studies paid off, and so did the JD. I never wasted the second chance you gave me – I couldn't. Thank you again."

"You're doing better than eighty percent of our class, and earning it honestly, without special connections. Congratulations." I pause, remembering I'm not here to catch up. This isn't happy hour, or even a sales meeting. It's cold business of the most personal kind. "I won't keep you long, I hope, calling in the favor. Just be here by Thursday, wear my ring, and put on your best act."

"Hope you're right. I kind of have a life now," she says, quiet and unsure. It's like I'm able to hear the guilt sticking on her tongue, thick as chewing gum. Her voice wavers like the fire she readied to hurl my way just had cold water poured over it. "That's why I called. I wanted to talk before pulling up stakes, before we do...well, this."

Marriage. Or at least a pretend engagement.

She can't bring herself to say the unspeakable. Fair enough. It's not like I'd expect the shiest girl I ever met to handle this fake fiancé thing with a laugh and a song.

I only need her to follow through. My brow curls because there's some reasonable doubt creeping into her tone. I never fucking liked second guesses.

Doll better not disappoint. There's no Plan B, short of hiring some clueless broad dad would see through in a heartbeat.

"Are we doing this, or not?" I ask, brusk and pointed.

There's a considerable pause. It's stifling. I'm about to end the call and throw my phone off the balcony when she lets out a slow, soft sigh. "I guess. How long do you need me?"

"Ninety days ought to do it, but probably less," I tell her. "Doubt my father lasts through summer. It's him we really need to convince, before he pushes daisies. If you're able to take a leave of absence and meet me for a month or two, we'll be even. I'll pull every string I've got to make sure there's still a place for you in China, if that's where your heart is anchored these days."

"God, Cal. I'm sorry about your father. Of course I'll be there," she says, sympathy I didn't ask for oozing through my phone. "The company wants me back in the States next week anyway. I think I can be there by Thursday."

"Perfect. There's a charity auction on Friday I'm attending, and I'd like you with. I'll show you off to the movers and shakers, let the tabloids tell the city the disgraced son everybody forgot the last seven years landed a normal woman."

There's an awkward silence. She must remember I have zero tolerance for comforting bullshit, like if she starts telling me the litany: *it's not so bad, I'll find my way, and disgraced? Surely, I'm exaggerating.*

I've heard the same bullshit from my two best friends, Cade and Spencer, a thousand times. I don't need more empathy. It hasn't gotten me anywhere.

"Just tell me one thing," she says nervously. "Why? The details aren't making sense. You mentioned your father, his illness...are you trying to make sure he sees you happy before...you know?"

"Before he croaks? No, this isn't some ego trip, doll.

I'm not looking for his sad, selfish approval. There's a condition in his trust before he goes: I need a wife to rehabilitate myself, or I get virtually nothing."

"I see," she whispers. In fact, Maddie doesn't have a fucking clue, but what else can she say? "Well, whatever I can do to help, Cal. Just like I promised."

"Anything," I say, repeating her last haunting word to me after the disaster. "Put on a good enough show for the public, for whoever I ask you to fool. Maybe I'll let you sleep in a separate bed."

She gasps. My tongue slides against my teeth, loving how wickedly close the air escaping her mouth is to a moan.

"Um, I did say anything, but I don't know if I can –"

"Relax. I'm not interested in getting my dick wet where it's not wanted. You're paying your debt with this fake fiancée act. Not with your body."

Honestly? I want her at ease, sure. It won't do either of us any good if she shows up at the auction full of wide-eyed sexual tension, on edge because she doesn't know when I'll push her into the nearest wall and rip off her clothes.

Yet, it's no more than three seconds before I regret those words.

After all these years, I still want to fuck her. Once, I was after her cherry. I'm sure that's long gone, stolen by some other lucky bastard. But I remember the short, sweet taste I had of her lips seven years ago, before I walked out on the schoolyard that day and let fate pull the trigger, blowing my life to pieces.

"I'll see you soon," she says, timid as the old Maddie I remember. "Is there anything else you want?"

"Just you, doll. Friday. Come bright-eyed and madly in love with me, a come fuck me dress on your hips and a pair of heels on your feet. Pick whatever you want online and text me your choice. I don't care how much it costs. I'll put in an order."

She's quiet for a moment. "Really? Is this how it'll be the entire time? I thought we left Maynard behind, Cal. We're in our late twenties for Christ's sake!"

It's finally upsetting her. Don't know why the hell that's so amusing.

"What happened there never left me," I say, picking up my wine glass, letting the dark red sweetness drown my tongue. "Friday, Maddie. We have a lot of catching up to do."

I hear her start to form another word, but I disconnect the call before she gets it out.

If she's still feeling sorry for me, I don't care.

If she's offended, I care even less.

I've protected her enough for one lifetime. I'm done treating her feelings like eggshells.

This artificial engagement is on because I don't have a choice. It's my only shot at convincing dad to hand out more than a few measly million, to open the doors I've earned keys to before it's too late, and to set me up to continue the good work I've done for the firm started by my grandfather.

It's bound to be hell on us both. Maddie doesn't want to be here fawning over my sorry ass any more than I enjoyed the year off my life in jail for her.

That's how this works – *quid pro quo.*

Friday, we do what we need to. She starts paying off

her debt. If I decide to have a little fun while this shit show hits the road, then so be it.

* * *

"Holy fuck. I know he always said you'd get *nothing*, but you're telling me he means it?" Cade looks at me, running a hand through his thick blond hair. His angular jaw clenches in sympathy. The genes from his Icelandic blue blood father couldn't be more obvious.

I nod once. That's all it takes for him to spin his chair around, breaking out the emergency flask of vodka he keeps under his desk for just these occasions.

"Double shot for me," Spencer says from the corner, looking up from the stock prices scrolling across his phone's screen. "I'm doing time with the boys from New York this evening. Neolithic. You both know what that means."

My brow furrows. "Yeah, absolute ball busters."

The prestigious investment firm from Wall Street doesn't fuck around. Neither does Grant Shaw, the founder, who's sent his boys to the other coast sniffing for new business partners.

"Go easy, Spence. Your miracles always happen sober," Cade says with a frown, passing us both our drinks across the desk, a single shot for everyone. "I'm fucking floored, Cal. How could he just cut you off at the knees? Nobody in Seattle gives a shit what happened seven years ago. Can't believe your old man still thinks it makes you a liability for the firm."

He knows that isn't true. *Plenty* of people care, but I let his lie off with a dark glance.

"I'm not the one he ever wanted sitting here. It was always supposed to be John," I say.

Deep down, when I plow the darkness and come face-to-face with everything I'll never admit, I think my big brother might've done better than me. Hell, I practically *know* it. He had discipline, heart, and a set of brass balls that got him slaughtered protecting his fellow soldiers.

He also didn't have a prison record and a sickening trial that had half the city clucking their tongues, thankful they never raised a 'deeply troubled' kid like me. The other half got to enjoy several weeks of Schadenfreude. Comes with the territory when a billionaire's son lands himself in the deep, perilous shit I did. The poorer, angst types who pegged me for being born with a silver spoon in my mouth loved our misfortune.

"How long does he have?" Spence says coldly, staring at me with his eyes narrowed while he drains his vodka in one swallow.

"Six, seven weeks. Maybe less. Who the hell knows. It's not an exact science when the pancreas burns out and cancer goes everywhere."

"With all due respect, your old man's a prick if he sticks to his guns. He can't fucking cut you out," Cade growls, banging his fists on the desk when he brings them down. "You worked for your share, Cal. Harder than anybody here. We can't let him take it away from you just like *that*."

His fingers snap loudly, leaving a dull ringing in my ears. "Enough. Forget my crap," I say. "I'll work it out. Told you already, there's a chance I could change his mind if I meet the conditions he set in his trust."

"Oh, up and marry some broad? So reasonable,"

Spence rolls his eyes, sarcastic as ever. "What about an escort? They're not all fake tits and one night stands. I've paid plenty for girls who'll suck you off with stars in their eyes. Bet they'd glow brighter if they'd get their money without having to choke on your –"

"You can stop there. Shit, Spence, I didn't come down here to listen to your latest bedroom antics." I shoot him a dirty look.

Spence just grins. He purged his conscience a long time ago, shameless and proud of the high class notches in his belt. I ignore him, look at Cade, and regain my calm. "I have a plan. Might need a few extra days away from the office to get it going. That's what I really came by to ask for."

"Whatever you need, brother." Cade reaches across the desk and slams his fist into mine. He's too good a friend, better than I deserve, especially when I was drunk off my ass those nights after prison, after John died, deep in my rudderless misery while he was halfway through one of the hardest business schools in the country. "We had your leave on the books, anyway. It's no secret he's been closer to death's door. Already had your time blocked off over the next quarter for the inevitable."

"Just give me a few days. You can cancel the rest. If this goes off well, I'll have more reason than ever to hit it hard at the office. Won't need an extended absence."

Spence looks up, surprised. Cade stares through me, nodding slowly.

They know what I've been through over the years, how everything went haywire with my father after I saved Doll and no one could save John. They've watched me busting my ass for a pittance of a yearly bonus, without the cushy guarantee I'd inherit the stake they've always been entitled to from their dads.

"Cal," Spence calls my name, waiting until I turn around to face him. "Don't let this bullshit make you crazy. We've got your back if daddy dearest fucks you over."

"I know, and one fine day I'll repay it." Standing, I grab his hand, giving it a brotherly squeeze on my way out.

I may have lost the only family I ever had over the last decade to war, booze, and psychosis, but I'm thankful for the men who've stood with me since those days at Maynard.

It won't be the end of me, taking the crazy way out with a fake fiancée in a last ditch effort to fool my asshole father. It's going to work. And it'll be a massive relief when it finally pays off, and I don't need to rely on their support anymore to stave off disaster.

* * *

Thursday, Maddie texts me she's home. Same old neighborhood where her folks settled just outside the U of Washington campus. It's summer, and I hope she knows how lucky she is being able to hear herself think without the constant noise and frat parties.

She sent me links to the dress and heels she picked out before leaving Beijing. I vetoed her first two choices – far too plain and far too cheap for a charity ball where the median net worth in the room is right at thirty million – and told her to choose something that looks like it's suited for a Randolph bride.

She sent back a sleek blue dress with ocean trim,

matching heels, and a platinum necklace. Plus four different red-faced emojis I'm sure reflected how abruptly her heart stopped when I told her to stop screwing off, and send me something real.

Everything went on my Centurion charge card instantly. It also made my dick hard, picturing the little doll who always had a gift for making me hot in grown up clothes. I've seen her pictures over the years, and she's filled out nicely. Tomorrow, she'll show me a woman's curves in her classy new outfit, It'll make this job pretending we're on fire easy as sin.

Hell, maybe *too* easy.

I can't shake the curiosity when I'm home from the office that night. Impatient and horny bastard that I am, I break out my phone and pull up her number, typing out a text.

Cal: You've got a dressing mirror, right? Put it on and hit send. Show me everything. I want to make sure it's right for the ball.

It's the better part of an hour before I get a reply.

Maddie: How's this? Not showing too much leg for their crowd, I hope?

The V-cut down the middle rides straight to her bare hip, and I'm a fucking goner. My cock jerks hard in my trousers, its angry tip straining against my belt, ready to ruin everything before it's begun if I give it half a chance.

No. I can't let this do the thinking.

I have to get these pics the hell off my screen before the heat in my balls makes me stupid.

Cal: Perfect. I'll see you there at seven.

I'm glad she isn't looking for a proper date. I'm sending my driver around to pick her up after I show up at the ball half an hour early. It's how it has to be. Knowing what she's wearing, causing my prick to leak heat all over my thigh, I don't think I'd survive the ten minute trip in the back of the car without putting her under me.

I'm doubly grateful she never texts back. Gives me ample time to throw my phone on my nightstand and step into a long, cold shower. It takes the ice forever to soothe my blood, and I've got it cranked to glacial. I'm panting like a bull in rut by the time I step out, toweling off, ignoring the raging hard-on up to my six-pack while it hits me.

This fake fiancée act *won't* be easy.

But the faster it comes, the more I realize how its challenge has *nothing* to do with dad or even our screwed up past. There's a vicious chemistry between us I thought I'd be able to ignore. Thought it'd be dead after so many years apart.

Hour by hour, minute by minute, the march toward Friday evening warns me I'm flat out wrong.

Raw attraction is alive and kicking. It comes at me

with a thousand questions, but only one that's really important.

How the hell do I pretend I'm obsessed with this woman, and keep it professional, without actually fucking her first chance I get?

III: Jitters (Maddie)

I'm no stranger to old money, high class, and self-righteous pricks. Kinda comes with the territory when you're a rising star in a major international company. But glamor and egos aren't the main reason the butterflies in my stomach have teeth, making me woozy when I step into the sleek glassy building downtown for the first time.

"Name or party, madame?" An older man in a tailored suit steps up, swift as a secret service agent, looking me up and down.

At least my chic blue dress and heels pass the first test, and I'm not thrown out on sight. "Randolph," I tell him.

He grins. "Ah, so you're the lucky lady. My congratulations. Mr. Randolph has a table reserved. Right this way."

It's getting very weird, very fast. I follow him through the security line, and we head into a massive ballroom like something out of a fairy tale updated for modern times.

Several dozen well dressed couples mingle, their chatter a steady roil behind the soft piano music coming from the stage. My eyes scan the crowd for Cal. When we near the table with the RANDOLPH sign on it, at first I'm sure there's someone else in his seat.

The man dressed to the nines in his tux and silver tie looks preposterously mature. Gone is the handsome, slender boy I used to crush on, replaced by a tall, dark, and brutally handsome man.

Cal's looks were always good to him. Time has been even kinder.

I shouldn't be surprised. I tried to brace myself for this. Tried, and completely failed.

One good glance at my fake fiancé makes my blood steam down to my knees.

"Hello, doll. It's been a long time. Pull up a chair." The boy's deep voice is a man's now, several octaves lower than I remember. He stands, towering over me at least a foot, and readies my chair for me.

"My God." It's all I'm able to whisper as my butt hits the cushion.

His shoulders are broader. His muscles are bigger, firmer, and sleeker than his eighteen year old bones could've supported. If he's suffered over the years – and I'm certain he has – his body shows no signs. It's like the pain has somehow strengthened his rough beauty, carved more perfection into the jawline covered in a rogue five o'clock shadow, given his neat, dark hair a perfect wave, and deepened his eyes.

Those sky blue gems set in his handsome face are all I recognize of the Calvin I once knew. They're unshakeable. No different from the last day I saw them, full of fury.

Except now there's an added darkness in the blue halo around his pupils. It sends a sharp chill up my spine.

He strokes his chin, quietly studying me, impossible to read behind his gorgeous mask. "What are you thinking?" I try, breaking the eerie silence.

"I think it's too damn quiet. Glad you're happy to see me, doll, but I think you can be happier. Drink?" He waves to the bar in the corner, where there's a man in a vest shaking up a cocktail in a steel tumbler.

"I'd love to," I say, standing. I mean it.

I welcome anything that gives me a few more minutes to decide how I'll deal with telling the world I'm marrying this enigma.

I'm in a daze as I follow him to the bar, struggling to process how I've gotten here, back in the presence of a man I thought I'd lost forever.

I order my usual: a mimosa with extra citrus. He quirks an eyebrow and points it my way after asking for a scotch, more determined than ever to inflame the raw, confused pulse each look kindles deep inside me.

"Still love to play it safe, I see. Can't blame you. It's gotten you far."

"Well, to China, anyway. How are you, Cal? You look good." My cheeks bloom fierce red, transported seven years in the past as soon as the words are out. Why can't I compliment him like a normal adult?

"Miserable," he says under his breath. "Wouldn't have asked you to this shitshow if I didn't have a lot to lose. Let's get on with it, and do some introductions."

Apparently, he's never developed the patience for small talk. His hand drifts to mine a half second after we've picked up our drinks, and soon we're making the rounds.

"Mrs. Vernon, don't you look lovely?" he says to a plump, older woman near the stage, one hand holding her glasses. Yes, *those* glasses, the kind I thought were left behind in the nineteenth century. "This is my fiancée, Maddie."

"Delighted," the woman says in her haughtiest tone. Or

maybe it's her normal voice. "My, young man, why didn't I hear you were engaged? Tell me everything!"

"Met on business in China about six months ago. You remember that trip to Beijing, love? Rainstorm caught you outside Mao's tomb, without an umbrella. I was kind enough to share, and you were too beautiful not to. Found out fast we were both Seattle locals." He looks at me and winks when Vernon isn't looking.

"Uh, of course." Not. My head is spinning. I barely remember to nod, before the blush on my cheeks hits my brain, and turns me to stone. Good thing he does most of the talking.

"We fell fast and hard. Real whirlwind romance that'd give old Rhett Butler a run for his wind." Mrs. Vernon laughs when he mentions what I'm sure is an old favorite. "Proposed under a month ago. Can't believe how fast it's coming together, and how ready I am to be a married man."

He grabs my hand. So much for fixing this awkward tension turning my lungs to concrete.

"So charming! You're a lucky young thing, Maddie. I simply can't wait for the wedding photos." Mrs. Vernon goes doe-eyed. Her grin vanishes a second later. "And how's your father, Calvin? Is he close to...forgive me."

She trails off. I expect Cal's warm smile to die, but it barley softens. "He has a month, maybe two at most, or so the doctors say. They've underestimated him before. Dad's always been a fighter. I think he'll go down swinging, and surprise all of us."

"My sympathies, dear boy. If there's anything to settle in the aftermath, rest assured my Charles will be in your corner to put in a good word with your board."

THANKS!

"Thanks. Means a lot." He reaches out, squeezes her hand, and then we're on our way to a few more tittering couples.

He probably introduces me to half a dozen more I can't remember – always as the future *Mrs. Calvin Randolph* – before there's even time to catch my breath.

"Is this helping? Will Mrs. Venison or whatever her name was help you? It sounded good," I say hopefully, looking for any excuse to slow down this bewildering meet and greet with millionaires.

"No. Charles is a thirty year baller and has a lot in our hedge fund, but the board's vote is shackled to dad's will. There's no overriding the pull a founding name has in the company."

There's so much to these delicate politics I don't understand. It's not like he gives me a chance to catch up because we're still moving.

"Cal, Cal, I thought I'd see you here!" A lean man in a grey suit holding a tablet runs up, slowing our approach to the next group of VIPs.

"Turner. Surprised you're taking precious time away from fishing for secrets from tech titans to talk to me. What gives?" Cal eyeballs him suspiciously.

"Actually, I came over to see if you'd have an in for me with Spencer Emerson. Is he here? Heard he'd landed a lucrative deal for your firm to inject new liquidity into ShopUp, and I'd love to have a word."

"He isn't around, and he wouldn't want to talk to you if he was. Nobody at Randolph-Emerson-Turnbladt got where they are with loose lips, especially when it involves multi-billion dollar deals with start ups heading to the moon."

"Ah! So it's *billions*, plural. Got it." Smiling, he holds up his tablet and quickly types his comments into what looks like software for press professionals.

"I can't believe anyone wants luxury brands shoved in their faces when they could buy affordable and efficient, but what do I know?" I say. I can't hold my commentary.

ShopUp is an app designed for rich people, where they can type in any old thing, and receive only recommendations from 'the best of the best.' In practice, it also means the most *expensive*, a reverse bargain approach suited for the ones who hang their lives on having the most bling.

Turner's eyes go wide, and he gives me a soft smile. "Forget ShopUp, Cal. Who's the fox with the mouth?"

"This is my lovely fiancée, Madeline Middleton. Soon to be Mrs. Randolph after we have our wedding in Tokyo in a few months. She can't wait for the honeymoon. I hope you'll forgive her snideness. I'm quite looking forward to our sixty day cruise around the South Pacific. Her uncle did a lot of missionary work on a lot of islands. This woman knows them all like the back of her hand. Isn't that right, doll?"

I didn't know a nod could be so heavy. The white lies are getting much darker.

"Tokyo? fiancée?" Turner looks like he's struggling to keep his jaw off the floor.

Honestly, so am I, because the improv stories Cal keeps making up about us just keep getting crazier. What's next? Telling them I'm already pregnant with the twins he's probably written into his script for a perfect life?

"Don't look so stunned, my man. I just handed you an exclusive." Cal slaps him on the shoulder and gives it a squeeze that rocks the skinny young man roughly our age. "We've got a lot of people to see, though, so why don't you get cracking and send me a link to the story in the morning? Good way to announce our engagement for free."

"Hold up, hold up! I've got questions...can't I at least have a picture?!"

Turner chases us like a hopeless puppy. Cal leans in with a heavy sigh, whispering in my ear. "Play along. It'll be good practice for dad soon."

"Fine, one good picture to go with your article. As for the details, you fill them in. What's fit to print isn't always honest. Here, I'll get you started: we met in Hong Kong doing charity, we're both Seattle natives, and I love the hell out of this girl. You've got five seconds to get your camera going."

Under five seconds warning before I'm in his arms. Cal seizes me, locks his powerful hands around my waist, brings me to his chest, dipping his face toward mine.

Oh, God. Isn't it a little soon for –

Our lips collide, destroying my thoughts. It's more explosive than I dared imagine.

The big bang happens all over again in our ten second kiss.

Whole worlds are born in a shower of sparks. They glow, they burn, fading into the molten shock flowing through my blood. So sudden, so unexpected, and so relentless my body reacts on pure instinct.

My brain hasn't caught up to what's happening.

But my heartbeat, my pulse, and the shameful fire building between my legs...*mother mercy.* They're as hot and bothered as a ShopUp user laying eyes on a five figure toaster, and my tongue melts against his far more naturally than I'd like.

Resistance? Restraint? Common sense?

Gone.

My brain may be screaming *no, no, no*, but the moan that slips out of me, and into him when my nipples turn to hard peaks through my dress is a simple, unmistakable *yes.*

This kiss is living memory. It takes me back through time, retraces all seven years to the first and only night he first laid his lips on mine, a carnal promise we never had a chance to act on.

Maddie, what the hell are you doing? My senses return, and I'm pushing hard against his chest with both palms before he eases up a second later.

"Was it as good for you as it was for us?" Cal asks, an eyebrow quirked at the blogger. I'm catching my breath, surprised Turner's glasses haven't fogged over from the scene he just witnessed.

He never gets a chance to answer. Cal leads me away, leaving him speechless.

I guess that makes two of us.

We're done making the rounds and in our seats when my thudding pulse finally lets me speak. "Okay, what *was* that? I thought we were keeping it professional, retaining certain boundaries, just like you said..."

"Practice, doll. Professional doesn't mean ice. This has to be believable. If we're never physical, no one will buy it. Besides, Turner's got a good track record making this crap viral." Cal looks at me and smiles like we're talking about nothing. "Would you rather he show us off in a series of Tweets, or should I march you up on the stage for a repeat performance?"

God, no. On so many levels. If kissing him is practice for this farce we're putting on, I never want to see the grand finale.

I'm saved from a retort by the first speaker stepping up to the microphone, announcing the charity auction underway. Turner isn't the only person fixated on us. Low, hushed jabber flies around the room, impossible to ignore, more than a few middle aged couples pointing our way, and smiling.

At least they're happy. The gossip mill is a lot less pleasant when you're steering it. It's hard to even look at him as the bidding starts on a priceless sculpture by some wonderfully weird and gifted artist. I'm reeling in silence, frozen in disbelief that I gave in.

It doesn't matter that there wasn't a chance to put up my guard when I didn't know what was happening until he'd taken a nice, long sip of me. I caved, went weak in the knees for this crass, strange man I owe my life to.

It's terrifying how little the distance the years have put between us means. My body responds the same way it did when I was young and clueless. I'm in grave danger.

Three priceless art pieces sell for six figures each before Cal says anything. "Watch this," he tells me in a hushed voice, holding up his sign.

It's hard not to gasp. Bidding for the huge white urn with the soft pink roses brushed by hand up its sides starts at a hundred thousand dollars.

Not even a year's salary for me. And he's the one roping me into this stupid fake fiancé thing, worried about *money?*

"Two fifty," he says simply, holding up his sign.

"Two hundred and fifty thousand dollars! Do I hear two seventy five?" The auction hawker beams, scanning the room for fresh competition.

Another sign goes up across the aisle, several seats down. "Three fifty," a portly man in a vest says, giving us a quick glance with his beady eyes.

Just because the money is going to a good cause doesn't take the sport out of it. My heart leaps into my chest as I realize what I'm really seeing: a dick waving contest for rich people. And I'm seriously afraid Cal is going to get his slapped hard before it's over.

"Four hundred even," Cal says, his deep voice louder.

The auctioneer at the microphone blinks. He never expected a bidding war over the most boring item yet. Low whispers roll through the crowd. I hear several cries of "really?" and "they're crazy!"

Whatever the Victorian vase is worth, it's already smashed through its ceiling. I lean in, hand halfway over my mouth. "Cal! I don't know what you're trying to prove, but –"

"I've got this, doll. Keep watching." He cuts me off, a wicked smile pulling at his lips, waiting for his competition to up the ante, or else slink away with his tail between his legs.

"Four fifty," the man a few feet over growls. I see his wife clutching his shoulder from the corner of my eye. We share a brief look of solidarity. Saving men from themselves is harder than breaking up dog fights sometimes.

"Do I hear –"

"Four seventy," Cal says, his jaw subtly clenched. The

bidding slowdown to smaller increments means they're both nearing their limit.

"Five hundred even!" A new voice says. Half the audience gasps.

The portly man looks defeated, red in the face, and suddenly goes quiet. Cal, he's ice next to me, revealing very little of the tension pulling him apart inside.

He *needs* to win. I sense it in every wolfish glance from his eyes.

"Five hundred thousand for this marvelous hand-painted relic from a nobler time!" The auctioneer squawks. "Do I hear five ten, ladies and gentleman? Five ten for this glorious, one-of-a-kind piece with roses sure to make your own gardener jealous?"

There isn't a sound. Just swift, crushing silence.

Cal's fingers twitch once on his sign, wedged against his thigh. I wrap my fingers gently around his rock hard bicep, squeezing it through his suit. "Let it go. You did your best."

He pushes me away softly, and stands. "Five fifty."

The floor drops out. I'm hanging my head, wondering how I was ever so stupid to believe this brash, crazy man would've sobered up with age. He's just as reckless and determined when he senses a fight as he was when it all went to pieces.

My heartbeat swallows my ears, making me dizzy. I feel like I'm reliving the incident all over again.

"Five hundred and fifty thousand!" The auctioneer sings, his smile becoming a grin. "Do I hear five seventy five? Five seventy five?"

I'm shaking, counting the seconds. He can't go higher than this. Five slip by before I hear the final countdown.

Going once!
Going twice!

"Sold, to the handsome young man from Randolph-Emerson-Turnbladt with the heart of iron!" Auctioneer man sings. "My lovely assistant will be in touch to wrap it up and find out how you'd like to bring this beauty home."

Cal drops into his seat, a thin halo of sweat on his brow. He wipes it quickly with his sleeve as the vase is wheeled off the stage, and they start setting up the next piece.

"I sure *hope* you know what you're doing," I mutter, leaning into him and whispering it as softly as I can, without surrendering the sharp worry in my gaze. "Over half a million dollars for art? Are you *sure* you need me to do this? Seems like you're kinda loaded."

"This thing just cost me a decent chunk of my cash reserve, Maddie," he says, calmer than ever while his words make my heartbeat ten times faster. "You'll help me make half a million a drop in the bucket after this marriage gets me what I'm owed. Also, what kind of loving fiancé would I be if I let that piece of history go? Didn't you recognize the cream background? The roses?"

"Obviously not!"

He's lost his mind. I'm still shaking my head when it hits me.

When I look up, a nervous wreck, he's smiling. His lips close in, leaving a peck on my cheek, and then I feel his hot breath oozing into my ear. "Now, you remember, yeah? Those roses on white...exact same pattern you wore on your dress the day I went on the field with Scourge. I'd be a fool to *ever* let us forget."

***

He asks me to hang onto the huge vase wrapped up in thick newspaper as we crawl into the back of his limo. I clutch it like a kitten hanging onto a tree, so jittery over accidentally banging it against the car I'm about to explode. The nerves he's soaked in kerosene and lit on fire for a dozen other reasons aren't helping either.

We're halfway to his penthouse downtown before I finally find my courage "I can't do this if it's going to be crazy. We need ground rules," I say, meeting his blue eyes in the darkness.

"What did you think we'd discuss tonight at home? What kind of lingerie I'd like you to wear when you parade around the house?" His smart slays every part of me his words don't reach. "I never operate in chaos, doll. I'd have never gotten my life halfway back on track if I did. Of course we'll have a plan."

There he goes again. Making me feel small, restless, stupid.

That's the Calvin Randolph I remember. If that weren't so infuriating, it might be charming because it's familiar, a ghost from a simpler time when I didn't have a life complete with an impending fake marriage to worry about.

"Why did you really kiss me so hard in front of the reporter? I don't believe that was just 'practice.'" I let loose the other question eating me. "Something softer would've worked. You didn't have to put so much into it."

"It's called passion, Maddie. You should try it sometime. Real emotion makes people excellent liars. No, you're not truly my blushing bride, doll. You just taste fucking good to me. I don't need to lie about that. If you're asking my permission to half-ass this arrangement, don't. I need you here, all the way."

I can't hold his eyes. *Ass.*

I'm forced to look away, staring sadly out the window. A thick Seattle rain hits the glass and forms rivulets. It's pouring by the time we pull into his heated private garage. He tells me to leave the vase on the seat – the driver will take care of it – and I do.

The icy tension between us doesn't get any better on the elevator ride up his tower. When it reaches the top and I hear the ding accompanying the door sliding open, my hands are trembling on the gold banister behind me.

Sighing, he steps forward, and punches the button to close the door, giving us some privacy. "What's wrong?"

"What does it look like, Cal? It's too much." No lie. It's overload. "I can't believe I'm back here, doing this, with *you.* I should be in Beijing for another week, working contracts in English and Mandarin. Not taking a leave of absence from my career to settle our old score from half a lifetime ago."

"I know this is hard." He steps in front of me, slides his strong hands on my shoulders, his fingertips pushing gently into my skin. "Believe it or not, I appreciate you, Maddie. Even if I have a twisted way of showing it sometimes. Stay strong, and we'll be even. You'll never hear from me again."

That isn't what I want! I'm prepared to scream it after him, torn because he wounds me so easily, but always does just enough to remind me there's a soul somewhere behind his freezing looks.

He takes me by the wrist and leads me out, down the

hall to a tall, ornately carved door, one and only entryway to his million dollar condo.

If he hurt his finances tonight dropping over half a million on charity art, it won't hurt his standard of living. His place looks like the kind I've only seen in platinum card traveler's magazines, and sometimes among the new desperate-to-impress money in China's business elite.

His world is lush.

Overstuffed leather chairs next to windows oversee the city's best view, towering over Pike's Market, stretching out to a picturesque shot of Bainbridge Island and the mountains beyond. An obscene mantle attaches to a fireplace probably able to produce enough heat in the winter for a small army. And a sleek glass liquor cabinet yawns full with wine, fine spirits, and imported beer, most of it totally out of reach without using the library ladder on the shelves.

I sit while he walks to a long fancy table. When he returns, there's a thin stack of papers in his hand. He pushes them into my lap and hands me a black pen. "Read it and sign, doll. Had my lawyer cook up something to protect us legally."

"Fake fiancée, defined here as Ms. Madeline Middleton, agrees to pursue the duties outlined below in the strict spirit of non-disclosure..." I read the words slowly, letting each one slide down my throat and pool in my stomach like ice water.

My fingers page through it, and the dread only grows. There are so many clauses in cold legalese. Nothing seems unreasonable. But that doesn't make it any better.

When I look up, he's smiling, sitting in the chair next

to me with another God forsaken smirk on his lips. "Is this *really* necessary? There's so much here."

"It's for your protection as much as mine. Here, look at the last page," he says, reaching over, pulling the last sheet out and putting it on top. "I knew we'd be pressed for time, so I asked my guy to spell out all the rules in a neat little list."

My eyes skim more. He's not kidding about the little part. It's three short phrases that could mean anything if they weren't backed up by longer parts:

No sex. Both parties agree to keep their relationship strictly professional.

No money. Fake fiancée understands this arrangement guarantees no compensation, beyond what Mr. Randolph decides to spend on gifts, expenses, or direct rewards.

No disclosure. Fake fiancée agrees to keep this agreement strictly secret, until such time it's terminated, and further agrees any disclosures to the media without prior approval by Mr. Randolph are prohibited.

I'm shaking my head. He grabs the pen, pushes it into my hand, and holds it up in a writing positioning. "What's wrong, beautiful? Anything you'd like to add?"

My eyes bleed fire when I look at him. I seriously contemplate asking him to add *no teasing* to this stupid agreement, if it wouldn't sound so ridiculous.

"No. Let's get this over with," I say, sighing as my wrist glides over the paper. I scrawl my name and initials on several pages, drawing on my legal experience to take one last quick look to make sure there's nothing buried that can bite me.

When it's done, he grabs the papers, and throws them into a leather case on the table. "Perfect. I'd say 'pleasure doing business,' but then that's a given when I'm dealing with you, doll."

It still doesn't sit right. I press my hands together, looking away, staring at the city's winking skyline through his windows. "I know what we need to do. I signed it. Tell me what else you need."

"So thoughtfully boring. How about a drink to celebrate?" he asks, helping me sit on one of the posh chairs next to a massive window.

"No," I whisper, blinking back my tears, wiping them beneath his unrelenting gaze with my wrist. "I just need a moment."

For half a minute, he's quiet. Then he sits down across from me, takes both my hands, and gives them a reassuring squeeze. "How do I make this easier?"

Easier? No such thing. There's nothing in the world that will make this faux engagement with a man who has his kind of history a breeze.

"Let me in," I tell him. It's the one concession that might give this a shred of normalcy. "Treat me like a friend if I supposedly want to be your wife. Talk to me about life, where you're going, what you really want to achieve after this madness."

He looks away, dropping my hands. "We're actors, Maddie. Just like the contract says. We aren't old friends, and certainly not lovers. We were classmates who got in too deep, and on the wrong asshole's worst side. We did some stupid shit it's taking years to undo. Why do you want to complicate this?"

"Because it *isn't* simple. Not when you shove me into your arms and kiss me for the first time in years! God, Cal. I know it can't be easy, everything that's happened, but do you have to be so heartless?"

He reaches up, scratching his clenched jaw. His sky blue eyes pierce mine, angry and electric, like it's almost as hard for him to sit here with me, and re-live the past.

I'm a fool for asking him to step back with me into the pain, I know. But honesty never hurt anyone, and right now, it's the only thing that'll let me process this screwed up arrangement without feeling like a plastic accessory.

"I picked you because we have a certain history, doll. That's undeniable. I need it to fool the world, and make sure my father coughs up what belongs to me before he's gone. Don't see any sense in this burning need you have to rehash hell at the academy. Let's put it behind us, and keep it the fuck there. Let's play our parts. You're here to be my fiancée. Not my therapist."

His harsh look threatens to set me off all over again. The tears stinging my eyes worsen because I haven't even had a chance to sleep off the jet lag.

I hate this. I hide the tears behind my palms, turning my face, willing him to shut up and disappear.

"It's been a long day for us both. Let me show you to your room."

"No!" I'm on my feet, clearing my eyes one more time to give him a harsh look. "Just point me to the right place. I'll find it myself."

With a savage glance, he points down the long hallway starting under a crystal chandelier. "Last room at the end. Sleep in tomorrow. I'll be out all day. Won't need you again until Sunday, when it's time to visit my father."

I storm away, resisting the urge to head for the front door instead, and find my way out.

By the time I clean up and lay down in the Egyptian

cotton sheets, my new headache is worse. It's shocking how much the four hours I've spent with him are like staring into a mirror, expecting familiarity, and seeing only distortions.

He's the same. It's the Cal Randolph I remember in all his arrogance, his wit, his ruthless good looks with the ocean eyes able to melt any panties he desires, whether the women wearing them like it or not. The boy who teased me, who turned out to be my savior, always showed the same smirk, same poise, same bottomless energy and focus as I see in this man.

But there's also something different; a dark, cold, and very adult aloofness in his character. The old Cal wouldn't have shuffled me off to bed if he'd seen me cry like this. He would've swept me into his arms, kissed away my tears, and carried me off to join him in bed after making certain I wore a smile again.

This new man, who I've agreed to marry, and pray it won't ever go that far, I don't know. He confirms my biggest fear I've carried around for seven years: our tragedy changed Cal forever, and not for the better.

GET FIANCÉ ON PAPER AT YOUR FAVORITE RETAILER!